IT HAPPENED IN SILENCE

~ Karla M. Jay ~

This is a work of fiction. All the characters, organizations, and events portrayed in the novel are either products of the author's imagination or used fictitiously.

Printed in the United States of America
Book Circle Press

Cover designed by Emma F. Mayo

Photo: Lynda Smart-Brown

ISBN: 987-0-578-79251-4 (paperback)

I dedicate this book to anyone who's had their voice silenced through fear, injustice, or discrimination.

"Where justice is denied, where poverty is enforced, where ignorance prevails, and where any one class is made to feel that society is an organized conspiracy to oppress, rob and degrade them, neither persons nor property will be safe."
~ *Frederick Douglass*

"The web of our life is of a mingled yarn, good and ill together."
~ *William Shakespeare*

OTHER BOOKS BY KARLA M. JAY

When We Were Brave

IT HAPPENED IN SILENCE

Karla M. Jay

HAPPENINGS OF THE DAY
MAY 1921

WANTED:
Man of God for
Traveling Preacher Position

$100/yr + A Good Horse

Northern Georgia Baptist Circuit

Stewart Mountain, Georgia. May 1921

-1-

Willow Stewart

Our ancient rooster, Cockle, splits the morning calm with his scratchy crowing and rips me from an eddy of a daydream I prayed I could hold on to. That bird has been irritating since he hatched, but today he sounds worse than a metal scoop scraping the insides of an empty cookpot. I'm fully awake now, reality reaching into my chest and squeezing my heart. I fight my bucking chin, trying to hold back tears, although I know they have a mind of their own and can't be intimidated. I was dreaming of Mama. She wore her playful smile, and her bubbly laugh filled my ears. Then Cockle ruined it all. My insides and outsides hurt as if I've been tumbled in a rock-slide, though nothing the likes of that happened. But the notion that death isn't fully done hunting my family is pounding me from all sides.

I've a long day before me, heading off our mountaintop to find a traveling preacher. The baby's birth went bad, and Mama is laid up inside, doing poorly. On this sad morning, I'm angry at the birds for singing their fresh tunes, for welcoming the spill of warm sun across our rocky peak.

My one wish is to hear Mama say my name again. Soft, like a breeze through tree boughs. *Willow*. People's voices create colors in my mind, and Mama's is creamy peach. I want her to tell me everything will be fine, that she is just worn out and resting. Sorrowfully, she stopped talking hours ago.

My sister Ruthy, to be married after she turns eighteen in three months, enters the kitchen from the parlor. The blue of her eyes stands out against the bloodshot white, whether from the constant irritation of crying or the long sleepless nights. She has our Poppy's brown hair, but it's a messy bird's nest this morning. I inherited Mama's Scottish red mane and managed it into a braid last night or I'd look the same mess. She catches me staring at her hair and runs her fingers through it.

Ruthy reaches for my hand and gives it a quick squeeze. "You go sit with Mama, Willow."

I nod. Born mute, I sign my question to her. *"Has she talked again?"*

"She's still unconscious"—she straightens her flowered shift—"but breathing regular."

My heart thuds as I push into the sitting room where we spend most evenings in the fall and winter. The oil-fired heaters that will warm the room again wait in the barn for the first cold snap. They've barely been packed away. Two windows are open. A spring breeze sweeps in the smooth lemony fragrance of magnolias mingling with drying mud and the biting scent of newly sawn wood. The neighbor men worked through the night building the coffin in case it's necessary. It waits alongside the cabin, next to another smaller one. I used to love fresh-cut pine scent but now it's ruined. I jump ahead in my mind and see Mama's burying box, decades from now under the cover of moss, rotting there, never needed. I pray God is listening to our prayers and deciding that fate for the box. That we won't need it. Calling home one Stewart kin member this day is pain enough.

In the center of the room, Mama lies on a single bed. A ray of sun strikes the ornate oil lamp hanging from the center beam above her. It casts a rosy glow through its hand-painted floral glass shade. Mama looks at peace, her folded arms rising and falling on the white sheet covering her. Her pale hands like two sleeping doves.

The menfolk moved great-grandmother's Colonial-style cedar chest from the center of the room to the far wall next to Mama's favorite padded chair and sewing stand. The stitching hoop still holds the last of the pillowcases she's embroidering for Ruthy's wedding to Leeman Castlelaw.

I sit in the spindle chair next to her bed and hope Mama knows it's me. Her "silent gift" as she calls me. When it was clear as moonshine I'd never speak, she and I created a hand signaling language that works well. My older brother Briar caught on and was often my translator, especially if we ever found ourselves in unfamiliar company. But that was a rare event due to how far up in the hollow we live. Poppy, Ruthy, and my little brother, Billy Leo, understand me sometimes—but only basic ideas. If my thoughts are simple enough, like following water skeeters across a pond's surface, they understand me. But for my below-the-surface opinions, I need Mama or Briar.

My eyes move to the three-shelf bookcase below the window. The top shelf holds one of Mama's favorite books, *Black Beauty*. A tale about a horse's early years and what his doting mother teaches him. The binding is worn from all the times she read it to us. When I recite the whole story in my head, word for word, it's my mother's voice I hear. I'm lucky that way. Most folks must hear their own voice when they think or have an inside-the-head conversation. Since I've never made even a squeak, I have mama's speech tone in there, especially when I'm reading.

I study her hands and picture her fingers flying over the piano keys, my Poppy slapping his knee and saying, "Della Rae, you play like an angel in a vaudeville show."

Those fingers. They braid my unruly red hair and tickle the backs of my legs. And Mama is a hand-holder. She always says holding hands is a promise between two people, a way to speak without words.

Reaching for her now, I wedge my fingers under her palm. The coolness surprises me and races straight to my throat, threatening to stop my breath. Why have I not held her hand more often? Spent more time in the house with her and less time in the forest? *I'm sorry, Mama*, I scream in my head. *I'll be around more. Just as soon as I get back from fetching a preacher. And trying to coax Briar home.* I sob and choke and cry some more. My stomach tightens, and silence twists through the room, snake-like, burrowing through my fifteen years of happiness. If Mama passes, I wouldn't care if I follow her into the next world because I don't know if anything can fill the holes if I remain behind.

Ruthy enters with my youngest brother, Billy Leo, twelve, groggy and clinging to her side. She's going to marry in a few months. Appears to me Ruthy doesn't mind that Leeman reeks of the wild onion sulfur-like stink from digging the rare bulbs he sells to lowlanders at the Broken Fork Country Store. I know for sure I'll be giving any future husband a good sniff before I ever agree to marry. That is if anyone will have me. At fifteen, it's looking mighty doubtful.

"You best get going, Willow. I packed you a food parcel by the door. Poppy's waiting on you outside."

When I lean closer and kiss Mama, my tears splash her cool, dry cheek. *I'll be back tomorrow. Please be here when I get home.* I wipe the moisture from her face, then turn to my sister, wrap my arms around her for a hard squeeze, and accept her kiss atop my head. Billy Leo lets me run my hand through his messy hair. The smile I try to form jitters around on my lips. Seems I know I've failed at offering a spark of optimism.

I leave the room, but Ruthy's voice, with its scarlet-red cheeriness, pokes at my heart as she tells Mama that Billy Leo has come to sit a spell. When Ruthy marries off, I'll be Mama and Poppy's main helper, cooking and tending the gardens, working the old mule with Poppy in the fields. Ruthy won't be but five miles away, though in the dark surrender of winter's reach, distance increases tenfold.

I open the screen door and cut my eyes to the left.

Lucille and Everett Tate sit in rockers on our wide porch, sipping sassafras tea. The soft blue-green color of the porch ceiling reflects onto Everett's white shirt. Although the paint color keeps the evil haint spirits from crossing our threshold, it can't shoo away folks like these two. Mama and Poppy welcome everyone to our house, but some folks they're less enthused about. The Tates are kinfolk. Cousins on Poppy's side. But so far removed it would take exploring the family Bible back to when his relations first reached these mountains to figure how they fit in with our Scottish kin. Poppy likes to say if Everett ever had the notion to work his own crops, that notion would die of loneliness. Instead of being self-reliant farmers like the rest of the folks in our community, the Tates pester the circuit preacher to point them toward the next deathwatch or funeral where food is abundant, and gossip, singing, and a secret mug of liquor fill an evening.

"Sorry about your baby brother, Willow." Lucille Tate is taller than her husband with a scowl between her eyebrows that ofttimes smooths out when her hair is pulled into a tight bun. Today is a loose-hair day, and her scowl's so deep it looks likely to sing if handed a hymnal.

"We attended the four-county revival meeting just last week," Missus Tate goes on to mention. Her voice swirls like gray ashes in my mind. "Reverend Cox done a bold meeting. Dozens of folks walked the aisle and was saved."

The Tates believe they praise God's glory more than the rest of us. Poppy says truth be told, they do seem busy in the eyes of the Lord, following His word to every pic-a-nic and church supper they catch wind of.

"We did an altar call in your name, Willow, asking the Lord to heal your affliction." Lucille smiles. "You just wait, child. One day, He will answer."

I sign, *"Thank you,"* but feel like a traitor, and heat flares in my neck. There are more important prayers that need to be sent heavenward than that of me talking someday.

My hand is clenched on the wooden railing. I release it and exhale as I walk down the three steps to stand by Poppy. He's tall and solid, with bushy eyebrows, the left one cocked higher than the right, as if to say he is wise to the ways of the world. His fair skin, permanently seamed with wrinkles and laugh lines, will be bronze by summer's end. He generally wears his whiskers only in the winter, but a two-days' growth now spikes his chin and cheeks.

"They're here," he says, his usual hazel-blue voice a threadbare version of itself, worn thin from greeting everyone while under such strain. He points a knuckled finger toward our last kinfolk to arrive on our side of the Stewart mountain. Uncle Virgil with his crooked leg from the world war, and Auntie Effie with plum-size eyes that say she is stuffed full of more sadness than she knows what to do with.

They are my favorite relations.

Auntie and Uncle lead their horses to the crowded corral. I study the yard full of folks gathered round the makeshift tables of old wooden doors set across sawhorses. An hour ago, Ruthy and I served up fried rabbit and squirrel with wild horseradish pulp and early lettuce from the garden. Thirty-eight people have arrived for Mama's deathwatch. Pans of cornbread drizzled with bacon grease and honey disappeared in one passing.

Poppy reaches for my hand.

"C'mere, Pumpkin." He pulls me closer, then slowly rubs my arm, wrist to elbow and back. He wasn't a hugger, but his calming way of smoothing out the wild side in our livestock works on us children too. Affection from him is rare. He's done become a hardened man these past few years. Tragedy has nearabout wrung the happiness out of him.

My nervous insides feel as if they might burst out like a bottle of shook-up pop. I lean into his warm hands and enjoy the moment.

"You'll soon be on your way, Willow." His voice sounds full of tiny river pebbles, stonier today than usual. He returned from the war with a lower, crackling voice, surviving a mustard-gas attack that killed many a soldier. Now, like the rest of us, he hasn't slept since Baby Luther died yesterday. "Just to the church in Helen and back. You remember my directions?"

I nod. The church is the easy part of my trip. Finding my twenty-year-old brother, Briar, might take me longer. He needs to come home. Fifteen months is long enough to heal old wounds.

Cornhusk mattresses and extra chairs cover our grassy yard. Past that is the corral where my horse, Jacca, a ten-year-old red roan with black points, mingles with the guests' horses. His name means God's Gift. Poppy bought him off the local Cherokee chief two years ago for a handmade chest of drawers. My pa is a right good furniture maker and Briar was taking an interest before he left home. The chief said Jacca was terrible for hunting because he was the talkingest horse they ever heard. Nickering and snorting, always trying to get his way. I smile. He's at it again in the enclosure, trying to push his way around a huge draft horse to make eye contact and beg oats from the big guy. It surely is a gift from God that a mute girl should own a horse that's pert and pushy.

Aunt Effie reaches my side and pulls me into a full-chested hug. My aunt and uncle would have arrived yesterday with the other relations and neighbors after Poppy rang the large dinner bell. Five quick clangs meaning our family needed help, and then after a moment's pause, he added one more for Baby Luther's passing. It was right then, before the startled birds returned to their morning song, a heavy rain broke loose and stayed hard at it most of the day. The river swelled, forcing my aunt and uncle the long way up Stewart Mountain to reach our cabin.

I breathe in Auntie's lavender soap scent. A warm memory sweeps through me. Mama and my aunt sitting out on our front porch in the slant of the evening sun, breaking apart dried lavender heads into a pot of warm lard and lye and laughing about menfolk or family antics as they make enough soap to last the winter.

Uncle Virgil steps to Poppy and shakes his hand, then leans in to give me a quick squeeze. He and Aunt Effie treat me good, like nothing's wrong with me. When I was younger and my cousin Len was still alive, I spent a lot of time at their house. They live right in our holler across the ravine. In late fall after the hickory oaks drop their leaves, their house and butcher shed peek through the scattered pines. With Aunt Effie being Mama's sister and all, she and Ruthy will take over organizing the household duties while Mama is getting better.

My plan is to follow the old road off our mountain, make a left at the Chattahoochee River, and parallel it all the way to the lumber town of Helen pitched along the big river. Never been there before, but it isn't more than eighteen miles away.

Poppy rubs my back as he speaks to my aunt and uncle.

"Willow is about to get busier than a moth in a mitten, but she's up to it."

Warmth moves through me at his praise. He's been afeared that Mama might follow Baby Luther into the grave, and this has softened him.

"You travel safe," Aunt Effie speaks into my hair, "and come back right quick."

I try not to feel too proudful that Poppy asked me to ride out to fetch a pastor. God will easily slap down a person chock-full of pride as easy as batting a fat tick. It comes down to the fact that I'm good on a horse. I'm also the best reader and writer in the family and at the right age to be off on my own. I'll find the first Protestant church I come across and hand them a note, asking for the next traveling preacher to offer a respectable funeral at our mountainside cemetery. Poppy said it don't make no never mind which religion shows up. The pastors all know how to wrestle God's attention for a time. Then on to a post office to get a message to Briar explaining the baby he knew nothing about died, and Mama is in a bad way. That's the secret part of my journey.

"You don't have a care now, Willow," Aunt Effie says. "I'll spend time with your ma and help the other womenfolk with chores."

I squeeze my hands together over my heart. My sign for thank you.

Without a voice, I use hundreds of homemade hand signs, but my relatives understand very little. It isn't their problem and it doesn't bother me. At age ten, I shed my ill feelings about not being able to make a sound. Mama read the story from the *Atlanta Constitution* about a woman who has it worse off than me. That Miss Helen Keller can't see or hear, but she gave a talk in a meeting hall. She said the greatest gifts in her life were curiosity and imagination. Mama said Miss Keller might as well be mountain folk with her message that the only excuse for being in this world is doing things to help one another. That's how we live.

"Don't you let folks get ugly to you out there." Uncle Virgil's brows knit together.

I nod and try to force a smile, but I've got no happy in me, just a stomach full of wriggling worries. I reach for the charm string round my neck. My fingers move across the four buttons there, finding the pink mother-of-pearl from Mama's wedding dress. I rub the raised floral pattern between my thumb and forefinger, and my body eases. Mama called it a forever charm, passed down from her own mother's wedding dress bought from a fancy store in Paris, France. It's left over after making Ruthy's bridal dress and my first happy ornament. The other three buttons are for remembering people who passed.

A pressed pewter button from Uncle Stewart's Civil War uniform, a burnished brown one from older brother Luther Junior's only suit coat, and a wooden one from my cousin Len's hunting jacket.

Ray Finch, the holler veterinarian, walks by carrying a heavy burlap poke, darker at the bottom where it's wet.

"Virgil. Effie," Mr. Finch says. "Good to see you, although the circumstances are a cryin' shame."

Mr. Finch brought ice from his cave deep in Gumlog Gulch, and extra camphor. Baby Luther's body has been kept cold in his tiny coffin with camphor cloths placed over his face to keep his skin from turning black.

Mr. Finch turns to Poppy. "How's Della Rae doing, Luther?"

Poppy is the first Luther in our family. My older brother Luther Junior died in a mining accident on Pigeon Mountain fifteen months ago. He was barely twenty. The explosion happened only six months after Poppy returned from France, sick and dog-tired. Those days after Luther Junior was killed were a blur. All-day crying, no one able to believe Luther Junior was really gone. Poppy fighting with Briar over what had happened. The sharpest image I hold from that day are the shiny nailheads in the wood, where someone overdone the hammering to shut the wood-slat crate they sent my brother home in. A note came attached, stiff with condolences from Mr. Mercer, the Estelle Mining owner. Other scrawled words said the company believed they'd recovered most of my brother from the explosion but warned us not to open the lid and check.

After he was buried in the family cemetery on a high knob, the neighbor men left their handmade leather boots outside the cabin, covered with fresh earth from Luther Junior's grave. I studied that dark dirt, stuck on the notion that it unfairly exchanged places with my brother. The black soil was free to watch the sunshine poke daggers of light through the morning fog while my brother was destined to darkness. I was only fourteen but learned an oak-size life lesson that day. In order to pack down the pain of losing a loved one, adults turn their talk to everyday concerns, such as how months of foggy mornings could rot through a birch outhouse faster than one bad winter.

Now our new Baby Luther isn't with us anymore. Appears as if God wants only one Luther in this family.

"Willow will be back tonight." Poppy squeezes my arm and his eyes squint, a move I know dams back tears. "God hasn't called Della Rae home yet, and she's a strong woman. In all her years of healing everyone else, she's taught Ruthy how to help her now."

He swipes the back of his hand across his eyes where it comes away wet. His next words are nothing more than choked sounds, and I hardly recognize his voice.

"Better she's here if she passes."

Hearing Poppy admit Mama may be dying sets me to crying big silent sobs. Snot running down the back of my throat threatens to suffocate me. Not only am I mute, but the airway parts in my throat don't work like they do for other people. I have room for either phlegm or air but not both at the same time. "Narrow tubes," the visiting doctor told Mama when I was four.

Poppy gently pounds my back and my breath returns.

Before Mama weakened and stopped talking, she asked me to be strong. I can do that.

"Let's get you going, Willow. Do you have your whistle?"

I pat my dress pocket and nod.

He picks up my burlap sack with the food Ruthy packed. Before he takes a step, he says, "I have something for you." Secretive-like, Poppy reaches into his pocket and pulls out a square wrapped in cloth.

I feel my eyes go wide at seeing the peanuts through the cloth. Mama's skillet-made peanut brittle.

Poppy must see the surprise on my face.

"Ruthy insisted you have a special treat for the ride." He tucks them inside my burlap sack and tightens the drawstring. "You enjoy this during your travels."

I swallow hard. Poppy always says, *"If you light a lamp for somebody, it will also brighten your path."* This treat cheers me for the moment and puts a tiny rip into the uncertain veil of death hanging over the day.

Poppy's face is full of emotion as he lays a hand across my back and plays with my braid. "Jacca looks ready."

We walk across the yard toward the corral, so filled with dandelions the ground might as well be a soft buttery blanket. It begs me to lie down on top to let its velvet yellow petals tickle my arms. I'd pour out my pain into their simple cheery stamina. That's the thing I like about dandelions. They're strong, all busting out from cold earth the moment the spring sun chases off winter's icy fingers. And then overnight, the dandelion turns to a white puff-ball, and the first time a holler wind reaches up the mountainside, it blows the puff to pieces, sending the bits traveling to places far afield never to return.

Today I'm like that puffball, except I'll be back to my home in no time.

Poppy is no hand-holder, but our arms touch on purpose as we cross the yard. Everywhere I look reminds me of Mama. The yellow roses she's trained to climb a fence. The newly planted vegetable garden. Her favorite chair on the porch, with its slightly crooked rocker and pleasant *creak creak* on the old boards early in the mornings when she's shucking something or knitting. Her hands always busy. Sassy, the goat Mama bottle-fed when Poppy told her to let it die, stands below the clothesline looking lost and confused. Where's her morning scratch behind the ears? Mama's blue gingham dress, the last one she wore before giving birth, hangs empty over the poor critter's head.

I'm feeling as hollowed out as that piece of clothing.

The guests sit on their thin mattresses, spread out like horizontal head-stones in the yard. Some folks are asleep. Others are smoking corncob pipes and trading stories. The woven scents of honeysuckle, fresh churned dirt, and cherry tobacco make me dizzy, and for a moment, the world blurs at the edges. I sense the guests' eyes following me as I open the gate and coax out Jacca. They all know my purpose in leaving. To find a preacher to give Baby Luther a Christian send-off. But they don't hear the prayer playing through my head.

I pray that if I ride fast enough, using one of the skills God granted me, nothing will happen to Mama while I'm gone. Burrowed deep inside my heart, a tiny voice, one I don't recognize, speaks in golden tones. It says Mama won't pass with all of her children home and by her side. It's why I've secretly vowed to find Briar, even though his parting words to Poppy were that he'd never set foot on our homestead again. Perhaps time has picked away his feeling of scorn.

Slipping the sack's long drawstring over my head and across one shoulder, I climb onto Jacca's back. I touch my necklace, return Poppy's wink, and head off Moss Lick Knob, or as our kinfolk call it, Stewart Mountain.

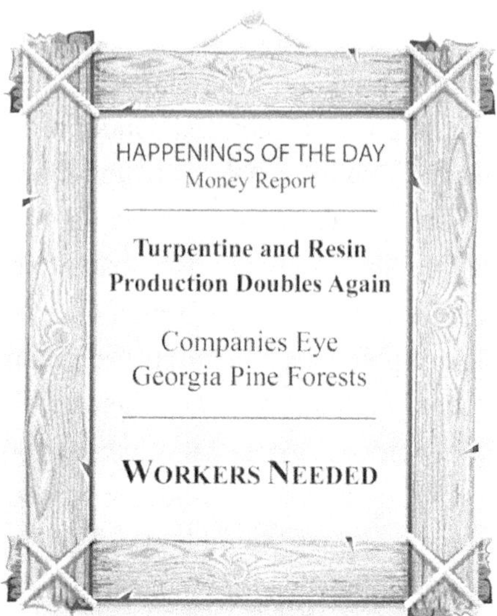

HAPPENINGS OF THE DAY
Money Report
Turpentine and Resin
Production Doubles Again
Companies Eye
Georgia Pine Forests
WORKERS NEEDED

Timberland Mountain, Georgia. May 1921

–2–

BRIAR STEWART

My heart thumps in time with the axes, V-cutting the pines in the woods at my back. If Daryl Brown, prisoner number 16, ain't back in another thirty seconds, I'll have to call over the dog handler and he'll set the hounds loose. Then when them animals find him, Daryl will be a dead man 'cause the boss, Boyd Taggert, will shoot him. Taggert's the work gang supervisor, and he loves nothing more than target shooting while perched on his horse. He'd shoot a Negro easy as a poorhouse rat and won't never think twice about it. "One of you dies," he often announces to the dog-tired convicts, "just phone up the warden and I get me another."

Since I moved up the convict ranks to a work gang trustee, the convict escape rate is zero, and I aim to keep it that way. Any prisoner on the run means I lose the few freedoms I earned before my sentence is over. It ain't much, but sure beats swinging a pickaxe.

We're trying to finish up slashing the loblolly pine faces and setting the turpentine jars on a tract of ninety-eight acres south of Cartersville. Been at it for three days and should've finished up by now. The Pearson-Gysse Lumber Company didn't care how we worked the trees as long as we met their quota. With twenty-four convicts, that amounted to cutting eleven thousand trees a day. We're behind now due to a real frog wash of a storm that hit two days earlier and two dead convicts.

"Daryl." My voice ain't none too pleasant as I push away the underbrush, following the direction he headed after he called out for permission for a squat break. Five minutes is all he's allowed and that's passed. "Back to it now."

The man was a steady chipper, and I'd hate to lose him. Good with the axe, he'd slash seven hundred sap trees a day without a whine. Chosen to work in the forest, it spared him from the terrible conditions in the coal mines or rock quarry. A big Negro, he was sentenced to the County Prison Camp for two years for speaking to a white girl. Taggert handpicked him from the camp stockade, always choosing the biggest fellers with the longest sentences. Never one to be crossed or made to look the fool, Taggert will hunt Daryl all of the twelve miles back to the penal camp if'n that's what it takes to kill him. Leave him half buried in the woods and never file a report to the warden.

A mighty easy feast for the black bears and mountain lions.

"Over here, Mr. Briar," Daryl says, hardly loud enough for me to hear. If'n he thinks I'm gonna be part of his escape, he's dead wrong. Four months and fifteen days. I done held onto denial 'bout the cruel conditions forced on the work gangs, kept my head down, and turned a blind eye to the beatings and deaths. Four months and a few sunrises until my nine-month sentence is served. And no one's gonna drag me backwards.

I push through a pocket of sweetshrub, the clover scent of the blooms trailing the brush of my hands. Off to my right, Daryl stands stock-still next to a pile of boulders. His face has gone as pale as my behind.

"You're not thinking on doing something foolish, are you?" I ask.

"No, sir." He stretches his eyes wide and drops his gaze to a spot in front of his work shoes. The leather is ripped. His toes peek out of the right one.

In the thick carpet of brown pine needles and dead leaves, a huge copperhead is barely visible, coiled, his head pointed at the convict. It's fixin' to strike, but I sure am relieved Daryl ain't made a run for freedom. With the crooked judges in the south, there's no such thing as freedom.

"That's a big son of a bitch," I say. Daryl's not carrying his hack, 'cause all convicts must leave their axes fixed in the last tree trunk when they call a break. Even as a trustee, I ain't allowed any weapons. "You know he's just as scared as you."

"No, sir. I don't knows that."

Daryl's black-and-white-striped pant legs are shaking. The snake can't hear, but it sure can feel vibrations through the ground. I gotta do something quick.

"I'm gonna distract it." I reach for a long stick on the ground. "If'n you have any fast left in you, jump back behind that boulder when I yell. Can you do that?"

"I jumps wherever I has to."

The snake's four feet away. I raise the stick, and as I hit the ground behind it, I yell, "Now!"

Daryl disappears like dust in a hurricane, and the snake spins toward the stick. If'n I had more fellers with me, we could circle it and beat it to death, darting in and out like dogs on a caught raccoon. But today don't feel right for testing fate.

I soft foot it backwards. Six feet, then eight. Old No-Shoulders unloops himself and slides away, creating a dry scraping sound of steely muscle, contracting and expanding through the dead underbelly of the forest.

"C'mon, Daryl. Walk you back." The Negro falls in step behind me. Even in this position, I smell his dirty clothes, drenched with a week's worth of sweat. The convicts don't get to change out prison garb except on Sundays.

He and I come out into the work area. The thick odor of hot rosin rolling off the bubbling turpentine still hangs in the clearing.

Taggert is on his Palomino, rifle laid across his lap. He squints hard our way.

"Why the fuck is that blackie behind you, boy?"

This was a trail position Taggert warned against. *You want to get killed, put a convict with nothing to lose at your back.* I have no such worries. These men are defeated, not dangerous.

"Leading him away from a fat copperhead, sir." I turn to Daryl and point to the tree with his hack in the wood. "Git back on over there and hit it hard."

"What you taking up with his side for?" Taggert's scowl puckers his face like a dried-up apple, and he scratches his fat belly through a gap in his tight shirt.

"Weren't doing that, sir. I went hunting him and found him froze in place with a snake at his feet." I nod the truth into my words, waiting to see if Taggert reaches for the bullwhip coiled on his saddle horn. My back healed, but the stinging pain that left the scarred welts will stay in my mind till my dying day.

"Make sure that boy misses the next two water breaks."

The heat's been rising all day. The workers in the distance are wavy images of black and white set against shimmering brown trunks. Two water breaks in the morning and twice in the afternoon ain't hardly enough.

Daryl, convict number 16, is surely gonna suffer. I didn't sass back, but I wanted to remind him we can't afford to lose another prisoner.

Our work gang moves its convict cages to a new area of the woods in five days. We're about twelve miles south of the County Prison Camp, cutting on a remote pine mountain. Every two weeks, a few of us pick up provisions and a couple more workers from there. A week and a half ago, we started with a crew of twenty-four convicts, but one dropped over dead the second day as we climbed the slash of red dirt high into the green hills of timber. One got mouthy and forgot his only answer to everything said to him was “Yessir.” Taggert shot him. No record’s ever made when they get killed. The accounting of laborers is barely kept for those who die while working. Escaping is a different path. With that, they hunt for you forever.

Fellers have perished, but so far not a one’s escaped.

Out in the woods, we’re a chain gang with no shackles but still slaves to the state.

The Pearson-Gysse Lumber Company pays the prison system a cent a tree, which goes toward Taggert’s thirty-five-dollar-a-month salary. Taggert don’t pay us nothing.

The rest of the day ain’t worth mentioning. I keep my eye on Daryl, hoping he don’t keel over. A body can endure most anything unless the mind gives up. But I don’t reckon that’ll happen. The convict told me he’s got a wife and baby boy near Savannah and plans to see them again.

In the hillside glades, the shadows bleed together. Taggert blows his whistle. Three long blasts. End of another workday.

The weary men weave their way out of the trees to the clearing with the prison wagons, which look an awful lot like circus cages. There’s two of them, parked side by side, waiting to be moved to the next cutting area by the mules. Each car is ’bout the size of half a boxcar placed on wheels, with wooden sides that hinge and drop down to let air flow through the iron bars. A little mobile jail for twelve men per, with a bunk for each man and one slop bucket.

The convicts wash up at two pails of water, sharing the same rag and cake of soap.

The cook’s been at it for an hour. The iron cauldron hung above the fire pushes out an inviting scent that claws at my hungry insides. The whole camp setup reminds me of my short time hoboing across the country, night-time in the camps called Jungles, partaking in a cautious brotherhood.

“Washing up,” I call out to the three other trustees. Calling out our every intention is a part of our confinement. ’Bout the only thing we don’t ask permission for is the right to breathe.

“Wash up,” one calls back.

I head to the rain barrel behind the trustees’ tent. The other three will each get a turn when I'm done. As a trusted convict, I advanced from the filthy stained prison stripes to two sets of blue work britches and shirt.

Stripped to my drawers, I wash the sweat and red dust off. The cold water is a healing power all its own. Grew up playing and fishing in streams. It's a comfort to me despite the cold.

A stick snaps behind me in the woods, and I slowly turn expecting to see a deer. A white boy stands in the forest looking my way. He then takes off running. Who could be way up here? Nothing but tall trees for miles with Timberline Mountain running up against other smaller forests speckled with towns.

The boy might've been in his teens but carried that starved build, runty and spindly. I pushed the forlorn look I saw on his face out of my mind. When I set out on my own over fifteen months ago, I wrapped my heart in iron so no hurtful sights or words could get to me. The boy is hunting trouble if'n Taggert spots him. The supervisor would slap on a false crime, like spying, on the feller and induct him into our work gang. Just like that, he'd be lost to the world. Another nameless fool.

I get dressed in my clothes and that cloak of denial that's kept me sane. The boy might be out hunting with his pa for all my cares.

Back in the supper area, four long tables made of planking over sawhorses serve as eating space. We're all seated outside when the weather is nice. Rainy days force the convicts into their jail cells under lock and key and the rest of us into our tents.

I scratch one of the coon dog's ears when his handler ain't looking. Convicts and the two dogs are supposed to stay wary of each other in case one gets to running, the other to chasing.

When everyone's washed, we fill the table benches, sitting one trustee to every six convicts. Taggert eats alone, off to the side at a small table he had me make. Fancier than the man deserves, if'n you ask me.

The tall dark pines grow blacker as dusk moves in. Hoot owls start up deep in the woods while the flit of bat wings move overhead. A night of insect feasting has begun.

The cook drops two squares of cornpone, a pile of lima beans with pork chunks, and a big spoon of sorghum onto everyone's tin plates. Soon the scraping of forks on metal echoes through the woods, a respectful time as darkness wins over the day. Unlike suppertime on the other chain gangs working the cotton fields or rock quarries, our food's passed around for second helpings till they run out. And we often get meat, slim pickings for other gangs.

The image of that boy in the woods comes back to me, the look of hunger hanging on him. Thousands of fellers are off on their own. Many took to the rails. Told to leave home 'cause there ain't enough vittles, or left orphaned when the Spanish Flu passed through a mite more than two years earlier. Then they were made to leave the orphanages after reaching the legal work age of fifteen.

Hundreds of stories being told, all filtered down from days that won't never get much better, but in the long run can't get no worse.

The reverse of that is my tale. Things that can't get no worse are about to get a whole lot better.

The convicts have forty minutes till they're locked in the cages. Once inside, they head to their bunks, since there's little room to stand in the narrow aisle down the center. Huxley, a bearded trustee from over Savannah way, picks a soft banjo tune. The moon pulls itself up behind the trees, heading for the deep gray of the night sky. Flecks of stars sink lower to the Earth, pressing down.

I lean against a tree and recollect my hoboing days last year. I miss swapping newspapers with other hobos when I was riding an empty from St. Louis to Wyoming. Learning hundreds of hobo signs left on fences, walls. We slept in the nearest barn, worked the endless wheat fields, listened to men like Rhymin' Bob recite poetry while decking on top of a flyer.

In hindsight, I could've learned more hobo signs. That's the truth. Didn't recognize the sign for *the Town Has Corrupt Police* when I waltzed into Euharlee. Didn't have a clue that every free man wandering the street is gonna end up in shackles.

Was only after I lost everything that I now truly understand freedom. Four months and fifteen days. I ain't never gonna feel the bite of shackles again.

Marietta, Georgia. May 1921

3

Ardith Dobbs

Oliver is crying from the upper floor of the house, dragging down my good mood with shrieks of "Mommy." A voice in my head retorts, "Hush up!" with each screech. I have so much to accomplish today, and the child barely went down for a nap. Where is Josephine? The girl has one child to take care of and she can't even do that.

"Josephine!" I set my pen aside, careful not to ruin the ledger. The other ladies admire my penmanship, and I don't take my duties as secretary and treasurer of our newly organized Daisy Ladies' Society lightly. "Please stop that child from screaming," I shout while seated behind my mahogany desk.

"Coming, Miss Ardith!" Josephine dashes by the door to my office, holding up her long blue skirt before she thumps down the carpeted stairs. I follow the thud of her footsteps as she crosses the room below me. I can't discern what she says to the five-year-old, but he immediately quiets down.

In my favorite room, I arch my neck and study the high ceiling with the flower pattern stamped into it. Cream-colored walls and my new light green silk curtains frame the two tall windows. Morning sunbeams push inside and lay ladders of yellow across the two butter-cream armchairs adorned with near-scandalous red pillows. I remember begging William to buy this house two years ago, even though his advertising agency wasn't doing as well as it is now. Thank goodness today is full of optimistic consumers who will buy any new product that's just invented. Been no better time in America, I'll bet.

The baby rolls inside me. I rub my swollen middle, trying to calm her. Yes. I know it's going to be a girl. This pregnancy has been so much different than my miserable time with Oliver. I had a miscarriage last year, but only two months in. This is Katherine. That's the name I'm choosing. She hasn't caused me to vomit even once. William doesn't care for the name, but he won't have much say. The other night while we played bridge with our best friends, Frank and Teresa Greer, Teresa laughed at him for being such a fuddy-duddy and thinking name picking is left to the head of the household.

I still can't believe how testy William got over Teresa's question concerning what we'd name the baby.

"We're still discussing names," William snapped.

I know my eyebrows scrunched together because I remember thinking I'd get age lines if I didn't relax them. The truth was, we'd been arguing over names seconds before our guests arrived. I made it clear that no child of mine would be called Hester or Chester.

Frank saw my consternation that night. "William, ol' boy." He clamped a hand on my husband's shoulder. "We're in trouble now. We gave them the vote, and by darn they think they have the right to name their babies."

Teresa snorted. "Gave us the vote? The law passed alright. Did you vote last fall, Ardith?"

I shook my head, careful not to show too much displeasure. William didn't care for Teresa's vocal opinions about events he would call "men's issues." Frank Greer is the Marietta City attorney, and William has needed him more than once, including early last week. Frank unearthed the loophole that forbids that Jewish family from opening their dry goods store next to William's advertising and insurance business on Main Street. For this reason, William held his tongue when Teresa railed against the rules she believed confined women.

"I didn't vote either." Teresa slapped her cards against the table edge. "But women in Utah did. Wyoming. Idaho. Those backward places followed the new law. If we don't get a chance this fall, I'll organize a women's march like Atlanta has never seen."

A statement like that always made the men nervous, and both William and Frank flinched.

And here I am at my desk organizing Marietta's Spring Festival with a parade for all the new women who joined our organization. Not really a march, but we will put on quite a show.

I return to my ledger and add the last of the names and mark off they paid the annual ten-dollar dues. I'm pleased with the new inductees. Three schoolteachers, a midwife, a social worker, the bank president's wife, and three women from the gardening club. Of course, the majority of our new members switched from the Dixie Protestant Women's Political League once they realized we shared the same goals to carry out our Christian duty and that we are a social order for social purposes.

Two hundred new members this month alone. Two thousand dollars to spread the word.

Soft footfalls come closer in the hallway. Josephine lightly knocks on the doorframe before stepping into view. She is a big girl, not fat but taller than I am and strong. Her hair is fashionable, worn swept up in a chignon bun. One characteristic I liked about her when she interviewed last year. Most Negro gals wear their hair in a twisted-up rag, and she has a few of those. I let Josephine wear them on her own time and have told her to keep those dirty old cloths out in her sleeping quarters attached to the house. Josephine is what we call a high-yellow colored. Her mother is white. We assume her father was black. Thanks to the civilized laws of our land, her mother is confined to an insane asylum in Virginia for having relations with a blackie, married him even. Then they were found out. Her father was killed working off his crimes in the brick foundry near Atlanta. So far, Josephine doesn't appear to have too many of the destructive genetic outcomes that arise from interracial breeding, except for her sexual promiscuity.

She is hugely pregnant, due a few weeks before I am to deliver. I was furious and fired her the day the growing bump under her housedress became impossible to hide. How dare she? Who would look after Oliver and the new baby if she has one of her own to worry about? Then I remembered my friend Nancy Withington, Sheriff Withington's wife. They have four children she's handed off to wet nurses after they were born, just like in her parents' days. I unfired Josephine as she was slinking away, carrying her carpetbag and wearing that ugly head rag. William will have to understand that I need a nanny and a housekeeper whether she's tending her own baby or not. In these years since Oliver was born, I now have social duties I've pledged to follow through on just as William does, and Josephine will be an asset.

By the looks of the enlarged mounds under Josephine's bodice, she will be able to keep her child and my baby well-fed. She won't say who the father of her child is, but I've seen her talking to the neighborhood bootblack who services the wealthier houses. A black-as-coal boy indeed.

Josephine is holding Oliver's hand as he quietly stands beside her. "May I take Oliver outside to the terrace?" How she gets that boy to behave, I'll never know. As long as she keeps doing it, I'll never care.

"Yes. Please do. I need to walk some papers over to the Greer house, but I won't be gone long." I gather my ledger and the envelope with the dues.

"Hi, Mommy," Oliver says.

I raise my eyes. He has a big grin on his face, resembling his daddy with his big gray eyes, auburn hair, and chin cleft.

"Hi, sweetie. Now you do as Josephine asks. Run along, and I'll see you when your father gets home."

His smile evaporates, and he disappears along the hallway. Is every child this needy? Shoot-fire as we say back where I came from. My ma and pa barely paid us a minute of attention unless we stopped hauling water, boiling laundry, or scrubbing the cabin floor. I need to toughen up Oliver. He's too delicate for his own good.

I drop my paperwork into a brown leather satchel William bought for me the last time he was in Atlanta. "For the businesswoman in my life," the card read. I was tickled he recognized I have important duties, too, and am not just his bed partner. He had no choice but to marry me. I flirted with him so hard, taking him to the edge on every date. I made sure he knew he'd be satisfied whenever he wanted. Now, six years later, I have more important duties filling my time. I'm glad he recognizes how busy I am, although I know he's often frustrated when I beg off.

In the hallway, I stop so I can view myself in the full-length mirror. Who knew the daughter of a railroad fire-knocker, one of the dirtiest jobs the Southern Atlantic offered, and a mother who never rose above working herself to death in a moss-covered shanty, would grow up to live in a mighty fine house with wealthy friends and neighbors? Surely not my folks. It took me tiring of a family secret to drive me away from Hickory Nut Hollow and to show me the world. I learned that having money is not evil. After a winding path of missteps and some small luck, I created a new image in Atlanta. That's where I met William.

The mirror shows the reflection of a fashionable woman in a bright lime green and white lace dress. She has foregone the modest Puritan look and could be a woman right out of the *American Vogue* fashion magazines she peruses. Thank goodness women no longer bind their middles to the circumference of a canning ring. Women in old newspaper advertisements always looked like ants with big bottoms on one end and big heads on the top. My new straight dress has a drop-waist sash with a wide green bow tied in front below my bump. The shift is loose enough to cover my curves in keeping with modesty at all times but is also so freeing. And that's the motto of women today—we're free.

Free to vote. Free from being told we have no ideas worth hearing. Free from the chores of only raising children, cleaning, and cooking meals. My women's group raised money for milk for the public-school children and put together food baskets for the poor. We have a say in the community and in helping our husbands and other members of the Klan keep Marietta pure.

We pay attention. We report. We preserve our town's Protestant heritage.

I smile at my reflection. I am a Kligrapp, a secretary, and the Klabee, the treasurer.

William and the other husbands on our street are Kleagles, paid organizers, inviting men of good heritage to join them. I love our secret names, all the creative K words.

I touch my stomach. Baby Katherine will be our newest member.

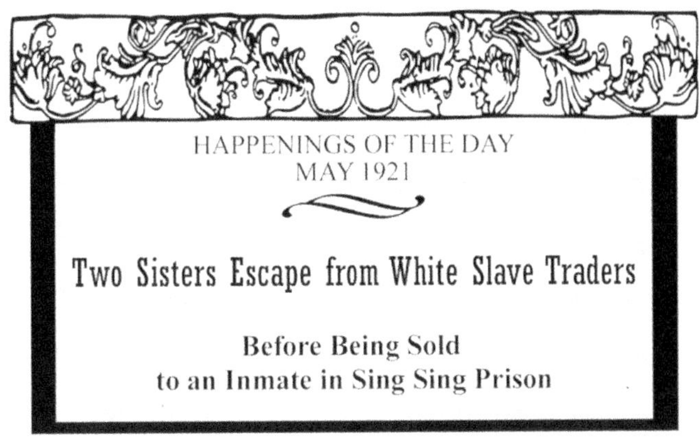
HAPPENINGS OF THE DAY
MAY 1921

Two Sisters Escape from White Slave Traders

Before Being Sold
to an Inmate in Sing Sing Prison

Stewart Mountain. May 1921

4

Willow Stewart

Jacca follows the deer trail into the thick forest. The morning woods vibrate with the hum of locusts, rising and falling as if they're in a church sing-along led by a master insect. The trail is a shortcut. It will be slow going, but once off the steeper part of the mountain, we'll make good time. Morning fog rises and twists toward the sky, and like a magician pulling away his white handkerchief, reveals lady slippers, trillium, and jack-in-the-pulpit along the forest floor.

Twenty minutes later, I catch the first rumble of Ransom Creek. It cuts through the base of the holler, separating Uncle Virgil and Aunt Effie's hillside from ours. I'll cross it at the Miller Coal train bridge. When the rains come down like they did yesterday, the face of that peaceful summer creek, full of hidden crevices and muttered secrets, distorts into something ugly. It turns into a violent and unrecognizable downward rush of green and white water that can sweep a body off the lower wooden bridge we often use. It will strain that person through snarled boulders and logs before his last cry echoes from the dense forest.

Auntie and Uncle were forced to cross this higher-up bridge this morning, leading their horses across the train trestle. The same dangerous crossing that killed their son Len nearly four years ago. His mare spooked in the center of the bridge when the rails began vibrating underfoot. The animal tried to turn back moments before the daily coal train hurled around a blind curve, forty minutes later than scheduled. He knew the time of day by the set of the sun in the sky. What he didn't know was that the daily train was forced to stop at a rockslide. Although the railway men worked fast to clear the tracks, the engineer couldn't make up the lost time.

Len and I were twelve at the time. He was my favorite cousin. I touch his coat button on my necklace and try to remember his voice. It was somewhat moss green, I think, like fine wool unspooled across a cutting table. Some shade of green for sure since we spent so much time in the woods, digging roots and gathering plants for my mama. She has a deeper knowledge of herb care than most folks in the highlands.

There aren't more than two hundred and fifty people on these peaks, and all our houses are linked by dirt roads and winding passes along the ridgeline. I go with her sometimes to check in on the sick. There's a lesson to be absorbed in visiting other countryfolk. Take the word poor. It's like striated rock ledges, with different meanings of the word at different levels. We mountain folk are self-sufficient and don't rely on outside goods to get by. But one day, we came across a new level of down and out, where it was as clear as daylight something had gone sideways.

We found a rotting cabin backed up against a granite ledge, the shingled roof sloped near to the ground. A dark and woeful setting. The father had died from the Spanish Flu nineteen months earlier. He'd been off to war when the disease caught him, like millions of other people in the outside world. Poppy and Uncle Virgil made it back from France without the flu snatching their breath away. The ravages of mustard gas were enough to abide. Earl Scoggins, the traveling tool and knife grinder, told us most mountain folk stayed free from the deadly disease. Relatives heeded the message to avoid the cities because there the flu outran righteousness. At that dark house in the woods, I remember the children. All twig arms and legs. Faces unwashed for a season. The hateful poverty nothing more than an afterthought to the grieving mother. We took food back a day later and located some kin who soon drove them away in a brittle, rusted truck.

Jacca nickers and suddenly stops. The wispy hairs on my neck stand up, and I cut my eyes from side to side. I trust the horse's senses. He heard something. The silence lasts half a minute and then the forest sounds begin again. I don't find what spooked him, so I tap him on his side with my heels, and we move ahead past the chaotic mass of boulders and down toward the river crossing.

About twenty minutes later, Jacca's hooves clomp across the train bridge, and I send a prayer heavenward for Len, letting him know he's in our thoughts. We head down a wider trail with the river to our right. In an hour, we'll meet up with a two-lane paved highway Poppy calls "The Fancy Road." It will take us into Helen. There is another way off these hills, but it's a winding dirt road. Tray Mountain Road leads from The Fancy Road right up to our cabin, past the neighbors, but it's miles longer. It also connects with Indian Grave Gap Road, an area that births most of the holler's ghost stories. I never like riding by there. I've not seen one of those restless spirits, but in all my growing-up years, heard tales of them stealing souls. Our cabin has haint-blue ceilings, a color used to confuse the spirit into believing it's underwater. And our outhouse has newspapers pasted to the walls because everybody knows evil spirits will be too distracted by all the words and pictures to bother a person having a personal moment.

I have no paint or newspaper and no reason to believe I'll need them on this trip.

The breeze off the river scrubs the air clean. I breathe in the fresh scents, ripe with sun-warmed grasses, rotting bark and leaves, and wet earth. Fallen trees blanketed with moss line the bank, pointing downriver. A pile of rocks creates a jumbled island, water slipping over wet stones, leaving them shiny like they've been greased with a layer of lard.

Having lost myself in the welcoming caress of the woods, I've let Jacca slow his pace. I nudge the horse, and he walks as fast as the path will let him. He's surefooted, and with our silent bond, he reads my changes in leg pressure and my pats on the neck even better than a tug on his reins. In an emergency, Jacca follows commands with the wooden whistle Poppy carved.

Before long, the ruckus of the river is behind us and Ransom Creek flattens into a wide stream. I stop and dismount so we can drink. Jacca follows deer prints into the creek and loudly slurps from a clear pool. I make my way upstream from him, avoiding exposed tree roots, and pick my way over pebbles to the stream's edge. This is my only pair of leather boots, and they need to stay dry. I cup my hands and scoop the cold water, taking notice of the small fish flashing beneath the surface against the riverbed's mottled greens and browns. Jacca is making all kinds of racket, overturning stones with his hooves. They clack against each other, a loud hollow sound.

A flutter sets down in my chest. I've been off the mountain with Poppy before but never alone. We aren't but a quarter mile from the paved road and the Chattahoochee River ahead, though we won't cross that river. Thanks to all the rain yesterday, I imagine it's a rushing waterway that will wash a person's poor judgment straight into eternity.

Jacca is a great trail horse, but I worry about the twelve miles of paved highway into Helen. If we can travel through side fields and stay away from logging trucks and other vehicles that might spook him, we'll make it fine and dandy.

I hear a moan on the wind, a sound that has no business disturbing this peaceful setting. My mind could be playing tricks on my ears with my earlier musings concerning haints. I click my tongue, and the horse heads my way. Until I get him out of the water and away from his slurping and rock rolling, I won't be able to tell for sure what I'm hearing. I lead him up the bank and rub my hand along his warm flank, calming my rapid breath. Stopping to pull several handfuls of new grass from alongside the river, I offer it to him. The tickle of his whiskery chin as he eats from my palm is one of my favorite things.

I hear the sound again. It's a man, his hollering coming from farther down the path. Off to the left, away from the stream. Most of our neighbors and relatives from the mountain are at Mama's sitting up, so who's on this back trail? Chills run through me. He must be in a passel of trouble to be yelling six ways to Jesus. My heart's pounding, and it's with little hope I pull open my burlap poke and search inside, supposing Ruthy packed a knife to go with the food. She didn't. My small notepad and pencil, dried butter beans, bread, cheese, and candy are no protection against whatever has this man bellowing.

I square Jacca on the path, once again pointing down river, and climb onto his back. He must feel my fear. He sniffs the air and pitches his ears forward. I lean over him and give him a quick hug as if to say, *it's fine*. Three clicks from me and he's up to a smooth gait. More than anything, I want to ride on past whoever or whatever is ahead, but not trying to help a fellow man is a lowdown sin.

Jacca's hooves beat the sun-mottled path. The bushes scrape against me, but my split skirt and calf-high boots prevent scratches. My breath is coming fast, and I keep an eye out for what's waiting on our left. Through the trees, I spy an open field. Two horses stand hitched to a peddler's wagon. I pull Jacca to a stop and squint in the direction of the rig. It's the same Mr. Coburn, who visited us no more than four days earlier. His voice now sounds like broken red glass. I hop off Jacca and lead him through a tree line to the field. A broad-winged hawk circles overhead and lets out the uncaring cry of a hunter.

On the far side of the wagon, Mr. Coburn sits on a wooden stool and hasn't noticed my approach. His trouser legs are rolled up past his knees, and he's slapping at his bare legs full of spots. Jacca whinnies and snorts and tries to pull away.

Mr. Coburn jumps to his feet.

I raise my hand to say it's okay and lead Jacca to stand beside the two weary-looking horses. Pulling this loaded wagon all over the back hills is a job for animals bigger than these poor creatures.

Keeping my distance, I turn to the peddler. His white shirt is rumpled, and he's dressed in a plaid vest and brown trousers. His bowler hat is on the wagon steps, and the sun bounces off his bald head, leaving only a half wreath of graying hair circling the back side.

He clears his throat.

"Young lady, I apologize for my cursing. I sat a spell over yonder"—he points to a grassy area—"and the chiggers got to me."

Wet grassy fields are always home to the tiny red bugs, especially in the spring. The peddler told Poppy he was from the city, and right as rain, he just proved it. The man's legs are splotched with dozens of red sores, each the size of a buffalo nickel. I motion to stop itching them by pretending to scratch my arm and then slicing both hands in the air away from me.

"Well, shit fire and save matches. You're that mute girl from up the hilltop."

I back up a few steps. We only met the man that one afternoon when he arrived at our homestead, his wares rattling and banging against themselves, as his merchant wagon climbed the washboard road. The horses looked plumb wore out even then.

He claimed to hail from Charleston, South Carolina, but said he recently began as a traveling salesman in northern Georgia which put him in our neck of the woods. Poppy was leery of him at first and didn't lower his shotgun 'til he felt for sure Coburn wasn't a revenuer looking for moonshine stills. The country's new anti-alcohol rule was only eighteen months old, but raids take place on our mountain every month or so. The officers go away empty-handed, and not because we don't have corn whiskey. Everyone in these hills does. They just aren't practiced at looking in all the right places.

Mr. Coburn's wagon held dazzling merchandise, and Billy Leo gathered around it all big-eyed and gawking. It was like having a Sears & Roebuck catalogue fling wonders from its pages onto our doorstep. There was gum and candy like Beeman's, Black Jack, and Necco Wafers. Mr. Coburn apologized for not providing every newfangled candy offering, but it wasn't like we would buy any if he did have it to sell. He also hawked suspenders, thumb tacks, and boxes of Old Dutch pot cleanser. Mama studied the claims on the box before putting it back saying, "No thank you, sir. My ashes and vinegar recipe is working finer than frog's hair."

When Poppy shook his head against all offers, he added, "Get some feed and water for your horses and come on in for supper."

Once seated around our heavy wooden table, Poppy offered thanks for the food and safe guidance for the peddler. Mama served chicken and dumplings and mushroom soup followed with a special treat—boiled custard.

Mr. Coburn spent the night bedded in our barn, and Poppy kept his rifle inside the front door. The man seemed fine enough, but one never knew what foul wind might blow our way.

Before heading out early the next morning, he complimented Mama on her cooking.

"We grow or pick everything fresh. These woods will feed a family if you know where to look."

Poppy didn't wave as the man rattled his way down the hill.

Now here he is boiled up with bites, and Mama's words run through my head again. *Doing a good thing to help another is why God put us here.*

So I have a solution for the man.

He calls, "Where you heading?" as I turn to the stream bank to find jewelweed. In a patch of sunlight, I spot the hairy green leaves and pluck a handful. Mama calls them miracle greens. The smashed leaves cut down pain and heal skin irritations.

I drop the leaves in his hands and mime that he should rub the leaves into a pulp and put it on his skin. I have no problem being neighborly, but I'm not about to touch those hairy, bug-bit legs.

He scrubs the green paste on the bites and seems to hold his breath, waiting for something to happen. A smile grows on his lips, and he sits up straight.

"You're a choice bit of calico, aren't you now?"

I shrug. Of course, Mama taught me a few healing tricks.

Mr. Coburn studies me for a moment then speaks. "I knew another girl back home who was simple in the head, and just as sweet, but the family didn't treat her so well as yours. She burned to death in the little shed they locked her in whiles they were at church."

I recoil. Locked in a shed? Because she can't talk? Who does such a thing?

"Appears you've got skills."

I point to my head and nod, then open my hands, pretending to hold a book. I have no way to explain I've read one hundred fifty-six books so far. The only thing slowing me down is the traveling librarians who have a hard time getting up into the hills in winter. Sometimes I fancy that one day I could do the librarian's job. I'm comfortable on a horse, pulling a small wagon, and would know which books to recommend to all the holler folks.

Mr. Coburn's face changes to serious. He must feel bad about calling me simple. I hold no grudge because he doesn't appear to be a mean feller. I understand folks expect the world to always match their beliefs about what's normal. They aren't used to bumping into exceptions. And maybe in some cases, a person who can't talk might be a bit slow in the head.

"I thank you for stopping and helping." He tilts his head to keep me in sight as he lowers each pant leg. "Why are you so far from home?"

I pull out my notepad and write, *going to find a preacher in Helen*, and hand the pad to him.

He takes a long time to read those few words, so I assume he's not good at ciphering. He nods. "That's where I'm heading, into Helen and then beyond." He squints one eye. "I owe you for your medicinal knowledge... um, and your horse is sure to spook out on the highway. Why not send him back up the mountain and I'll take you the rest of the way?"

The man has put words to my biggest worry. Jacca and the highway. He's as important to me as anyone in my family, and I can't undertake the idea of anything bad happening to him. Jacca knows his way home, and with three short blasts from my whistle, he'd head that way.

I study the peddler and his wagon. I don't really know the man, and Poppy *was* wary of him at first. Is it immoral to be alone with a man if he's only half a stranger? He'd eaten at our table.

He squints toward the sky. "If we get a move on, you will be home before the Lord lowers a blanket of stars over this day."

My mind's running in tight circles with indecision. The wagon seat looks wide enough for me to sit a proper distance from the man. And the town of Helen is no more than an hour away. Then I imagine worrying Poppy when Jacca returns without me.

Mr. Coburn is packing away his scattered belongings, preparing to leave. The idea that I'll be home tonight at Mama's side helps me make up my mind.

I take out my notepad again and write a note to Poppy. I slide it under Jacca's saddle. It says I've caught a ride with Mr. Coburn and will be back before dark. I pat Jacca's neck and pull his head lower and press my forehead against his. My way of telling him everything is all right. I lead him to the trail and point back the way we came. Three tweets from my whistle and he heads home at a comfortable trot. I feel a bit offended he didn't glance back or hesitate, but it just means I've trained him well.

When he rounds a bend and disappears from sight, I turn back to Mr. Coburn's wagon. He's opened the back doors of his truck and is leaning inside. A selfish thought sneaks into my mind that maybe he's choosing a drink for me before we head out. Never tried that Coca-Cola he has in there.

He turns, pointing a silver pistol my way, and then sweeps the gun toward the interior. "Get in. I'm keeping you for mine."

His voice, now a dung-brown color, matches the ugliness on his face.

I fumble for the wooden whistle. One short tweet followed by two long ones and Jacca will come charging back. My breath hitches in my throat. I get the whistle to my lips and give it the first short chirp, all the while backing away from the man.

"Confound you!" He lunges and reaches me in five paces, rips the whistle from my hand, and throws it into the field.

I scratch and claw, trying to get away, but he punches me in the stomach, and I drop to the ground. I've never been hit before, so I'm momentarily stunned. Tears roll from my eyes, and inside I scream for Poppy. I want to be small again and climb onto his lap, to feel his hand rubbing my arm.

Fear takes ahold of my soul, freezing me in place with shouts echoing in my head. *Get away!* The world flickers and breaks in bitty snippets.

The man's yellow teeth flash through his cruel smile and send chills through me.

A hawk circles overhead.

The wind's fingers whisper across the tops of the spring grass.

I scramble to my feet, but he grabs my hair and pulls me backward to the wagon, cussing. "Kee-riste! You're worse than a rabid polecat."

At the open door, he pins me against the wood slats with one elbow to my neck and shifts the gun to the back of his pants. In one smooth move, he hefts me into the interior, leaving me crumpled between his loaded shelves of goods. I'm on my feet and lunge for the doors as he closes them. He reaches in and pushes me back, snagging my charm necklace.

The last thing I see before the doors shut are my precious buttons spinning away, silhouetted against the blue sky.

HAPPENINGS OF THE DAY
MAY 1921

SONS TO TESTIFY AGAINST FATHER

White Farmer Kills 3 Negro Workers
as Crop Prices Sink

- An Impartial Jury Will Be Difficult -

Timberland Mountain, Georgia. May 1921

-5-

BRIAR STEWART

The next morning, Taggert struts around the camp, just shy of gnashing his teeth like a demon on a mission. The early heat is already so thick it's worth wearing. The supervisor came to realize his request for two prostitutes from Cartersville ain't been honored. Taggert pays a feller to ride young gals out to the camp three days before some of us trustees and a couple of strong Negroes head in for supplies. I can't find words to talk to the abused gals on the way back, once Taggert has used them up. It's a chore I hate. They're usually young, godforsaken waifs, abandoned to the streets for a dozen different reasons. I don't know what could've went wrong with them not showing, but Taggert's been cracking his whip at the heels of the convicts all morning. He ain't cut skin yet, but with the men stripped down to their waist, all the fellers are as twitchy as cats surrounded by a slew of mangy dogs.

The Negroes ain't even singing their hymns and folk songs. Trustee Huxley often plays the banjo along with the convicts' tunes, but he left the instrument at camp after Taggert threw him the stink eye. Even the forest seems to have built a wall against the supervisor's wrath, preventing a cool breeze from blowing through the timber and leaving us fighting vexing clouds of gnats.

"Mind your potatoes!" he snaps at me when I suggest Clyde, the water boy, make an extra round before dinner break.

Clyde. He ain't a boy at all. He's a string bean of a man, with a red nose and orange-peel face. An old-timer who claims to have spent forty of his sixty years in and out of jail. And prohibition ain't stopped him from drinking or making hooch. Once drunk, he goes forgetful and staggers to the closest town and gets nabbed once again for *devilment.*

A convict calls out for a break to retie his boot because it's raising blisters.

Taggert crosses the space between the trees and faces off with the convict. "I ain't worked you no harder than anybody else. Look around you, blackie. They all still working."

"Yessir."

I move closer, worried another worker gonna get himself killed. Taggert pokes the prisoner.

"You need your mammy here to keep your shoe tied, boy?"

"No sir."

Taggert shakes his head. "Let me see what you crabbing about, John Henry."

The convict pushes his right foot forward and steps out of the back of his boot. An inch of pink skin shines along the side of his heel. It's bleeding round the edges.

"Piss on it," Taggert says.

The convict raises his eyes, a dangerous move that often begs the bite of a whip. His face is frozen. His mouth gapes open. Confused.

"I said, get that cock out and piss on it!"

I step forward, my eyes latched to Taggert's. "Sir. We're wasting daylight on this." Don't know a man alive that can piss while filled to the brim with fear.

"It heals cuts and blisters." Taggert pushes me away and takes out a pocket watch attached to a leather thong. He growls to the convict. "You have two minutes or I'm whipping you red."

The convicts close by stop their cutting. The air in the woods tightens.

"Get back to work!" Taggert yells to the others. He turns to his victim. "Tick tick."

The prisoner's got his britches unbuttoned and holds his member. His hand shakes as he begins praying in a quiet childlike manner.

I hold my breath, as if'n I can stop the unfolding of those seconds. That's the thing 'bout time though, ain't it? It's never all the same. Some hours or days go by and you don't take no never mind of it. Then, the opposite can happen. A little minute stretches your senses until all you can do is notice the frightful passing of precious blinks of time.

The sound of splashing liquid takes hold and refocuses my vision. The convict sags in relief as he keeps soaking his foot and boot.

Taggert shakes his head. "That's enough. Tie that shoe and get back to work."

He walks away and I follow him.

"Ain't never heard tell of piss being a cure," I say.

"Because you're a dumb mountain hick," he sneers. "What would you do back home?"

"Apple cider vinegar, or if we hike to a sunny knob, find aloe vera leaves."

"Ya don't say." He adjusts his hat on his head. "See any of that round here?"

"No sir, I don't. That's why I was asking about the piss." I know I'm poking the bear. But he's ignorant and always prideful of his lack of knowledge. He even challenged my story 'bout riding rails through Utah on the way to California, him saying Utah set up next to Canada. And I'm the dumb one?

Taggert sighs and stares at the sky. Not a cloud showed up to help out today. He slaps his leather gloves against the back of the wagon and turns to me.

"Wasn't there a farm about three miles back? Sits off the trail?"

"I recollect it. Might be a bit farther though." What's he want to know that for?

"You're gonna fetch me some milk. Stomach's full of fire ants today."

This is the first time he's trusted me to go off the mountain alone. If'n I keep riding, how long will a search party stay on the hunt for me? I picture the homestead of Stewart Mountain, my pa, ma, sisters, and brother. As a crow flies, it ain't much more than seventy, eighty miles to the east. But tales tell of wardens hunting down family members, forcing them to take the place of the escaped criminal. The last guilt I need in this here world is bringing more sorrow to them.

He walks to his tent and returns with some limp dollar bills.

"Buttermilk would suit as well. And ask about blackstrap molasses and biscuits." He crosses his arms. "Can't take much more of what the cook is putting out."

This is why men with more smarts don't sign up as supervisors. They may get to let loose their cruel side on the job, but they eat convict fare along with the rest of us.

"Yessir." I look over at the four horses and the mules. "Which one you want me on?"

"Take Bayou. You 'bout the only one can handle him."

Bayou is a dark dapple gelding, five years old, although he acts like he's only months from being unbridled and unbroken.

I nod and cross the short field and open the thrown-together pen. My pa and me didn't agree on much, but one thing Poppy always said was when we ride a horse, we borrow the wind. That sure is the truth. I think of Willow and her horse, Jacca. They know each other so good. I don't want to shadow Willow's sun, but when I lived at home, I was plumb jealous of their abiding tie. Although I tried to hide my covetous heart, it was like trying to slip sunrise past a rooster. Willow always noticed and often let me take Jacca when we rode all over our mountains. A wash of sadness fills me. I push away the good thoughts of the nineteen years I had there. Before the accident. Before the anger. Now I'll never go back.

I make a clicking sound. The horse comes to the fence and eats long grass from my hand. When he's done chawing, I put my hand under his chin. The bristles are prickly, like an old broom sweeping on my skin. I lean near his head, breathing in his smell.

"You ready to be outta here?" I slip his saddle and bridle on, glad he doesn't try to bite as he's wont to do. Probably just as happy as me to be getting away. The last items I add are two empty burlap pokes fixed across the saddle with a rope.

Turning the horse down the rutted trail, I raise my hand and Taggert does the same. The path cuts across a small area full of high grass and wildflowers, then enters a pine forest thinned years ago for its logs. The jays are screaming curses to the squirrels, and a red-tailed hawk circles overhead in the trees' openings. The forest noises, right down to the whispering at night, make me the happiest. Sounds that sit peaceful-like in my mountain soul.

Farther on, the trail winds through a rocky landscape where a big ol' twisted rhododendron casts a crisscross of shadows on the path. Ferns unfold, framed by big rocks covered in green moss and silvery lichen.

A dirt road shoots off to the left. In the distance sits a barn. I turn Bayou in that direction. In a small gully, we pass the rubbish pile. Next comes a scraggly apple orchard. Split-rail fencing lines the road, leading to a corn crib, a well with a hanging pail, storage shed, chicken coop, and outhouse. Not as pretty as Stewart Mountain but laid out 'bout the same as our homestead.

Except for the house.

We got ourselves a fine cabin. Sturdy. Waterproof and windproof. This here house ain't no more than old boards and rotting wood shingles covered with moss under a pecan tree.

A weathered man in overalls is pitching hay into a pen next to his barn.

"Howdy!" I call.

He straightens and shades his eyes with his hand. "Howdy."

I continue forward, stop near his fence, and dismount.

"Come from down the work camp. Hoping to buy some milk off you."

I reach in my pocket and pull out the money. “And biscuits and syrup if’n you got some to spare.”

“Aya. I figgered that’s where you from.” He points to my britches and shirt. “The blues is a dead giveaway.” He studies the money. “Glad to see you’re willing to plow straight. Had another work crew come through a year back. Stole a couple of my chickens. That was a fine howdy-do.”

He spits a stream of brown chaw to the side and raises his eyes. One’s gone white and the other’s milky brown. Poor man can hardly see.

“You safe enough living way out here?” Folks with bad intentions could surely take advantage of him.

“Safe enough. Got a wife and son helping me.”

Was his son the boy I spotted in the woods?

“How old’s your boy?”

“Thirty-two. Third generation working the farm. Grandad got the lands by the lottery after Indians swapped out for Oklahoma. Last century.” He swipes at a trickle of sweat running down his cheek from under his hat. “’Course Grandad was looking for gold like most folks during the big gold rush in these parts. Found none of that. The Cherokee he took the land over from had a right good layout here. Already had the orchard, some cane fields. Wasn’t too hard to turn to farming.”

The man leans on his pitchfork, seeming tuckered out from the telling.

“Ah.” Not one to argue, I know the Cherokee didn’t volunteer to *swap* these lands to head out West. Ma had us children study about the local Creek and Cherokee’s forced march west under President Jackson. The Trail of Tears the Indians called it because thousands of them died along the way with their own Negro slaves in tow. But some Cherokee hid out in these hills and refused to leave. Pa trades with two local Indians up on Indian Grave Gap Road, not too far from our homestead. They’re good folks. I smile and add, “Read where the Indians in Oklahoma discovered heaps of oil under their new homestead. Guess they’re richer than all the gold rushes put together.”

“Hunh.” His face knots into a bed of deep wrinkles. “Don’t have time for reading, boy. ’Sides, newspapers will say anything to squeeze a nickel a month outta you.”

Bayou is stomping the ground. He's a kicker and not a horse to keep standing round.

"'Bout what I come for. Could we buy them supplies off you?"

He reaches for the money, folds the bills without looking at the amount, and stuffs it in the front pocket of his overalls.

"Back in a jiffy."

A light breeze blows the sweetness of honeysuckle my way, and I breathe deeply. It smells like freedom. I picture taking the farmer's offering then heading on down the road, riding into town and disappearing. I'd have pert near an hour's head start on Taggert realizing I wasn't back yet. Another half hour for the coon dogs to reach this farm. Time enough for me to hop a train and head west.

Except for the threat of harming my family.

I sent them money early on from harvesting wheat in Montana and later from picking apples in eastern Washington State. California, Utah, Missouri. I should've stayed out West. They must think I gave up. Last letter I sent from Rome, a town not far from here, was the stop I made before I got arrested in Euharlee.

The farmer comes back with a burlap poke and sets it on the ground at my feet.

"This what we got extra." He pulls out two one-quart glass bottles of milk held shut with a metal doohickey over the glass stopper. A small jug of molasses, five large turnips with the greens, and a tin of biscuits.

"I thank you." Taggert's mood should lighten. I load the two burlap sacks so they're hanging off Bayou on separate sides and the bottles won't bang together. "I'll get the bottles back to you in a piece. Might come by here again in a few days when we head off the mountain for supplies."

He scratches his jawline, making a sandpapery sound.

"Wouldn't mind if they were full of turpentine tar when you do come. Roof's riddled with holes."

I laugh. "Seems fair. You get yourn and we get ours." I swing up onto Bayou. "You take care."

He nods and spits to the side.

"Hey." He reaches into his back pocket and pulls out a flat bottle with a clear liquid. "You want some spark to get you back up that hill?"

"No, thank you. Not allowed to drink."

He chuckles. "Me neither. The wife rears so much sand about drinkin' I do it in secret." He tilts the bottle, and I watch the gristle in his throat jump up and down as he chugs the fire water. "Ah." His eyes water as he wipes his hand 'cross his mouth. "That's finer than snuff and not half as dusty."

It's been fifteen months since I've tipped a bottle, but I can almost taste the corn liquor at the back of my throat.

"Sure is." I touch my fingers to my hat brim. "Got to get on now."

Bayou remembers the way up the trail, so I don't have to do much directing. I think back to my days as a traveling worker. Saw lots of broken men in the hobo jungles who couldn't go a day with no spirits. One freezing night, riding the blind outside Kansas City, a drunk feller forgot to hang on and toppled off the blind platform at the front of the baggage car. Cut in half under the wheels.

My last drink was the day my brother Luther Junior died. Truth be told, most good things in my life died that day.

The recollections fly off as something at the edge of the woods catches my eye. I squint. It's that dang boy again. He's standing by an old rotten house that's struggling to stay erect, held up by thick vines twisting 'cross its walls. The chimney done gave up and is halfway crumbled. There's a pile of stones at the base.

Haints are known to haunt folks with a guilty past, and I wonder if this is what I'm seeing. But the ghost raises his hand, waving me to him.

I keep riding. Got no time for another stop. Can't afford to get busted back down to convict stripes, and Taggert would gladly do it.

I go another hundred feet then take a gander back at the shack. The boy's still looking my way, his arms hanging loose at his side.

Dagnabbit. I can't go ahead 'til I see why in tarnation this boy is way out here in nowhere and beyond. Kid looks as young as Billy Leo, who ain't no more than twelve.

I turn Bayou 'cross the grass and tree stump field 'til I reach the hut.

The shack looks worse up close. Part of the roof is caved in and the windows ain't nothing but two black holes.

"What you doing out thisaway, son?"

"Ve don't have place to go."

He's fair-skinned, has messy blond hair, and his clothes are all dirty and torn. I think he's a mite older than I first figured, maybe fourteen. And the way he talks ain't nothing like I ever laid ears on.

"Who's 'we?'" I look around but don't see no one else.

"My brother inside, he sick." He crosses his arms hugging himself. "I can work in woods camp for food." He points up the hill in the direction of our gang.

Good Lord. He'd be deader than a swatted skeeter in just one day.

"You don't wanna do that. How old might you be?"

The boy seems beat down by my question.

"Fifteen. Just little for age." He makes a muscle by cocking his arm. "But strong."

"Your accent. Where you hail from?"

He pauses, then speaks. "Boston."

If'n he's from Boston then I once rode Noah's Ark.

"Just some verk for to buy medicine." His chin jitters, and I try to still my heart.

I slide off the horse and open one poke and hand him a bottle of milk. His eyes light up.

"Hold the bottom of your shirt out."

He sets the bottle carefully at his poorly shod feet and makes a bowl holder with his shirt. I place half the biscuits from the tin there, leaving four for Taggert.

"Get on into a town. Emerson's 'bout seven miles due east but it don't have much in the way of offerings." I point to the north. "Cartersville is 'bout eight miles thataway. Got a good doctor there." I shake a finger at him. "Son, listen to me. You do *not* wanna work for my outfit. It pays in bad vittles and nightly whippings."

He flinches at those words. Hopefully, I've scared him away from here.

"Zank you." He smiles. The thankfulness in his eyes is strong and tries to grip me.

Bricking up my soul, I climb onto Bayou again. I can't help this boy and his brother. My goal is to get out of Georgia. Away from the dark times I been living through here.

"You do what you gotta do," I say. "That's the way I always done."

I ride off without looking back.

Four months, fourteen days. Not that long now.

HAPPENINGS OF THE DAY
MAY 1921

WANTED:

Salesmen & Solicitors

Men of Character
to Represent an Association Backed by
Leading Businessmen of Atlanta

Must Be Morally Ambitious
and Willing to Travel

Marietta, Georgia. May 1921

6

Ardith Dobbs

"This is delicious, Ardith." William smiles from the head of the table, sitting tall in the pale green velour-covered chair as he cuts another bite of pork chop. The new chandelier above our dining room table reflects golden patches on the cherrywood and adds a spark to his eyes.

He's grown more handsome in the six years since we married. Those gray eyes, straight nose, and the characteristic Dobbs male chin cleft. His brother and cousins all have that deep groove set in their strong chins.

"I asked Josephine to make it." William and I finally have a quiet moment together. We've both been busy with our social activities, and it feels as if we never talk anymore. Oliver is eating in the kitchen with Josephine, which they both seem to enjoy. "I know it's one of your favorites. Something to cheer you up after your hard week."

He shakes his head and snorts. A sound that marks his frustration.

"That Society for the Prevention of Cruelty to Children," he says. "Of all the nerve! They should stick to solving the problems in their immigrant-infested cities up north and leave us alone down here."

"Nosy northerners. They need to hear about all the good we are doing in the South."

The SPCC organization wrote a scathing story in the *Atlanta Constitution* about Dobbs Advertising and Insurance, William's company. It claimed Prudential Life Insurance, the national company that provides life insurance policies for William's customers and his agents, is insuring babies and young children with the sole purpose of making morticians rich. And unfortunately, it's partly true. A few local undertakers have adjusted their bills higher to match the burial benefits an insured customer receives. But that wasn't William's doing. The undertakers are to blame.

The SPCC reported that baby mortality rates have risen since insurance companies started offering life insurance. Ridiculous. Babies die just as often as they always have. The Beck Infantorium crosses my mind. The large statue of an angel beside the large columned house. The cemetery out behind. I shake the memory away. That was seven years ago. It's most likely out of business by now.

"Did Pastor Dalton refute the article?" I ask. He's our Methodist pastor and belongs to many of the same men's groups William joined.

"He wrote a sterling rebuttal." William sets his fork down and wipes his mouth on a cloth napkin monogrammed with a D. "It comes out this week. He emphasizes how child life insurance has saved cities, churches, and taxpayers money by cutting in half the number of pauper burials. I had him go through the books and get some facts. Even at the usual mass grave rate of nine dollars a child, several cities near Atlanta have saved tens of thousands of dollars because children are now insured."

I reach for his hand and squeeze it. "You just need to show people that there's a huge demand."

When he's too busy, I often help William collect the weekly insurance payments of ten cents per child. In certain areas of town, I take Josephine since she's comfortable talking to everyone. When given permission, that girl is a chatterbox. I'm surprised her tongue hasn't worn down to a thin flap of pink skin. But she helps by being so verbose. I get distressed when I see a struggling family, with five skinny children and a baby on the way, count out their fifty cents for the insurance premium. I have to remind myself this is a good thing. If one of those children dies, the twenty-eight dollars they receive will go a long way to invest in the remaining children. The mother will never feel the shame of letting the poor lost soul be hauled away to a pauper's grave. Still, I can't look the pitiful mother in the eye, so I make Josephine do it.

This reminds me. I set my utensils down. "We're out of promotional pamphlets."

"I'll get Betty to print off another fifty." William's advertising agency has expanded to three employees in the last year. Companies are making more products than ever before, and people are willing to buy them. He settles back in his chair and loosens his tie. "Just be careful who you're giving the brochures to. That newspaper article called us baby baiters. Maybe avoid following leads from the obituaries for a time and meet new women outside of the social welfare offices."

"It's so unfair." I slump, feeling chastised. "The parents are more than grateful for the life insurance money. Especially since they never paid any premiums on *that* particular child who passed. Pastor Dalton needs to say we're informing the uneducated on how their family can be comforted if another child should die." What's wrong with people? We give them the money for one free funeral and show them how to insure the rest of their sorry brood.

"I'll talk to him about it. But we don't need the courts involved."

I'm never sure why William worries about the courts. Most of his friends are in legal fields and have each other's backs.

Josephine comes into the room and clears away the plates and takes cups from the sixty-inch buffet that came with our dining set. It's filled with William's family china and silverware, passed down three generations. When he asked about my family inheritances before we married, I said everything was lost on that ill-fated *Titanic* along with my parents.

"That was a very good meal, Josephine." William sends her one of his winning smiles. "Thank you."

"You are welcome, Mr. Dobbs." She waddles around the table pouring coffee. She seems to get bigger by the day. I squint. What if she's carrying twins? That would ruin my plans for her nursing Baby Katherine when she arrives.

"Josephine, do you mind getting Oliver ready for bed after you've cleaned up?" I smile her way. William is always overly polite with her, so I try to mimic his manners when he's listening. Sometimes I want to scream, "Girl, are you paying attention?"

"My pleasure, ma'am."

After she leaves the room, William frowns. "Did I mention that I have to go out tonight?"

"Yes." He's told me twice. I'm sure with everything spinning through his mind he forgets if he said it or just thought it. I do that so often. "Where are you meeting?"

"At York's." He drinks the last of his coffee. "He's called in the mayor and most of the city council so we can address the quarry's and brick factory's production rates. With the new road going in and the new city hall being built, we can't let them run out of workers."

The mayor's brother owns the enormous Bellwood Quarry nearby and a smaller one in Cartersville, forty miles north of Marietta. The quarries provide granite and limestone for other buildings, but lately workers have been harder to find with so many Negroes moving up north.

"What does York have in mind?" We're good friends with Sheriff York Withington and his wife, Nancy. I have no idea how Nancy manages four little ones while spreading her time among the Women's Christian Association, the League of Women Voters, and anything to do with prohibition. She coined the famous slogan "It's a Man's World Unless Women Vote." Every woman wore a button or pin promoting that saying during the suffragette protests last year.

I've offered a few catchphrases when I'm around Nancy, hoping she and the other women in our Daisy Ladies' Society would like them, but none of my mottos have taken hold. But I'll keep working on it. Loads of cornpone sayings run through my head from growing up in the sticks, such as "Don't blame the cow when the milk goes sour—Vote!" But I need a high-class idea about women being industrious and making a difference.

"The sheriff's suggesting a change to some of the town's laws. Probably going to get harder on petty criminals. He's proposing all crimes, no matter how minor, become felonies, so we get more work time out of the men. The governor has been hounding private companies to increase their work contracts, so this should appease him."

Like in other counties, convict labor improves our highways and constructs our buildings. And the ongoing problem of criminals sitting around being useless in prisons, as in states up north, is solved. Georgia has no prison system, just a chain-gang program. Seems other states are watching closely to see why we're so successful. We're ahead of our time on lots of civil issues.

William stands and gives me a peck on the cheek. "How are you feeling with the baby getting so close?"

"My feet hurt a bit, but overall I'm doing fine." I slide an arm around his waist. "Two weeks at the most, the doctor says." I can't wait to hold my little girl. William is a great father, and when he has time, he takes Oliver everywhere and plays with him in the backyard, roughhousing, doing boy things. I'm looking forward to being in charge of girl activities.

"Good." He draws me back to look into my eyes, and I melt under his gaze. I'm so lucky. Or as folks would say back home, "*You didn't pick up no crooked stick when you found him.*" I give him a big smile. If only he knew my roots. I've told everyone the story of the loss of my parents aboard that doomed ship. How I was fortunate to have arrived in New York on the *SS La Provence* with my aunt from England—may God rest her sweet soul—the year before. It was the easiest way to wipe out Hickory Nut Hollow.

"Since you're feeling well, how about you spend some time with Oliver tonight?" He kisses the top of my head. "You'll be busier once the little one arrives, and I know you were gone all today."

I keep the anger from showing on my face. My meetings today with the other wives were to support our husbands. To help him. Who did the men think organized the church suppers, catered the rallies, and helped spread the men's mission of promoting racial separation in keeping with sustaining white Protestant supremacy? I spend all day with Oliver. Sure, Josephine is a great help, but the boy is always around.

"Yes. I was planning on reading to him once you left."

I walk William to the door, and once his car pulls away, I move into the sitting room and sink into the soft couch across from our elaborate brick fireplace. The four tall windows are draped in pale gold Cretonne with a subtle flowery pattern. William complained he could've bought a car when he saw the price tag for the new draperies. But I know he's pleased with all the compliments we receive for how beautiful our home is.

I'll read to Oliver in a few moments. I wiggle off the couch and climb the stairs to my study. I've scrawled appointments across the desk calendar's face. William has hinted that once the baby comes, I need to back off the outside women's meetings and should settle in at home. Except when he needs me at his office.

I simply can't do that.

Women across the country are highly involved in the men's Klannish activities, but here we are kept to the side. Only two weeks ago, a dedicated Klan wife in Dallas tipped off her husband about some shenanigans she saw on the street. The Negro boy caught associating with a white woman was taken out by masked members, whipped, and as a reminder to his friends, had the letters *K K K* burned on his forehead with acid.

That's the kind of information we wives can provide. I want to be more influential, to help our country. Women of the KKK are organizing in other states. When they reach Georgia, I plan to join. Maybe because my life has been built on secrets so far, I fancy the prospect of belonging to a hooded society kept hush-hush through oaths and rituals. And it protects our children and their future from inbreeding, immigrants, and the immorality of Catholic teachings.

I pause in front of my bedroom and listen for sounds coming from

Oliver's room. Josephine is humming, the last kindness she does every night as she rubs his back, sending him off to sleep.

I walk to my bed and lie back, enjoying its welcoming embrace.

Josephine softly closes Oliver's door and whispers, "Goodnight," as she passes by my room. Her living quarters are attached to the house, near the kitchen.

And since Oliver is already asleep, I'll read to the boy tomorrow night.

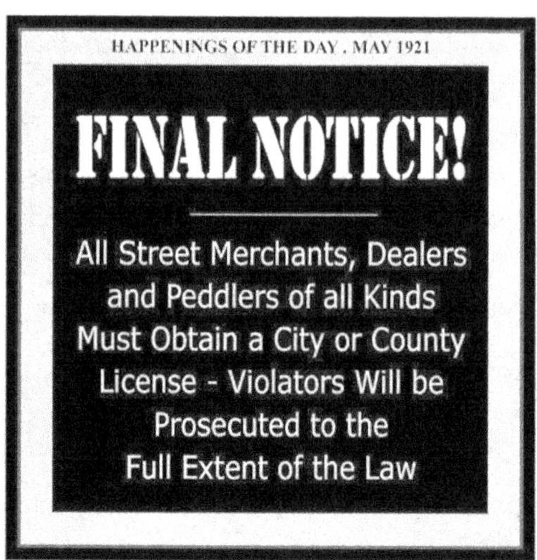

On the road to Helen, Georgia. May 1921

7
Willow Stewart

The wagon bumps along, and I balance inside, clinging to the wooden shelves to keep from falling. I've never been this afraid, not even the time Briar and I scared up a bear cub from a clover patch, and his mama set her mind on killing us. That day, my brother waved a large branch around and yelled as we backed out of the predicament.

I need Briar and a big stick right now so bad it hurts.

My stomach tries to toss what little is left from breakfast, but I fight to keep it down. The doors are bolted from the outside, and I've slammed my weight against them until my shoulders and back ache. I peek out of the crack running across the top of the doors, and the jerky view does nothing to calm my racing heart. We're following a logging trail, moving deeper into the forest, and by the angle of the shadows, we're not headed toward The Fancy Road. I send a prayer heaven-bound, asking for salvation from the dishonest Mr. Coburn. Poppy always says, "Let's save tomorrow's troubles for tomorrow." I can't heed his words because today's troubles are a mite bigger than he was talking about. I wonder if I will even see tomorrow.

Like a dead leaf in a stream caught in an eddy, swirling round and round, the peddler's been singing the same eerie song over and over. His voice is the color of a bloated boar carcass, and the words sting like hornets.

"There's sweet peaches down in Georgia / The beauties there / Pick one for a peach of a time / There's a preacher preaches down in Georgia / Always happy to say, sweet peach / Will you love and obey?"

Sour rises in my throat. I'm nearing a respectable marrying age. I've worried no suitor will find my silence love-worthy even though Mama assures me love is not about words but about being *fully* seen by someone. If this man defiles me, I won't even be a sight for sore eyes. Tears run down my cheeks and my legs shake. To calm myself, I reach for Mama's wedding button to roll between my fingers. My chest hitches as I touch my bare neck, recollecting my charm necklace is lost to the earth, where the living pulse of grass and other plants will eventually absorb the precious buttons from sight.

I sink to the floor where so many shoes and boots have stood, searching for something to buy. It's also where the peddler must sleep during foul weather, and a chill races through me like the first blue lick of winter through the chinking in our cabin wall. Disgusted, I return to my feet.

What's he planning? I had one chore to do today, and I've failed Poppy and Mama, my kin. I'll be talked about as the girl who went off to find a preacher but wound up dead. The truth sits ugly on my character. I was enticed into wrong choices by accepting a quick way into Helen. And that he seemed to be a respectable man, a vendor. In the dim light, I study the shelves loaded with cans and jars and brightly packaged candies. They might as well be serpents slithering around for all the evil they represent. We mountain folk only leave our homes out of necessity—to find a doctor, veterinarian, or a preacher. My now shameful predicament is why we keep the curiosity door to the outside world locked. The Bible warns against trickery and deception. I sure fell into this man's evil ways.

The wagon slows. I peek outside and notice we're deeper in the woods. Through the door's narrow crack, I inhale the scent of pine and stagnant water. A woodpecker drums out an alarm as the wagon stops, the bird's proclamation of danger banging the same beat in my chest.

An unknown feeling shifts in me. I sense a gathering of contrasting desires that in the last hour were no more than scattered yearnings, like acorns dropped onto a bed of pine needles. There for the gathering. I can't name them all, but I know I want to find Briar, to hear Mama laugh again, and I want to fall in love one day. And none of those will happen if I don't escape.

Mama always says, "We mountain folk are built for uphill climbs," then adds, "although you'll never climb the same mountain twice, not even in a memory."

I want this mountain behind me and the memory washed away by a flood like no one has ever witnessed.

The springs in the driver's seat creak and the wagon shifts. He's climbed down. I hold my breath, anticipating how soon the back doors will open. I nose around the shelves for a weapon and grab a can of Campbell's vegetable soup. His footfalls go in the other direction.

"There you go, Old Blue and Keewah. I reckon you're worn to pieces." His voice has rusty streaks in it.

The horses' bridles rattle. He must be releasing them from their neck collars.

"Yonder is grass and water. Starting in the morning, we have a big day looking back at us, so rest up."

He's whistling that same peach tune as he nears the wagon again. The metal bar scrapes across the latch, setting my teeth to chatter. This might be my only chance to best him. I lift the can and wait.

"I figure you're madder than a wet hornet in there, lassie." The doors don't open but he's talking. He clears his throat. "I'm only wanting some company in my travels. I mean you no harm. I can get you purty dresses and you'll have good food."

The man may try to honey-coat his desires, but they still carry the stink of sin. I am traveling nowhere with him.

"When I open the doors, I'm hoping for that neighborly spirit you showed toward me earlier."

I don't wait for him. I push one door wide and swing the can onto his head, recollecting a similar feeling of helping Poppy pound a piece of leather laid over a rock.

He yelps and staggers backward.

I jump to the ground and spot a tree line. I know the forest better than almost anyone. If I can reach it, he won't see hide nor hair of me again. Grasses whisk against my boots as I cross the field, and my arms windmill away a netting of gnats. My legs are stiff and won't cooperate at first, but I push them faster. I send a prayer skyward that my narrow breathing tubes don't fail me.

"You no account woman!" His voice is akin to river stones rolling over each other. "You're testing my patience!"

I'm almost to a stand of sycamores and white pine when a pain zings across my left arm, the reverberation of the gunshot blasting past me and wearing itself out in the trees.

I'm going to die here.

Choking back a sob, I grab my arm and drop to my knees. I picture Poppy reading the note I left under Jacca's saddle, saying I caught a ride with Mr. Coburn and will be back before dark. Poppy would wait until dusk, then be torn about following my trail and leaving Mama's side. He'd stay awake all night, praying that at dawn's first shine, I'd come home with a preacher. I would be overdue, but his mind would stay calm, knowing I knew my way around the mountain. What he would never know is what is about to happen in this field.

The peddler reaches me. His face is blotchy, his skin purple and white with a river of blood tracing down one cheek.

"I nearabout kilt you and it's all on your head." His eyes are full of menace, and heat rolls off him as he yanks me to my feet by my good arm. "Where's your Christian compassion?" Spittle flies and I turn my face away, but wet flecks splatter my cheek. I wipe them away. "All I was asking for was the company of a fine lass, and now you've gone ornery."

He pulls me to the wagon as I condemn him for judging me to be non-Christian. The man wouldn't recognize Jesus if He descended from the blue beyond, toting a sign declaring *I Have Returned.* Coburn is as heartless as a chicken gizzard.

My arm is sparking fire, and I'm feeling swimmy-headed. After he ties my hands behind my back with rough twine, he spins me around against the wagon's side. Pressed against me, his breath pulses hot and sour on my face. He jams his hand up the leg of my wide riding dress and pushes his fingers inside me. I squirm and fight, but he digs deeper, hurting me. I spit on him and he pushes me away.

"You contrary woman!" He wipes the spittle from his cheek. "You will get used to that and much more."

My insides quiver like a squirmy nest of baby snakes. I look to the forest and the sky. I won't have my last vision on God's green earth be his scowling, beard-stubbled face.

He continues to cuss and call me names as he paces about five feet away. I ignore his berating voice and shut off the pain in my arm and privates and immerse myself in the world that will go on long after I'm gone. Fluttering leaves accept their dance, following the rhythm of the wind, a light *flap flap* high above. Treetops split the sun into slanted beams, bonding the forest floor in shared spots of gold. A grasshopper whirs past, his life's adventures fulfilled in short leaps. Stones press through my thin-soled boots. If only the ground could open up and swallow me. I don't want to die but would rather that happen than have this man take my virtue.

He reaches for me again, this time tearing my dress open at the shoulder. I kick him and he backs off. My shoulder is wet. That's when I glimpse my bare arm, where blood flows from the gunshot wound.

The world swirls into an ever-shrinking tide pool of greens and blues and then disappears altogether.

I awaken propped up against one of the rear wooden wheels, my hands still tied, my legs outstretched on the ground. My throbbing shoulder is bound in a rag. Coburn is about fifteen feet away, back turned, stoking a fire under a hanging metal pot. I assess how my body feels, relieved I haven't been further violated. He'd reattached the shoulder piece of my dress with a safety pin. It's afternoon, and by the length of the shadows, I've been unconscious for about half an hour. If able to stand without making any noise, I can slip around the wagon and be gone. I need to reach the deep embrace of the forest to lose him. A man who doesn't know about chiggers has no notion of the hidey-holes for a person determined not to be found.

Balancing on my backside, I lift my legs and pull my feet toward me, careful not to touch the ground. I rock forward, trying to get my boots under me, just as one of the horses nickers.

Coburn looks to the horse and then swings around to face me, catching me mid-stand.

"Hell-fire and damnation! You're more stubborn than a corpse."

I cross my legs and sink back to the dirt. As long as his temper doesn't turn on me, I'll get my chance to escape.

He scratches his face and shakes his head.

"But it *is* serendipitous you've just awoken. I'm standing in need of that mushroom soup your ma made." He points to a board near the fire, where he's been chopping mushrooms and wild onions. "Thought perhaps you'd show me how to make it."

I stare back at him. As hungry as I am, I won't indulge his made-up fantasy about us. We are not coupling up in any way. And I'm not taken with the idea of teaching him to cook.

He shrugs and drops the vegetables into the pot and reaches for a burlap poke set nearby.

"That look is a bit hateful, you know. But it don't trouble me none. I'm a single man now, and I can learn to make do. Finally got rid of my wife, Reppie. Her sass-back was well above her raising and I tired of it, you know."

He empties the sack onto the board and reaches for his knife again to slice the mushrooms spilled there. My breath catches. They're Death Cap. Country folk know how to spot the deadly fungus, but to an untrained eye they look like regular white mushrooms. I stretch my eyes wide and shake my head when he looks my way. Tales have it that right before folks die from everything inside of them shutting down, they claim Death Caps are the most delicious food they ever ate. There's not one healing herb in the world to turn our fates around if we eat these.

"Oh, yeah. Reppie's mouth ran like a boarding house toilet. Her father wasn't no better. Ask him the time of day and he'll tell you how to build a watch." He drops the poison mushrooms into the pot and slowly stirs. "I borrowed money from the bank for the wagon and horses and set out. But it's lonely. You must know what that's like with your handicap."

I point my elbow toward the pot and shake my head again. Of course, the man can't make me eat these any more than he can make me talk. But if I let him die, is that murder? The Bible takes no weak-kneed stand on killing.

He stops stirring and peeks in the pot then back to me.

"What's wrong?"—he shrugs—"Oh, I reckon I'm not making it the way your ma does." He chuckles, then turns back to his stirring. "I know us being together is new on you, but you'll come around. I sure am thanking the Lord for a silent woman after my Reppie chewed my ears to nubs."

I close my eyes and try to think how to tell him about the deadly mushrooms, but he keeps yakking.

"I owe the bank money, but I've not sent them penny one of it. And I sure picked me a bad mountain to try to sell my wares." He reaches for two tin bowls and ladles the soup. "Take your daddy…he bought nothing but ten cents' worth of candy. Pshaw! A lousy chicken can scratch together more money than that. Your pap's probably so cheap he wouldn't give a nickel to see Jesus riding a bicycle." He stands and heads in my direction with the soup.

Hot anger rises in me like never before. Loyalty to God and family are the rules worth wrapping your life around, and Coburn's words are pure blasphemy about my Poppy.

He sets the bowls on the ground near my legs and leans in close enough so I can clearly see the cloth threads in the green and white buttons on his vest.

"I was gonna untie you, but your eyes say you're not half-broke yet." He points a spoon my way, and a buzzard smile appears on his lips. "I'll tame you, girl, you wait. I'll ride you and tame you good."

My stomach heaves at his plans. I choke back sour stomach juice.

He reaches for the bowl and brings a spoonful to my lips. I clamp my mouth shut and turn my head, not even daring to breathe in the scent.

He shakes his head and picks up the other bowl.

"I'm a patient man. You'll get hungry." He scoops the first bite into his mouth. It's lumped high with mushroom chunks, and he slowly chews, smiling. Talking around the mouthful, he says, "Delicious. This will go to bad if we don't eat it. Wasting food is a downright sin. Didn't your ma ever teach you that?"

If I could talk, I'd say my mama taught me plenty about sin, enough to know that long before nightfall, Mr. Coburn will stand in front of Our Maker trying to explain his sorry self.

But of course, I can't talk.

HAPPENINGS OF THE DAY - MAY 1921
LIBERAL
COMMISSIONER
Moves Women and Children
off Chain Gang to
Work in Penal Gardens
"Even Convicts Need Vegetables,"
he states.

Near County Prison Camp. May 1921

8

BRIAR STEWART

In two days, I ain't seen neither hide nor hair of the boy from that shack. I hope he took his brother and went to town to get help. I'm heading off the mountain with Tuck, the fourth trustee on the work gang, a feller a couple years older than my twenty. The trip will take us into Cartersville for supplies and back. Taggert stays behind with Huxley and Clyde. Clyde, he never leaves the work gang. Any town with a whiff of alcohol and he's done for. Prohibition is in force, but a man can find a bottle of hooch if he knows where to ask.

We take the mule and wagon and two of the convicts. The Negro with the foot blisters is hobbling round worse than ever, and Taggert don't seem inclined to see the prisoner piss on himself again. Besides, the convict's messed up foot caught an infection that made it swell to double in size, so his boot won't fit. Now I'm even more doubtful of Taggert's healing wisdom. And we're carrying in a white feller who took sick with the fits and has been spouting crazy talk ever since. Just shouted, "When the magpie comes back, give him three licks with the asparagus." Both prisoners will be sent from the County Prison Camp to the State Penitentiary in Atlanta for medical attention.

Taggert handed me some letters and a list of supplies. A sealed letter is for the warden at the prison camp. Another is to be mailed at the post office to Taggert's wife. The last is a scribbled note to be dropped off at Miss Lily's Threads & Things on Main Street. I took a quick gander at that note. Couldn't help myself. Taggert threatens Miss Lily that if'n she don't send three "Things" by the end of the next two weeks, he'll get the sheriff interested in her side business.

Tuck and me made this very same trip 'bout fourteen days ago. He's good company, a country boy from Alabama told to leave home and earn his way two years earlier when the boll weevil killed off the family's cotton revenue. He roamed a bit, living off church charity in each new town. They arrested him near Atlanta for cussing in public while standing outside a feedstore where he had hopes of working. Two sorry good-for-nothings picked on him for his grimy clothes and commenced to spitting on him. His cusses trailed after them, and to his misfortune, into the ears of a policeman.

He's serving nine months, five to go.

We left at first light, moving through the heat and rising steam. The day was fixin' to be a scorcher. We got four miles behind us—the first part of it is winding logging trails, crick crossings, and then scrawny back roads before we reach Cartersville. It's faster going down but'll take longer coming back, all uphill, loaded with supplies and four new convicts.

Once out of Taggert's sight, Tuck rides up front with me. This leaves the prisoners unguarded in the open wagon. But they ain't going nowhere.

I guide the mule down the path to the farmer's place. "I got one stop couple miles from here," I say. "You mind?"

"Naw. Glad to be out of camp." He chews on a thumbnail and spits something to the side. "It gets to me, you know."

"Me too." I ain't sure what "it" is. The smell of dirty convicts, the cussedness, the bad food, being a prisoner? Could be one or all.

We come out onto a clearing with a view to the left. The unrolling of the forest below looks like a quilt, many shades of green closer up and deep blues in the distance. I picture my home on Stewart Mountain, scrubbing away the vision and my old man's parting words. "Jesus might love you but that's about it." Couldn't never please Poppy. Knew I was mostly a failure in his eyes, but that, *that* was the final cut.

"Do you know what's gonna end these chain gangs?" Tuck has a far-off look on his face.

"New laws?" I learned whilst traveling that the South is about the only part of the country still holding the idea that punishment means working a man to death.

"They already changed the laws. In 1908. Georgia legislators passed the Prison Reform Act. Got rid of convict leasing. But they still needed all us poor fellers to do their free labor, so they created chain gangs."

I cut my eyes to him. He's a mite smarter than I first figured.

"You a lawyer?"

He shook his head. "Naw. I got a year into the University of Alabama, Tuscaloosa, studying law. Then the KKK torched the church that sponsored me. They don't take a shine to Catholics, you know."

"They got a whole fistful of hates, I read." I shake my head. "You peel a person's skin, and everyone looks the same inside. I was raised to believe a black heart is evil. Not black skin."

The path leads down through more pine. It's an old trail where the needles settled over the years, making a spongy cushion in the ruts. A pleasing wind swings 'cross the treetops, swaying them in unison. Ward Creek gurgles off to the side, showing up and disappearing as it makes its own means down the mountain. Squirrels skedaddle before us, then curiosity takes hold and they hang onto the side of trees, upside down and staring with shiny black eyes.

"Yup, we all bleed alike." He pulls his hat lower to shade his face. "But you watch. No one working convicts like this has a drop of decency. It's all about bending the rules to make money. And if you surround yourself with others who like twisting them rules, nothing's going to change."

"It ain't fittin' the way it works round here." We pass a rusty wire fence and thickets of blackberries ahead. Then I spot the path to the farmer's house. "That's our stop, up yonder."

I turn the mule down the dirt track. Not that far ahead, the old man is standing next to a fence post, chawing a long blade of grass.

"Howdy," I say. "What you doing way out here on the loose end of your property?"

"Pshaw!" He slaps some dirt off his britches leg. "Heard you coming for days. You fellers squawking loud as a bunch of magpies."

I laugh. "S'pose we were." I like the old coot. I hop off the wagon seat and reach in behind and pull out his milk bottle, now full of tar. "Here ya go."

He reaches for it and holds it close to his good eye.

"Gave you two bottles."

In front of Tuck, I can't tell him how I left one with the lost souls in the woods. If Taggert ever got wind of it, he'd add a few more months to my sentence. My time with the boy will be a secret between the kid, the forest, and me.

"Still got one at camp. Tar is worth more than milk."

He *harrumphs*. "Costs me good money to feed my darn cow. You get them pines that God gave you for free."

I nod at the truth. "I'll be by again and bring the other."

"Be waitin' on you."

Back up on the seat, I slowly turn the wagon round in his dirt yard. A woman is sweeping the porch and stops to look our way. Tuck and me raise a hand in greeting. She nods and returns to her chore.

The farmer is halfway 'cross a fallow field, moving toward a small shed. He must know every inch of his land, 'cause he don't walk like no blind man.

"You drink that other bottle of milk?" Tuck says, stretching a grin.

"Naw." Not sure why, but I don't want him to know about the boy and his brother. "Broke the damn thing on the way back. Should've toted them bottles in separate pouches, but they banged together. Couldn't let Taggert know."

"That's the truth."

Ward Creek runs north and dumps into the Etowah River. Dozens of streams pour out of the hills to meet the big river, which we'll chance upon in no time at all. Critter trails stretch away to nothing in the thick woods. We come to an area that's second growth and thinned where fire licked through it some time ago. Many trunks still blackened. An eerie sight.

"When you get out, you gonna try to get back to college?" I say. We hit a good-sized rut and the wagon jumps. I look over my shoulder. Both convicts are still lying down, sleeping.

"Hope so. Railroad is always hiring. I might work there a year, save money, then go back."

"Good to have a plan. I tried my hand at woodworking in Saint Louis. Feller that hired me said I had a good eye for design. Might try to be a furniture maker." I'd never said this out loud before. "Rich folks'll pay pert near fifty dollars for a handmade supper table and eight dollars for a chair."

"Darn good money." He scratches skeeter bites on his arm. "You rode the trains. Which job you think is best?"

We're dropping down a twisty road into a holler, and I hear the crick before we reach it.

"I spent a night with a tower operator looking over a big switching yard near Kansas City. That feller's hands was busier than a lint picker in a cotton mill. He was shifting a long lever to switch trains from track to track. Had to change signal lights to tell train crews the route was safe or there was a wreck. Nothing boring there. And I gamble he makes good wages."

"Huh. Might not be boring but sounds like he's stuck in one place. Like prison." He snorts. "Had enough of that."

I laugh. "Hear ya." I slow the wagon as we draw nigh to a wide rushing crick. "Porters in the sleeping car set up the berths at night and turn them back into sitting rooms at first light. They travel for weeks at a time, making darn good tip money."

I stop the wagon at the edge of the Etowah River. It's wide but shallow at this crossing.

"Water break."

Tuck helps the lame Negro out of the wagon. The man hops away to do his business behind a wide oak. The white young'un is mumbling 'bout snakes and badgers as I get him to his feet. He walks away and leans against a tree.

"Ten minutes," I call then turn to the stream and step out onto the rock beds, where the water burbles over the stones and falls from one ledge into a pool on the next lower one. I squat on my heels and drink from the stream, lifting the cold water in my cupped hand. It's sweet with a thin taste of iron and so cold it pains my front teeth.

What's stopping me from driving in another direction right now? We just crossed the Old Alabama Road. Say I turn back and decide to head west instead of north? I can drop Tuck and the two convicts off on the outskirts of Euharlee just west of Cartersville. Let them disappear into the four winds. Otherwise, once we reach Cartersville, the shackles go back on the inmates' ankles. They'll be chained together on the way to the hospital. The feeling of freedom they tasted while working the pines will soon be scrubbed from their senses.

And as always, the choice not to cut and run often circles back to shame. I don't want my folks to know I've amounted to no good. Vowed to myself when I left home to do right by my family name—and did for near a half a year. Made sure to send money to prove myself responsible, too, 'cause I had failed so miserably in Poppy's view.

Bugs buzz in the heat. My mind wanders. When I let my protective shell crack open, I confess I miss my kin.

This time of year, we'd fill most evenings on our old wraparound porch, shaking off the last recollections of winter's yoke. I picture Mama knitting in her favorite rocking chair or shucking early peas. Billy Leo might be studying a jar of lightning bugs, trying to figure a way to sneak them into the house. Many a night a few have escaped from under our bedsheet, bouncing round inside the log walls while I hunt down his *tiny lanterns* and set them to freedom out the window. Willow, almost sixteen now and mute, is always reading. Each night she keeps right at it until the pages are near impossible to cipher in the heavy gloom of twilight. Poppy is forever tinkering, fixing something, or whittling, while humming a tune. If he's up to it, he'll get out the old fiddle and we all set to foot-tapping. But mostly he's wore out.

My oldest sister, Ruthy, has a voice clear as a spring morning. She's a good shape-note singer like most folks who never learned to read music. Just before I left home, she'd barely caught herself a boyfriend at a local pie day, where the hillfolk gather at the old Methodist church to swap six months of gossip and helpful fixings to each other's problems. That night, Mama pushed her to the front of the dance floor when the fiddles came out. Ruthy sang "Barbry Allen" so mournful, it'd make a buzzard cry, and then she switched to "Wreck of the Number Nine."

Leeman Castlelaw, a hard-working onion seller from the Castlelaw clan of Bear Trap Holler, heard her sing and fell for her. Willow thinks he smells like chopped onions and uses her hand signs to say her eyes water when he's nearby. But that's our Willow. She picks up on smells and sounds like no one else can.

Maybe Ruthy has found a better-smelling feller by now.

What I miss most 'bout home is the quiet that comes with the dark skies. Out here I'm surrounded by more than twenty snoring, moaning men. I got a few peaceful nights like back home while riding atop a train. There the skies come to life, filled with so many living sparks, shifting in a swirl of streaks from one side to the other as the train takes bends on the track. The lights pull me. A million bright flickering bits, touching my face, my arms, almost drawing me off the Earth.

A cowbird cries over my head. I splash water on my face and close my heart. All this recollecting is wasted thoughts. Time to skedaddle.

We're back on the trail minutes later. I steer the wagon down Old Goode Road to Cartersville.

The convicts go back to sleep, and Tuck tries to play a tune on a cockamamie whistle he made from a pine knot. Sounds like a crow with a nut stuck in its throat, but I let him entertain himself.

The pine trees peter out and give way to wild fields. Then dry dirt roads show up, splitting the cotton from the wheat. Every mile or so, set back aways from the dusty lane, there's a hardscrabble house and old outbuildings circled by large shade trees.

It's now late morning and the heat's rising from the fields, from the road, wrinkling the view ahead. In a clean-swept dirt yard, two old women sit on rickety steps fanning themselves, while the young'uns play near their feet. Older children run around, chasing without seeming to notice the sun bearing down on their curly dark heads.

A low rumbling sound comes out of nowhere and I slow the mule.

A dog barks at the shack as a single-engine airplane rises from over the tree line and swoops down low over the fields. It sprays the crops, the women, and their children with clouds of white dust. They wave it away from their eyes, but their faces remain turned upward in delight toward the retreating airplane.

It's not a sight many folks will ever behold. In all my travels, this is only the third time I've seen one.

"That beats all!" Tuck says, a wide smile on his face. He leans closer. "Maybe we can catch a ride out of here."

"That would confound Taggert, wouldn't it?" I chuckle. "Empty wagon seat, everything else in place."

We continue on past the road that leads to the Tumlin Indian Mounds and to the outer parts of Cartersville. The road gets wider and the houses are closer together. We round a street corner, pass the flour mill, and spot the airplane again. It's parked in an open field like a small bird, nose up and sitting on its haunches. Dozens of people—no womenfolk—stand around talking to a man in riding britches and boots, leather flying jacket, and leather head protector.

"Let's stop and hear what he has to say." Tuck is on his knees on the wagon seat, looking off to the side as we pass the field. The convicts are awake and sitting up as well.

"We'll be late," I say.

"Ten minutes don't matter. When we ever gonna be up close like this again, Briar?"

I can't hardly argue. "I reckon we can take a gander."

I steer the mule to the edge of the field and hop down. Tuck follows.

"What about them?" Tuck hooks his thumb toward the convicts.

I address the two. "You run now, and you'll catch a back full of bullets. I don't want to see that. You understand that, right?"

The Negro nods while the other guy mumbles something 'bout going to a circus.

"Enjoy the show from here." It's then that I notice the line of black-and-white-striped uniforms in a field in the opposing direction. The Negroes are chained together so's to work as a unit, chopping at stumps in a cleared field. I point. "Don't want you back in the chains."

"Yessir," the colored man says.

We cross through weeds, coming up short of the pilot and his plane. He's answering questions from the crowd, made up of men and young boys.

"I sleep in a hammock strung between the struts."

He's clean-shaven with chiseled features and has a full-of-himself stance.

"How much for a ride, sir?" A boy is breathless, perhaps having run here from wherever he first spotted the plane.

"Three dollars, son."

The boy drops his head and arms.

"You got any money?" Tuck asks me.

"Not here I don't." I stashed some outside a town called Kingston west of here. It'll be my first stop when I get out. "Steep price, but I bet it's worth it."

A man hands over some money and pushes past the boy to shimmy aboard. Soon the pilot gives the propeller a spin, and the plane kinda bounces down the field before turning around again. It thunders toward us and the road before lifting off.

My heart pounds, imagining what leaving the ground must feel like. The airplane disappears over a small hill, the engine noise growing fainter. Then before we know it, the airplane is right over our heads again. He flies so low, I feel as if I can reach up and touch the bottom skin of the machine.

The pilot is showing off now. He turns the airplane around over the town, pulling up sharp and rocking it on its side. He glances down through what looks like support rods and flying wires and waves. The fare payer's face is stuck in a fearful stare, his arms braced against the door.

Once again, he circles low over the field and lands his plane.

I chuckle on the walk back to the wagon. "That was worth every dollar that man paid."

"Sure enough." Tuck nods. "I aim to do that someday."

"You'll be the Flying Lawyer."

"I'll give rides all day." He slaps his knees. "Then I'll buy one of your fancy dining tables."

I turn to the Negro in the back. "Say. What's your given name?" Taggert called all the Negroes John Henry.

"Frederick Sharp, sir."

"Well, Frederick Sharp. What'd you think 'bout that?"

He's all smiles, showing several missing teeth. "That was better than two singing Sundays."

"Sure was," I say.

The other convict is talking to his hands, something 'bout a porcupine. Not sure how that fit messed with his mind, but the boy is lost to the world. May just be a kindness from the Good Lord.

"What you in for, Frederick?" I'm always curious what got a man in trouble. Add it to my list of *whatever they done, I ain't gonna do.*

"They got me for 'walking without a purpose,' sir."

"How long you get?" Tuck turns in his seat to ask.

"Two years, nine months."

Tuck whistles, a long slow sound that fizzles at the end.

I shake my head as I steer the wagon onto the road again. Walking without a purpose? What kind of no-good made up law is that? Might just as well arrest a feller for breathing while living.

We come in on Indian Avenue. I turn the mule up Chain Gang Hill, as the locals call it. At the top sits County Prison Camp, a layout of U-shaped wooden barracks inside high barbed wire fencing. One guard tower is at the corner of the barracks.

The prison holds a couple hundred convicts, most out this time of day on the county work sites. Same as we passed in the stump field near the airplane.

I used to believe we are all a fruit of life's lessons. Bad or good. But what lesson is there in being made to work in cruel conditions 'cause some highfalutin so and so with power claims walking without a purpose is a crime? A man can stand brutal force, but brutal reasoning will break a feller in two. How can a man fight against laws made for the sole purpose of supplying free labor to the rich? It's all so wrong.

I drive through the guard gate. The four of us had seen something full of wonder today—the airplane. The hope of flight that was only a wild idea some eighteen years ago.

Minutes and days ahead might get ugly, but I'm gonna hold on to the magical vision of that airplane. A symbol of freedom. I hope these other fellers do too.

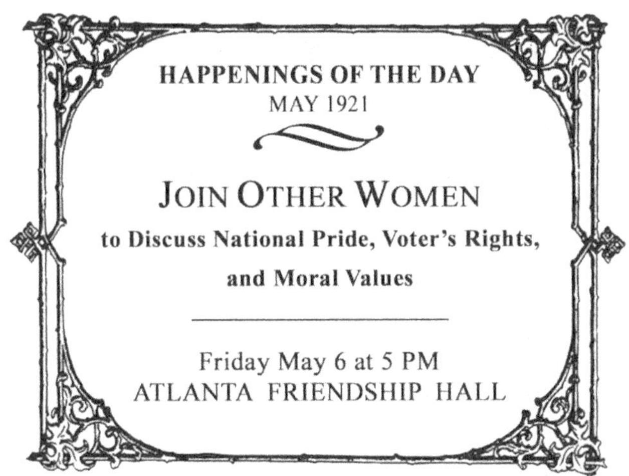
HAPPENINGS OF THE DAY
MAY 1921

JOIN OTHER WOMEN
to Discuss National Pride, Voter's Rights, and Moral Values

Friday May 6 at 5 PM
ATLANTA FRIENDSHIP HALL

Marietta, Georgia. May 6, 1921

-9-

Ardith Dobbs

I put the finishing touches on my hair and admire my new dress in the mirror. This one is a pink and pale yellow sleeveless chiffon shift, perfect for a fine May day and the important ceremony this afternoon. I can't believe it's finally happening. Our meager group of the Daisy Ladies' Society becomes official members of the WKKK today in Georgia.

Josephine took Oliver to the park and later will watch him while she cleans our house one last time before she needs a few days off. She mentioned she thinks her baby is close to coming. Any day now, she predicts. William will enjoy his father-son evening with Oliver since I will be home late.

I rub my swollen belly. Baby Katherine has been more active today than usual. She must feel my excitement.

Deidre Barr from Indiana is coming with other Imperial and Realm Commanders from northern Klonvocations. Today's gathering at the Atlanta Friends Meetinghouse is heralded to draw six hundred women. Miss Barr is a celebrated Quaker minister, a temperance organizer, a political activist, and has preached in factories, garages, shops, and on the streets. I can only dream about how wonderful it would be to draw a crowd like she does.

An article my friend Teresa Greer wrote and submitted to the *Fiery Cross,* the Klan newspaper, caught Miss Barr's attention. Teresa wrote that we glorious mothers are powerful forces in society. The prime shapers of the values of home and family. That we are the foundation of a strong America. And that by not being allowed to join the men to defend the traditional moral standards against the vices of a modern society, a women's purity cause is half lost. This message is what Miss Barr has preached for years. That women are helpmates to Klansmen and should be duly inducted.

What I like are her progressive ideas about motherhood. She says it used to be the ideal fulfillment of a woman's destiny, but it's time for change. With equality on our side, our new roles as mothers extend to supervising our communities. To help our husbands uphold the tenets of pure Americanism.

As I'm leaving the house, Frank Greer pulls up in his new touring car. It's a beautiful sky-blue color with white sidewalls and tan soft-top. William said a lawyer's salary buys this type of car while an advertiser and insurance man needs to be happy with his new Ford. It's fine. Our house is nicer than the Greers' home.

Teresa slides out of the front seat and hops in the back with me, so I don't have to ride there alone.

"Frank." She uses a fake English accent. "You may now drive us to our meeting."

We raise our eyebrows to each other. *Aren't we special?*

Because Teresa grabbed the attention of the northern Women of the Klan, we get to meet Miss Barr personally after the ceremony.

"Are you excited, Ardith?" Her rouged cheeks are extra pink, and she's got a watermelon-wide smile fixed to her face.

"My heart is pounding faster than all get out."

She pulls away and frowns. "What a corny saying. Did you pick that up from your nanny?"

I will the heat to leave my face, realizing I've slipped in a saying from back home. I give a teensy chuckle. "I suppose I did."

She pats my leg. "Remember. We're helping raise the lower classes. Best not use your maid's phrases in front of Miss Barr."

"Of course. That would be ridiculous." I offer her my don't-be-silly face I've practiced a hundred times in the mirror, but inside I'm boiling. Sometimes Teresa is downright snooty. If she ever gets to heaven, she's the person who will request to see the upstairs.

Twenty minutes later, Frank pulls up to the large, one-story meeting-house. Lines of women snake out the two doorways, and I worry we might be too late.

"You ladies behave yourself." He turns sideways to look at us and smiles, saying "Don't go trying to run for government or anything."

We agree not to, and head to the front of the line with our special invitations and wait for the man at the door to check for our names.

I wish William was as accepting as Frank. We had a fight this morning about why I wanted to mingle with women who are opinionated enough to get themselves killed. William cited a mother murdered after she turned in bootleggers in Ohio, and another wife was beaten to death by unknown assailants, leaving her small children motherless. She'd recently passed out literature inviting Catholic women to leave their church and join the Women Against the Catholic Empire. To stop Papal Prisons and rescue girls trapped behind convent walls. I reminded William that in the end, they discovered the woman was killed by her husband because, in his opinion, she spent too much time away from her household duties. "Hopefully you're not plotting to kill me," I'd said.

When he didn't laugh, I added, "You know my focus is on poor immigrant women. We don't support the New Hope Charity Home for nothing. And like you, we're fighting the Catholics at every turn. Steering women away from the Sisters of Charity Homes. We're way ahead of them teaching women how to raise a better baby by joining our women's group. They swear to our moral code, get food, clothes, and advice."

I knew that would get to him. William loves babies and has rallied for the pursuit of only pure-blood children filling Marietta's schools.

"Come right this way, ladies," the man says. He's the only male in sight. Is he being honored or punished?

The interior is a large open room with dozens of rows of benches that create an inner square, all facing a pulpit in the center. A balcony above mirrors the same square pattern but appears to be for standing worshipers only. We are seated in the front row on the right side. A dozen other women are already seated around the interior. The room is unpretentious, without any ornamentation, but the benches' muted gray color and white walls are pleasing to the eyes.

Within minutes, the floorboards rumble as hundreds of women flow inside and squeeze into the pews, their colorful dresses creating an image of a flower garden against a gray backdrop. They are all talking, noisier than plovers descending on a swarm of grasshoppers.

I emulate Teresa, who is sitting near the edge of her chair, her back ramrod straight, a permanent smile on her much-too-red lips. This is a big evening for us.

Someone begins clapping, and women rise to their feet as three ladies enter from a side door. I recognize Miss Barr from the newspaper stories. She's smartly dressed in a light blue linen suit, white blouse, and smart cloche hat with a rosette flower on the side. She does a slow turn and waves to the cheering crowd, her round face aglow. My heart pounds, and I can't control my somewhat toothy grin. This is the closest I've been to a famous person.

"Thank you, everyone," she says, starting right in. Her voice is strong, uplifting. "Please be seated." As we all sit, she notices the women in the balcony section. "Or please find a railing to lean against." She pauses to wait for everyone to stop chuckling. "I am so thrilled to be speaking to you today. I've always wanted to visit your lovely state, but duty calls in so many cities. I'm here because you have a woman of justice among you!

Thanks to Teresa Greer, you have my attention." She scans the front rows, searching. "Teresa. Would you mind standing?"

I give Teresa a gentle nudge, but she lets a few seconds tick by before she stands. As we'd say back home, *she's milking this cow until the last teat goes dry*. Then I chastise myself. Her letter to the newspaper *has* brought us all favor. She stands to booming applause.

"And we have our Society of Friends here today. Could I have all of my Georgia sisters stand?" Miss Barr says.

This is so nice of her to include those of us who know Teresa. I rise and smile, but Teresa pulls me back to my seat and whispers, "She's talking about her Quaker friends."

I duck my head and study my hands like they've just shown up at the end of my arms. My face burns and I barely hear Miss Barr's opening words. I hope she didn't see me stand. I want to be able to make eye contact with her when we meet later.

Teresa murmurs in agreement. "That's right. And it's the truth."

I sit up straight and tune in.

"…and we are all here together. Joined in one brave, noble cause. I see representatives from the Ladies of the Invisible Eye, the Grand League of Protestant Women, Queens of the Golden Mask, who have traveled here from the Midwest. We have the Hooded Ladies of the Mystic Den, and Puritan Daughters of America. We are not different groups any longer." She raises her hand in the air and women clap and catcall. "We are here to stay. History will tell of our righteous fight to safeguard the white race against a rising tide of color. We prevent juvenile delinquency, loose morals. We support segregation and fight every moment against miscegenation."

We cheer louder.

If William could hear Miss Barr, he would agree with her ideas and not think of her talks as radical. He and the others have combated the same vices for six years since the Klan started up again in 1915. That circuit-riding minister, William Simmons, proclaimed the rise of the second KKK atop Stone Mountain, not that far from Marietta.

"But I insist that in all things you act with the modesty and with the virtue of your womanhood and be careful not to foster masculine boldness or restless independence. Leave political strategizing to the men but support the politics in the communities. We hope one day to open these doors to our children. I want to see our southern sisters sponsoring parades like the one we just attended in Indiana. My heart was warmed by one float in particular. It featured a little red schoolhouse surrounded by happy children dressed in miniature Klan robes. The banner read 'Ku Klux Kiddies.'"

"We should do that in our Spring Fair," Teresa whispers. "We can have a sewing bee to make the children's and the babies' regalia."

Teresa and I have paid our ten-dollar Imperial dues. Finally, in tonight's initiation, we will receive our robes and hoods. We've already been calling ourselves by the Klan's organizational names that the WKKK in the North and Midwest are using. But tonight, I will become a true secretary and treasurer for our group. A Kligrapp and a Klabee in our local Klanton. Perhaps one day I could move up to just the secretarial position over a province, which would cover our whole county. And what if William moved up the ranks? To be married to a Grand Dragon. That would be most exhilarating!

Teresa jabs me in the ribs. Can the woman hear my pious thoughts?

"She asked who is ready to take the vow," she says, leaning close to me.

Hands are raised all around the meetinghouse, and Miss Barr is turning in a slow circle with a celebratory air about her. I jam my hand upward before her eyes move to our side of the room.

I am ready.

I'm not sure I have ever been as excited or as filled with a sense of patriotism as I have at this moment. Baby Katherine is extra active, and I can't wait to tell her about this when she's older, about how she was involved too. We are more than two hundred and fifty robed and hooded women gathered on a high hilltop outside Atlanta. Miss Barr and the local Klansmen arranged streetcars to carry all of us who were ready to join to the edge of the city. We walked with linked arms the rest of the way to the remote hilltop. Only moments ago, the sunset presented a magical ending to the day, which perfectly matches my mood. As dusk settles, the chief officer of the province, a Grand Titan, and his other officers, known as the Seven Furies, walk to the fifteen-foot wooden cross and light it on fire.

"This is to remind you to act like Jesus Christ and serve the Klan. You are in God's army against the enemies of God's chosen people." The fire flashes yellow against our white robes. "You are masked to hide your individuality, your social class, and to make you all equal as you go forward in Klankraft. Remember your motto, 'Not for self but for others.' As you look upon each other robed in white, realize you are now on a common level of sisterhood."

That's the swell of pride I'm feeling. I finally have an honest group to belong to. No more running from my backwoods roots or the lie about how I'm the only one left in my family due to an iceberg. This is the first truthful endeavor I've ever participated in.

"In a few minutes, you will take a sacred vow. If you ever break that vow or disclose what you've learned today, you will answer to a tribunal. Failure to obey our laws or the command of an officer results in harsh punishment, from suspension to banishment altogether. Spies, and there have been a few who have joined, are eventually discovered and no longer report to anyone."

I swallow. The weight of what I'm about to do hits me in the chest. I will be a member of a secret army. The reason America will recover from its depths of impurity.

"We are the invisible empire, and you will be able to identify a sister or brother Klansman by our secret Klan words. Learn them well."

I've rehearsed the new names for the Kalender. The days, weeks, and months, but it's a lot. January is *Dismal*, February is *Mystic*, March is *Stormy*. The secret saying for today's date, the 6th day in the first week of May, is the Dreadful day in the Woeful week of the Horrible month. I've tried to practice with William when we are alone, but he's often not as thrilled as I am. He said the words are to be used in emergencies, when a brotherhood connection needs to be validated. Not just for a notification of a run to the market.

I disagree.

"Let the ceremony begin," the Grand Titan says.

Miss Barr and her female officers approach the makeshift altar after kissing the American flag and slipping fancy blue hoods over their heads. The rest goes by fast, and I try to savor every minute. We sing one verse of "Onward Christian Soldiers," then an officer repeats a litany over our symbols. The Bible, the fiery cross, an American flag, a sword, water, mask, and our robe. Then they pour water into bowls on a long table.

We line up and move forward until we each reach the water. I dip my fingers in and do what the other women ahead of me have done. I touch my shoulders and say, "In body." I touch my forehead and say, "In mind." I wave my hands in the air. "In spirit." And finally, make a circle around my head and say, "In life."

When we've all completed the water ritual, the Grand Titan speaks, his voice deeper now. Like a loud rumble against the wavering fire.

"With this transparent God-given fluid more precious than the sacred oils of the ancients, I set you apart from the women of your daily association, to the great and honorable task you have voluntarily allotted to yourselves as citizens of the invisible empire…women of the Ku Klux Klan."

Chills run through my body.

He continues. "May your character be transparent, your life's purpose as powerful, your motive in all things as magnanimous and as pure, and your Klan membership as real and as faithful as God has commanded."

We line up again, this time to approach Miss Barr, the Grand Titan, and his Seven Furies who congratulate us. When I reach Miss Barr, I lean closer and say, "I am Teresa Greer's friend. I want to thank you for the special invitation to tonight's ceremony."

"Ah. The one who wasn't sure if she was a Quaker or not." Her voice sounds like she's kidding, but behind the hood, who can tell.

"Yes." My voice is pathetic, and I hate that I'm coming off in such a bad light. "I'm sorry I misunderstood the 'friends' comment."

She pulls me a bit closer. Our cloth head coverings touch.

"It's your job from now on not to misunderstand anything you see." She squeezes my arm and then turns to the next woman.

One of the Furies extinguishes the cross. "You may remove your regalia," he calls above the excited conversations.

I neatly fold my robe and hood and try to find Teresa. We've been offered a personal ride home by Miss Barr's group. I wander through the women and return *congratulations*, but I still don't see Teresa. When I return to the altar area, Miss Barr and the dignitaries are gone.

I'm furious. How could Teresa leave me like a bloated pig in a well! I'm going to jerk her bald when I get close to her again. Tears prick my eyes, and I will them away. I don't need to be treated extra fine like Teresa does. As I said in my oath, "May my life's purpose be powerful."

With Miss Barr's touch lingering on my arm, I follow everyone down the hill, walking carefully in the dark. The trolley will deposit me three blocks from home. I head back to my daily life, now a secretly changed woman.

HAPPENINGS OF THE DAY

MAY 1921

POLICE LOCATE RUNAWAY GIRL

Lured to her De-flowering by
Promise of Candy

Sent to
Home for Wayward Youth

The Road to Helen, Georgia. May 1921

-10-

Willow Stewart

Mr. Coburn isn't dead, but death stalks him where he dropped face-down onto the ground many minutes ago. His body bucks, and my efforts to deafen my ears to his woeful bracken-brown cries of agony are useless.

Got to free myself.

The sharp edge of the wagon's rusty metal frame works nearabout perfect to cut through these ropes. Now free, I rub my wrists and check the gunshot wound on my arm. The bullet only nicked me, and it will heal though there might be a scar. I need to grind some burdock root and make a plaster.

Coburn is quiet. I walk to his side and prod him with the toe of my boot until he rolls onto his back. He doesn't respond. Shootfire! His face has gone the color of smoke, and for sure he's gone, no longer pondering the secrets of death but witnessing them up close. Lord, a man with a tarnished character like his probably got sent to *Haints Holler.*

I study the field. A wind slides through the tender grasses, pointing green fingers my way. A message arrives on the ripples, that one day I may be judged for letting him eat the poison. And it isn't too far-fetched in my superstitious nature to wonder if evil will trace its way up Stewart Mountain and punish me by taking Mama to her death.

What would we do without Mama, without her laugh? She makes every chore, no matter how hard, more fun. She'd see us fading on the job and would call out, "Let's put a tail on it, children!"

Then break into a funny song.

Make a game of tossing shucked pea pods into a bucket.

Or let us draw purple faces on each other during blackberry picking time.

The thought that she might be gone makes me feel heavy and stuck, like a butterfly with its wings torn off told to keep moving.

A cold shiver slithers down my back. I must get to Helen.

Burdock likes dark, moist areas, so I hunt along the forest floor for the big plant with wide wavy-edged leaves. There it is! I pull a handful of stalks. With my teeth, I strip the outer covering and spit out the bitter skin. The fibrous insides are what I need. Back at the wagon, I find a clean tin bowl and smash the plant into a paste, place a handful on my wound, and wrap it with a strip from my torn sleeve. There's a can of BC Powder on a shelf somewhere, if my recollection hasn't run off and left me. The powder is good for tooth pain, headache, and both the curse and muscle cramps. Since I helped him with his chigger bites, I reckon taking this from him wouldn't mean I'm stealing. It's a simple trade. Besides, his behavior toward me wasn't worth a cuss, and I'm certain as May mud that his poor wife isn't missing him and his shabby morals. I rip open the packet and stir the powder in water and swig it down.

Right now, I'm so hungry my stomach thinks my throat's left these parts for the big city. The wagon is loaded with food, but again my mind pages through my Christian standards. Is it stealing, or reckoning from the man who fondled and shot me? My stomach growls a fierce answer, and I remember the food Ruthy packed for me. I hop out of the wagon and grab my draw-string sack left on the ground where I fell.

I eat all the food except the peanut brittle. I might need those later. Soon, I'm ready to go.

Since there's no way I can lift the man into the wagon, I have no choice but to leave him. Grabbing his feet, I tug him closer to the bushes. His coat hikes up round his shoulders, leaving a drag trail of turned-up dirt from where I moved him.

Now for the horses. Can't very well leave one and ride the other. When night falls with no campfire, wild animals will move in. Mr. Coburn won't know what's happening, but the horse would be attacked. And since I can't ride both, I'm obliged to drive his rig into town.

Not quite sure where I am, though, and for a flea's second, I consider going home. Poppy and the other menfolk could take over dealing with the dead peddler. But I could no more return without a preacher than choose to speak. I need to follow through with my promise.

Stepping through the white clusters of Dutchman's breeches, I reach the center of the field. From there, Tray Mountain is in view. Coburn moved us eastward a mite and we're closer to Anna Ruby Falls, still in the thick of the northern forest. I raise my hand to block the sun from directly piercing my eyes and measure its position in the sky. By turning the wagon round, I'll be headed west again toward the Fancy Road. Not as much off course as I feared.

I close and latch the wagon doors and then glance at the dead man once more. His gun lies near his crumpled body. I pick it up and empty the bullets and toss them into a patch of tall thistle. Then I drop the gun into the pan of hot soup and kick dirt on the fire below to put it out. My bandaged arm aches. Today could very well have ended even more catawampus, with me dead or toting around a life-changing bucket full of regret because I really might have tried to kill him if he hadn't killed himself.

I slowly approach the horses, praying they don't have a side of ornery I can't handle. To get better acquainted, I rub their necks and make eye contact. Soon, they let me hitch them back into their harnesses, and my shoulders relax.

I spot the trail where the peddler entered the field, climb up onto the seat, and click my tongue to get the horses moving. At first, trying to manage two horses is like attempting to braid eels, but I get the feel and keep the wagon in the tracks and upright. I conjure up the character Mr. Toad in *The Wind in The Willows.* It's when he's fixated on his new horse-drawn caravan. Although I have no friends like Rat and Mole to join me, I picture Mama by my side, telling me to be strong.

I should make Helen before sundown, but now I need a preacher *and* the law. I don't like that I'm delivering bad news all around.

Forty minutes later or thereabouts, by the look of the sun's movement, I turn left onto the Fancy Road. The smooth gray surface feels foreign, and the wagon sides no longer clatter and creak. Along the motorway, forsythia sways in the ditch, its yellow blossoms starbright against the grassy fields.

Over the clomp of hooves, I hear a far-off clank of a tractor and see a fallow field dotted with black tree stumps. The sound tells me a farmer is nearby. A truck approaches and my heart quickens. I slow the horses and wave my arms, hoping the person will alert the local police for me, and I'll have less writing to do to describe what happened with that no-account Mr. Coburn. The rusted truck, piled high in the back with tied-down furniture and two scrawny boys riding on top, doesn't even slow. The hunched over driver looks as if he has his own troubles that stretch into next year.

Never felt so alone, but I keep going. Faith and hope are fuzzy say-sos wheeling around like swallows in my head. *Faith* I will get a note off to Briar telling him he needs to come home, and *hope* I'll return home to find Mama making a turn for the better.

A speck grows larger on the road ahead. It's a shiny black car. Lord, be praised! Once again, I wave, but he keeps going. As it passes, I see POLICE written on the hood and a badge on the door. Why isn't anyone stopping? How many young girls are driving merchant wagons, wildly waving their arms for attention? I know he saw me. A squealing sound cuts the day in half. I look over my shoulder, and like watching a flock of birds suddenly change direction, he spins his car around and heads my way.

I nearly wilt like a pulled weed.

I direct the horses off the road and stop at the edge of a barley field. The late afternoon sun eases toward the horizon behind scruffy strips of clouds. Dusk—when shadows stretch mighty long—will recolor the sky in about two hours. A whippoorwill's sad call floats across the field, matching my deepest concerns. There's no chance I'll return home tonight.

The police car stops behind the wagon. I take my notepad and pencil from my burlap poke and write, *I need to fetch a preacher in Helen.* I slip the note in my dress pocket. I close the poke and climb down from the driver's seat. Two sets of policemen's leather-soled shoes slap the road as they approach. I hold the reins on the jittery horses as the men stop a few feet away.

They study me. I study them. One is taller and has a birdlike face. His eyes are red-rimmed, as if they dislike sitting in their sockets. Both men have deep rows of weathered skin at the back of their necks. The shorter policeman has oversized, disorderly eyebrows, looking for all the world as if baby muskrats are plastered there. With one hand in his pocket, he's jingling something metal, maybe coins.

"Are you driving this rig all by your lonesome?" Furry Eyebrows says.

I nod.

How do I explain what's happened to Mr. Coburn? Would they believe the kidnapping account? Snatching and keeping someone is rare, according to Mama. Years back I asked her what kidnapping meant. She explained and assured me folks stealing children happens about as often as the five-year locust, and usually, that locust has come dipped in gold, and money is the allure.

Well, Mr. Coburn was misinformed concerning the riches he'd find coating our stomping grounds. The only things golden atop Stewart Mountain are the gilded ribbons the sun trails across our peaks from morning to night.

Bird Face steps closer. "You own this here wagon?"

My heart drums. Since a lie would follow a person halfway round the world to trip him up again, I shake my head. Reaching into my pocket, I flip a page in the notepad and write, *The owner died in the woods.*

"He your kinfolk?" Bird Face squints at my note and hands it back. He turns to Eyebrows. "She might be from one of the deviant families up in the hills. Seems to have a defect."

I start to make hand signs and realize they mean nothing to them. I scribble, *My mind is fine but I am mute.* I show them my earlier note about needing a preacher and going into Helen.

They confer as if I can't hear.

"The wagon has a registration tag from South Carolina." Bird Face adjusts his heavy leather belt. "No sparrow-sized girl drove that wagon this far without a mess of trouble straggling behind her."

"By the looks of her, something transpired. Ripped dress. Her arm is bandaged." Muskrat Eyebrows points at my arm, and I take a step back.

A train whistle echoes in the distance. Its hollow sound courses through me, wrapping my heart in pure loneliness. Home feels so far away. I shake my head and begin to write more as they keep talking.

"You take the horses and rig," Furry Eyebrows says to the tall man. "If she's running from no good and needs a preacher, I'll drop her at the Center Baptist Church. She'll need doctoring too."

I hand them several pieces of paper. *My Mama is very ill. I was heading to Helen when the peddler shot me and tied me up. He ate poison mushrooms. My horse returned home. I had to take his horses and wagon to reach Helen.*

"You didn't know this peddler?" Bird Face raises his eyebrows.

I shake my head.

He continues. "Were you begging food off him? I know some of you folks are a sorry lot."

I don't like his attitude. He doesn't know my family. I write again but realize I'll run out of paper with all their questioning. More than that, they're wasting daylight.

I stopped to help him, and he turned no good.

"I'll carry you on into Helen and get you some help." Bushy Eyebrows reaches for the horses' reins and hands them to his partner. "Get a head start, Earl. Leave the wagon at the station but let the horses graze next door in McGregor's orchard."

Earl bunches his forehead. Evidently, the idea of being stuck with the peddler's wagon sticks in his craw like hair on a biscuit.

"What about the dead peddler?" His voice has changed from assured navy to whiney lavender. He climbs onto the seat and waits for an answer.

"I'll have…" The muskrats above the policeman's eyes rush together, like long-lost kin embracing each other, and then scuttle apart. "Excuse us, miss, but what's your name?"

I write Willow and that I'm going to meet my brother Briar. I want them to think I won't be alone and will be with a man.

The policeman reads off what I wrote and nods. "Those are good mountain names."

Earl mutters from his perch above me. "Probably named the others Dead Log and Pond Scum."

The muskrats throw themselves at each other again and stay locked together above flint-blue eyes. "That's uncalled for, Earl."

In the same instance, anger sweeps through me like fickle autumn weather. How dare he make fun of our names! In these hills, kin loyalty is above anything or anybody else's laws. Neighbors have been known to hide a relation out in the laurel, carry him food, keep him posted on the whereabouts of the law, and help him break jail if it comes to that. Mama's needlework that's framed and hanging on our kitchen wall proclaims,

Blood makes you related,
loyalty makes you family,
and that is the gosh-darn truth.

I force a smile, knowing if Poppy heard what Earl muttered, he'd have knocked the man's teeth backwards and watched him spit them out single file. I make hand signs telling him he's a mean polecat. Earl asks me what I said, but I pretend I don't hear him.

The nice policeman looks my way.

"Can you draw a map so the coroner can go fetch the dead man?"

I nod. I sign that it's not far away, no more than a few miles back, and then realize they have no idea what I'm saying. Might as well be chasing away a crazed hornet for all the hand gyrations I made. I miss Mama and Briar, my translators.

"Good. At least that's what I think you're gesticulating. We'll have you draw that when we reach Helen. Earl, you best get a move on with those horses."

Earl lifts his hat and sets his mouth in a hard line. "See you in town," he says as he waggles the reins to get the horses and wagon going. The wooden wheels creak, and stones crunch under their weight.

I watch them pull away, and the grace and beauty of those two animals make Earl appear to be a better man than he thinks he is.

"Let's get you to Helen." The policeman starts to put a hand on my back but pulls it away, uncertain. "My name is Sergeant Vissom. Peyton Ray Vissom if my mother's hollering it."

His voice is dusky blue, the same color that hovers at the edges of the sky right before the last soft orange of the day blinks off. A trustworthy sound.

As we walk to the car, my legs wobble from a heaping case of the jitters. I've never ridden in a motorcar before. And do I dare trust another man?

Mr. Vissom opens the door, and I hesitate before sliding in. I have no choice. Walking to Helen after dark would leave me in a pickle. Where to go? Who to trust? Once settled inside, I rub my hands on the seat. It's soft like Poppy's favorite chair, and the car's insides smell of cigarettes and gun oil. When he pulls out onto the road, and the car picks up speed, I grip the seat with one hand and the door with my other. The windows are open, and the air is ripe with manure and thick pine.

He laughs. "First time in a car?"

I try to look brave, but my jaws are clenched tight.

"Think of it as a faster horse." Mr. Vissom moves to the wrong side of the road for a moment as we pass Earl and the wagon. Earl raises a hand our way. He must've come to harmony with his duty.

"That's what Henry Ford said, you know?" The policeman shoots his eyes my way. "Or maybe you don't know. Anyway, Ford invented the first motorized car, and he liked to tell people, 'If I had asked you all what you wanted, you would have said faster horses.'"

Because I can't talk, the man assumes I'm dumb and haven't learned anything. I don't take offense. But Mr. Vissom is wrong. Mr. Henry Ford did not *invent* the first automobile, but he figured how to make one more folks could afford. Librarians cover our hollers and leave months-old newspapers with us, understanding our delight in the accounts of the outside world. Mama recited the stories to us while Poppy rocked in his chair and smoked and repacked his corncob pipe. Later, when I learned to read, Mama and I raced to be the first to find the plumb craziest story within the pages.

I can't relax with the car going this fast, so I hang on tight. The world zips by, blurring things together meant to stand apart. Barbed wire fencing, signs lost in high weeds, white milkweed flowers, two cows, and shredded rubber tires.

"Glad you're not one of those juvenile delinquents tearing this country to pieces, listening to dance music, wearing britches, smoking. So unladylike."

With quick sidelong glances, I inspect the driver. I'm glad I'm wearing my riding dress and not my berry-picking britches. Since he's never headed into a thorny patch wearing a dress, he's never experienced how prickers can twist a hem tight enough to cocoon a body. Only a good pair of snippers or the Coming of Christ can free you. Pants aren't a sin. They're a necessity.

"You're lucky you live in Georgia. We still have our values, and for a young girl that counts for everything. Chicago, New York City, now those are places breeding immorality faster than clergy can preach it down. Boys and girls together unchaperoned. Women smoking, cussing"—he shakes his head—"Plumb shameful."

Mama and I read a piece in the *Montgomery Monitor* about young women being arrested for defying the decency law by rolling their stockings below their knees at the beach. Others hemmed their dresses nine inches from the floor, well above the acceptable three-inch length. They scrub rouge on their knees and cheeks. Mama said it's because women finally feel equal to men. In many states out West, they vote just like men. They learned menfolk skills while their husbands or fathers fought in the Great War and now don't want to be told what to do. It seems silly that men are in a horn-tossing mood over a shorter dress. Any practical man would realize his wife is saving money by buying less cloth. I can't wait to tell Mama about these other big city sins Mr. Vissom shared.

My throat tightens at my last image of Mama. Has she opened her eyes or asked for a glass of her favorite sweet tea? Barbs of worry gnaw at my insides.

But worry won't take away my troubles. They'll only rest like heavy fog over my mind. I reset my thoughts and shoo away the worry.

The land flattens out, and the thick woodlands disappear behind us. A road sign reads *Robertstown*. We top a hill where below, the Chattahoochee River opens up, a winding blue ribbon across a colorful green quilt all the way to Helen.

Mr. Vissom points. "I'm taking you to the Center Baptist Church. Pastor Dean Holcombe and his wife Dorothy will help you."

I marvel at the wonder of how quickly we've arrived and twist my hands in excitation.

We drop into a small valley, and ahead, the road disappears again into the next woods. A right nice storybook picture.

Mr. Vissom barely slows the automobile as he pulls out a cigarette, steering the car with his knee so he can strike a match and light the tip. The unwelcomed scent of the blown-out match drifts by me and dies off out the window.

He smokes in silence for a few minutes.

"You been to Helen before?" Mr. Vissom squints at me around the curling smoke.

I write on my tablet and hold it up.

He squints to read my words. "Only to Folsom, huh? Not much to see there. A dry goods store that's more dry than goods. Small hardware building. I heard the newspaper closed down last year."

Two years back, before Luther Junior died, Poppy took Briar and me along on his trip to Folsom Creek. Poppy rode Big Blue while we sat behind on full burlap sacks in the wagon. Poppy was trading dried ginseng for a new brand of corn he'd heard tell of. Coming off the hills on washboard roads left my bones jiggling inside long after we stopped, but my first ever taste of a MoonPie made up for it. Makes me wonder if Briar has eaten another MoonPie now that he's working in the lumber business and can buy store-bought goods.

"That's all Byrd-Matthews woodhick camps there." Mr. Vissom points to neat rows of one-story wooden shacks. "Ever since the Morse brothers bought the lumber mill a few years back, the town's sprouted wings."

I flinch as someone working a loud horn blasts a long signal, and swivel my head looking for the source.

"Mill whistle. End of the workday."

We reach the fringes of Helen and pass slow-going train flatcars loaded with trees. Briar last wrote from the town of Rome, and I know from a map it's west of here. Course, we've heard nothing for several months now. He might think we don't care none, but even Poppy has softened and asked Mama what the last letter said. He nodded when he learned Briar was working in the lumbering business, and the five dollars Briar sent went into the crockery jar meant for emergencies. It will be good to have him home.

I'm feeling nervous again. With the sun hanging behind the tops of the trees, its shine time was near used up for another day. By the looks of it, I'll have to sleep in Helen overnight and head home at first light. No way I'm walking past *Haint Hollow* at dark.

"Almost there, Willow." He must sense my jitters. "Let's put the preacher into action." He turns the car up a short drive and parks in a dirt-packed lot beside the church. The parsonage connects behind the main body of the white building, and that's where Mr. Vissom points, once he helps me figure out how to open the car door.

A tall woman unfastens the parsonage screen door and waits on the stoop.

She smiles and says, "Deputy Vissom. It's nice to see you." Her light brown eyes drop to study me. "Who have you brought with you?" As she talks, her head pecks forward and backwards like a chicken. She's wearing a sensible hair bun and a long yellow print dress. "Bring her on in here." She steps inside and we follow.

The room smells of aged wood and fresh-baked bread. In the center of the kitchen area stands a wooden table big enough to seat the Last Supper with the Lord's followers, but my eyes are drawn to a shelf against the far wall filled with books. The multicolored spines gleam like a candy store shelf, and I hold my urge to rush over and run my finger over their leather and cloth covers. Never spied so many books in one place.

"This here's Willow, and she's come to notify your husband he's needed up in the hills."

"My husband's gone at the moment, but won't you stay? With it being suppertime and all, I'll set two more plates."

I smile. I'm not even half hungry. The food from home has filled me up.

Mrs. Holcombe cocks her head to the side, and while her eyes stay on me, her words are meant for Mr. Vissom. "Is she deaf and dumb?"

"She hears just fine and has a good hand at writing"—he smiles my way—"Just can't talk."

"Her ma and pa. Are they related?" She isn't being accusatory, just a mite puzzled.

I shake my head at the same time Mr. Vissom says, "I don't think so."

I open my poke and reach in for my writing tablet and pencil. I write, *They met on a train.*

"That's good, Willow." Mr. Vissom scowls at my open poke. "What else do you have in there?"

In the bottom, the wrapped candy is by its lonesome. I pull it out and hold it up.

"Did that peddler give it to you?" Mr. Vissom says.

I shake my head.

He then retells what little he knows of my story to the preacher's wife.

"Willow was heading off Stewart Mountain when a peddler grabbed her and tried to have his way. She wrote that he's dead."

Right off, Mrs. Holcombe gasps and throws a hand over her mouth. Her owl eyes drill into me.

This wouldn't do. Mr. Vissom made me sound like I killed the man. I cart out my tablet again and turn to one of its last pages and write, *He died from eating Death Caps while I was tied up.*

Mrs. Holcombe reads the words over the policeman's shoulder. She clicks her tongue and shakes her head.

"You poor dear." She crosses the room and drops an arm around me, a motherly embrace I happily lean into. My mama is a wraparound hugger, like the porch on our cabin, both arms enveloping the person who at that moment has caught her affection. But I'll take this one-arm squeeze for now.

"You've had a day awful enough to make the angels cry," she tsks. "Not more than an hour ago, Hank Fry came down the mountain near Moss Lick Knob. He was in Bear Paw buying deer hides off the Cherokee. Hustled in here, telling my husband to pack the Good Book. That's where my Dean is right now. Preaching on Stewart Mountain."

I feel my shoulders slump as tension runs out. Although I failed in my attempt to summon a preacher, the man was there nevertheless, overseeing Baby Luther's passage to heaven. Now, my only chore is to reach out to Briar and head home.

I write on the paper, *Yes. My baby brother died.*

Mr. Vissom's furry eyebrows are moving every which way, undecided at best. His face sags. A weight seems to pull down his shoulders.

"You mentioned that your mama was ill. I'm sorry to hear there was a baby that died."

I sign thank you and think he understands the hand signal.

Mrs. Holcombe steps away from me and leans her backend against the table. She hugs and unhugs her midsection—a nervous movement—then her hands drop to her sides like dead doves. She's chewing her bottom lip, her eyes flitting between me and the ceiling.

I can only reckon her nervousness is because she lost a child during birth, and Mama's situation circled sadness back her way.

"Child. I'm sorry. When Hank Fry was leaving the mountain, he heard the dinner bell ring dozens of times, signaling an older person had passed. My husband left saying he had two funerals to preach."

Her words land like big old rocks on my chest, and I fight for air. Mama's gone? I roll my burlap sack into a quivering ball and then unroll it before squeezing it again. I tied my hopes to the notion that with everyone on the mountain praying for Mama, she would recover. Dark sorrow arrives and severs my hope, cutting any string that's kept me upright. I collapse.

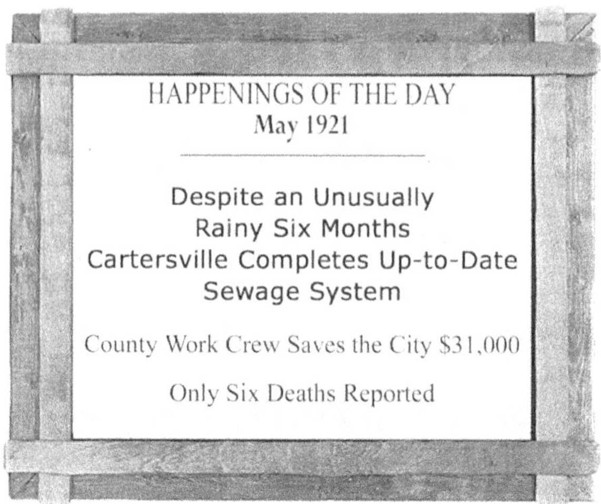

HAPPENINGS OF THE DAY
May 1921
Despite an Unusually Rainy Six Months
Cartersville Completes Up-to-Date Sewage System
County Work Crew Saves the City $31,000
Only Six Deaths Reported

County Prison Camp. May 1921

-11-

BRIAR STEWART

It's that part of nightfall when the sun has gone but daylight still hangs on. I'm facing the barracks on the Ladds Mountain side. Above me on the hillside sets the Ladd Lime & Stone Company buildings, built on wooden crisscross stands to reach high up against the tall butte. The first part of my jail sentence was on a chain gang, working in that limestone quarry. Hot, dusty, mind-numbing work for fifteen hours a day in chains that killed off many a feller. The ankle shackles chewed scars into my legs, now forever proof I was a no-account convict. Never again.

Vagrancy. That was my crime. I had forty cents on me when a policeman stopped me in Euharlee, nine miles west of Cartersville, where I planned to hop a ride on the W&A Railway to Atlanta to find work at the Fulton Bag Company. The judge in the county court claimed a man needed to have a dollar on him to be judged worthy to walk the streets.

The rub was that the day before, I'd hid my money near there, not putting my trust in a small bank. Poppy hammered home his distrust of banks after the panic of 1907 when a small bank in Diviner Gulch closed between nightfall and dawn, taking the mountain folks' money with it. Poppy lost all of twenty-three dollars, but the bigger loss was his trust in the government, a trust that had roots as deep as an old white oak. The Mason jar hidden behind the woodpile is the Stewart family's new bank.

Didn't have me a jar, but I found a right nice hidey-hole until I get back.

Tuck and I eat supper with the trustees away from the other prisoners. The guards and Warden Hauser take their meal in a clean dining space in the warden's house. Nice house or our low-slung barracks, the vittles never change. It's the same grub dished up three times a day in camp. A square of cornpone with grease, red beans, and a spoon of sorghum syrup.

One black woman with a three-year sentence for disorderly conduct works in the cookhouse. There's an eleven-year-old colored girl to help her. She's a sad little bitty thing. Skinny as a rail with one eye that turns out, gawking at Lord knows what. She got a year for "stealing a ring" she found on the street in Emerson. I asked her if her parents knew where she was, and she mumbled she didn't think so. That's not right, but it's just another thorn in my shoe that I got to button my mouth and not complain about.

I push my plate away. Everything tastes like ash and dirt. Ain't barely fit to eat. Cornmeal comes here from warehouse floors, and all taste is cooked out of the beans. Plump maggots would give more flavor. Tomorrow, Tuck and me will load up on some pork with the other foodstuffs. Enough to last the next two weeks in the timber. Hauser already pointed out the four new fellers we'll take back to the turpentine hills. Strong but defeated, strappy but obedient. Three coloreds and a white feller.

"I'm gonna walk," I say and leave the trustee table.

The County Prison Camp sits on a hill above the downtown. It's got five buildings and one guard tower. When facing the U-shaped compound, two smaller buildings are to the right. One holds work equipment, and the smallest is the warden's office. Another small shack is to the west of the barracks, down the bank and slightly to the rear, pretty close to the chicken coop. I got no idea what the building's for, but it's tucked in the woods and a mite hard to see. We ain't never allowed near it.

The prison quarters themselves are as rotten as all get-out. Ain't nothing more than drafty wood-frame construction surrounded by a gated fence and barbed wire. Convicts made Georgia's road system one of the best in the country, according to the newspapers, but we ain't allowed to build a better prison camp for its slave laborers.

Inside, the building is laid out with rows of narrow cots, each with a pillow with no fluff and an itchy blanket. A small potbelly stove sits on one end, but in winter it might as well be a pile of cold stones for all the heat it puts out. That's what I'll remember from my days here. The cold. The ruination.

I walk to the hill jutting out over the Etowah River. I followed it when I was heading into Euharlee. Should've walked around that town. Why had I kept moving east? Was I circling closer to Stewart Mountain to test my decision? I said I'd never return home, and I meant it. But time's worn down my anger, and I've thought of climbing that mountain and peeking through the trees to see how the family was doing.

But what would come of it? More harsh words? Mama crying again? No. Once I get free and land a good-paying job, I'll write and send more money. The mail is brought to the homestead by a crier on horseback half-weekly, coming from Indian Grave Gap. In some ways, I hope it pricks Pa that I am doing just fine.

I sit on a rock. Muffled explosions come from Ladd Mountain. Luther Junior and me worked in a gold mine six months before he died setting dynamite. It was good pay that we sent home every week. Pa had barely got back from the war and couldn't push a harrow at the time 'cause his lungs was so damaged. Whilst Mama and Ruthy strapped themselves to the plow, and Willow and Billy Leo planted and weeded, we all chipped in to keep the homestead going. Pa got stronger every week. He said the clean mountain air healed him, and it sure seemed like it did.

On our one day off from the gold mine, my brother and me hunted in the hollers or caught a swim in the lake near Pigeon Mountain. Luther Junior was a decent storyteller, even though he wasn't much of a reader like Mama or Willow. He had dreams like no feller I ever knew. Flying machines, talking critters, another world going on inside our Earth. He also had an easy laugh and a temper faster than greased lightning. And often, he had a gift of knowing something would happen before it did. A coiled rattler, a small cave-in. The good Lord must've give it to him.

So how come he didn't know there was danger the day he died? That thought's pestered me worse than a hat full of hornets. Or did he know and send me out of the mine to save me?

I swear I've heard his voice. One time at his graveside before I left home. *Don't stand by my grave and cry. I ain't there.*

Some days I'm so full of fury. Why can't we peel back time and tinker with the bad events lying there? If'n I could, Luther Junior would still be here. I'd be gone. His death cut me, and the knife twists deep when I see a lake and hear laughter float out over the chilly waters.

I swipe tears from my cheek. I'm a gosh darn fool for trying to live backwards.

The sun's gone now. The rooftops on all the town's buildings have all turned dusty pink. I head to the outhouse to piss before turning in at the trustee quarters. The outhouse door is locked, but behind that, the empty building in the woods offers cover, so I head that way to take a leak.

Lightning bugs blink messages to each other. Songbirds done gone silent for the day but as if on cue, the birds of the night are talking. The spooky songs and whinnies of screech owls cut the silence. The moon climbs higher, splashing down a silver glow, and makes the trees look like shadows against the dark purple sky.

Voices come from the woods behind the building. Quietlike. In the next moment, I hear the sure sound of a shovel turning dirt. I slowly inch closer and slide along one wall to get a closer look. Something's off. All the work crews are s'posed to be inside at dark. Since I ain't never known a guard to lift a shovel, can't imagine who'd be working out here.

In the telling moonlight, two men in regular work clothes are digging a rectangular hole. They seem to be arguing in whispers.

"Alls I'm saying is, the camp does an awful lot of 'special burying' these days." The man looks around like he might've heard something.

"And alls I'm saying is, we're paid ten dollars to dig holes and shut up." This man has a cigarette clamped betwixt his lips, and when he talks, the tiny orange glow of the tip bounces up and down. "I got you this work to keep Betty off my back. If you don't wanna take five dollars home four, five times a month, let me know."

"No. We need money." He slices the shovel back into the dirt and heaves the scoop on the big pile next to them. "Digging holes after dark. Something wrong going on here and I don't wanna have any more trouble with the law."

They're burying convicts out here? Other side of the camp has a perfectly good graveyard for those who die. Helped wheel a prisoner or two out thataway during my time up here.

"Warden said these two come in dead from working the pines," the smoker says. "Not asking how or why."

The hair rises at the back of my neck. Sure, hundreds of work gangs are spread out all over Georgia with logging companies, but far as I know, my work crew's the only group "working the pines" from County Prison Camp. My guts roll, and a bad feeling settles in my chest. I move closer. A twig snaps under my foot. Dangit!

The men freeze and slowly look around. Seconds tick by.

I hold my breath and daresn't move.

After what seems like God's eternity, Smoker Feller says, "Deer."

"We done dug deep enough." The first feller's voice has gone higher, reaching into gal territory. "Let's roll them in and beat it back to town."

I peek round the building again as the men drop their shovels. While they are situating themselves round the first body, I move closer, slipping behind a big pine. Sideways.

They lift a body clothed in convict stripes by the legs and hands and swing him to the hole. The moonlight hits him suddenlike. It's Frederick

Sharp, made haintly white in the light. Blood covers the side of his head. Dark stains cover his shirt.

I hush a gasp. Don't need to look too close to know the white guy who had the fit is next. The warden shook my hand when I brought these two in. He's so dishonest I should've counted my fingers when we were done just to make sure.

The two convicts needed doctoring, not killing. Both their heads look smashed in. One guard here is hired to be The Whipper. Loves cutting up everyone with his braided leather crop 'til they're bleeding like a pig. And laughs all the harder when they beg him to stop. He's the one I bet done this at the warden's bidding.

My stomach's spinning like an eddy, and I fight to keep my supper down. It ain't right. But who to tell? I know where I stand on this kind of injustice. It's plain rotten to the core. And staying silent is a betrayal to my Christian rearing.

No way I'm approaching the warden here, but Taggert needs to know. His workers didn't get sent to the State Penitentiary Hospital. They were killed and dumped in a secret grave.

The men finish up and pack their shovels through the door of the shed. They leave through the woods, a lantern lighting their way, and finally disappear out of sight.

My legs shake, as if fighting to hold me up, all the way back to the trustee house. One small light burns at the end of the building, and I'm grateful for the dimness as I drop onto my cot. Tuck is snoring and the others are settled under their blankets.

Being arrested and put on the chain gang was me hitting rock bottom. Or so's I thought. I never suspected there was a whole nother level below that.

This must be what hell's like.

The morning blooms bright, which makes no kind of sense because of what I know happened after dark. Sometimes I think deep in the night is the hardest time to be alive. All my worries and dark secrets swirl in my mind like in a thick muddy swamp.

My eyes burn from no slumber while I pull on my pants.

Tuck is up and running off at the mouth. He looks my way. "What's wrong?"

"Didn't sleep, I guess." I splash water on my face and use my shirt to dry it instead of that dirty towel everyone else uses.

"I'll say. You do look lower than a bowlegged caterpillar." He chuckles and punches my arm. "You up to driving the wagon?"

I'm so hopped up to get away from this place, nothing will stop me from leaving.

"Not a worry. Been steering a mule since I was wagon-wheel high."

"Let me know if you need me to take over."

After rushing through breakfast, I feed the mule. I push my face into his side and breathe in his strong animal scent, calming my nerves. I gotta pull myself together. Seeing prisoners killed for minor trespasses ain't new. It happened at the quarry. But two fellers doing their time, needing medical help? It don't sit right with me.

Speaking up's what I should do. Getting through my sentence and leaving here is what stops me though. Only way to get past last night in my mind is knowing one day soon, I can tell. I'll fly to a bare branch like a crow and scream what I know. Newspapermen are always looking for stories.

But will anyone listen? This world's chock-full of despair—yours, mine, theirs. It's a lot of telling and not enough listening.

The work groups are counted and sorted for the day's gangs. Groups mosey off to workplaces within walking distance. Five miles or less.

The four prisoners for our work gang are waiting with a guard by the wagon. Tuck and me let them settle in the back before we leave the prison camp. They looked relieved to be going someplace new, a feeling that's fresh in my mind.

Downtown Cartersville is coming to life. People stop and watch us go by. When I was on the quarry gang, we walked in long chained-up lines to Ladds Mountain. Families set up along the roadside with blankets and vittles as if we were a parade to behold. Boys taunted us and some threw bottles. We were told to keep our eyes down and mouths shut.

I pull to a stop at the J & L Mercantile. Tuck heads inside with the list of eats we need. Don't know the convicts well enough to leave them alone. After a few weeks together, we learn to trust each other, but that ain't today.

Two young women come out of the Ross & Bradley Lunch Counter 'cross from where I parked. I turn my head when they look my way. Even without the striped clothing, they know I'm an inmate.

One day I'd like me a steady gal. Had one for a time in Nebraska last year until her pa heard I come in on a train. She was a candymaker at the factory pert near my boarding house outside Lincoln. She had these pouty lips that were soft and sweet. I swear, before and after we kissed was like someone parted the air and said you can't go back to that old way of breathing. We would go for breakfast at a diner like this one 'cross the street. Pancakes and bacon. Lordy I miss hearty vittles like that.

I miss her too.

Tuck returns with the grocer at his back. They set five burlap pokes in the wagon betwixt the convicts.

"Get the bread out," I say to Tuck. We learned on the last journey to town, we don't need to watch our backs as much if we feed the convicts. And Taggert didn't take no notice that a loaf was missing. The convicts nod their appreciation 'cause many ain't tasted bread for months, or maybe years.

The next stop is the one I dread. Miss Lily's Threads & Things is two blocks over and sells hand-tufted bedcovers, a fast-growing at-home trade. So many of these types of stores opened up along the Old Dixie Highway, it got the nickname Bedspread Boulevard. Guess *bedspread* is what high-minded folk call them. Back home we just call them covers.

I whoa the mule again and we stop in front of a shop. Fancy wood scrolling gussies up the door and windows. Lacy white curtains hide the fact that in the back rooms, other than deals on covers are conducted.

"Be back directly," I say.

I carry Taggert's note inside. A young girl with clipped blonde hair sits behind a table, working on a cover. Shelves along the walls are filled with folded ones arranged by color. Other areas sell sewing stuff. Ribbon and pillows and thread.

"Good morning. Can I help you?" she says. The girl stands and walks to me. She's wearing a real purty dress that my sisters would label snappy and stylish.

I slap Taggert's folded note against my leg.

"I have a message for Miss Lily."

The girl's gaze hardens a might too quick for my liking.

Now I'm embarrassed. "Not me. From my boss." Don't want her to think I'm hiring gals for wicked purposes.

She drops her voice so I can barely hear her and looks around in all directions.

"Give me the paper and get out."

I lean forward. She snaps it from my hand faster than a snake striking.

"I'm sorry." My face feels like it's burning. "I don't have any choice in the matter."

She moves away from me and narrows her eyes so much, all I see is her lashes.

"Sometimes a hard choice and the right choice are the same thing."

Got no time to explain myself or why I'm stuck with no recourse, so I nod and leave.

"You get in a quarrel in there?" Tuck says as I climb onto the wagon seat. "You look like you wanna kill somebody."

"Not hardly." I slap the reins and steer the mule away from Main Street. "Just feeling cross. Townsfolk guessing what my life's all about without knowing me."

"The martyr type," Tuck says. "Them's the sort that get my ire up. Makes me wanna yell for them to climb off the cross 'cause someone else can use the wood."

I laugh and it feels good.

My body relaxes as we leave the last houses behind and climb Old Goode Road. I steer the wagon through coltsfoot. The small, green, leafy plant blankets the forest this time of year and fills the air with a balsam scent. The trail crosses a small wooden bridge, and the *clomp clomp* of the mule's hooves on the timbers echo like thunder through the woods. Moss and fern line the path in shades of bright green that stand out even more against the iron-rich orange dirt. The convicts are singing folk songs behind us, the fresh air a liberating feeling, I guess.

About five miles to the new camp, we break free of the trees and into a meadow. A ways off, a storm is fixing itself in a mighty form, like a monstrous big gray genie, filling the sky with angry black clouds. Lightning spikes toward the ground, announcing its intention to set our nerves on edge. With the heaping gloom, it'll be dark-thirty before we reach the camp, and the men in the forest could be struck if they don't hustle outta there.

Taggert's gonna be furious if he loses another day of nicking trees.

"Will we beat it?" Tuck says, his face turned to the sky, thumb and pointer finger pinching the skin on his throat.

I raise my eyebrows and offer a maybe, maybe not look.

"My poppy used to say, 'If'n you want help, look to the ends of your arms first.' I'm gonna give it my purest effort. Hang on." I flick the reins and yell, "Giddy Up!"

The mule sets off at a faster clip, bouncing us on the seat. The prisoners grip the wagon sides and hang on for dear life.

Blue-white stingers knife down from the mean-looking clouds and nearly singe the treetops with crooked fingers. I push the mule harder, and we finally leave the open pasture and get into the blackening forest. Now *we* are in danger. Thunder grumbles and growls. Probably angry that lightning is always the spectacle, while thunder trails behind rumbling a late-to-dinner warning.

Day's light turns to dusk. Ground twisters full of leaves spin inside the woods, and I squint to keep the flying bits outta my eyes.

"Almost there," I call over the rumbling storm. The first drops splat big and fat against my skin, and I turn in my seat. "Hunch over them bags back there. They need to stay dry."

The fellers do just that.

Up ahead I see the blurry shapes of the convict cages.

"We're here," Tuck calls out.

I get the mule stopped. The ground's now covered with little streams and puddles. The trustees come running through the mud to grab the sacks and hustle them to a dry tent. Protecting the food above the convicts. But when you've known hunger for days, I reckon it's the natural first choice.

The girl's words from Miss Lily's Threads & Things come back to me. *"Sometimes a hard choice and the right choice are the same thing."*

Right now, I got no choice. I'm riding out my sentence.

Taggert struts toward the wagon like a cantankerous hell-bent rooster, whip coiled in his hand. He always likes to greet the convicts thisaway. Rain pours off the back of his hat.

"You S-O-Bs are mine now. The warden might have picked you, but don't mean I gotta like you."

He hooks a thumb over his shoulder.

"Get on over to the cages."

He turns to me as I unfetter the mule.

"You get that note to Miss Lily?"

I hate the guy. These young girls are all he can think about, though he's married and all.

"Yes, sir." A fenced-in area has been built since the gang got here this morning. I hustle the mule there and run back, heading for the trustee tent.

Taggert meets me there, standing under a tarp the fellers raised above the door flap.

"Everything else work out?"

I need to tell him 'bout the warden killing the convicts. But a strain in his voice stops me cold. He's testing out what I know.

A chill sweeps clean through me. The letter I handed Warden Hauser from Taggert. What did it say? "Yup. All fine and dandy."

Maybe the warden was abiding Taggert's orders to kill the workers. Then I recollect something Taggert said before I left with the maimed convicts, and I know my hunch to be true. He was mad 'cause the two men couldn't work no more. Muttered something 'bout it costing thirty cents a day to treat them at the hospital. Money that comes out of his earnings.

I duck my head to hide my look of shock but reckon I shouldn't be surprised. The feller's heart pumps pure deceit instead of blood.

He's side-eyeing me like a hunting hawk. In his mind we are like mice, his to do with as he sees fit.

I need to hold that in *my* mind the next four months.

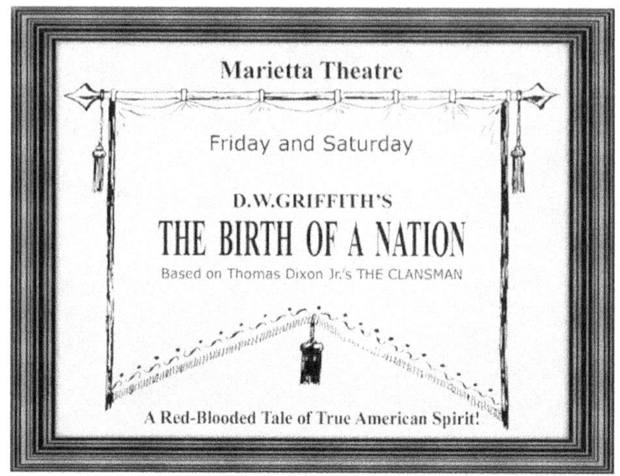

Marietta Theatre
Friday and Saturday
D.W.GRIFFITH'S
THE BIRTH OF A NATION
Based on Thomas Dixon Jr.'s THE CLANSMAN
A Red-Blooded Tale of True American Spirit!

Marietta, Georgia, May 1921

-12-

Ardith Dobbs

"Pay better attention, Oliver." We're almost to William's office, and I swear the child has stumbled every time the sidewalk changes from wood to cement to brick. I grip his hand tighter while I carry the basket of food in the other. "Daddy has a nice surprise for you as soon as we get there."

"My legs are walking as fast as they go, Mommy."

In one hand he holds a toy dirigible the Marx Toy Company sent to William's advertising office. I need only to write to a company and tell them my husband has a popular advertising company in Atlanta, and they send samples of what they're promoting. Oliver is dressed in brown tweed shorts and knit sweater two-piece romper from The Charles Williams

Stores of New York City. With boys' clothes running up to $4.89 for a good suit, and the way he grows out of them so fast, I have no problem writing letters every day. I already have a bureau drawer full of baby gowns for when Katherine arrives. I keep the fancier ones with the pastel lace and embroidery, and the plain ones I give to the women I visit for insurance collection or send them to the New Hope Charity Home we sponsor.

We walk by the Walthour & Hood Bicycle Company. William says the main building in Atlanta is almost a city block long and five stories high, built from local bricks like most of Atlanta. The window displays the newest in Roadsters, Bikeabouts, and the specialty bicycle called the Motorbike. William threatened that he will get one for me if I ever dent the car again. I knew he was teasing. It's such a small ding, and the black paint to fix it is the same one everyone uses.

I slow as we start to pass the Ludlow Steamship and Train Travel Adventures shop. The Great White Fleet has a poster for a twenty-five-day cruise to Cuba, Jamaica, and the Golden Caribbean "*where the pirates hid their treasure*." I once suggested a steamship tour to William, and he was aghast that I would ever get on a ship after what *happened* to my parents. That *Titanic* lie worked when I needed it, but it circles back like bad cider when my memory gets unreliable.

Displayed are brochures from all the major railways. *See Yellowstone, Yosemite, Glacier National Park. Book a luxury train from Chicago this summer!*

"Let's go in here for a second." I pull Oliver inside the travel company and approach the man behind the counter. "How are you?"

"Fine, ma'am." He sets his wire-rimmed reading glasses on the counter. "May I help you with something?"

"Yes. I'm curious about the train trips for this summer. What would something like that cost for my husband and me?"

"For you?" He studies my swollen midsection.

I pull Oliver in front of me to try to hide. How impertinent. "Yes. My husband and I have often talked of travel. You may know him. William Dobbs, two doors down?" I will have to ask William what he thinks of this man.

"Of course. He has two fine companies." He clears his throat and reaches for a leaflet behind him, showing Yellowstone National Park. "This trip takes fifteen days from Chicago and includes all of the meals and a sleeper car with a private sitting room. That's two hundred and twenty-one dollars a person."

"That sounds wonderful." William would choke on that amount, considering he just paid $465 for our new Ford. "I'll take that information, and William and I will discuss it."

He hands me the brochure before we leave.

"Are we going on a train?" Oliver asks, his tipped-up face full of delight.

"Mostly mommies and daddies go on these tours." His face falls. "But when you're older, we can all go on a trip. Okay?" I picture the four of us and a nanny traveling across the country. This baby will be my last. Miss Barr's final words to me ring in my head every day. "*It's your job from now on to not misunderstand anything you see.*" I can't stay vigilant with a passel—I mean a large family of children, now can I?

"Okay." Oliver takes my hand, and we head to William's building. It's a two-story structure with a fifteen-foot black water tank perched on the roof. Two large windows offer views from the first floor, and the second floor has four taller, more narrow windows. That's the insurance company, accessed by climbing a flight of interior wooden stairs.

We enter and Oliver yells, "Daddy!" Noisy printing machines are clacking in the back room, and the place smells of ink and paper, not an unpleasant scent.

William scoops up Oliver, who throws his arms around William's neck and snuggles close. My husband sends me a dimpled smile. "We'll be right back. I have something for our little man."

He disappears into another room where all of the new products are stored.

"Hi, Walter." I set the food basket by the door and turn to the young man who sits at his drafting table across the room. He's the main designer. Walter is fresh out of the University of Florida, although we joke that we don't hold that against him. William calls Florida the Spanish colonial sauna that's turning swampland into a Northerner's folly. I think William's just angry he's missed out on the land boom after one of his friends told of making $19,000 on a sale there.

"Hello, Mrs. Dobbs. How are you today?"

"I'm fine. Just stopped by to borrow the car to run my errands."

"I hope no fence post jumps in your path." He's bent over a drawing, but I see the smile at the edge of his mouth.

It's been a decade since Alice Ramsey showed men that women are competent behind the wheel of an automobile by driving all the way across the United States. Somehow, we ladies still have to hear this. "I'll try to be careful."

I step to William's work area and study his desk. He has stacks of requests for advertisements and has already laid out a few that will go into the local Marietta Daily Journal and three newspapers in Atlanta. Milk seems to be a popular sell. Horlicks Original Malted Milk claims it's great for infants and invalids, and Borden's Milk has the slogan, "The more Borden's Milk you drink the better and wiser you think!" Here's one I've never tried, Jelke Good Luck Margarine. It shows a boy making a fist and showing off his bicep with the script, "The Fine Taste Satisfies. The Low Price Gratifies."

It looks like William has suggested adding the swastika, a sign for good luck, to the ad. It reminds me I need to call Mary Trowbridge, who's been in charge of our sewing club. After we finish another ten good luck baby quilts, we have to switch to making the Klan regalia. Mary took the oath the same night I did, and she'll understand swapping out the darling pink or blue swastika quilts to start making the baby and child robes. We'll just have to hand over the adoptive babies to the New Hope Charity Home in regular cotton blankets for the time being.

Oliver comes running back holding an object that has the stem of a pipe but is shaped into a bird above the pipe's bowl. He blows into it and a loud bird sound comes out. "I'm a canary."

"That's creative, darling." I drop a hand on his back. "What a great outside toy."

"I know you love birds, Ardith." William smiles and watches Oliver.

"It's the water you put inside it that creates the realistic sound." He spies the brochure in my hand. "What do you have there?"

I show him, and he looks it over and hands it back. "Maybe one day." His face is set in a patient mask I've seen him wear way too often when I have new ideas. "Right now, we have little ones to raise."

"We do." I smile. What a bore sometimes. "And right now, I have appointments to keep." I reach for Oliver's hand and scoop the basket up when we reach the door. "Come on, son."

William follows me out to the car parked along the tree-lined street. It's a new Ford Model T Sedan with an electric start. I never could hand crank our last vehicle—such a limiting device invented by men.

"Stick to the hardtop roads." William's arms are crossed. "And no faster than thirty. If you hit anything, I don't want it to hurt Oliver or the B-A-B-Y."

I wave away his comments. "We're going to be F-I-N-E." I notice he doesn't mention *my* safety.

Oliver climbs into the front passenger side, and then I walk around the car. The Marietta Movie Theatre is across the street and catches my attention. The small building, covered with ivy, is sandwiched between two taller ones and has changed its marquee. It now announces the hottest movie out there, *The Birth of a Nation.*

"I see Mr. Rutledge decided he needed to get in step with what the mayor was asking." A national group for Colored people is trying to stop the showing of the movie, but it plays to packed theatres in Atlanta week after week. Local mayors, wanting to show unity, asked their movie house owners to run the film more often. There were consequences for those who rebelled. One movie theatre owner in Cornelia who refused to show it was beaten, tarred, and feathered. He got his picture in the paper, looking less than proud of his disobedience.

"He said he's going to show it until people stop buying tickets," William says. "Could run all year the way it's selling out now."

"We have the best town." I slide into the driver's seat and pull the door closed. I start the car and make a show of slowly pulling out. And thirty miles per hour? William has no idea I handle the car going much faster than that all of the time, especially on the Dixie Highway. And why not enjoy that road? We pay for it with our motor fuel tax. I'm sure it's what William and the men are talking about when they speak of highway robbery.

Oliver is flying the airship around in front of him, making motor noises. It's better than the annoying bird pipe but still irritates me.

"Why don't you get on your knees and watch out the window? The tank will be coming up soon."

The British Army placed one on a concrete slab below an America flag. A thank you to the United States for their participation in the war. But now it looks like a rusted potato with caterpillar tracks running around it. It's more than five miles from where we are, but Oliver will watch for it like it's around every corner.

Oliver tires of making airplane noises. Finally I can use the quiet time to think about Josephine and the next few days. It's clear she's about to have that baby whether I'm ready or not. William and I discussed letting her try out the new Colored Hospital at Grady in Atlanta. Actually, that was his suggestion. My thought was to have a midwife deliver the child in Josephine's room on the side of our house. We finally agreed to that. My obstetrician, Dr. Hugo Grange, covers the foundling and lying-in homes in the area and is adept at delivering at home. He's not prudish about providing for unwed girls like Josephine and has a good reputation for using the new Twilight Sleep drugs. I got his name from a Klan sister who swears he does what he's paid for and goes on his way. All of my friends know about Josephine, and they understand our acceptance of her distasteful condition. But she's a hard worker, is respectful, and there's the added bonus of having a wet nurse at my fingertips once my baby girl arrives.

"There it is!" Oliver has his face pressed against the door's window. "See it, Mommy?"

"I do. Now have a seat. I brought you a candy to eat while I make my visits." I reach into my pocketbook on the floorboards and pull out a banana taffy on a stick.

"Thank you, Mommy." He removes the yellow wrapper from the three-inch candy. He will be entertained for thirty minutes. I know. I've timed him.

I slow the car and turn onto a smaller road, careful of the crushed-stone surface. The crunch of the stones under the tires vibrates all the way to my fingertips. We pass a small clutch of shacks I suppose are houses. They're raised off the ground, supported by flat rocks or blocks of wood. One says *General Store* but it doesn't look any more special than the other shacks, though maybe a bit bigger. A wooden church with a surprisingly tall steeple is off to the side. If it was ever painted, the evidence of it is long gone. Colored children play in the dirt and sand that surround the shacks. The adults are nowhere in sight, probably working their sharecropper fields. Poverty has drained their spirits. The children's eyes are huge, their faces vacant. I know preachers would have quoted Matthew and said, "Blessed are the poor in spirit, for theirs is the kingdom of heaven," but I would bet a quarter of these families would like a little taste of kingdom here on God's green earth, or in their case, God's dusty acres.

Frederick Hoffman, a statistician at Prudential Life Insurance Company, once claimed that the excessive mortality rates in the American Negro were not due to their daily conditions of life but was an inherent racial trait. During slavery, the Negroes were healthy and disease-free. But since emancipation, their race has been on a downward grade. He predicted their complete extinction by 1930.

My Daisy Ladies' Society has had the poverty discussion over and over. What to do, how to encourage women to make the needed changes and reduce the social evils of poverty and unwanted babies? Abortionists say they have the solution, but Lord knows that's an after-the-fact evil. We need to stop the creating before the next baby is made. Eugenics is the simple solution for decreasing births, whether of the feeble-minded or those less intelligent and unfit to parent.

Margaret Sanger, a feminist and nurse said, "More children from the fit, less from the unfit."

The more they breed, the more they need. I just came up with that. I nod my head and smile. I'll share it with The Daisy Ladies' Society. I might finally have a saying they'd want to make a project around. Banners. Buttons. I'm getting good at this.

Fiona Elsmore's house is another mile down Chicken Branch Road. Our women's group has fifteen board members, or as we call ourselves in private, Kleagles, just like the men. We're in charge of looking for new members to join the Women of the Knights of the Klan. We've each pledged to find five new women a week who share our ideals and who can afford the membership fee of ten dollars. In trade, we offer charity.

I'm checking back with Fiona. Her husband Roy is not a Klan member, but on my last visit to drop off baby clothes for her new daughter, she said she'd be ready to join in a few weeks. Roy works on the Western and Atlantic Railroad, and according to Fiona, has an on-again, off-again nervous condition left over from fighting in the Great War. He needed a government rest camp, but with no physical malady, they never accepted him. She takes in washing every day to make money for the times he wanders off his latest job in a fog of discouragement.

Her two boys, ages eight and six, are sitting on the breezeway opening, their thin legs swinging back and forth. A wave of sadness washes through me. I was raised in a similar Cracker-style house outside of Hickory Nut Hollow. Built out of cypress wood, the house has wide covered porches. Raised up on rock pilings, the crawl spaces beneath the homes work for ventilation, and the floor cracks throughout the home make sweeping away dirt and crumbs hardly a chore. 'Course I think that's where it gets the name cracker. Fiona and Roy keep a few chickens under there. The birds get the morsels that fall below and also eat fleas and other bugs.

I park and turn to Oliver. "Play with your toys, and I'll be back in a few minutes."

"Can I go sit with the boys?" Oliver points to the house.

They should be in school. Marietta has a fine public school system. "No. You have on new clothes. Just stay here." I reach into the passenger footwell, grab the basket, and head to the house. The children are thin and pale. "Hi, little ones. Is your mother inside?"

The older one leans forward trying to see in the basket. "Did you bring food?"

Well that was really rude, but there's no reason to correct the poor child's bad manners. A question deserves an answer. "I did." I reach under the cloth and find a bread roll for each of them. They snatch them away and bite into the food like feral animals.

I sigh. This is the Daisy Ladies' role—to teach parents how to raise their children. One lesson at a time. I climb the steps to the open breezeway and turn to the left, where the eating area is. "Knock, knock. Fiona? It's Ardith."

The door is cracked open, so I push it inward. "Yoo-hoo."

Fiona is sitting at the small table with room for only two wooden chairs. She's holding her baby girl wrapped in the blanket I brought to her during my last visit. Her gaze turns my way, but it's empty. "I need your help," she says in a quiet voice.

My heart pounds. I hope she's not asking me to clean because the house is dirty and smells like soiled diapers. Something has happened. I set the basket of food on the table and pull the cloth away, revealing the contents. "Look. I brought bread, a ham, and some winter potatoes."

Her eyes slowly slide over the food, and she nods. The baby hasn't made a sound but is sleeping against her shoulder. "Roy is gone for good."

"What? He's dead?"

"No, he left us."

He's been known to wander off before, mostly at night when he can't sleep. "He'll be back. It's just his nervous condition. Give him some time."

"The railroad cut his wages again. Said they don't need so many workers now that people drive automobiles."

The state does seem to have chain gangs putting in newer roads everywhere. "When did he leave?"

"Three nights ago. Finished his work shift and come home." She runs a broken fingernail along a crack in the tabletop. "Before bed, he supposed he could try and find a mill job, get away from the railroads, you know. He woke up middle of that night a'screaming and making no sense." She shifts the limp baby to her other shoulder. "Ran out of the house and hasn't come back."

What help does she need? "Do you want my husband's men's organization to find him? The Klan can help him get a job. Especially if he isn't drinking and wants to join a civic-minded group." They've hunted down a dozen men in the county. Abandoning a wife and a family is illegal.

Turning them in to the police and having the men spend time in jail helps no one, so the Klan somehow talks them into returning home. I heard the *talking* may involve a beating and strong threats.

She shakes her head. "Roy told me straight up he was done trying. He's a broken man from the war and can't see his way out of it."

"What is it you want me to help you with?"

"I want you to find a home for Anna." She hands the two-month-old off to me, and I have no choice but to take the tiny blanketed package since Fiona quickly releases her grip. "She deserves better than this." Tears fall down her crumpled face that looks closer to fifty than her twenty-five.

The child is warm in my arms, just her nose and closed eyes showing in the swaddling cloth.

Fiona stands and crosses to a tan crockery jar on the shelf, takes off the lid, and brings out a handful of crumpled money. "I was saving this up to join your women's group, but I recollect you said there are folks that will take in babies for twelve dollars and adopt them out." She drops the money on the table. "That's what I need. A right good home for my baby girl."

How awful she must feel. With my baby almost here, I can't fathom the pain of giving her away. My past surfaces and I remember another baby, but I push those recollections away. "Fiona. Are you sure? Once they find a home, she can never come back."

She squeezes her eyes tight and nods. "Please. She's been sickly off and on, and I can't keep paying the doctor three dollars every time he comes out."

"What does she have?" Diseases are running rampant. Some even say the Spanish Flu is circling back for another bite out of the population.

"She had whooping cough, but that's passed. She's got a delicate stomach. Can't keep breast milk down, but she's fine with goat's milk." She points to a wicker basket that's packed. "I've filled several bottles to go with her."

She already has the child organized to go? "If I hadn't come along, what were you going to do with Anna?"

She drops her gaze to her hands and picks at the side of her thumb. "I didn't know what to do, so I wrote back to an advertisement in the newspaper.

It was a little bitty notice hidden away in the livestock section. A foundling home said they'll pay me eight dollars for Anna and adopt her out." She looks at the baby. "I packed up for when they give me a holler back."

"What's the name of the home?" I know most of them around here. Some are downright unscrupulous.

She moves papers around on the table and comes up with a torn-out portion of a newspaper and slides it across so I can see it. "*Beck Infantorium.*"

WANTED:
No questions asked, no birth certificate needed. White
baby girls under four months old. Receive $8 and the
comfort of knowing we will find her a good home.

I'm momentarily dizzy with a memory from seven years ago. That was the first and last time I was there. My secret no one need learn. "Um… you don't want them. They take mostly high-risk babies and infants born in scandalous circumstances." Magda and Herta Beck, the sisters who own the home, like to say they cover up the county's dirty secrets. I reach for the money and tuck it in my jacket pocket. "I'll take her to the New Hope Charity Home. They do a nice job of tending the infants, and if I remember right, they might even have a goat or two."

"Thank you. Do I need to sign papers?"

"New Hope can keep this a secret if that's what you want. I assume you don't have a birth certificate." The baby wiggles in her blanket and tries to push her tiny hand out.

"We don't. Um…I don't."

I stand. "That's fine." I remember her other sons. "Why aren't your boys in school?"

A tear slips from her face. "They're too weak to walk. It's not much more than four miles yonder but they ain't eaten in two days. This food is a ray of sunshine."

"The school formed a Parent-Teacher Association. I'll call them from home after I stop at New Hope. They will make sure the boys are fed and can get to classes."

The baby is light enough to cradle her in one arm while I lift her wicker basket with the other. "You sure this is what you want? How will you explain it to Roy when he comes home?"

"He ain't coming home." She shakes her head. "His daddy's rifle is missing and he ain't one for hunting after all he witnessed in the war." She swallows hard. "One day someone's gonna come knocking to tell me they found him in the high weeds or out in them woods."

"I'm so sorry." I'm not much for hugging strangers, and besides, my arms are full, but I think I would've done it if I could have. "You take care of your other children and don't be afraid to ask for help."

I leave the room and come up alongside the boys.

"Where are you taking our baby sister?" The oldest boy jumps to his feet, his face knitted into an angry scowl.

I stop and smile. "Your mother asked me to take her to a nice home where she can get lots of food."

"But she's coming back, right?" The younger one is on his feet.

What to tell them? The hard truth can't be easier to hear than a little white lie. "Yes. Your mother can go get her as soon as she feels strong enough." I descend the steps and they follow me, as if staying near their sister may prevent her from leaving. "Now you boys go on back to the house and take good care of your mother."

"You can't keep her." The younger boy reaches for the blanket and starts to pull her from my arm. Tears cut pink trails down his dusty face.

I use my big stomach to block his grasp, then open the car door and set the basket in the footwell.

My Oliver is startled at my quick movements. "Mommy?" His voice is strained.

With my free hand, I grab the dirigible and hand it to the younger boy, then take the whistle from Oliver's grip and give it to the older. I plop the baby in Oliver's lap. "Hold onto her, Oliver."

I close the door and face the children. "Your mother has food inside for you so skedaddle."

They slowly back away and soon turn and run to the house. I needed to be firm. They were acting like rabid dogs moving in for an attack.

The car starts on the first try, and I make a circle around their house as I'm not keen on backing up. That's how I bent the fender the last time. We crunch our way back down the road as I shoot glances at the baby. Her eyes are open and she's looking at Oliver. "Her name is Anna."

"Are we keeping her?" Oliver pulls the blanket away from the baby's mouth, inspecting her whole face.

"We're taking her to a place that's like a hospital."

The baby is making cooing noises and I smile. Who doesn't like a baby? They only have eyes for the person holding them. That complete devotion fills my heart. So sweet.

The baby's hand pops free and is swinging in the air, trying to locate Oliver's face. "She has spots all over her. Good thing she's going to the hospital," he says.

Spots? I slow the car and lean over the infant. "Hell's bells!" There are red sores around the baby's mouth and on her hand. Some of the sores have burst and developed honey-colored crusts. It's impetigo. "Don't touch her! Wrap that blanket back up around her hand."

"What's wrong, Mommy?" Oliver's face puckers and his arms shake. I swear this child is more thin-skinned than a rotten tomato. He doesn't move, so I reach to rewrap the infant.

"It's fine." I take in a big breath. "I don't want you to catch those spots. They can make you really itchy, and you remember poison ivy from last summer."

Oliver's lip quivers but he freezes, still as a statue.

This is a fine howdy-do. Fiona must have seen Anna's skin disease. I'm out here doing charitable work, and now I'm stuck with a hard decision. Impetigo spreads so quickly. New Hope Charity Home will know what to do to treat Anna and keep her away from the other babies, but what will they think of me? Bringing them such a poor-quality child? It makes me wonder if Roy's mental condition has passed down to this sickly child.

I turn north on the Dixie Highway toward Cartersville. The turn to New Hope Charity Home comes up in five miles. The Beck Infantorium comes to mind. It's not much past the turn to New Hope.

The Beck sisters will never remember me. I was there all of three nights, and they never ask names if a gal isn't forthcoming. Which I wasn't.

I weigh the decision. In either place, the baby will get a cradle and someone to feed her. Both places offer adoption, and with her being white, she has a really good chance. We've often joked at the Daisy Ladies' Society that every baby that expects to be adopted ought to be born with blue eyes. The dark-eyed girl or boy might be just as pretty, but it was hard to make the discerning family believe so. I've heard that an attractive infant sells from fifteen to a hundred dollars. Usually paid in installments since not many of the adoptive parents have the larger sum just lying around. The newspapers run the slogan that it's cheaper and easier to buy a baby for a hundred dollars than to make one of your own.

Isn't that the truth.

When I don't slow for the road to New Hope Charity Home, I realize I've made up my mind. It's the paper that Fiona showed me. The Beck Infantorium's advertisement indicated they are seeking a new baby that matches Anna's description. The bonus is they won't have to pay for this one—she comes with money. Fiona won't know or care. She's relieved her daughter won't suffer the sadness and hardship that's in front of her and the two boys.

Oliver is quiet as a mouse and following my direction not to touch Anna. "I'll buy you new toys, Oliver. Those boys didn't have any to play with, and I know you understand helping others."

He nods. "Maybe I can have a circus car with animals like Horace."

Horace is one of Sheriff Withington's sons. "That sounds like a nice idea." I'll have to ask Nancy where she got it and see if I can write away and ask for one.

We bump down a back road and to the Beck sisters' home. They have a large piece of property, although I remember not being allowed out behind the icehouse and food storage. A cemetery shows up first, running off into the woods at the back of the large white house. A tall granite angel towers over a sign for burial lots. I pass that and pull into a circular driveway.

I carefully scoop the baby out of Oliver's lap and tell him to hand me the basket. The wide porch has a Baby Box where a person can drop a baby and leave with no questions asked. It's the humane answer to mothers abandoning them in alleys or drowning them in ponds.

The doorbell chimes a happy tune, and moments later, a tall, raw-boned woman answers the door. It's Herta. "Hello," she says and looks to the driveway and then back to me. "I see you brought us a little one."

"Yes. From a family in a pickle." The woman has barely aged. I know I surely look different than the poor girl from Hickory Nut Hollow who once staggered across their doorstep.

"Dill or sweet?" She tilts her head to the side.

"What?" I must have skipped a question.

"Just a pickle joke." She smiles and a wolf's grin comes to mind. "Won't you come in?"

"My son is in the car, and we must be getting back to town." I raise Anna at an angle so she can see her. "The mother has run into hard times, and she's asked to have her baby adopted out. She paid twelve dollars."

"Oh, the poor dear." She studies Anna and reaches for the bundle. "White parents?"

I pull back a little so she can't accept the baby. I need to let her know what she's taking on. "Yes, both white but the father has a nervous disorder from the war, and this one has been sick quite often. Right now, she has impetigo." I remember the basket. "And she needs goat's milk, but there's some in here."

"We take in sick babies as well as the healthy ones." She reaches for Anna, and I hand her over. "You say the mother paid for relinquishment?"

I pull out the twelve dollars. "Here it is." I hear babies crying in the back of the house. I don't remember that much commotion. It sounds like dozens. "How many infants do you have at one time?"

"We can take fifteen. We have room just now for three more." She pulls back the blanket and examines Anna. "This is much better than diphtheria." She rewraps the baby. "We'll get her healed and then find a good placement."

"Thank you. You've solved a big dilemma. And maybe in the future, my women's organization can make a donation to help wayward mothers."

She turns the door handle, pushes the basket inside, and then says, "That's very nice, but we are self-sustaining." She raises Anna to her shoulder. The door is nearly closed when she says, "It was lovely seeing you again."

I feel faint. My feet are glued to the porch boards. This is very bad. What if the sisters tell someone about me? Then I remember she doesn't know my married name. And my given name of Sissy Belle Strunk from six-plus years ago ceased to exist once I arrived in Atlanta.

She nods and heads into the house, the swell of wailing sounds closing off behind the door. How many workers does she have now? With fifteen babies, she and her sister must be slaving day and night.

I feel deep-down tired. It doesn't take much these days with Baby Katherine about ready to arrive.

I climb into the car and pull past the house. Another woman with her hair tied into a scarf struggles with a wheelbarrow behind the home. As it tips to the side, it appears to be loaded with small melons. Must be Magda. I never asked if they were ever married or had children of their own. And if they are spinsters, they aren't all that old.

Everyone has a different calling in life. They have chosen a hard path, raising other people's throwaways and covering the men's chores too.

Oliver has fallen asleep, and it's a peaceful drive as I head back to Marietta.

As for me, I'm satisfied with what I've accomplished today to help out poor Fiona, and happy knowing the WKKK's charity outreach in the state legitimizes us. We have a robed event in a few days. Dressed in our impressive lady's regalia, we will visit a children's hospital to hand out gifts. The parade is coming up in another week. Five hundred women strong will walk through Marietta and end with a picnic in the park. A wonderful show of the power of white Protestant women and what we can do when we unite under one banner of purity. The national figures say the WKKK has reached half a million members this year. We will cleanse the United States, one community at a time, and make it a better place for all of us.

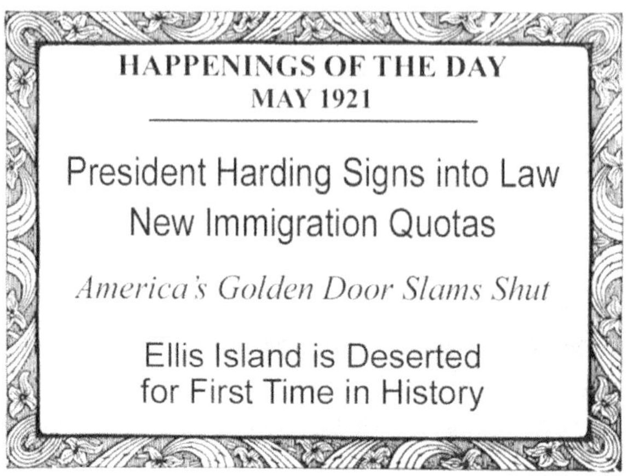
HAPPENINGS OF THE DAY
MAY 1921

President Harding Signs into Law
New Immigration Quotas

America's Golden Door Slams Shut

Ellis Island is Deserted
for First Time in History

Helen, Georgia. May 1921

-13-

WILLOW STEWART

Somehow, I've been carried to the table after playing dead like a curled-up opossum on the floor. Mrs. Holcombe and Mr. Vissom talk about me as if I lost my hearing along with my mama. They decide I'll stay at the parsonage for the night, and I don't even try to lift a pencil to scribble out an argument. Like a yellow thread in a stack of hay, I'm lost.

Mr. Vissom asks for an ink pen and paper. "Willow, once again, I sure am sorry to hear of your family's losses. I'll be on my way to deal with the peddler and all. Give us a quick drawing of his whereabouts, and we'll take that worry off your head."

The peddler's location and his death feel unrelated to me, like a fantasy story from a book I might've read. I draw a shaky map and slide it across the table. Mr. Vissom touches the brim of his hat and thanks Mrs. Holcombe for watching over me. He leaves, another mumbled condolence trailing charcoal gray heaviness behind him.

Mrs. Holcombe makes a switchboard call to the local doctor to come check me out first light. She insists she cannot let me return home tonight in the sad state I'm in. I believe she's right.

I have no idea how to accept this twice-terrible news. I sit in a stunned pool of stagnant despair while the preacher's wife prepares supper.

Maybe it was someone else who died and not Mama. Anything could have happened like a fall, or someone choked. I shouldn't wish another person dead, but God's plan may have called someone else home.

My insides hurt, and I know I'm wishing for a rainbow to appear out of a dust storm.

Mama is dead. She was so alive three days ago, sewing, cooking, getting ready for the baby. A fat, dark cloud feels permanently settled over our sunny mountaintop.

I barely eat the bread soaked in warm milk and honey Mrs. Holcombe prepares. It goes down hard—the sorrow knotting my gut. Every time the woman sly-eyes my way, I close mine, afraid to witness the sympathy in hers. Earlier, my silent gasping sobs scared her. Time stops for me, pinning me in a place of sorrow with no way out. A gloomy forest with no sunlight. My cheek muscles are in spasm after my one long paralyzing cry, and it hurts to eat.

When it's obvious I'm done with the food, Mrs. Holcombe attends to my injured arm. She cleans it, and I barely register the pain. She applies some goo from a blue jar called Vicks VapoRub and wraps a clean bandage on it. My wound burns like a small fire, but I welcome the sting. I should hurt everywhere since Mama's gone.

She guides me to the outhouse thirty yards from the back door. Darkness has arrived in its sneaky way, nearly graying out the spaces between the trees. The night air feels cool, and a new pain arrives, as I picture home with its refreshing evening breezes.

Back in the house, I wash at the kitchen sink, splashing cold water on my swollen face. Mrs. Holcombe settles me in a tiny alcove off the kitchen with a single bed sidled up next to a wooden stand. She explains she'll be right around the corner, preparing her Sunday lessons for the children's groups. Probably to take my mind off Mama's death, or maybe it's because she doesn't know what to do with a mute, she has talked non-stop about her and Dean's obligations overseeing a rural church. Besides pastoral care and preaching, they pay the church's bills and prepare the budgets.

"My Dean will take the Lord's word anywhere need be," she says, "and no offense, but folks around here only pay in sacks of walnuts or ham hocks. But with God's grace, we get by. That kind of meager compensation worked out all right when he was single and a circuit preacher down near Savannah, riding all over God's green acres. But it wore him down something awful. He used to say there's no such thing as bad weather, just a weak countenance, but that was before he ran up against the hurricane of 1910."

I have no response. I'm suffering through an onslaught of bad weather myself.

She leaves me alone, and I stand at a small window and watch the moon rise, tonight a weaker version of its usual bright self, as transparent as steam. I can relate. Part of me feels as if I'm dissolving, losing myself like soda ash tossed into water.

I sink onto the soft bed. Inside my head, I replay the sound and rhythm of Mama's voice. Like the seasons and the plants and the river, she lived in daily harmony with everything and everyone. I can't imagine life without her. Will our broken hearts ever seal back up? Or will it be like a busted hand that never heals straight and true? It pains you to close it, but you go on hanging the wash, cradling a baby, or shielding your eyes to watch an eagle soar across the face of the sun, recognizing the hurt every time you move it.

Memories flash behind my closed eyelids, each recollection to match every beat in my chest. Mama humming as she does her needlework, all of us gathered in the parlor, warm against the cutting wind that scrapes down the mountains, dragging eerie whistles through frozen boughs. Using a foraging knife to cut stinging nettles pushing up through the snow and brown patches of winter leaves. Forcing Poppy to dance a jig on his birthday. Sewing Ruthy's wedding dress. Making clothes for the new baby out of scraps from our outgrown clothing.

And just like that, with her last breath, everything stops. Our sign-language conversations.

Newspaper reading. Reassurance.

For a long time, I've shared my fears with Mama about what might happen to me. Would I ever marry? Have a family? Many days I'm satisfied with the notion I'd stay near our home fires and not be out in the world, hungry for other cultures. Unless books give out, I can do all my exploring from home. I'd help Mama with the folks who come to her with ailments, educate myself in her herb-healing knowledge. She always told me I can do anything my heart desires, even if it means moving off the mountain and into a township.

But after what I've experienced today, I can't see a safe place for me outside of my hill family.

Mrs. Holcombe is flipping pages at the kitchen table, her pen scratching on paper. I carefully turn over on the bed, arm aching from the wound. Fresh tears spring free and I have no mind to stop them. Perhaps the hot salt will wash away my guilt. As I look back on the day, I surely committed a sin. I could have kicked the mushroom soup out of Mr. Coburn's hands and taken his punishment. He'd still be alive. I'd be defiled but safe in the knowledge my wickedness had not taken Mama's life. Everyone knows the Devil waits for a sinner to break one of the Ten Commandments and then he gives them the what for.

And what a walloping he unleashed.

I want time to stop in that moment before Mama passed. Then I could live the rest of my life there before it changed forever.

I imagine it all. Pastor Holcombe arrives too late to our homestead tonight to properly funeralize. He spends the night in the parlor on the guest cot that's seen many a wayward traveler or sick person who needed Mama's close watching. The neighbor men dig the grave, while the women weave wildflower wreaths and line the coffin with one of Mama's best quilts. Was it the one we all played Toss the Cat with last fall when the cat skedaddled to the corner that Ruthy held? The cat's prediction of who would marry next was right—Ruthy got engaged a week later.

In the morning, Mama and Baby Luther would be laid in the coffin, feet placed toward the east so they can face the rising sun. The morning view of the mountain ridges is splendid and one of Mama's favorites. The peaks poke like dark islands through a sea of soft fog, changing from gray to apricot as the sun pushes through. If ever a soul heard the voice of God, it would be there in the cool of the early day.

I long to be there with Poppy rubbing my back, Billy Leo wrapped around Ruthy, the family and neighbors singing "In the Sweet By and By," Mama's beloved song. I picture Poppy lost in a forest of sorrow. Can he imagine ever finding his way to a better place?

Mama is thirty-nine, Poppy going on forty-one. Both came to America in 1898 on separate ships and with different stories. Mama and Aunt Effie never knew dire poverty. Her parents raised the sisters in Invergarry, a village in the Highlands of Scotland. Mama's voice softened to dusky green whenever she spoke of her childhood, playing in the lush glens surrounded by towering mountains. Her father was a crofter, a working man on a twenty-acre farm, and held a small portion of the land in his own right. After both the cereal and potato harvests failed, he sold everything, wrote to a great uncle in the MacDonell clan in northern Georgia, and bought ship fare for four. Two weeks into the passage, Mama's parents died when their wet coughs turned to pneumonia. Mama was seventeen, Effie fifteen when their parents were buried at sea. When they reached New York City, the First Presbyterian Church housed them for one night, took up a collection to purchase train tickets for them to travel to Washington, DC, then through the Carolinas with the final destination of Dalton, Georgia. Great Uncle Alistair MacDonell met them there to transport them the last one hundred fifty miles by horse and wagon to MacDonell Mountain.

Poppy was on that train from the Carolinas.

He was one of eight children living near Ardgour on the western shore of Loch Linnhe, Scotland. After the failure of the fishing, linen, and kelp industries, his father became a cottar, a farmworker with no land of his own. Life was hard, and Poppy ate spoiled wheat for days on end. He left home at age seventeen to reduce by one the mouths his parents tried to feed. When he tired of using the Free Church's charity, he made his way to Glasgow and found passage on the *Anchoria,* an immigrants' ship bound for New York City. He also had an uncle in Georgia.

Poppy thought he was in sorry shape until he saw a large group of immigrants who boarded, half-starved and half-naked, young children in rags—shapeless fragments of what must have been clothes.

Poppy helped the crew convert empty bread bags, scraps of old canvas, and blankets into basic coverings for them. He swore that if he ever had a family, he'd create a life where his wife and children never went hungry, always understood they were loved, and developed the character to step forward in times that called for kindness and courage.

Once in America, he and Mama set out to do exactly that.

It began in earnest the day Poppy, Mama, and Aunt Effie stepped off the train in Dalton, Georgia. His uncle had a place a few hollers over from Mama's relatives, but Poppy went straight to work on the MacDonell farm, her homestead.

Poppy always said life wasn't about living but was about having something or someone to live for. What would happen now?

All I know is I will return home, and in four months, Ruthy will marry and move away. I will take up Mama's and Ruthy's chores, making sure little Billy Leo sits up straight, remembers his manners, and learns to read and write. I'll work hard like Mama, who is as tough as a pine knot. Was. She *was* as tough.

A sob catches in my throat. Billy Leo had only felt Mama's warm hugs for twelve short years. I will have to tell him the stories from before his recollections started, from before he was born. And that was the best reason for me to remain on our homestead. If I was off on my own, the worst part of holding onto the memories would not be the pain, it would be the lonesomeness of it all. Memories need to be shared if they are to live on, and at home, I could do that.

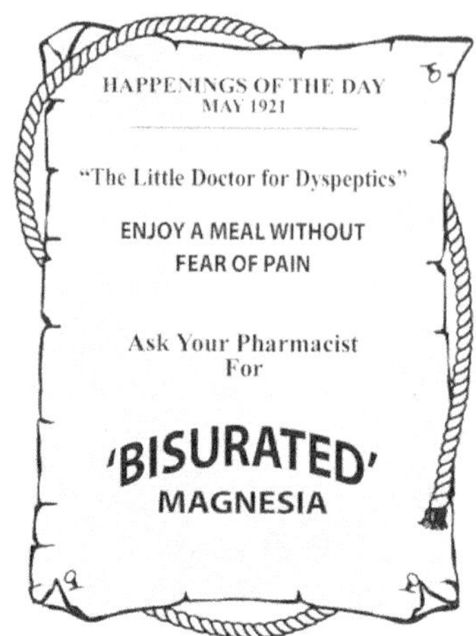
HAPPENINGS OF THE DAY
MAY 1921

"The Little Doctor for Dyspeptics"

ENJOY A MEAL WITHOUT
FEAR OF PAIN

Ask Your Pharmacist
For

'BISURATED'
MAGNESIA

Timberline Forest Camp. May 1921

-14-

BRIAR STEWART

It's rained off and on for two days, changing from pouring to sprinkling to back again. Foggy days, steamy nights. Convicts remain locked in their cages, just getting a few minutes outside every eight hours.

Even though the sun's finally out, Taggert's stuck in a dark, foul mood. We're dozens of sap barrels behind, so he's working the convicts, including us trustees, sixteen hours a day. I done chopped wood to stoke the fires under the turpentine vats until my hands are blistered. The others, they're sharpening hacks, clearing brush ahead of the choppers, and making sure the dippers ain't spilling a drop of valuable gum when they empty the cups into buckets.

The new convicts settled in. The white feller, Bub Belknap, is grumbling 'bout the long days. His woeful story is that he claims the boy was in the middle of the road when he struck him dead. The lad's sister told it different. They was off to the side, gathering cans to resell for food when Belknap run him over. Wherever the truth lies, Belknap got sentenced to one year. I remind him of why the turpentine gang is better. Better air, less crowded living quarters. But his muttered cussing still trails behind him.

The dipper has surely got one of the easiest jobs. He follows the lead choppers at first pass. Once they make their V cut, he nails the Herty cup to the tree below it. Second pass he removes the full cup of gum and dumps it in a bucket.

This morning, he's got molasses in his drawers.

"Belknap." I approach him, with my axe over my shoulder. "What you trying to do out here?"

"Got too much to do." He lifts his hat and slides his arm 'cross his sweating forehead. "I'm doing two fellers' work."

"You're doing no more than the rest of us. Now stop looking for sundown and supper or you're gonna catch more than you huntin' for."

"This ain't right." He slumps against a tree and swipes the clay cup off. It breaks apart when it hits the ground.

I take a gander over my shoulder. Taggert is on his mount circling the work area, but I don't see him right now.

"We'll catch up with our quotas tomorrow or the next, then drop back to routine schedule. If you're fixin' to blame someone, blame yourself for what you done that landed you here."

"You a criminal too. How do you get special treatment?"

"Worked my way up the hard way." I point to the trees. "Get a move on."

He slowpokes to the next tree and kicks the cup. It breaks, and sap runs in a clear stream down the bark.

"Whoops." He smiles and heads to the next tree and smashes that cup too.

I hurry to his side, grab his arm, and whisper. "Knock it off. You gonna catch hell."

He twists away and breaks the next cup. "Already caught it, you ask me."

Boy flies out of control, running from tree to tree, tearing off the cups, stomping or slamming them with his hammer.

"The hell's going on here?" Taggert yells, coming up behind me on his horse. "Stewart. Stop that idiot from destroying them damn cups."

I make a rush for Belknap, but he's running like a scalded haint. He looks back once and I catch his eye. I've seen that look before. If he'd had even a smidge of hope, it took off and fled just before.

Tears of downright rebellion run down his cheeks. He's giving up!

Belknap weaves and disappears into the trees, heading downhill.

"Get the dogs!" Taggert yells toward the camp tents. He turns his horse and cocks his rifle as he rides off in the direction Belknap set.

Sour throw-up hits the back of my throat. I need to keep the other fellers operating or we gonna get more trouble to answer to.

I move through the pines, pushing the convicts to stay at it. Assuring them they're okay. There's fear in their twitchy movements, and I smell it on me. We all taste the fright the hunted man must feel.

The coon dogs are really telling it now. They're closing in on him.

What made him give up like that? Feeling beaten down is something we all have hanging on our shoulders in this here prison camp. But it's short-term. His decision is permanent.

The gun fires twice, just moments apart. Each shot pinches my insides.

I get back to chopping wood, letting the logs take all of my anger and fear.

Taggert rises up the hillside, the dogs happily loping alongside his Palomino. A successful day for them.

"How many these cups he break?" Taggert calls my way.

"Two, three dozen I reckon." I rest on the axe handle, trying to quiet my shakes.

"Shit." He scratches his neck. "Didn't have that many to spare."

"We can try to plug up some of the old tin ones," I say. It don't sit right with me that I'm so helpful, but what choice remains?

"Goddammit. Why'd the warden send me that S-O-B?"

"Can't say, sir." *Maybe he wanted to get rid of him before he had to bury another feller in the secret graveyard.* "You want some of us to fetch Belknap?"

"Leave him for the animals. Besides, his face is shot off. Nobody needs to see that."

I recollect my last sight of Luther Junior, dead in the mine, and all that remained of him. Forgetting something like that is hard, but always keeping it locked in my mind is even worse.

"Forest ranger swings by here off and on," I say. "Recollect he said he don't like finding body parts. I could bury him."

"He's not gonna see anything from those damn bird perches or overlooks. He shows up, we say nothing." Taggert suddenly groans and grabs his stomach. "My damn guts. I didn't need that excitement today."

Hefting the axe, I turn back to splitting logs.

"Stewart. I need you to ride into Cartersville."

"Was just there." I tamp down the excitement. Any venture away is fine by me, and it sounds like I'm going alone. Unheard of. "What'd we forget?"

"Guts are killing me. Grab me a coupla bottles of Bisurated Magnesia from the pharmacist. The pills, not the damn powder." He pulls out his watch. "You leave now, you'll get there before he closes for midday."

"Sure. Anything else while I'm there?" I'm still testing the idea he's letting me go without another inmate by my side.

He pats his shirt pocket and pulls out a half-empty cigarette pack.

"Need some more gaspers. Might as well keep my throat and lungs healthy since my guts gone to shit."

"Woodbine again?"

"Prefer Chesterfields but if not, yeah."

"I'll take Bayou again. Him and me get along real good."

He opens his wallet and hands me a ten-dollar bill.

"Head out." He squints and clears his throat. "Remember, you try anything funny, I'll take you down harder than any no-account criminal."

"Always on my mind, sir." I fold the money and tuck it deep in my shirt pocket.

I saddle Bayou and point him down the logging trail. The first two miles are the steepest, mostly switchbacks. Ain't worried. He's sure-footed and I ain't in no hurry. I can cover seven miles and back in no time. Once sat a horse for fourteen hours, him getting feed and water just every so often. Worked branding season for a rancher in Wyoming. A hard job for sure, but it made a man feel worth his salt.

Off to the left, a steady rolling stream makes a low throaty rumble. I lift my face to the sun, letting its light and the tree shadows dance 'cross my skin. Smells of old wood and wet pine paint the air.

Maybe when I get out, I'll look into what it takes to be a forest ranger. A month back, when we were cutting on the other side of the ridge, a big feller rode into camp. He talked up a storm around the vittles we shared. Said living out on his own is lonely. Checks in just weekly with the ranger headquarters from call boxes nailed to telephone poles, usually not far from the ranger's shack. That big ranger had a fine sense of humor. Named his high rocky roost Last Step Lookout 'cause below his wooden perch looks to be 'bout five hundred feet of a granite-faced cliff.

He talked 'bout measuring distance to the first spiral of smoke using a compass and a map. I'm purty good at guessing distance. He also has to know all about shoeing a horse. And in case the feller takes sick, he has to know healing herbs. Nobody'd need to teach me either of those.

The thought settles nicely in my head.

I'm passing oak hollows where squirrels are *quaa-quaaing* away above me. A few nuts fall to the ground, and I ain't sure if they're meant for each other or me. Ahead, a dead oak stands black and twisted off the trail, out on the edge of a hill. Yonder, I catch a glimpse of Cartersville. Tiny curls of smoke rise from factory chimneys. The houses and buildings are all situated like white and pink stones cozied up together in a riverbed.

A lone crow sits near the top of a dead oak tree. A shiver fights its way up my sweaty back. Although the local Indians believe a single crow means something new or good is 'bout to happen, in my holler, it's a bad omen and foretells hard luck's surely 'bout to fall.

Wonder if it was sitting here when Belknap got killed. Sure as shooting don't want no more bad luck focused my way.

Round the next twist in the trail, I'm surprised to see that foreign boy squatting in the damp leaves. The tiny trail behind him must lead the back way to the same rotten cabin he's staying in. We've moved five miles farther along the mountainside, but here he is. I pull to a stop.

"Dangit, boy! Thought I told you to find a town."

"My brother vas too veak to valk." His face is a mask of hopelessness.

"How is he now?"

"No good." He stands and pulls up raggedy pants held to his waist with a graying length of rope. "He right there." Then he points to a sunny spot sprouted with ferns.

Can't see diddly from here, so I climb off Bayou and wrap the reins around a branch.

I follow the boy. "Is he awake?" His brother is curled up on his side, eyes closed, but his chest rises and falls. A rash covers his thin arms and skin-and-bone face. I start praying to myself that his next breath won't be his last. It's a terrible time when a brother loses a brother.

"I ain't got any vittles with me today," I say. "What you doing out here with him?"

"Need help to carry him to town." His shoulders slump. "To doctor."

My mind fights my heart. In my head, Taggert's warning wrestles the wrongness of leaving the poor boy here to die. *A useless soul is one who doesn't lighten the burden of others.* Dagnab my Bible upbringing.

"Let me sort this," I say. Can't hardly tote him into Cartersville because Taggert could hear of it. Euharlee is off to the left on Old Alabama Road, not more than six miles. Got arrested there last fall, but this time I got a purpose and money in my pocket. If I hustle, I can drop the boys off at the doctor's place and still ride to the pharmacist without losing too much time. "Ever been on a horse?"

"Yes, sir. Back home." The boy has new get-up-and-go written 'cross his face.

"Where's back home?" I fix my saddlebags 'cross Bayou to make room. "And dontcha say Boston again."

The boy kicks at the ground with his big toe.

"Russia. My family come after revolution, three years past. To Atlanta. Then flu last year take away everybody but my brother Cy."

"That's rough, kid." Maybe a home for orphans will take them in. "What's your name?"

"Ilya."

"Il yeah. Il-ya. Ilya, I'll put you in front of me in the saddle and your brother between us." I help him onto the horse. The boy smells like he's a few weeks shy of soap and water. I walk through the ferns and scoop up Cy. His weight is next to nothing.

"Keep him sittin' up 'til I climb on," I say, placing the child's legs 'cross the saddle and leaning him against Ilya's back. Once in the saddle, I make a sandwich out of us. "You push back a bit and Cy should stay right where he is."

"Zank you," he says, turning his head sideways. "Vat is your name?"

I start to say Briar and catch myself. Don't need the boy telling round who took him to town, so I use my middle name.

"Ray."

We drop off the hillside and come through the bottomlands. Hawks hunt over the sage grass, and a dozen cows huddle under the shade of river birch trees in a fenced pasture.

"Ve like milk you gave us," Ilya says, turning to the side. "My brother smile that day."

The sick kid is as limp as an eel out of water. Ain't sure what's wrong with him and also ain't free from worry his rash won't pester my skin later. Mama would know what to give him. She studied on all the herbs and healing plants. Folks come from several hollers away to ask for her help. But she ain't Briar Ray, now is she?

We ride the side of Old Alabama Road, giving space to the noisy automobiles and trucks. If folks don't look too close, we're just a family riding into town on an errand. Could be the youngest fell asleep between the two. Nothing hair-raising here.

I see the covered bridge before I hear Euharlee Creek rushing below it. It's a one-way pass-through, and I wait for a man with a wagon loaded with hay coming toward us. He touches the brim of his hat and I touch mine back. Once we enter the wooden cover, I ponder its length. I reckon it stretches a hundred, hundred twenty feet before the light of day falls on our heads again. The clomp of Bayou's shoes echo round the inside.

We exit and I turn Bayou away from the main street and town hall. Don't need a policeman asking 'bout us. Ahead, a woman walks with a little girl, both carrying parasols.

"Excuse, ma'am," I say as we draw closer to her.

She stops and lifts her face. "Yes?"

"We're in need of the town doctor. Could you offer directions?"

She raises her hand to her mouth. "Oh, your boy looks bad off."

"He's not my…" Why would I have this child with me if'n he ain't kin? I go with a lie. "Yes. My brother. Both are." I rest my chin on his head, wondering what all I'll be catching. "He's more wore out than anything." I tender a smile. "Who's the doctor in town?"

"Doc Jackson. And you're real close." She points down the street. "See the yellow house about six down? That's him."

"Thank you, ma'am," I say and nudge Bayou forward.

"Zank you," Ilya calls.

I look back, and the woman's forehead is knotted. Bet she's questioning why we brothers sound different. Folks tend to get worried 'bout anyone different than them.

A large painted sign in the front of the yellow house has Doctor Howard Jackson's name in black lettering on white. A smaller sign below reads, NO DOGS, INDIANS, OR BLACKS.

I tie Bayou to the hitching post at the side of the huge two-story house. It's an awful fancy one with black shutters and a great big tulip tree. The branches are loaded with pink flowers, reaching halfway 'cross the screened porch like a lady's fan.

I carry Cy while Ilya stays behind me.

"Rap on that door, Ilya."

He gives it three sharp knocks and we wait.

A woman opens the door. She's sturdy-built with graying hair twisted up in a knot at the back of her head. Her eyes are bright blue, trustworthy as a summer day.

"Hello. Looks like you need my husband."

"If he's the doctor, we sure do, ma'am."

She steps back but holds the door wide. The room's got half a dozen straight-back chairs set around its edges, with a fireplace and a braided rug in the center of the floor.

She crosses to an inside door and taps.

"Howard? You are needed."

Tall but bent over at his shoulders, Doc Jackson steps through the doorway. His eyebrows are bushy white to match his thick head of hair.

"He the one?"

I nod.

"Come in and lay that boy there."

He steps back to reveal a sunny room with cupboards and shelves and a small bed.

Once Cy lies down, I step back.

"Not sure what he's got, but he's been getting weaker and weaker."

"He's your relation?" The doctor pulls back Cy's eyelids and whites show.

"These're my brothers. Fell on hard times while back, been living meager in the woods."

The man opens Cy's mouth, looks inside, then presses round on his stomach. He sighs.

"It's pellagra. Seen too much of this lately."

"What's that?" I ask. If an orphan home takes the boys, they gonna want to know what's vexing the little one.

He folds his arms and studies Ilya and me.

"Best we know, it's from lack of certain foods. Mostly meat and eggs." He looks to us both. "Don't suppose you've been able to afford those?"

"No, sir." I stuff my hands in my pocket. This ain't a problem up in the hills. I touch the ten dollars Taggert gave. It'll buy some food. "How much is your fee?"

He squints. "You have any to give?"

"Got a dollar if you got change. Gonna use the rest for what you say. Meat and eggs."

Cy moans and mutters words, but they clearly ain't English.

Doctor Jackson steps back and crosses his arms.

"You got bigger troubles if that's Russian I'm hearing. Where you gonna live? Guy named Palmer has agents all over hunting for Russians. Sending them back home by ship, young and old."

"Think a home for orphans can take these two in 'til the little one is strong again?" I ask.

"How old are you?" the doctor asks Ilya.

"Fifteen. Just small 'cause of starving years before ve come here."

"Orphanages won't take you. Too old. But they will take your brother." He turns and washes his hands in a sink and dries them on a towel. "First, I'll get the wife to fry up some eggs and get the youngster a glass of milk. You think you can wake him up?"

"Yes, sir," I say.

"Come through here"—he opens another door leading into what looks like the kitchen—"and wait on the back veranda."

I tote Cy and we end up on a restful open porch, shaded from the hot sun by a sloping roof. I set him in one of the chairs placed round a lower table and give him a shake. His head rolls round like a rag doll missing its stuffing.

"You try," I say to Ilya. "Don't wanna hurt him."

He bends down and talks in the boy's ear, words I don't understand. He rubs his brother's arms and face. Soon the child's eyes crack open. They're as blue as Ilya's.

"Stay avake, Cy," Ilya says. "Ve now getting something to eat."

Cy's fixed look says someone forgot to turn the lights on in his head. Must have no idea how he come to be here.

"Okay," he mutters.

The door opens, and Mrs. Jackson brings out a tray and sets it on the table at our knees.

"You boys finish it all." She smiles. "Doctor's orders."

"Thank you, ma'am," I say. She's included small plates and cups to go with the pitcher of milk.

Ilya pours and helps Cy drink milk.

I reach for the ten-dollar bill to pay the doctor.

"Can you take this to your husband, please?" I hold it out to Mrs. Jackson.

"He won't take it now that he knows your plight. Said to tell you to buy food and the youngster should get stronger in a couple of weeks."

"Mighty kind. Thank him for us." Still have to explain to Taggert where his money ran off to, but I'll buy more food for the young'uns.

I let the boys eat the eggs and drink the milk. The smell of the eggs calls to me to take a few mouthfuls, but these boys need it more. 'Sides, I'll have all the eggs I want in a few months. My worry is where to take these fellers. Tearing them from one another at an orphan home's door don't seem right. But to keep a bigger problem from befalling me, I need to get on my way to Cartersville for Taggert's supplies. Opposite direction.

Then I recollect when I passed this way before being arrested. I spent time in a large cave with about thirty dry rooms 'bout four miles northeast of here. Where my money's waiting. Was saving the trip back there until I got out, but a quick drop-by won't delay my return to the work gang by much. Going to have to tell a tall tale to Taggert the way it stands.

"You boys ready to get back on the horse?" They finished the last of the vittles, and Cy looks a sight more bright-eyed but not so bushy-tailed yet.

"Where you take us?" Ilya says. "Ve together, no matter what, da?"

"Oh, I plan to keep you together." I motion them off the back porch and to the horse. "But first, we got a stop to make."

Soon we're headed back to downtown Euharlee. My plan for the Russian orphans is so clear to me now. The Bible reminds me, "Do not boast for in a moment you may reap disgrace." I won't crow about my idea, but inside I do feel mighty pleased I thought of it.

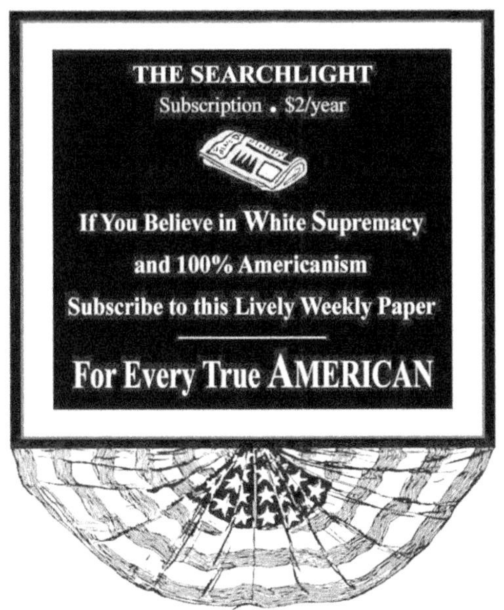

Marietta, Georgia. May 1921

-15-

ARDITH DOBBS

"Bedsheets and pillowcases?" Teresa Greer taps the *Atlantic Independent* newspaper page, a scowl on her face. "Leave it to a writer from New York to not see us for what we're about."

Teresa, Nancy, and I sit around my dining table, properly set with my finest china, tall crystal glasses, fine embroidered napkins, hot tea, and homemade cookies—my old grandmother's recipe. Josephine serves Earl Grey and then leaves the room. She has all seven children corralled in the playroom, entertaining them for the next hour, despite having birth contractions since this morning. We're squeezing in one more planning meeting before she's off work a few days having her baby.

We're looking through the local newspapers for articles written about our WKKK march through Atlanta last night. I'm still thrumming from the delight of pulling off a sixty-women march—led by mounted police, thanks to Sheriff Withington. Though most were Klan, they weren't robed. Dressed in their finest black uniforms, they had a sharp but menacing presence. We women assembled at the Methodist Church, and when we were all outfitted, marched quietly down the main street carrying our signs of patriotism. Mine said "Stronger Women, Stronger Homes." I wanted "The Awakening—Now and Forever," but another woman grabbed it first. The exciting part was that people packed the sidewalks. The many announcements we hung around town publicizing our "Walk for American Values" worked well.

I remember the hush that fell on the onlookers. They seemed to sense our force, respect our unknown power. Some may have been afraid. Good. Chills had raced through me. I mean, I boss Oliver and Josephine around, but I've never held sway over groups of people before.

When we reached the park, the local librarian Mrs. MacDougal stood on a platform to announce the social activities we were involved with and how we were solving problems across the country. She was robed, of course, so only we knew who she was. Some people may not have liked the idea that the woman who hosts Reading Time for their children also thinks of nuns as the pope's whores. She talked in general about what type of women join the Klan, while the rest of us handed out new flyers inviting "the better educated and connected woman" to a lecture session. That's where we get down to the truth about the Catholics' dirty little secrets. We also cover the sneaky Jews and the sexually promiscuous Negroes.

I circulated through the crowd, telling everyone that our group was a fun thing to do with friends. That it got me out of the house for a few hours. About how I loved the emphasis on family, home, and women's rights.

"Good Lord." Nancy is reading from the *Miami Herald*. "Listen to this garbage." She folds the paper, aligning the column in front of her.

> "Astonished Atlantans watched in shock as robed Ku Klux Klan women took to the streets of the downtown last evening. The organization has frequently been investigated in crimes against ethnic minorities, in particular, Colored people. The Klan hides behind their masks and robes while spreading hate and fear throughout the south. The irony is that for all of their dislike of the Catholic faith, the Klan wears the Church's pointed hood, the *capirote,* a way for self-confessed sinners to repent in public without being recognized by fellow churchgoers. It is fair to say the members of this rapidly growing Klan are not using their disguises for the same apologetic purpose."

We all snort and hmmpf our disapproval.

"How dare they!" I'm furious. "I bet a Catholic wrote that."

Teresa sips her tea and gently places her teacup in the saucer. The Royal Albert Azalea design always reminds me of fuzzy purple caterpillars, but I could never ask William to replace his family's wedding gift to us. *My* family would have sent chipped blue enamel cups if they'd had any idea I was married—or even alive. Sissy Belle Strunk has been a missing person all these years, and one day the search for her, for *me*, will simply fade away.

"Frank said that Congress's investigation has helped him recruit men faster than ever," Teresa says. "And higher-class members, especially in rural areas. They say they didn't know we were a true American organization until Congress stuck their noses in our doings and the newspapers carried the failed investigations."

"That's what's going to happen here. You watch." Nancy closes the *Miami Herald*. "We have our local paper to praise. Ardith, William did a magnificent job with the advertisements he placed around the article. Flag and Bible sales, our bake-off to support deserted children." She opens the *Marietta Daily Journal* and taps the photo of five women in full regalia with the headline.

Women of the KKK March for Charity

"That's what we need more of." Teresa takes a peek. Points to another ad on the page. "Oh. Have you ladies tried this?"

The photo shows a bottle of Lysol with the tag line, "For complete Feminine Hygiene rely on Lysol. A Concentrated Germ-Killer and more."

Nancy Withington laughs. "Yes, in my kitchen but not my privates."

"It says it's recommended by leading gynecologists." Teresa leans back with a satisfied expression on her face.

"People are paid to say those things. Right, Ardith?" Nancy says. "William must see these false claims every day."

"Just snake oil, companies trying to get a person's money." I try not to look at my ankles as I feel heat rise in my neckline and pray I'm not perspiring. Because I've wasted money on Melto and several fat-reducing creams, the only thing that changed on my waist, legs, or ankles was potent swampy smells coming from me by the end of the day. "It's like that Gillette Company trying to get women to shave their legs and armpits. Shameful." I add another exhalation to show my disgust.

The other two are quiet for a heartbeat, then Teresa shrugs. "Frank likes my legs smooth. I've been shaving for about two years now."

"Me too." Nancy removes her lightweight embroidered jacket off one shoulder to show and rub her armpit. "Nothing there. I swear I grow more hair than York."

How could I have missed this? This is why I need to get out more often and not immerse myself so much with Oliver or cleaning. I swallow and resist the urge to fan my warming face.

"I meant that the ads of half-clothed women are shameful. Once I can see my legs again, I'll try out the newest razor." I pretend to bend over, but I'm stopped immediately by my big belly. I change the subject. "Let's get a list ready of *I Caught You's*"—I grab a tablet and pen—"and Nancy can take them to York to look into."

"Me first," Teresa says. "I don't know the man's name, but he works at the Atlanta Pencil Factory." She leans forward, eager to share what she's discovered. "He's always on the street in front during the dinner hour, handing out pencils that read, 'You won the vote—Use it.'"

"Does he seem to have a political leaning?" Nancy asks. "I'd like to finally see women vote this fall."

"He's only handing them to Negro men and poor immigrants, so..."

"The one-dollar poll tax prevents most of the poorer folks from even registering," Nancy says. "That and the literacy tests, of course. Not sure a pencil's going to matter."

Teresa pulls one from her pocketbook and puts it on the table along with a brochure. "He's handing out *helpful* information that may get more Negroes interested."

My mind jumps to my folks in Hickory Nut Hollow. They never would've paid one dollar to register to vote. And take it from me, their opinions weren't worth hearing. A century of staying locked away in the hills, circulating their backward logic? My pa would say, "Life begins with hospitality, but if you want happiness, that requires a powerful emphasis on *leave us the hell alone.*"

"Well, we don't need this man trying to change the voting numbers," Teresa says.

"I agree," Nancy says, as she tucks the brochure in a folder. "York can send out a deputy to get this man's name. Maybe a late-night visit will put him back on course." She smiles at Teresa. "Well done. This is a good *Caught You*. I'll go next." She brings out a newspaper clipping of a wedding announcement. "This priest named James Coyle performed a marriage last week between an Episcopalian girl and a Puerto Rican immigrant. Several days before the wedding, Ruth, the wayward gal, converted to Roman Catholicism. We can only assume under pressure."

We *tsk* and agree the minister needs to be punished. Nancy slides the clipping into her folder.

"What do you have, Ardith?"

"Two things." I pull out a dollar bill. I've torn off the upper right corner where the pope inserted his image. "The bank needs to go through all of its currency and purge its vaults. Why, after four years, are we still finding these...these blasphemous things?" The arrival of the pope as the emperor of the United States was imminent if we did nothing. Rumors circulated that the Catholics plan to build a palace in Washington, DC to allow the pope to oversee his empire. Everyone knows Catholics in the United States, whether citizens or immigrants, are spies for the Vatican.

"You want the Klan to go after the Marietta Bank?" Teresa lifts her eyebrows, turning her eyes into large sapphire marbles. "We all deposit there."

"Um…only a conversation. Not a punishment." I swallow hard. That didn't impress them like I hoped. "This leads me to my *Caught You.* Roy Elsmore, out on Chicken Branch Road, has deserted his wife and two boys. The wife, Fiona, went so far as to put her darling daughter up for adoption." I remember the impetigo and shiver. That child was a mess. "I'm sure Roy can be found and brought back."

The truth is I hadn't put any time into spying on the townsfolk because this week it was too hot out, and I am too tired. After the baby, I'll get my prying eyes going. Offering up Fiona's husband was my easy way out this week. The Klan will discover what Fiona already believes—Roy is most likely dead.

"Oh, we can't have that," Nancy says. She makes a note on a pad of paper and puts that in her file, then pushes away from the table. "I'll round up my kiddos and head home. We've had a good week, fellow Daisies."

Teresa agrees, and as she leaves, two little ones trail behind her. Four follow Nancy. I sink into the chair in the front room. William will be home in two hours, and I haven't had one thought about what Josephine should make for supper.

I smile. Our ladies' club is what I've needed in my dull life. Because of us, three secret deeds will take place to improve our community.

"Miss Ardith." Josephine is standing in the hallway. She clutches her belly, and the front of her dress is wet. "I am sorry to disturb you, ma'am, but my baby is coming."

If she lost her water in the house, I will be furious. "I see that."

"I was outside when this happened." She looks at her wet dress. Her face scrunches together. It's obvious she's fighting pain. And that'll be me soon enough, but of course, I'll suffer worse. Colored gals can tolerate pain better than white women. I mean, everyone knows that. Thank goodness, Dr. Grange will give me something for the pain.

And because we like Josephine so much, he'll provide that for her too.

"Okay. Head to your room and I'll call the doctor."

This means I have Oliver for the next three days while she recovers. It'll be draining, but I can manage. Then a happy thought bubbles to the front of my mind.

Today is Friday, or Deadly in Klan-speak. William will be home on Dark and Desperate to help me.

Helen, Georgia. May 1921

–16–

Willow Stewart

Cooking sounds from the rectory kitchen draw me awake. For several seconds, I try to remember where I am and why I'm here. When I turn over, pain shoots through my ailing arm like raccoon's teeth chewing at it. Then vexing reality settles in the room. Dust motes dance along a beam of sunlight, unaware that dancing is forbidden after a death.

I push out of bed, and the squeak of the springs mocks my throat's inability to make even a sound as simple as that. At the window, I study the clear morning sky and pray that God has favored Stewart Mountain with the same pure sunrise. During the night, the rain drumming on the roof matched my tears. Eventually, the Sandman won out, and I slipped into sleep.

"Good morning, Willow." Mrs. Holcombe stands in the doorway with a tentative smile on her face. "I made porridge."

I smile back and gesture that I'll use the outhouse first.

Outside, I close my eyes and breathe in cool ribbons of fresh air. I cross the grass, heading for the edge of the woods. The puddles of rainwater squish between my toes under the soft give of spongy ground. Mama loves—she *loved*—the air after the rain. I draw in another deep breath on her behalf. A quiet hissing comes from the forest, the tiny water droplets drizzling down from a thousand leaves. Nearby are the lavender blossoms of the Lenten rose and pink trilliums. They have to hurry through their whole life before the trees finish leafing out, blocking the life-giving caress of the sun. My chest tightens. Everywhere I look, something is struggling to stretch time for another chance to celebrate the orange traces of sunset. To soak in the pink of the next dawn.

I wish I'd spent more time with Mama, helped her more than just these last few years when we shared the duties of healing a neighbor's maladies. Or when we huddled over a new book or newspaper. But until I was about twelve, after our chores were done, Briar, Billy Leo, and I spent our days in the forest, building log dams, making pretend homes in tree branches, or picking herbs for Mama's remedy jars. And lying in thick wide patches of purple violets that lifted us to heaven on earth with their scent.

Guilt sits heavy on my shoulders as I return to the parsonage and enter the kitchen. Two bowls of porridge face each other across the table.

"Do you think you can eat something?" Her voice is a soft mauve, a careful color.

I nod and take the seat where she points. A cup of milk sits next to the bowl.

"Pastor Holcombe won't be home until midday. Officer Vissom is on his way."

I reach in my dress pocket for my pencil and pad and remember I've run out of paper. I hold the stubby pencil and mimic writing and shrug my uninjured shoulder.

"Oh, wait. I have scratch paper round here." She steps to a desk and brings back a pad of paper the color of buttermilk.

I write, *I can walk home. Thank you.*

She studies me so hard I feel like a fly stuck on tar paper. What is she thinking? I drop my head and scoop a few bites of the food and force it down. The milk is cool, a strange sensation in my throat. I spot the built-in blue metal icebox, advertised in newspapers as, "Spoil yourself as you keep your food from the same fate." Mrs. Holcombe must've been enticed. The cool milk soothes the rawness in my throat, and I see the advantage of the indoor icebox.

"Nonsense. You just eat and relax. I need to ring a friend…a sick friend." She wipes her hands on her apron. "Won't be away but a minute. Will you be okay?"

I smile. After she's gone, I shake my head, not believing all this. I'm forever being treated like a baby. Why would any fifteen-year-old girl not be okay sitting at a table eating, unless they were thought to be simple? I can hear her tapping the switch on the telephone, and I wonder how on God's green earth she got trained to be a telephone-hello lady. Having a telephone and *knowing* how to reach other people are two different things, and that would take training.

I finish the porridge and feel a wave of might move through me. And I thank the good Lord 'cause I need to buck up for my walk home.

She returns to the kitchen, beating up her apron again, wiping her hands over and over, as if they fell in a river and she had to fish them out. Surely they can't be wet.

She holds out a folded piece of paper. A one-page booklet of sorts. The photograph on the front shows a large white building. On the steps, dozens of girls of all ages are dressed in their best, flanked by two women looking like they had their fill of sour mash just before the photographer's bulb flashed.

She pats her hair in place, although not a lock has moved atop her head. The woman's hands stay busier than a blind judge at a beauty contest. That's something Briar used to say.

"I want to talk to you about something. We'd like to send you out to Cave Springs. To that school." She points to the paper.

I have no time for formal schooling. Mrs. Holcombe has no idea how busy we women are at home, always staying in front of our work. The writing across the paper reads, GEORGIA SCHOOL FOR THE DEAF.

Why in tarnation would I attend a school for the deaf? I shake my head before handing the leaflet back.

"It's a right nice home for white girls although the property has two other homes. One for boys and one for Colored children." She sets the picture on the table again and pulls an envelope out of her pocket. "We pass the plate each Sunday, and a portion is set aside for young folks who need taking in."

I don't need taking in, but I sure need to get going.

I write, *I thank you for your kindness. I'll be on my way,* and hand her the slip of paper.

She reads it and moves closer, carefully reaching out a hand, checking to see if it's safe to touch me. She leaves her fingers on my wrist and their dampness sends a shiver up my arm.

"I will tell you the truth, if you do the same." Then she leans closer and peers into my eyes. She pulls me by the hand and leads me into the parlor and points to a green upholstered couch. I take a seat, unsure of what she is about to say. She settles beside me, sitting close as kin, and I get an uneasy feeling. "Deputy Vissom and I are worried about you. We think you're a runaway, but afraid to tell us what you're running from."

I feel scolded. I've told them the truth. Did they think I killed the peddler and stole his wagon just to get away? Why would I wave down the law if I was running? I would've kept going.

"I know about family loyalty." Her smile is crooked, perhaps an apology for the story her brain is mustering together about me. "With your ma sick and all, a father might turn his attentions…" She clears her throat. "Might get the idea—"

I brush her hand away and jump to my feet and head to the kitchen where she follows. How dare she insult my poppy! Cuss words race through my head. The woman is lucky they have no way to exit my mouth. I breathe deeply to try to cool the heat pushing off my face.

"You can't help what's going on at your homestead. We are aware of the inbreeding." She's standing. Her hands flutter again, uncertain where they should be. "This is why your kinfolk pushed deeper into the hills to escape ridicule." She takes a step toward me and I take one back. "We want the best for you. God guided you off the hill and into our hands. As a half orphan, you'll be surrounded by others like you. Many single parents have allowed schools and orphanages to raise their children. What a blessing the Lord is bestowing. Think about it. If a mute can get as much learning from books as you have, imagine what you could learn in a school program surrounded by normal folks."

I'm suddenly sorry I wrote that I've read a passel while admiring her books.

I've been taught to never be rude to an adult, but if I don't get away, that's about to change. Mrs. Holcombe seems dug into this school idea like an Appalachian tick. A large clock ticks loudly on the wall, and an image of a skipjack beetle comes to mind, and how he clicks out his steady warning just before flipping himself in the air, evading danger. I have more than a few clicks building up in me at the moment. But being angry isn't what I need. I can get glad in the same clothes I got mad in, so it's time for me to act like I am hearing her out before I get on my way.

I reach for the piece of paper on the table and write, *Can I send a note to my Poppy before I go to the girls' home?*

She looks pleased, like she's treed a fat raccoon.

"Lord Almighty! You write what you have to, and I'll have the police drive it up. Your family needs to know you're in good hands."

I don't know about the good hands part. When I leave this church, I do know I'll be in more trouble than a person standing in a black snake pit toting one hoe. I write, *You've met the preacher. His wife is taking me to live at the Deaf School for Girls in Cave Springs. You will have to milk the herd without me. Love Willow.* I fold the note several times and hand it to her. She slips it in her dress pocket, still smiling. If she reads it before I'm gone, she'll think I'm leaving with her. Poppy will know I'm in trouble with the last line. We milk one cow, a Miss Mildred, not a herd. "Milk the herd without me" has always been our kin's warning message that we are in danger.

We've used it only once before. Federal agents swarmed the mountain looking for moonshine. Briar came charging out of the woods yelling out the secret sentence. Mama rushed to hide the five bottles in the piano bench before the two men reached the cabin. They searched the house and found naught. Before they left, they appreciated sweet tea and Mama's piano playing before heading off on a new pursuit.

Mrs. Holcombe hands me the envelope. "There's seven dollars in there for your first month at the home. After that, you'll be assigned chores to pay your way." Her eyes crinkle at the corners, pleased with her charity.

I accept it but have no intention of crossing the stoop of that school. If I don't take it, she'll wonder what I'm up to. The Bible says that when a person lets the devil have an inch, he'll throw the door wide open. Yesterday, I let a man die, and today, I'm stealing from God's servant. Within a day, I've gone and chipped two commandments right off the face of Moses's stone tablet and made them my own.

Tires crunch on the pebble drive.

"That will be Deputy Vissom. He's offered to drive you to your new home in Cave Springs. You may not know the county, but that's about a hundred twenty miles west of here."

Not only do I know where Cave Springs is, part of our home learning was to memorize the history and the layout of all the towns in Georgia. Briar's last letters home came from near there, west of Cartersville. That was five months ago, but I reckon he's still working in the logging industry there.

I pocket the envelope and write, *I'll be ready once I use the outhouse again.* I grab my burlap poke on the table. Mama made it for me, and I won't abandon it, even though it's only candy.

I run a short distance like a gun is pointed at my back. At the edge of the woods, I duck behind an old oak tree as Mr. Vissom calls hello to the preacher's wife, and the car door *whumps* shut just as the screen door opens.

"Is she inside?" His voice is a strange brown, also tight like barbed wire wrapped around his words. "Did she take to the idea of the deaf home?"

"She'll be right back. I think the idea set real nice with her."

"Not that she has any choice. Her father can try to find her, I guess.

I'll wager within a few days, she'll want to stay after she's enjoyed indoor plumbing. I also need to talk to her about that map she drew."

There's a saying that all secrets are witnessed in the forest, but as I stand in the trees, I'm not prepared for Mr. Vissom's next words.

"It led us to a field where the ground was chewed up from hooves and wagon wheels, but there were no poison mushrooms. No dead man."

That peddler was graveyard dead when I left.

"She was quite upset when you asked her to sketch the map. Very easy to make a mistake." Mrs. Holcombe's voice sounds thin, whitewashed with raggedy nerves. "Maybe animals got to him."

"No blood. Even with the rain last night, animals leave parts behind. Clothes. I'm not sure what happened there."

Mrs. Holcombe clucks her tongue. "Must have been a mind-fuzzing event. Getting captured like that. Easy to forget details."

It sounds like he spits tobacco. "I'll talk to her on the way to the school."

"She wrote a note to her father."

"Tear it up," are the last words he speaks before the house swallows them up.

I already have more troubles than I can say grace over. And God knows the truth about the pickle I was in with Mr. Coburn. My throat tightens. How will I ever return home if I'm locked up in a school for deaf girls?

I glance to the sky, check the sun, and take off through the woods heading south.

In the opposite direction they expect me to go.

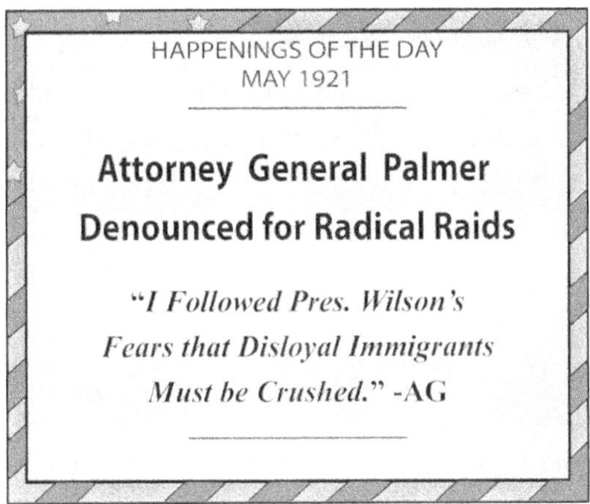
HAPPENINGS OF THE DAY
MAY 1921

Attorney General Palmer Denounced for Radical Raids

"I Followed Pres. Wilson's Fears that Disloyal Immigrants Must be Crushed." -AG

Kingston Saltpeter Cave, Georgia. May 1921

-17-

Briar Stewart

We veer off Sugar Valley Road and cross Ashpole Creek, heading to Saltpeter Cave, the saddlebags full of grub. Chicken, cheese, bread, bacon, and eggs. Milk, lard, and potatoes round out the vittles that I pray will last 'em a good two weeks. Had money left over from Taggert's ten dollars to buy a fry pan, matches, candles, and two sets of tin plates with knife and fork. Fresh water in the cave and hours of sunshine at any of the two openings should have these two fellers right as rain in no time.

They're both old enough to work in the cotton mills. Train runs from Cartersville to Atlanta, pert near to dumping a feller at the doors of that Fulton Bag Company. They even got a whole town suited for the workers, with a hospital, library, and company store. Called Cabbage Town 'cause so many folks come from the hills to work there. Never heard tell of a mountain person who don't love a good plate of boiled cabbage.

Was headed to Fulton myself when I got arrested.

"You are here before?" Ilya asks as we wind up the sides of Knox Dolomite Knob.

"Spent a few days last winter," I say. "You'll be safe inside. Nobody mining here no more."

The main entrance is to the east and comes up as a little bit of a surprise, tucked in a shady fold near the top of the mountain, bearded by hardwood trees. The other entrance comes out northwest, but it's a mite smaller. To get to that side, you gotta crab along on elbows and knees in some spots.

Bayou picks his way through the jumble of rocks to the tall opening. I help Cy down. He's wobbling a bit but standing on his own.

I sling the saddlebags over my shoulders and turn to Ilya.

"You help your brother. Once inside, we drop down 'bout three hundred paces at a fair steep angle. Then we reach the rooms y'all can stay in."

"It cold inside?" Ilya says, following behind me.

"Yeah. Can get so cold, we mountain folk call it a 'two-dog night.'" I see the puzzlement gripping Ilya's face. "That means you need a couple dogs to keep ya warm. 'Specially deep inside. But near the entry it's warmer. Best sleep outside at night." I tip my head to the side near the opening. "Under that overhang is a flat area. You'll find an old kiln. Do your cooking there. Wash in the pool right next to it."

I stop to light a candle and tell 'em to follow me. Then I lead the way into the mouth of the cave and crunch through sticks and dead leaves. We slowly descend on a path that must've been cleared for hundreds of years between piles of rocks. The bright sunlight thins as we move inward. Ilya and Cy stay right behind me. The scent of damp rocks fills my head. My heart thuds like it wants to come out of my chest. This smell always brings back the day Luther Junior died.

We reach the first room without a hitch. It's smaller, 'bout the size of the inside of our cabin back home. The walls are jaggy, probably carved by water 'fore dirt was invented. Water plinks somewhere deeper, and a small stream dribbles in a back corner.

"Y'all should be safe in here, but if anyone comes, there are more rooms a mite past this one. Get to the big one with over five hundred names scratched into the walls."

"Can you show us?" Ilya lowers Cy to a flat rock in a dry area.

We could spend hours in here studying the wonders of pillars sprouting up from the ground or hanging down from the ceiling. Stalag-something or another Willow calls them. Even has a room with a rock shaped like a giant jug.

"I'm on an errand for the boss and he don't take lightly to tardiness." I set the sacks with vittles in a corner. "I might can circle back in two weeks. But don't wait on me. Y'all get stronger, head on down to Atlanta and grab some work."

"Zank you, Ray." He smiles.

I wonder for a second who he means. "My pleasure. Travelers need to stick together."

"I hope you come back."

"I hope y'all find a nice place to live and work. You two ain't known a minute's peace out there on your own."

Ilya told me how his kinfolk made it to America after nearbout starving like millions of others in Russia. His folks saved them from becoming part of the thousands of children who yoked together after the 1917 Revolution, hunting and robbing so's they could eat.

Boy told tales right out of a horror book. Folks following gravediggers, waiting for the black of night to dig up the fresh dead. Cooking legs and arms. His family of five ate grass from the fields. One sister died on the passage. His parents grieved but were mighty thankful for a new country, a fresh start. Then the Spanish Flu took them.

Got one more stop inside this here cave.

"Y'all get washed up in that pool over yonder." I point to a dark hollow where water drips in from above. "Be right back."

I light another candle and head to the next room. Ain't no more than a wide hallway but directly opens up into the large room. Not the biggest one, but it's got a dozen stalag things—pillars—and lots of hidey-holes.

A worry pecks at me. What if someone's been snooping round in here and found my money? I cross to a pile of stones, the top one covered on purpose with bat shit. Then I lift three rocks off to the side of the pile and lean over. It's still here! The gunny sack is settled in the hole just as I left it. I undo the drawstring and pull out ten dollars. But I hesitate. There's another thirty-five in there. Enough to live on if'n I was to catch a fast-moving freight away from here. I'd leave Bayou with a farmer to steer Taggert and the hounds in another direction away from the boys and me. But a life on the run ain't a dependable way to be living. A feller'd be looking for storm clouds at every sunset. And I sure as shooting don't want Taggert anywhere near my kin back home.

I close up the sack and cover it again with the rocks. I stop for a moment to look up. Hmm…still there. Names. Carved in the flat stone ceiling. Carrie Smith, Mary Harold, and seven other gals, with the year 1896. Some twenty-five years ago. I spent many an hour talking to these past seekers when I wandered through before. Wondering what they was doing down here. I found human bones in a small space deep in the back. Just parts. Not a whole person worth. What happened there is a secret only this old cave and the good Lord know.

I head back to the boys. Cy is naked, and Ilya is pouring water over him with a tin pan. The puny young'un is covered real bad with angry sores. If'n Doc Jackson can be trusted, the vittles will heal all that before long. Said pellagra is a starvation illness.

"I best be going. Cook the chicken first off 'cause it won't last long even in this chill." I pat Ilya on the back. "You take good care of your brother." *Because I sure enough know what it's like to be careless and lose one.*

"I vill." His eyes say thank you, and that's worth all the extra trouble today.

Back on Bayou, I ride off hell-bent for Cartersville. The pharmacist is opening up after his dinner hour, and I buy the pills and cigarettes. Chesterfields. That might soothe Taggert's ornery spirit.

Nothing's changed when I reach the cutting area. Tuck waves and goes back to sharpening the blades.

"Where the hell you been, Stewart?"

I raise my hand to stop the conversation. Once I get Bayou back in the corral, I turn to Taggert. His face is rooster red.

I hold out his items. "Chesterfields, sir. Your lucky day."

He snatches them from me along with the change I produce.

"Not what I asked. Why the fuck it take you four hours longer than it should to get there and back?"

On the ride back, I practiced a few excuses for being late. Stopped to watch an airplane, or got swept off the horse by a tree branch. I try out the one that makes most sense.

"Tried to take a shortcut going down, sir. Got slowed by a jumble of logs. No work crew in sight, but somebody's doing a heap of cutting."

"Don't pee down my leg and tell me it's raining, boy. You smarter on a horse than most. No way you'd put your mount through that."

I shrug as if to say that's the plight I was in.

He taps out a cigarette from the pack and lights it. After inhaling deeply, he draws pert near close 'nough to kiss my nose and blows that dadgum smoke in my face. I fight to keep from coughing, but he got me good. And I fight not to move as I stifle a cough.

"I'm gonna be watching you. And next trip into Cartersville...ain't gonna include you."

"Yessir."

"Get back to chopping wood." He unscrews the cap on the medicine bottle, palms two white pills and throws 'em back. Swallows. "You ain't getting supper tonight neither."

"Yessir."

Don't bother me none. I can miss a meal knowing them two Russian rascals are fixin' to eat right good tonight. Bet they sleep like babies swaddled in a cradle.

I know I will.

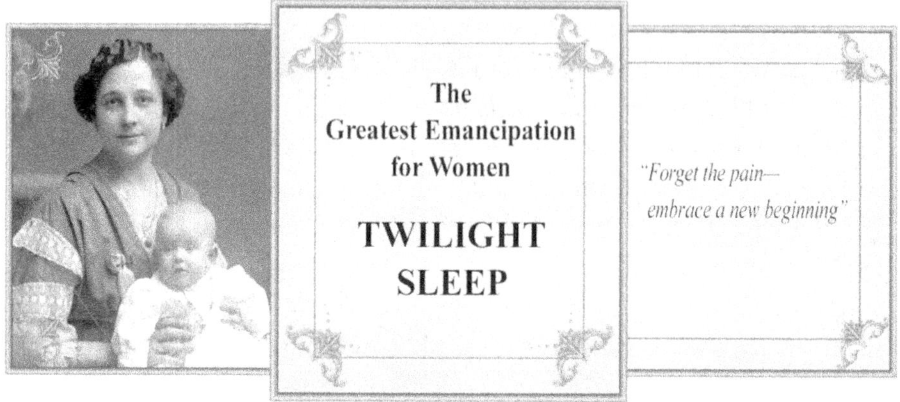

The
Greatest Emancipation
for Women
TWILIGHT
SLEEP
"Forget the pain—
embrace a new beginning"

Marietta, Georgia. May 1921

-18-

Ardith Dobbs

Dr. Hugo Grange has arrived. He's dashing for an older man, with silver streaks in his dark hair and bright sapphire eyes. And quite the ladies' man, always giving me sidelong looks when he thinks I don't see. He's my personal doctor, of course, so all modesty evaporated after the first time the man viewed me half-naked.

But he's attending to Josephine now.

When we first hired her, William redid the mudroom and toilet area attached to the house, turning it into a comfortable living space with a bed and chair. There's also a mirror and shelving and pegs for her clothes and personal things. Two tiny windows allow for a nice cross-breeze, while our largest magnolia tree shades that side of the house. I haven't gone in her room very often, but when I've peeked inside, the room is always neat and doesn't smell foul as I'd always anticipated.

I checked in on her a few moments ago. Let me tell you, Twilight Sleep is the best invention any German has ever come up with. Josephine is covered in sweat, panting like a dog on a hot summer's day, and not making so much as a squeak. Dr. Grange said she can deliver anytime now.

"Throw it now, Mommy." Oliver and I are playing ball in the yard. However, the boy needs more time practicing with William. I know he's only five, but he catches like he's got ferns for hands. My brother Clem caught fireflies at dusk by the time he was three. *Used to catch.* Clem isn't grabbing at anything anymore.

I toss the baseball gently, and this time Oliver snags it.

"There you go," I say. He laughs and looks just as surprised as I am. My theory that Oliver needs more practice was just proven correct. Thirty minutes of tossing the ball and he's already gotten better. But William's busier than ever. Insurance and advertising are the fastest-growing businesses, and he heads to work earlier each day and comes home later. Who's the better parent now?

Josephine will need two to three days off to clear her noggin from the drugs, so I have many fun activities scheduled for Oliver and me. This afternoon, I'll show him the wooden wagon the new Liberty Coaster Company sent for us to try out. Tomorrow, the neighbor boy will earn fifty cents pulling Oliver to the park and spending the morning there. Then in the afternoon, I'm toting him along on my home visits to help collect insurance money. Money-strapped women hand over their weekly premiums more willingly when a little boy opens his tiny fist.

"Mrs. Dobbs?" Doctor Grange says from the doorway. "Come see."

Something in his voice is off. Is the baby deformed? With all the Negroes' careless breeding, birth disasters are common.

"Oliver. I need you to sit here and toss the ball into the air and catch it. Keep doing it while I check on Josephine and her new baby."

"I can count to a hundred. Want to see?" His face lights up. "Miss Jojo taught me."

"When did you learn that?" What else has she taught him? I pay her to entertain him, not fill his tiny head with too-soon knowledge.

"When we toss and catch the baseball." He tilts his head, the same movement William does when he has a new idea. "After Miss Jojo has her baby, she can teach you how to be a better thrower," he says. "With her, I catch the ball every time."

I want to scold him for his rudeness, but a baby's cry pulls me into the house. I brace myself. This might be horrifying.

I push inside. The air in the room is hot and clammy with the coppery scent of blood.

"It's a boy." Dr. Grange is finishing up with Josephine and the afterbirth duties. He flicks his chin toward the wiggling bundle in the sink. The baby's cocooned in one of the new white blankets I bought. "Appears healthy. Josephine did fine too."

Hmm. Why was he acting so strange if everything went well?

I glance at Josephine's naked body. She's unconscious and breathing steady. Clergymen protest anesthesia, saying labor pains are God's will. Well, thank you Billy Sunday. Let a muskmelon tear through a man's innards and we'll see who they're praising.

Thanks to William and my generosity, Josephine didn't die in childbirth like so many Coloreds, and her son arrived with her experiencing no pain.

This will be me in a week or two. But in a nice hospital bed. I'm glad Josephine is sleeping peacefully. She is a hard worker and a loyal helper. I refuse to call her a servant. That's so demeaning.

I glance at Josephine one more time. In the room's dim light, I'm reminded she could be a white girl being such a light-skinned Negro. Prettier than a mess of fried catfish, we used to say. If her mother hadn't fallen for the conniving ways of a Negro man, Josephine's life would've taken a much different course. With a mother in an insane asylum, her father dead, and the girl birthing out of wedlock, this is a fine howdy-do for the bastard child she'll be raising.

I approach the squirming babe and gasp. This can't be right! The boy could be Oliver's twin! White as down fluff with a cleft in his tiny chin. My mind plays with scenarios that explain why Josephine's child resembles mine. It's the situation. She eats the same food we do. She's surrounded by white folks, and it's rubbed off on her.

"What do you think?" Dr. Grange says. He has a smirk on his lips I'd like to swipe away.

I can't meet his eyes. There's only one explanation—Josephine beguiled William as sure as rats run the rafters. Hot anger rises in my stomach and I'm dizzy. How did William believe this would turn out? Especially when she showed herself pregnant. He could have demanded we hire another woman for any reason at all, and I would never have known what they had done. Men are so incredibly stupid.

No one can find out about this. Having sex outside of marriage is how men are exiled from the Klan. Or worse. And diddling a Colored gal? Downright sinful. No wonder Josephine is always puttering around William, swinging her fat sassy ass this way and that.

Anesthesia kills women all the time. Why couldn't it have taken Josephine? I shake my head. What to do? Whatever we decide, we need to do it fast.

I lift the baby and try not to look at it while I rock him. He's warm and snuggles into my chest and makes sucking sounds.

"Dr. Grange. Hugo." He must keep this a secret. "You can see my predicament here. I need your help."

He shakes his head. "No way to turn back time, Ardith."

"That's quite clear. But let's look forward. This baby will create a great deal of pain in our lives. With William's career. Our community *associations*." The doctor is a Klan member. He knows what I'm talking about.

"What is it you want me to do?" He stalls in his movements.

"I need you to certify that this baby was born dead. Deformed even."

He steps back and crosses his arms. "I can't do that. What do we tell Josephine when she wakes up and wants to see the baby?"

"That because she committed a sin, God gave her a hideous child. It died, and we needed to bury him." I stomp my foot. This is so unfair. My standing in the ladies' club will turn to dust. People will talk. We'll be financially ruined. "Isn't that what you do with babies that are malformed?"

"It is not." He shakes his head. "Ardith. You need to talk to William and sort this out. Josephine will be fully awake in half an hour."

Miserable man. How can I convince him? Then Dr. Grange's grown son comes to mind.

"How is Melvin? He still sneaking into widow Fraser's house at night?"

The doctor's face blanches. "What does that have to do with the problem at hand?" He points to the baby.

"Fornicating with a Catholic who teaches at the Good Tidings parochial school." I tsk. "*The Fiery Cross* reported that a man in Oklahoma was sufficiently beaten for doing no more than what your son is doing. Would be a shame if the local Klavern learned of this."

He drops his head. His fists double and relax and contract again.

I've hit his *facing reality* nerve.

"What do you suggest, Ardith?"

He says my name as if a crow crapped in his mouth. He should be thanking me. We're both in a tough spot, and we're solving this together.

"First off, I can pay you for all of this trouble." I've skimmed a little off the WKKK dues for an emergency. This predicament surely qualifies. "One hundred fifty dollars. In cash. Today."

His face is grim. "I'm not going to let you hurt that baby."

My mouth falls open.

"How dare you think that. As if I would. You only need to buy me some time." An idea is forming, and it's starting to look as sweet as a field of clover. "Give Josephine enough anesthesia to keep her knocked out. Just two more hours. While she's asleep, you do a little extra doctoring to make sure this can't happen again. And Lordy, don't let her die."

William left the car home today. He's duck hunting with the higher-ups in the local Masonic Lodge. Since sixty percent of its members have joined the Klavern, the Masons now let the Klan use their building for meetings.

"I'll be back. This will all work out." Before he can protest, I run out of the room with the babe still in its blanket, enter the main portion of our house, grab my bag and the money I stashed, and head to the driveway. "Oliver! Come here."

He runs to the car, still holding the ball, then rises onto tippy-toe to peek inside the blanket.

"I want to see Miss Jojo's baby."

"This isn't her baby. The doctor brought the wrong one." What does a five-year-old know about childbirth? "Get in the car, Oliver. We're going for a ride."

I hand the bundle to Oliver and show him how to rock the baby to quiet him. But I have to look away. The two of them together upsets me. The same gray eyes. The shape of the mouth. Oh, the fight I'll have with William. A water moccasin puts out less venom than I plan to inflict on him. And let him touch me again? Many moons will pass, as the Cherokee say.

While heading north on the main road, a new thought hits me. If my plan works, I'll have to keep my anger toward William tucked inside. The problem with Josephine will be solved.

My duty as a Klanswoman means I set aside all pleasure, and I take no pleasure in what I'm about to do. But mixing races leads to the downfall of society, and my duty is clear.

My ability to discern right from wrong is something I'm proud of. This is not revenge, though a lesser woman in my same circumstance might turn to that. This is about fairness.

For the first time all day, the wound-tight tension leaves my body.

And I drive.

This time Magda greets me at the Beck Infantorium. She's built like a man, strong in the arms, with broader shoulders than her sister's. It must be all the wheelbarrowing I saw her doing last visit. I explain why I'm here, and I hand the baby over to her.

She frowns and looks past me toward the car and then down her drive.

"It'll be our secret," I say. "And you'll make money and save yourself the trouble of a burial."

"We've never had this request before."

She's holding Josephine's baby. I *refuse* to think of it as William's.

"But you must have what I'm looking for." I raise my eyebrows in a challenge. "You deal in all types of…er…situations here."

"We take in the sick and poor in spirit. So yes. Many precious souls depart before we find them homes." She draws in a big breath. "I'll be right back."

I tap my foot and check my wristlet watch. Never have to ask William what time it is since the Hamilton Watch Company sent me their newest fashion statement.

I've been away from home now forty-five minutes. The sound of birds chirping in the trees is nice. It's a peaceful setting for so many little ones. At least for the healthy little ones.

Magda opens the door and presents me with a basket covered with a white cloth. I lift the fabric. The dead baby looks doll-like, as if it never took a breath.

"A boy, right?"

"Yes. He passed not more than a few hours ago."

He's the right shade of brown. High-yellow. Not too dark. I run my finger down his cheek, withdrawing quickly, startled at how cold his skin feels.

"We must keep the poor dears on ice until we can provide a proper burial out back."

I nod, then set the basket on the painted porch and count out thirty dollars.

"I added some because you've been so accommodating." I smile. "And to make sure your new baby boy finds a good Christian home."

"Is there a birth certificate?"

"There is not," I shrug. "The family is looking for privacy."

"Not a problem." She folds the money and puts it in her pocket. "There's times we don't get the legal paperwork."

Yeah. Like when I wandered in here ready to pop seven years ago. Came with nothing but a gross belly and left with twenty dollars. Never wanted to know who adopted my child. I *acquired* my new start soon after. Changed my name, stole some beautiful clothes from a shop on the outskirts of Atlanta. Reinvented myself. And I made up for those sins by raising a fine family, being an exemplary wife, and serving the community.

I thank her again and carry the basket to the car. Oliver is curled into a small half circle on the front seat. Mrs. Winslow's Syrup works every time. I'm not sure where morphine comes from, but the manufacturers need an award for excellence.

I slide behind the wheel and place the basket between Oliver and me. I love these quiet rides home. And once there, Oliver should sleep for a few more hours. He won't witness Josephine's grief when she wakes up to learn the awful *truth* about her baby.

No. No good mother would want her boy to hear all that.

And to be honest, I plan on letting Dr. Grange handle it. One hundred and fifty dollars says it's his duty. Besides, his son and the Catholic gal can do whatever they please. I only surmised that the two of them were canoodling, but I must've been right. Dr. Grange and I now share a secret. We're bonded in a good way, both getting something we needed. That's the best kind of friendship.

The operation I asked him to perform will make her sterile. Eugenics is very acceptable, especially the more and more we understand science and how defective traits are highly inherited. Today is a case in point. Josephine's sexual drive caused all of these troubles. She got that from her faulty mother. With Josephine's baby-making factory gone, she can focus on her job of nannying. Now that I think about it, the timing for what happened today is perfect. She'll be a wet nurse when Baby Katherine arrives.

The girl needs to keep making milk and stop having her corn ground.

I'm still furious with William. How could he? What a hypocrite! Night-riding and "taking care of" men who are crossing racial lines for pleasure. On the rest of the drive, I plan the lies I'll tell him. That'll feel good. Not revenge. Justice.

HAPPENINGS OF THE DAY
MAY 1921

Slave Trader Found Beaten in Hotel Room
2 Abducted White Girls Found Alive
Refuse to Talk

"Society's Shaming Allows Traders to Get Away with Horrendous Crimes."

Near Nacoochee Depot, Helen, Georgia. May 1921

-19-

Willow Stewart

This dewy morning feels like the end of the world. I've run till my legs are about to give out, keeping to the trees as much as Mama Nature allows. My injured arm is throbbing to the tune of "When Johnny Comes Marching Home Again." All that's missing is the fife and drums.

The occasional fence line announces the prospect of people. I follow a deer trail to a spring and trace it until I reach a shallow pool. Breathing raggedy, I bend over the water and scoop handfuls to drink. The clear water magnifies the flat rocks lining the bottom. Crawdads scuttle backwards, and when the water settles, my face stares back at me. My eyes are as dark as black walnuts. I can hardly recognize myself. My hair's come loose, hanging in stringers. My mouth is stuck in an air-sucking frown. I look like a ghost who's been haunting with no time off.

I don't aim to be, but I'm peeved at the bad intentions in the outside world. From Mr. Coburn's wicked plans to take me for his own pleasure, to a preacher's wife and a policeman trying to lock me away in a deaf school. They know I can hear just fine. Their belief that I have no purpose in returning home with Mama gone, that I have no life there, is so wrong. Labeling me a half orphan when there's no such thing. I pity everyone who's run afoul of these wayward thoughts.

Briar had an easier time coming off our mountain. Traveled some, which must've pleased his wandering curiosity. One of his favorite storybooks when he was younger was *The Wonderful Adventures of Nils*. Nils is a naughty boy who takes off on an aerial journey after climbing on the back of a goose. He travels around his home country. On his voyage, Nils learns about Sweden's geography and natural landscape. He has experiences with wildlife and strange people. He's taught valuable lessons about humankind and the folly in chasing after riches.

Briar must have many an adventure to share by now. Just got to get a letter to him about coming home soon, so he can tell them all to us.

I pull up wild greens and onions and wash them in the creek, then stuff them in my mouth and chew—sorry, Mama—letting the water drip down my chin. I hurry, knowing I can't stay in one place too long. They must be looking for me now that I'm a no-good runaway.

On my feet again, I follow the winding depression left by deer hooves, heading southeast. I recollect from studying maps left by the library ladies that a post office sits next to the Nacoochee Train Depot. It's no more than two miles outside Helen, so I should be there soon.

Can't count how many times I've stopped, thinking I hear something treading at my heels. This time it sounds like coonhounds baying. To make up for how ugly they are, God gave coonhounds the best noses on earth, and I didn't need them sniffing after me.

Keeping caution close at hand, I head for a thicket and push through. It's an overgrown mine opening. I step in. Dry dust on the rough walls reveals its years of idleness. The holes drilled for candles are empty eye sockets peeping my way. I take a few more steps inside. My boots scuff on loose rocks, and something small skitters away. Dripping water echoes from deeper inside, and even my breathing is exaggerated. Although the sound outside is muted, there are no shouts or barking hounds. The stale air tastes like minerals, and the chamber feels like it's closing in. I push back through the brush into the open air and fight tears. My older brother Luther Junior breathed his last in a mine like this. Did he know he was about to die? Possibly call out in alarm to alert others? Briar tried to talk about it, but Poppy beat him down with his fists and accusations.

I shake those terrible images away and press on.

Moments later, a train whistle loses itself over the valley, spilling its lonesome song into the town and above the farms. Through the ground, I feel the thrumming of the wheels on the tracks.

I come out of the trees upriver a mite and cross the Chattahoochee on a covered bridge. The train station sits on a sweep of shorn grass. It's a one-story white building with brick-red shutters framing a row of windows. The upper and lower rooflines cover the wooden walkway that circles the building, a dry waiting place for riders when the weather's not so nice. A woman and two children sit on the white benches, the children taking turns spinning a striped wooden top.

The stopped train is vibrating in place. People climb down from the two passenger cars hooked between the locomotive in front and five freight cars behind.

My heart stutters. Two policemen are talking near the engine. They laugh, and one slaps the other on the back. They don't seem to be in a serious discussion about a runaway gal.

I brush leaves off my riding dress, use my fingers to tuck the loose strands of my hair behind my ears, and head for the next building. The brick structure is about fifty paces away, with a big sign hanging out front saying one side is the Nacoochee Post Office while the other is the Henderson Mercantile Store.

Inside the building is a wall of metal boxes with small knobs on them. They're all numbered. 'Cross the way is a short wall with bars running from there up to the ceiling. In the center is a two-piece door. Its top half is open and makes for a counter. A man with a thick-as-dog's-hair mustache and wearing a smart cap waits on the other side.

"Help you, miss?"

I take a moment. *I need to send a postcard.* I hand it to him and wait.

He slowly nods, his eyes dropping to my neck and then back to my face, like he's looking for why I can't talk. Hmmpf. I wonder if Miss Helen Keller had her ears gawked at.

He turns and opens a drawer, pulls out a stack of cards, and spreads them in front of me on the countertop. I sort through them, shrinking from horror when I come across one with four Colored men hanging from a tree. I quickly choose the photo of the train station next door. Words across the front say, "Welcome to White County, Georgia."

"That'll be a penny plus another to send it." He puts the cards away.

I slide one of Mrs. Holcombe's dollars across the counter and get back a handful of change.

He hands me a pen along with the money and stamp.

"Just drop it in the slot when you're done." He points to the opening in the wall to his right.

Taking the few steps to a small stand, I try to decide what to say. Telling Briar bad news right off might not encourage him to come home. He and Poppy need to patch up their broken ties, but he might figure with Mama gone, there's no reason to try. She was the freshness in the air after a fast-moving rainstorm. The sugar in a rhubarb pie. The goodness in everything, whether hardship or daily pleasure.

Tears blur the white paper, and I blink them away, swipe them from my cheeks, and calm my jittery chin.

Briar. I'm sending this to say I have news of the family. We all miss you and your letters, including Poppy.

If you can get time off, come for a visit. It's about Mama. With Love, Willow

I look out the window and picture Briar reading this at his post box in Cartersville. Does it say enough or too little to stir him to come home?

It takes me a moment to register, but I hear a man outside mention my name. I shift to see who it is. Policeman Vissom! How did he know I'd come this way?

He's talking to the other policemen.

My heart stomps, and blood makes haste to my head. I'm in a mess. Mr. Vissom knows where I live. The law can easily come drag me off Stewart Mountain once I return. The forest could be a safe hiding place, but what kind of life is that? Poppy will need me at home. Ruthy is still there until she gets hitched the end of August.

Listen to yourself, Willow, thinking like a lawbreaker on the run. I look at the postcard in my hand. Briar will know how to help me. And Mrs. Holcombe's money will buy a train ticket to Cartersville, a place they will have no reason to try to find me.

I can tell Briar in person about Mama. I slip the postcard into my dress pocket.

With their backs to the post office, the policemen are talking to the conductor of the train that just arrived. Ducking my head, I slip out the door and head to the train station.

Once at the ticket window, I try to make myself small behind a man carrying a brown case, dressed in what I imagine is a business owner's suit. Poppy has one dress coat, but it doesn't hang as straight as this man's.

The paper and my pencil are still in my dress pocket, and I pull them out and write, *How much is one ticket to Cartersville?* I have no idea what it costs to ride a train.

When I reach the window, the ticket agent says, "Morning. Where to?" He's older than Poppy with swept-back dark hair and a gap betwixt his teeth wide enough to slip a strip of bacon through.

I smile and hand him my note.

He hands the note back, which I'm grateful for. I have only the few scraps left from what Mrs. Holcombe gave me.

"No direct route. Gotta go south to through Gainesville then Marietta, two train changes. Then northwest to Cartersville"—he points to a chart on the wall behind him—"It's a hundred twenty-seven miles. Rates are running near three cents a mile, so that's three dollars and eighty-one cents."

I hand him the four dollars and hope he doesn't mind that the bills aren't dry. They were in my pocket while I was running. I quickly wipe my hand on my dress because it feels dirty where I touched the stolen money.

He messes with a machine, and I watch it spit out a colorful ticket. Then he gives me my change.

"You traveling alone?" His voice is a blue hush of evening sky, the color of Poppy's when he speaks with worry.

I tuck the coins and ticket in my pocket and nod.

"Find a family or a woman to sit by. Shifty rascals ride these trains and they are so slick, they can sell salt to a snail."

He has no idea he's talking to a hunted thief. I smile, full of gratitude for the advice.

Next, I discover an attached washroom with private toilets. I do declare! Never shared this personal time with other people doing the same thing in a little bitty closed-off space next to me. When do people have their thinking time if they're never left alone?

The flushing spooks me, and I jump back, hoping my clothes don't get swooshed away. At the sink I wash my arms and face. I corral my loose hair into the braid again, but it still looks like a vexed red snake. A blazing signal, considering policemen are hounding for a red-headed gal.

Once outside, I slip around to the back of the building away from the tracks and draw in breaths to calm my worriment.

That washroom was a mite too tiny for what was happening in there. And Mr. Vissom said I'd be all wide-eyed and caught in a spell by indoor plumbing, but he's wrong.

Ten minutes until my train. I stay along the back of the building near the woods and move over to the mercantile store. Through a window, I see only a woman and small boy being waited on. I walk inside and choose a new style hat Mama and I saw in the newspapers that we laughed at. It looks like a pail got turned upside down on your head. I pay eighty cents for that *cloche* hat. Then I roll up my braid inside and pull the hat down over my ears. Hides my red-haired giveaway mighty nice.

The train whistle blows, and the engine and cars chug away. The police have crossed two sets of tracks and are talking to another man over there. I now understand why trains fascinate Briar and Billy Leo. Passengers sit safe, coated in the hardy metal wrapping, and are carried almost anywhere. Through cutouts in the mountains and over rivers and wheat fields, miles and miles of surprise unfold past the windows.

I piddle time away in the store and then slip round the backside of the building again. My train's arriving with a long blast of its horn. The brakes make a squeaky fuss. After a frightening croak of steam, I approach the rumbling metal machine.

Some folks exit, then I enter what I believe is the second passenger coach. I eye an open seat next to a fine lady in a fancy blue suit and feathered hat. I point to the seat and raise my eyebrows, my way of asking for permission to sit.

"It's free." She pats the bench and smiles. "But be warned…I'm all worked up and might talk your ears off."

Riders stow their small cases and other things they're toting under their seats. Now wondering if I look out of place carrying no travel bag, I drop onto the seat and keep my head down.

"I'm Alice Burns." She sticks out her hand and I accept it.

I pull out my loose paper. *I'm mute. Thanks for letting me sit here.*

Miss Alice gives me a long look-see and then says, "I think I would die if I couldn't talk."

I write, *I talk all day long. It just stays inside my head.*

She chuckles and it sounds like the tinkling of the high-note keys on the piano. Happy. Hopeful. I hear rose petals with fresh dew on them.

"Believe there's a lesson in that for me. If I live to be seventy, I won't have the time to take back half the things I shouldn't have said." She digs around in her bright blue bag, then stops fumbling and meets my eye. "'Course, my clock doesn't wind that way. If it needs to be said, I'll go right ahead." She pulls out a bright red tablet and pushes it toward me. "I'm not sure why your school hasn't given you more of these, but an independent young lady like you shouldn't be carrying around scrap paper to express herself."

I hold the tablet as if it's a shiny gold nugget. The Big Chief Pencil Tablet is fifty pages of wonderful clean paper. Only seen them advertised, going for ten cents each, but never owned one. The brown paper wrapped around store-bought goods works fine. And our neighbor folk save it for me the rare times they've left the hills to shop. Mama and I cut it into rectangular pieces that fit into my dress pocket, sewn on just for the purpose of toting my writing paper and pencils.

The gift is almost too much. Tears build in my eyes and are close to spilling. Mama would be so happy for me. Maybe she's peeking down from heaven. I open the red cover with the Indian in full headdress on the front and pick up my pencil and scritch out words on the top line of the first page. My writing instrument is a pioneer, treading its way across unexplored ground.

My learning has been at home. I never owned such a wonder as this. Thank you.

"You're welcome." She studies me some more. "Your eyebrows say you got red hair to match. Means you're covering up a fiery spirit. Don't let any man take it away from you." She crosses her feet at the ankles. "A word to the wise. Write what you want to say, not what others force you to say."

I nod. Her words about a man taking from me remind me of old Mr. Coburn. I could tell her about my close call with the peddler, but I don't want to remember what happened. And my heart still beats too fast from fear, knowing any second the police might board the train.

I like Miss Alice Burns. She seems sassy and brave. It's not every woman who dares go against proper dress and wear a feathered hat and a dress short enough to bare her calves. Lace-up shoes and boots are the only things we Stewart women wear, but Miss Burns wears two-tone blue and tan Mary Janes with T-straps I've seen advertised in newspapers. These open shoes are preached against at our mountain revivals, amounting to a scandalous affair for showing off stocking-covered legs. She's so pretty, like she's important. Most likely from a big metropolis. Hmm. I wonder if she's been inside a library, a dream of mine. Wouldn't surprise me at all if she has. But how does someone decide on just one book with hundreds to choose from?

I write, *Are you from Marietta?*

"I was born in Athens, got married, got tired of him cheating, and I got out." She laughs, shaking her head at a memory only she can see. "Pick wisely, young lady. Marry a man who thinks you're above him, not his possession."

The thought I'd marry a man above, below, or equal to me is a little bit like guessing what the wind will bring. It sometimes offers honeysuckle so powerful you're stuck in place by the weight of it. Or it can sweep by the swamp and drop a wet boggy smell that you could swear by all that's holy will ride your skin till the lye soap comes out. Every girl must fend off a few swamp gusts while she waits for a sweet breeze to blow her way. If that's God's plan, I reckon I will too.

The train's whistle blasts a long notice, and my innards jitter with excitement. I will try to memorize every detail of the ride once we get rolling. My ride to freedom. Billy Leo will want to hear all about it. He's forever running through the trees woo-wooing like a locomotive. My chest tightens at the sadness he's bearing right now. If only he could be here with me. We'd be on a grand adventure, ignoring the sadness we've pocketed.

"You're a brave one to be traveling alone." Alice's smile is easy, and her soft gray eyes are kind. "Where are you going?"

To avoid explaining my last thirty-six hours, I jot down, *To Cartersville to meet my brother.*

"How nice. I've got a sister who accuses me of dancing with the devil for my decision to divorce and a brother who spews preacher's words at everyone's feet while making gallons of sacramental wine for himself. He sells a few quarts to the priest at his church to make it look legal. I envy you your relationship."

The train jerks several times and pulls away from the station. Two men with satchels tied to their backs run alongside the train, visible only to the riders on my side. I point. Have they missed boarding on time?

"Hobos. They'll jump one of the freight cars behind, catch a free ride."

Is that illegal? I write small, not wanting to fill my paper. Hmm. Maybe they will distract the policemen.

"Sure. But the railroad detectives are too busy to catch them all. This joblessness. Thousands of men set loose, looking for jobs anywhere a train will take them."

The headlines I read back home say the *illusion* that the country enjoyed prosperity had run its course. Menfolk, who had served during the war, have set out foraging for work anywhere they can find it. Foraging. Makes me think of those poison mushrooms. That sinful Mr. Coburn. The start of all my troubles.

Anyway, not much ever changes for us in our mountains, but the bold headlines from the valleys below say men are feeling as useless as buttons on a hat.

Ms. Alice Burns smooths her blue skirt.

"You're meeting your brother, and I'm meeting my beau in Gainesville."

No wonder she seems like she has her trotting harness on, going someplace special.

I take up the pencil again. *You getting married?*

"Not while we're in the South, but yes, once we return to St. Louis. He's a defense lawyer there and often writes for the *St. Louis Post.* I work for the new Legal Aid Society. I'm a social worker. But right now, I just want to relax and let my mind go. Do you drink?"

She reaches into her bag, and I worry she's gonna offer me alcohol. I quickly shake my head no. I'm already in trouble with the law.

"Good. You're too young." She bumps my shoulder and winks. "But if you ever find yourself in a speakeasy, order a Gin Gimlet. It'll put the razz in your jazz. Anyway, I'll bet you enjoy a little chinwag about what women think." She chuckles, holding up a magazine, *Town Topic.*

"Gossip is the new drink everyone's clamoring for. The articles are frivolous, but tabloids like this are quite popular."

She hands me a magazine. The publication's contents are probably suggested by the cover—a good drawing of two women, their shoulders naked, one reading the magazine while the other reads over her shoulder. Right under the words, *The Journal of Society*. They're surrounded by ads for flowers, fancy dresses, and Bromo-Seltzer which is announced as a cure for "club, banquet, and holiday headaches."

Mama and I would have gotten a laugh looking through this magazine. Sadness tugs at the corners of my mouth.

I glance out the window as layers of dark-blue mountain fly past, stacked afar off. I try to imagine the world I know nothing about. A Golden Rule person, washed in the good Lord's commandments of right and wrong, could lose their way in the pages of a magazine like this. I don't want to offend Miss Burns, so I open the magazine and slowly flip pages. The buy-me temptations are boxed in lacy designs around the stories. I read that La-Mar Reducing Soap will wash away my fat and take years off my age. I can apply WINX eye makeup to look more mischievous or choose from one of eleven scented tins of Rigaud rouge.

Mama and I would've laughed over these, and Ruthy would cluck her tongue at the shamefulness of women so caught up in their appearance. We all know these products are as useless as the H in ghost.

Miss Burns is reading over my arm.

"Oh, don't do this one." She points to an ad with a sad woman viewing a man walking out the door. It reads, "Spoiled marriage? You must have neglected your feminine hygiene. Use Lysol Feminine Douche to put the loveable back in you." She adds, "I had a friend end up in the hospital after trying that."

The ads feel wrong. Why are strangers shaming women for every part of their life?

I fumble for my pencil and write, *Are women sad about these messages?*

"Not all. But in my opinion, it does strike a chord with way too many. I personally don't like these advertisements, but they pay the cost to keep the magazine going. There are some important articles in here women need to read. There's one about women taking new kinds of jobs and not just keeping with the professions of schoolteachers, social service workers, nurses, or secretaries. Like me. I lead a growing women's group taking on social issues. You could open a storefront, Willow. What would you sell?"

Her perfume floats around me. Something from the sweet rose family. My mind is spinning with so many newfangled notions, big oak-tree ideas for a girl no more than an uncurled fern, hoping for a sliver of sunlight. The thought that I could own a store was as far-fetched as turning over a frog and finding udders. And thinking too much of oneself and too little of others is the hefty sin of arrogance. The devil's pride.

"What's your passion? Is it writing a book? Art? Everyone has a dream"—she shifts to face me—"For me, I want every woman to be educated. White, black, blue, or red."

Miss Burns is a very knowledgeable lady if she knows about the blue people in the deep hollers of Kentucky. Forever, they've hidden from outsiders, like it was a command from God Almighty.

"Women need to know they can do whatever they want without being told they don't have the sense to make decisions. And voting." Her face is flushed with pink. "Women won that right in this country eight months ago, but did the state of Georgia let its women have a say last November? No ma'am. They did *not*. Our government has a love affair with its history of chains." She sinks back into the seat and closes her eyes.

Seems to me she's worn her words out. But my heart did get riled up with her ideas. To calm my stormy pulse, I settle my eyelids to darkness, then picture fluttering green leaves dancing to a pleasant breeze in the tops of trees. And think. People in towns and cities have mighty demanding worries. Keeping a husband by putting sink cleansers up your private parts, women starting businesses alongside men, and the state of Georgia still owns too many *chains*. I shake my head, trying to clear the jumble of concerns Miss Burns planted there. We have only three worries back home—uncontrollable weather, uncontrollable crop failure, and uncontrollable death. Other than that, we pull joy from each morning and enjoy contentment with each night.

I watch Miss Burns's head drop to the side. She's asleep. I was so taken up by her I haven't noticed the others aboard. Three rows up and facing my way, two boys not much older than me play cards on the seat between them. They wear tweed derby hats, loose jackets, and dressy britches. When one looks my way and nudges his friend, I drop my eyes and feel my face flame six shades to Sunday. Their laughter lingers too long, bouncing along the curved ceiling of the train.

An old couple sleeps holding hands, and I think of Mama and Poppy. It was a rare evening when they didn't have some hand-holding time, rocking on the porch or in the parlor by the stove. I worry about Poppy. He doesn't know how to do for himself with household chores unless we're there. What if he was alone in the cabin and something should befall him?

Thomas Monahan, the man who shod everyone's mountain horses, died after he broke his back trying to mend a hole in his spongy barn roof. The coroner said Thomas, who lived alone after his wife died, was most likely alive and suffering for two to three days. The scratches and drag-trails in the dirt told how hard he tried to return to the cabin before dying. Was only when he missed Charlie Howser's shoeing appointment that anyone went looking and found him twenty feet from his front steps. What a sad day. Jesus, please take care of my poppy.

The rest of the coach hosts young couples, some with children. Men in fine suits are reading or talking to each other. The man seated in front of me looks to be traveling alone. He's kinda lardy with a head to match. The gray hair that remains fixed above his left ear is brushed up his head, over the top, and ends at his right ear in a few cobwebby strands. He sure needs to buy a hat. That overstretched hair is not gonna keep that head warm. He explores the fleshly cranny of his right ear with his pinky finger, and even over the clicking of the train's wheels, I can hear the faint sucking sound as he twists it in and out.

The train rumbles on, bellowing quick horn bursts at railway crossings. I eat the peanut brittle, and my throat tightens round the thought this was the last of the candy Mama made. Miss Burns doesn't stir until the vehicle slows and comes to a hissing stop at the Gainesville Depot. She stretches. Smiles at me.

"It's a new world out there. People are tired of girding up their loins.

They are looking for freedom and fun." She pats my leg. "You and your brother stay safe but go enjoy yourselves." She digs around in her pretty bag again and hands me a card with her name and phone number. "If you ever need anything, write or have someone call for you. I like to help brave young girls like you."

Miss Burns has no way of knowing that my brother and I face a long stretch of mourning. First, I have to shake the trouble I'm in. I smile, tap the card, and touch my chest.

"Again, my pleasure."

People are leaving the carriage. I follow them out onto the small raised platform and try to stay in the middle of the group as I check my surroundings. Had Deputy Vissom supposed by now I've caught a train, or does he think I returned home? I have a heap of stories to straighten out soon as I get back.

Signs point me to a waiting place for Marietta. This platform is crowded, so it's easy to hide in the mess of folks standing here. Across the empty tracks, I spot Miss Alice Burns. She's chattering away, walking next to a light-skinned Negro man dressed in a fine suit and hat. He's smiling wide. Their bodies are bumping into each other. Playful-like. Her face is rosy, and she looks plumb happy next to her beau. I picture them married, saving $600 to buy a new house from the Sears, Roebuck & Company catalogue. They'd both have their very own typewriters at home, but maybe that's pushing my fantasizing mind too far. One is enough. Her beau holds open the door to the street, and they disappear into their forever after.

The next part of my travels goes smoothly. I sit alone in a near-empty coach, content to watch the stations and farms blur by.

And just like that, I'm stepping off the train into dusty air, onto a crowded platform in Marietta filled with noise like I never heard. Even my breathing sounds louder here.

But I don't have time to give another thought about the city as a man grabs hold of my arm and spins me around to face him.

"Willow Stewart?" He's a policeman with an angry scar running down one side of his cheek.

I swallow. Must remember to breathe and do nothing to let him know he spoke my name.

He pulls my hat off, and my braid tumbles free.

"Sure as shootin' you're the gal they're all in a fuss about. You're slipperier than oysters in a pan of butter." He pulls me away from the arriving train. "Before, you were just going to a nice home for other girls like yourself." He shakes his head. We're now outside the station and he's walking me to a police car. "Now you're going to jail until the judge decides what's best for you." His voice is swampy green.

There's no dam for my tears. They fall unbidden from my eyes as shame sits heavy in my soul. Not only is Briar not coming home, but I'm not either.

Hercules Steam-Distilled
Wood Turpentine
30, 10 or 5 Gallons
Quality by Professionals Who Care
From the Forest to Your Wood Project

Timberline Forest Camp. May 1921

-20-

Briar Stewart

"I piss in the barrels ever so often," Tuck says to me while we walk the outer edges of today's cutting. "'Bout the only way to get the mad out of me without getting killed."

I chuckle. "Thousands of barrels going to the naval store's depot. It'd be hard to trace, I reckon."

A light rain, not much more than a mist, dims everything afar off. The *thunk* of hacks V-cutting the pines sounds like woodpeckers at a once-a-year church picnic. All're talking and trying for the world to catch up on gossip before the day ends. I stop to check the fresh cuts and cups. Don't think we'll ever get this part done by the end of the day if'n the rain drives us out now. I study the sky. Looks heavy with darkening clouds. It sure ain't gonna blow over. Taggert gave the order. No matter the weather today, we keep at it.

"Keep their sorry asses out there. These white and black boys can work in the rain…they ain't gonna melt."

Taggert's under the tent overhang, smoking. Busy making his way through the logbook, corrupting the figures on the amount of sap collected. He answers to the Pearson-Gysse Company that has a contract with County Prison Camp. He needs to make sure they don't go looking elsewhere for workers if they don't like the results. And that would put us all back in stripes, busting rocks or mining coal, and Taggert back at the prison as a guard. No more special treatment for him. No girls brought in for his abuse. Same old food. Same old shit-tasting cigarettes.

A small creek chucks down the hill nearby and I think of them Russian brothers. Tuck gets his revenge for the unfair sentence he carries by pissing in the merchandise. But I got mine by knowing I helped the fellers out a week back with Taggert none the more aware. For those few hours that day, I was a free man. I'd never felt so good.

"Nice job," I say as we pass the cutters and bucket carriers.

We've got a solid laboring crew now. Turpentining is damn hard work. Fourteen hours some days. But most of these here convicts done seen the other penal job. They understand fresh air beats rock dust in your eyes and mouth. And nightly beatings by the lead whipper just for his amusement. Hopefully, all the beatings and killings is behind us.

Lucy, the friendly magpie up at our cabin, is most likely still tapping the window glass in the morning, wising Mama or Ruthy it's time to throw out the dinner leavings from the night before. Poppy said magpies live some twenty-five, thirty years. This bird's been round at least ten.

Lucy set up her home in the white maples round the family cemetery before reaching the bald outcropping on our homestead. Each year, she brought the young'uns around once they learned their wings. Got so Lucy recognized each of us as different and knew what we tolerated. When Poppy played his fiddle, Lucy stood on the porch rail and shifted her feet, a dance of some sort. Rewarded with corn, she two-stepped many a summer's eve. And she teased Mama by pulling loose the wooden pins from the clothesline.

I recollect the day that dang bird tugged Billy Leo's empty boots off'n the porch by their laces, making him search high and wide for 'em. All's while cackling from a tree branch above as he come closer and closer to finding them. Sometimes, she hopped behind me down the dirt rows I laid out in the garden, grabbing up bugs and worms, twittin' at my back when it was slim pickings.

But it was Willow who got the closest. Lucy ate berries out of my sister's open hand.

Tuck elbows me. "You thinking 'bout the gal back at Miss Lily's Threads & Things? Got a stupid smile on your face."

"Naw. Was thinking 'bout my baby sister, though she ain't a baby no more. She's fifteen now." I shake my head. Seemed not long ago we was running in the woods, talking, using our hand signs. "Trained a big magpie to eat outta her palm."

We reach the edge of the cutting area and head uphill to circle back another way. The air is thick with steam, but heavier rains stay to the horizon for now.

"She have a sweetheart?"

"Not when I left fifteen months ago. Could've changed by now."

It crosses my mind that when I get out of prison in September, I'll head on up to visit the folks, spend a day or two before leaving west again. We was a close family, even though I know I disappointed Poppy most my life. Couldn't never live up to Luther Junior's skills. He could do pert near everything, and I looked up to him too. Well, mostly. He didn't know enough about gases in mines to turn back when someone yelled. Weren't the unlit dynamite in his hands that blew him clean apart. Was the firedamp, the methane gas from the new opened chamber behind him that exploded.

"Your sister better looking than you?" Tuck says it with a smirk on his face. "Might need to come calling one day."

"Willow's a natural beauty. A rose with red hair."

Tuck slashes at underbrush with a stick.

Month ago, we had to clear the underbrush before starting. Back then, the land was jigsaw puzzles of hard clay. Fires start easily round turpentine. But with our off and on rain, it ain't been a problem of late.

"Tell me again where you live." He chuckles but I think he's only half joshing.

"Hold on there. You're off to lawyer school far, far away. And, I need to add, she can't talk." I raise my eyebrows in an aren't-you-surprised movement. I'm trying to keep her from heartbreak down the road.

"Not a word, or she is shy?"

"Not nary a one. Never has. Never will."

"I'm sorry. That must be hard."

"Not at all. Willow is smarter than the rest of the family. Reads everything she can lay her eyes on. Is a great writer. And we've a made-up hand speaking we use. Mama, Willow, and me is the best at it, but the others cipher good 'nough."

He shakes his head. "Well, don't that just beat all! Show me something."

I move my hands. "That there means 'Let's go fishing.'"

He does the movements. "Like you're casting fishing line."

"Yup. This is 'A storm's a-brewing, we need to hurry.'" He copies my clawed fingers, moving up and down in front of me, then fingers cutting off to the side.

"I like this." He's running his fingers round in the air in front of him. "How many of these do you have?"

"Me and her can talk all day. Specific names, she's got to write down. Like if she reads something in the newspaper before me. She's gotta write the names of places or people I ain't heard of."

"Show me more."

"Sure." I teach him a dozen more sayings as we move onto a deer trail, watching the laborers off to either side. "We spell with letters in the air, but you gotta do it backward, so's the person facing you sees it right."

Tuck tries out his name in front of him. He slows for the K. "Makes you think, don't it?"

"What the hell you two blabbing on about?" Taggert parts bushes on our right, nigh to twelve feet ahead on the trail. He got two dead rabbits by the ears in one hand.

"Just talking about Briar's sister, sir."

I act like I'm shuffling my feet as I kick him and whisper, "Don't."

We trustees have a rule. Don't trust anyone, specially the boss. Sure don't want him knowing anything 'bout my kin.

"Yeah?" He steps closer, and I shiver as he licks his bottom lip. "What about her?"

"She's ten years old yesterday," I lie.

"Oh. Good for her"—he holds up the rabbits—"Cook's gonna put a little extra something in the stew tonight."

"Didn't hear your gun, sir," I say. He ain't exactly a fat man, but I don't see him snaring a rabbit barehanded.

"Set two traps." He points to the cutting area.

"Where the men are working?" Tuck says with a frown.

"Thereabouts." He chuffs. "Set in plain sight. Gotta be dumber than a box of hair to not notice." He shrugs. "You know my thoughts on stupid. One dies…"

"…get another," Tuck and I say in unison.

"Right. Finish up out here and head in."

We walk in silence a bit. Tuck clears his throat.

"Sorry I almost told 'bout your sister."

"Close. S'okay. Taggert don't need to know nothing 'bout us 'cept our crime and our time."

We pass the workers. They're plumb droopy with tired. I know that feeling. Can't do one more lick or lift one more thing. Just kill me dead right here.

"Almost quitting time," I call out. "Supper holds a surprise."

We move on, each with our own thoughts.

Ever since I took Ilya and Cy to the cave, I can't stop thinking 'bout my brother.

I was hungover that morning. Once he smelt my breath, Luther Junior went back into the mine after working the night shift to cover my shift. Told me to sleep it off. Alcohol was legal, and even though the mine owners didn't want it on the property, the tavern down the road a piece served it up aplenty.

The explosion an hour later bucked me out of bed. Thirteen men died, sixteen bad-off hurt.

Poppy taught us a weak person lies, while a strong man can afford to tell the truth. I confessed the truth to him—that one time I should've lied. And I never let out a sound when he hit me. The slap echoed in my head for minutes. Can still hear Mama crying and praying, the whole family a mess of tears. The mine owner said it was no one's fault, but Pa blamed me in the end.

Luther Junior died at twenty, my age right now. What also vexes my soul is he had his eye on a girl a holler over. Dotty something or other. He talked 'bout her but never got the chance to bring her round.

Been punishing myself ever since. When Lead Whipper split my back open after a day in Ladds Quarry, I refused to cry out. Felt like I deserved beatings, maybe even death with what I done—or not done—for my brother. I owned those thoughts for a long while. Dared the devil many a day and night while traveling. But that fiend must not've wanted me.

The whistle blows for quitting time.

I only got whipped once, and boy howdy, that was plenty for all a soul's natural life. But it worked out in my favor. Taking the beating without making a sound seemed to raise me in the guards' eyes.

Soon after, I became a trustee.

Four months to go.

The skies might be clouding up, but the sun's shining down on me.

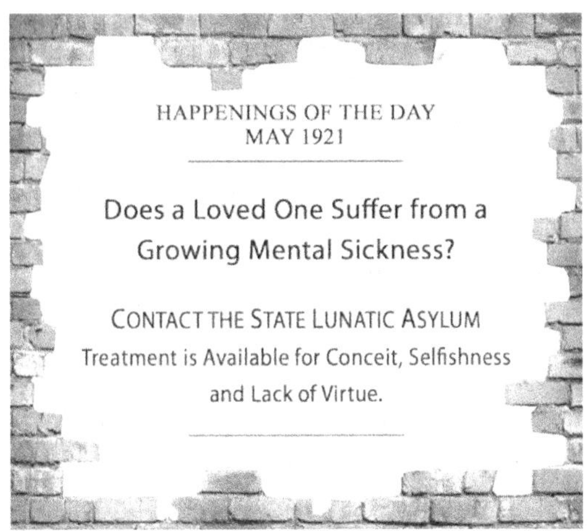

HAPPENINGS OF THE DAY
MAY 1921

Does a Loved One Suffer from a Growing Mental Sickness?

CONTACT THE STATE LUNATIC ASYLUM
Treatment is Available for Conceit, Selfishness and Lack of Virtue.

Marietta, Georgia. May 1921

-21-

Ardith Dobbs

"I still don't understand how it all went so wrong." William is upset. He came back empty-handed from fishing and then learned about Josephine. "We hired Dr. Grange because he's one of the best."

We're in the den. Sitting. He's in an easy chair holding Oliver, stroking his hair. The boy is out like a light. I may have overdone the soothing syrup, but I blame Oliver's grogginess on playing too much catch with no afternoon nap. As for me, reclining on our loveseat with my swollen feet propped up on the opposite arm is about as comfortable as I can get. My insides are shaking now that William is questioning me with his oh-so-righteous attitude.

The night turned chilly, rare for May. But it's not just the outside temperature. William is furious, and his words bite like frost. "You let Dr. Grange sterilize her? Josephine needed to be sedated when she found out."

"He said she would die if she tried childbirth again." The practiced lie runs off my tongue. "Everything was a mess inside of her."

He packs his pipe with Royal Albert, then tamps down the tobacco and lights it. His eyes never leave my face.

Why is he so suspicious? The doctor wouldn't have said anything about our secret, not if he wanted to protect his son. He might've acted nervous under William's questioning though. Inside my head, I scream, *this all went wrong because you decided to screw our nanny.*

"We'll buy a burial plot. I told Josephine that and she seemed relieved," I say.

I hadn't thought through what she would do with a dead baby. She cried throughout my whole talk with her, but I think she heard me explain how we were helping her.

I add, "Fourteen miles from here, in Buckhead. It sounds like a nice Colored cemetery behind the Piney Grove Missionary Baptist Church."

William smokes and rocks his head from side to side, still not saying much.

"She may not be able to go," I say. "Dr. Grange has had to sedate her again tonight. She tore out stitches earlier, dropping to the floor and throwing herself around."

"The poor girl." He shakes his head.

He feels sorry for her. *Hmmpf.* How many times did he have sex with her? May be why he hasn't been as amorous toward me in the past year. She must've left an extra soft spot in his heart.

"She may be temporarily insane." William truly looks upset.

"The medication can do that," I say. "She just needs some time."

"She was yelling to Dr. Grange that the baby is not hers. That this was all unfair." He knocks the ashes out of his pipe into a glass ashtray. "Doesn't seem like something a mother would say."

Josephine couldn't have known what her baby would look like. No one does before the infant is born.

"She can't understand how a dead baby could be hers. It kicked and moved around inside her. Then she wakes up to discover the babe never took a breath. It's unfair. Heartbreaking." I caress my large belly.

Josephine's mother went mad when they arrested her Colored husband. If Josephine loses her mind, she'll be locked away in the closest Colored asylum, way up in Virginia. My plans to use her as a wet nurse would dry up. But maybe breastfeeding wouldn't be as awful as it was with Oliver. A girl may not try to suck my nipples off. And if we have to hire a new nanny, I'll make sure she's homely. Like she's been beat with an ugly stick.

"What's going through that head of yours, Ardith?" William studies me. "You have that I'm-planning-something look on your face."

"I'd hate to lose Josephine. She's such a dear to have around"—*as you would know*—"and Oliver adores her. Maybe she could have some time to heal at the Leonard Street Orphan's Home in Atlanta. She could feed the poor abandoned babies." *And keep her milk going for Baby Katherine.* "You know. Feel like she's saving many children."

"We can talk to her. Seems a bit cruel."

"Lying out in her room crying all day, delirious with crazy thoughts, might be crueler." I heave myself to a sitting position. "We can ask Dr. Grange when he gets back in the morning. We have to drive near Leonard Street on the way to the cemetery. After, we could take Josephine to the home."

Still holding Oliver, William wiggles forward on the chair and stands. "This little guy can skip bath time tonight. I've never seen him so tired."

"He had a big day." *You have no idea how big.* I'm relieved William doesn't hand him to me. Boy's getting to be too heavy to lug around.

Before he heads up the stairs, he stops. "Did you take the car out today?"

How to answer? Is it parked differently than he left it? I've lied so much to the man, I decide to go with a part truth.

"I did take it. To the bank. I had a deposit from the women's Klan dues."

"Huh. It looks like you drove forty-five miles."

How in the dickens would he know that? "What do you mean 'it looks like'?" I make my voice playful. "Do you tell that by looking at the tires or something?"

"The speedometer has a device called an odometer built in. It tracks the miles."

Well, swat my hind with a melon rind. He never pointed out that part of the speeding gadget.

"I drove out in the country. The wildflowers are so pretty this time of year. Didn't realize I'd gone that far."

"I'd rather you use it only when it's absolutely necessary. Leave the pleasure rides for the weekend." He offers a tired smile. "We'll have a picnic. A country drive sounds nice."

I nod and smile. "Be up in a minute."

He climbs the stairs.

My head aches and I rub my temples. I worked hard today to save our family from disgrace. If there ever was an "*absolutely necessary*" trip, today's journey to hide his evil deeds was it.

Maybe one day I can scold him right back. Until then, I shove my anger deep down, like Ma taught me to do growing up in Hickory Nut Hollow.

The next morning, I go out early to check on Josephine. Her face is swollen. She's curled on her side, her eyes open, holding an empty gaze.

"How are you feeling?" I set the breakfast tray on a small table. "Here's some eggs, toast, and tea."

"It hurts," she mumbles. "I need to talk to Dr. Grange."

She looks as limp as an empty sack. Back home, women drank tea from boiled willow bark for birthing pain. 'Course those women never got their baby-making parts cut out. No need for that, since there were herbs eaten at the onset to stop pregnancy. But I wasn't about to peel a willow tree in our backwoods to help her with pain.

"Be right back. I have something that'll help." In the medicine cabinet of my bathroom, I push aside the Bayer Aspirin Powder, looking for the heroin tablets. Rumor says they are unhealthy for the mind, but the times I resorted to a tablet, I was filled with jubilation. Like the Rapture had come. Besides, not long ago the American Medical Association ruled heroin was a much healthier alternative to morphine and opium, two pain medications that hooked people into needing more. I think about taking a pill now but decide to wait until later. The focus needs to be on Josephine and giving her a good send-off for her son.

Back in her room, I fill a glass of water and hand her one pill. "This will help until Dr. Grange arrives."

Her look is wary. Like a trapped rabbit deciding if the offered carrot is safe to accept. She swallows the pill and settles back onto the pillows, keeping her head elevated.

I take a chair near the single bed. "I'm so sorry about your baby." And those words are true. Her real son will one day learn he was left at an orphanage. He'll wonder what happened that made him undesirable.

Before she woke up and first saw her baby, I spread some of her blood on the dead baby, then wiped it off. But not all of it. He needed to look freshly born.

She glances at the basket where the dead boy lies and scowls. "The doctor butchered me." Tears pour.

"You were going to die, Josephine. The birth took so long. I didn't know about Twilight Sleep. The drugs sedated the baby, and he stopped breathing. Dr. Grange said it's rare. William and I are heartbroken this happened to you."

"It doesn't answer why he cut me so's I never have another child." Her voice breaks into a sob. She drops her head into her hands and wails.

"If you got pregnant again and tried to deliver with a less experienced doctor or a midwife, you would bleed out and die. Dr. Grange saved your life."

"He ruined me for good."

"I heard my name." The doctor steps through the door and looks from me to Josephine. "How is our patient today?"

"She's upset of course," I say. "It's all so unexpected." I slowly shake my head.

"Are you in pain?" He sets his black bag on the floor and takes a few steps closer to her.

She recoils and tucks against the boards on the wall.

"Don't come near me! You had no right to do the things you did!"

He turns away from her and faces me. His eyebrows bunch together, and his face reddens.

See what you made me do? must be running through his mind.

He offers a pasted smile and turns back to her. "I had to make a difficult decision, Josephine. I'm never happy when childbirth goes wrong."

She spits at him.

I'm shocked. I hardly recognize this rabid being. Josephine is always reserved, mannerly, respectful. I tap the doctor's arm.

"She should calm soon. I gave her a heroin tablet a moment ago."

"I'm not gonna *calm*!" She throws a metal cup across the tiny room. Water splashes the walls. "I hate you both. You know what you did and soon everyone will know!"

My heart's racing, even though she has no proof of anything. The baby's skin tone is barely darker than hers, and he reasonably could be her dead child. She knows nothing. But for now, I need her to settle down before William hears her yelling.

"What is it you think we did, Jojo?" I hope using Oliver's pet name for her will quiet her.

She spits again, this time getting some power behind the spittle, and it lands on my dress. How *dare* she? It takes all of my effort not to cross the room and smack the living daylights out of her.

"I don't knows everything you did, but I do know that baby ain't none of mine."

"Having a baby die is upsetting," Dr. Grange says. "The situation can feel unreal. Plus, those sleep drugs can change the mind for days after. Feeling quite disconnected is not unheard of."

If he's shooting from the hip, he'd be a great cowboy. His words make sense to me. Now if she can accept them, life can go back to normal.

She carefully sits up. A knowing smile appears on her face, but it's not a happy look.

"I may be a dumb Colored girl to you, but I understand what gets passed down to a child." She wipes her nose on her arm, leaving a snail's trail of clear snot. "My baby would be white."

Hell's bells! She's going to admit bedding William. Is she trying to shock the doctor? He will have to act surprised when the truth leaves her lips.

"Why ever would you think that, Jojo?"

"Never call me that again. You the worst mother I ever met." She tightens the head rag that I loathe so much around her head.

Her words sting. She wouldn't know a good mother because she never had one. Taking her mama's craziness out on me is pitiful! And she just got herself fired. I can't abide having her here if she's gone crazier than an outhouse fly.

"Quinn raped me"—her words each have a space of their own—"several times when he stayed here last fall."

What? Quinn is William's younger brother from Dallas. He visited in August for a week. He and William look very much alike.

She's worked up and yells again. "My mama is white, and my daddy was half white. I's three-quarters white. That don't add up to me having a half-brown baby!" She throws a book this time.

Dr. Grange lets out a long breath. "Don't that beat all, Ardith? William's *brother* fathered her child. Sure makes these circumstances extra awful, doesn't it?"

She could've kept the baby and made Quinn pay to raise it. He's a smartass accountant. How was I to know?

"You should've told me about Quinn. I'm sorry he did that to you." We need to stick with our story. There's no going back now. "But be that as it may, this poor baby is yours."

She freezes for just a second, then springs off the bed and rushes toward me. "You lying!"

Dr. Grange grabs her around the midsection, and she lets out a painful scream and crumbles to the floor. While he holds her down with his leg, he reaches into his bag and pulls out a syringe filled with liquid and plunges it into her backside.

She thrashes and yells cuss words for twenty seconds, then goes unconscious.

He sits back and turns an angry eye my way. "Thanks, Ardith. I'm most likely going to lose my medical license if she talks." His jaws work hard. His face is tight. "How do you propose we solve this?"

What a mess. She seems bent on telling the world about what happened in our house. Raped by a family member. There's only one way to keep her quiet. Well, two ways, but I don't want to see her dead.

"You have to take her to that Colored Asylum outside of town. Check her in as insane. Then no one will believe what she says."

"To an asylum?" He rubs his neck, shaking his head. "This just sinks me deeper into the lies."

"She's going to keep talking, and someone might decide to check the orphanages around here for a newly dropped-off *white* baby."

"You should get her baby back. Tell her the truth. You thought it was William's."

"Then why did you have to sterilize her, Doctor Grange?" I draw out the word doctor, making a mockery of it. "Try explaining your medical reasons to her again."

His shoulders straighten. His face turns wooden. "Help me get her into my car."

"I was hoping you'd come around to reason."

"I'm not doing it for you. William is a Klan brother and I took a vow to protect him." He lifts her under the arms, and we each wrap one around our shoulder and drag her to the door. "And when you get ready to deliver in the next week or so, I'm not sure I'll be available."

"Fine. That's no problem."

And it isn't. I have a week to get a better nanny and an ethical doctor.

A fresh start in both cases feels good.

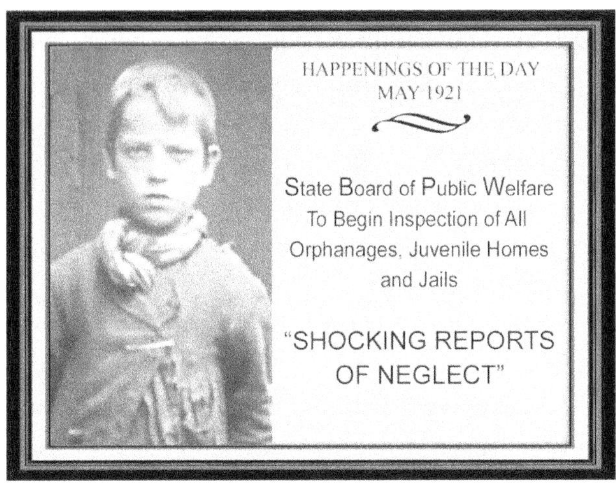

Marietta Georgia. May 1921

-22-

Willow Stewart

I write fast, needing to make the policeman understand he has misunderstood how I've come to be here. *Sir, I've done nothing wrong. Just arrived here from Helen with the blessing of my family. I'm to bring my brother home.* I'm sweating, and my hand trembles.

"Tell that to Judge Henry. He will hear your case this afternoon in Marietta." He pulls me to a black paddy wagon. "Soon you'll be a guest in their jail."

His smile is full of malice. His voice is storm-cloud gray.

He opens the rear door and pushes me up the two steps into the wagon. Benches line both sides. From a small window in the front,

I can see the driver. The windows look to be covered with thick wire fencing. To keep us from breaking them and escaping, I guess. Not that I'd even try.

The policeman slams the door shut and leans against it. Not wanting to look at him, I look out through the fenced-up windows. My train pulls away, leaving smoke and dust floating above the barren tracks.

The wagon begins to move.

This wooden bench is so hard, and my shoulders feel as if someone's pushing them down. I'm going to jail. The trouble I courted could fill my lifetime, but now I've invited it all in a matter of days. When Poppy hears of this, he's likely to cancel my birthright. He keeps his actions straight as a string, and here I am tangled up in a snarly mess. It'll be hard to explain I was arrested for doing nothing on my way to doing something. I don't count running from Mr. Vissom a bad thing though. He was about to send me off to a place I most likely couldn't have left. Seems like kidnapping to me. But I did take Mrs. Holcombe's church money. I'll send it all back to her if I can just get to Briar.

The paddy wagon rattles down the street. People stare. Shame fills me, knowing they must only see a dishonorable girl who must be kept away from society, locked in a cage. What seems like hours later, we stop, and I'm led into the backside of the Cobb County Courthouse in Marietta, down a hall, and into the jail.

The lockup has three separate rooms. The first room holds about five cages of white menfolk. The next room has two Negroes in a cage and one tied by his wrists to a metal pole near a dirty window. The overpowering smell of sweat, unclean menfolk, and utter despair come off that room.

"In here." The mustached policeman stops at the third section and points inside. A woman is curled up on the dirty floor in one cell, among bits of paper and dried mud. He directs me into the cage next to her. We're the only two women in the room. The clank of the closing door rattles through my being. If it didn't seem real before, this iron-bar pen just brought reality up close.

My surroundings are dark, but I cipher another kind of darkness in this place. The sadness left by folks before me. Four bunks line the cell and fold down from the wall and bounce back up when let go. A dingy quilt is folded on a short bench next to each one.

I sit on the bed and hold my eyes on the other woman.

Why did they just leave her on her back on this awful floor? Her head is twisted, facing the ceiling, and her eyes are open. Swollen. Red. As if stung by a sadness I never seen before. She's not crying now, but she must've offered up a powerful tear storm earlier.

Her eyes start to move, slowly searching my cell. They climb to reach mine.

"Help. Me." Her voice is the color of red coals. Only two words, but they seem to hurt her throat coming out. Not sure how I can help her though. In a nasty stew myself.

It just hit me that she's a light-skinned Colored gal. She's holding her stomach like she's sick or hurt. Must be why it's swollen 'cause she's tall, not fat.

I scribble out a note on my tablet and slide it through the bars.

She reads it then says, "I had my baby stole from me, and now they trying to send me far away."

What! Who steals babies? The newspapers say young girls get stolen and then made to do terrible things as a man's slave. But a baby? I signal for the tablet back and write again. This time I hold it up for her to read.

How is it you came to be arrested?

"The doctor told the police I was outta my mind. I was just distressed. They done me wrong." She pulls herself to a seated position.

I notice blood on the inside of one leg and more bloodstains on her dress. Lordamercy! What did he do to her?

We will see a judge. He might be better at understanding.

She shakes her head. Tears wet her face. "Men are deaf to a Colored's tale."

I don't know what to say.

My skin gets darker than hers in the summer, and with my red hair, my skin's not prone to browning much. Before I can write what I want to say to her, the door opens. The policeman is back.

"The judge left for the day and will see you both tomorrow." He smiles, but it's rotten. "Food comes around in about two hours. Those pails in the corner of your cells are your bathroom. Settle in."

He leaves. The only sound is the other girl crying softly. My chest hurts. She needs a doctor, not a night in jail. But it's apparent that no one will hear her pleas, let alone mine if offered on her behalf.

I reach through the bar and take her limp hand. Mama taught us the healing power of handholding. I plan on giving this girl as much of my strength as I can in this bleak situation.

The morning passes before a policeman pushes through the door.

"You two are up. Judge Henry's about ready to hear your stories." He unlocks our cages, and we follow him out. I hold the girl's elbow, since she's walking drunklike.

We enter a large room with fine wooden chairs and benches. Judge Henry is portly, with cherry-red lips he licks over and over again. Must've just eaten something good. He's sitting on a raised stage with deputies on each side of him. We're led to a row of wooden chairs about fifteen feet back from him.

I'm shaking and wish Briar or Poppy were here to take my side. But when I write this story later, I'll shorten it. Make fun of the circumstances.

I'm led to the line on the floor in front of the judge. I swallow a lump the size of a hickory nut. The policeman stands next to me.

A guard in a uniform that's a mite too tight reads from a piece of paper. "Willow Stewart, age fifteen. Arrested for insufficient guardianship, irresponsible conduct, and possibly becoming a menace to society."

I gasp. None of that's true! I shake my head trying to clear away the lies.

The judge's couldn't-care-less squint worries me. My legs are shaking like I've gone and murdered someone. And he's bored?

"She can't talk, or she don't want to," the policeman says to the judge. "Another reason she shouldn't be on her own."

That gets the judge's attention. "Can you talk?"

I shake my head. I hold up my pencil and mime I can write.

"Write something in your defense." The judge leans forward. Waits.

What should I say? My family is all catawampus and I need to pull it back together? That I have an older sister who'll act as my mother? They're so worried about me going back to a home with only a father. If they only knew what a good man he is.

I left home for two simple chores. To find the traveling preacher before my mother died. While I was traveling, she passed. Then I wanted to find my brother to let him know the sad news.

"What's his name and what does he do?" The judge seems righteously interested now.

Briar Stewart. He's working in the lumbering business in Cartersville.

The policeman steps forward and slides a sheet of paper in front of the judge, who sets a pair of spectacles on his nose and reads for a moment.

What's that paper?

He chuckles and shakes his head. "Deputy here looked up your brother when you told him his name." He taps the paper. "He's in Cartersville working in the pines all right. But he's been lying to you."

I scowl. If my thoughts could reach his tongue, it would be cut from his big mouth. Don't like him badmouthing Briar. Dear Lord, keep my mind. Don't let me take your name in vain because I'm fixin' to lose my religion.

Now a worry pushes through. Truth be told, Briar's letters stopped five months ago. Might be something new happened to him that he hasn't told us.

"He's serving time at the County Prison Camp, out on the turpentine gang."

My head spins. Briar was arrested? All this time I've been happy he's satisfying his wandering spirit, while he's been stuck in a jail. And Poppy's heart changed toward him, trusting he was a working man.

How long will he be there?

The judge looks at the paper. "Let's see. Done five months and has four months more." He clucks his tongue. "Criminal tendencies must run through your kin. Because here you are too."

What can I do to change any of this?

He sits back and folds his hands on his chest like he's studying me.

"You're going through a rough patch, your ma dying and all. Because I'm not a bad man, I'll help you both out." He motions for a pen and takes up a new sheet of paper. "You can serve two months in a labor industry and that will reduce his time by two months. You'll both get out together."

Two months! I write real fast. *Could our time be shortened, sir?*

He frowns at me. "You'll pay your debt to society by working it off where we see fit, girl...and help your no-good brother too."

He can't mean that I would work in the forest, can he? What if it's a sneaky way to put me in that deaf school? I can't trust anyone.

Where will I work? I'm trying not to cry but can feel my throat pinching toward a good bawling.

He reaches to the corner of his desk and drags a black book closer and opens it.

"This has the recent requests for girls."

Huh? How many gals get arrested? With the police and their made-up crimes, maybe more than I could ever imagine.

"There's a sewing job in Cartersville, or a local woman here needs a nanny." He adjusts his spectacles to look closer at the page. "A Mrs. Ardith Dobbs."

The Colored girl jumps to her feet and screams.

"Lordy! That lady is puredee evil! Lying Jezebel done killed my baby and sent me here." Her fists are balled up tight at her sides. "She the one needs arrestin'!"

"Quiet down!" the judge says, his voice thundering, face scrunched like an old bulldog. "One of you bailiffs take her out of here until we're done."

"I need to speak to a legal person!" Her red-striped voice fades as she's taken outside.

But her words, that nearabout echo through my soul, rattle me. That kind of house sounds mighty awful. Besides, Cartersville is where I wanted to go in the first place. I cast a fine stitch Mama always said. Sewing for two months, knowing I'm helping Briar? That's my choice.

Please send me to the sewing job. I wait, my chest fluttering. But he doesn't seem like a man who wants someone telling him what to do.

He scribbles on a paper and hands it to the policeman who brought me here.

"Get her transportation up to Cartersville." He looks my way again. "I sentence you to two months' labor. At a place called Miss Lily's Threads & Things."

I sag in relief. Briar's sure gonna be surprised when he learns about this.

The policeman driving me north is lanky, with combed-back dark hair and a dark shadow above his lip. What a thin mustache. His eyes are cloud-gray, the color that builds before the rain spills out. But dark circles under his eyes show he's been ill-acquainted with a full night's sleep for a time now. He gives me a too-quick smile when I'm handed over to his care.

Before he says a word, we're in farm country.

"Did you meet Sheriff Withington?"

I shake my head.

"My brother-in-law. Our men's group is meeting up here today is why I can drive you. You can't talk at all?"

Again, I shake my head.

"When you get out of custody, you can cleanse your evil ways by joining the women's branch of the Klan. Put you on the right path of wholesomeness. Just stay away from immigrants and Negroes. We're working fast and hard, trying to cleanse the world for pretty white gals like you." He taps out a beat on the steering wheel. "We're only the best men, and now women, in every walk of life. You can't hardly find a doctor, lawyer, or banker that hasn't joined."

I nod but don't like his words. I don't have evil ways. Just got caught up with bad-intentioned folks. Newspapers outside Georgia write worrisome stories 'bout the Klan killing in the dark of night. Like he says, important men belong, so the papers say everyone looks the other way.

"We don't have to stay secret anymore." He's smiling. Looks to be more proud of his belonging than a God-made soul ought. "We sponsor parades, picnics, even beauty contests. Donate money to churches and hospitals. Last year, the wife and I showed up at Christmas parties for orphans, me wearing a Santa suit and handing out gifts. We're what America is all about."

My insides are hopping around like I swallowed grasshoppers. Got the willies about what's ahead for me, can hardly tolerate this man's boastings. Proverbs says don't brag about tomorrow, since you don't know what the Lord has planned.

What should I do when I get to my labor job? Can I ask where Briar is working and try to find my way there? Do we get days off from our work? It would be nice to spend a day with him.

I wonder if he looks much different. It's been a whole fifteen months. I think he's kind of cute—for a brother—with his dark hair and bright blue eyes. But I'll never tell him that 'cause he'd make fun of me.

We reach Cartersville, a town two times bigger than Helen. The policeman stops in front of an appealing shop. Miss Lily's Threads & Things is printed on the window in frilly cursive. Bedcovers in many colors are stacked in the window.

"I was told to take you in the back way." He gets out and motions for me to follow him between this and the next building, a shoe repair shop. The back of the bedspread store looks like a house, sided with white boards and pink trim. Must be where we sleep when we're not working.

The policeman opens the door and lets me step inside.

"Here she is," he says, handing my papers to a woman. "As promised."

The lady looks me over and nods. "Hi. I'm Miss Lily."

I nod and look her over too. Her face reminds me of a hawk, with those sharp lines and angles. And her name don't fit her at all. Prickly Thistle would suit better. She's wearing a Sunday-best flowered dress. Two other girls are sitting round a table, working on pieces of cloth in front of them. They don't stop but glance my way before turning back to their work. Funny, they both look scared. Why?

I'm self-conscious about how I look. My riding dress is a mess, my hair is loose in places, and I must smell nigh close to a horse that's been rode too hard and put up wet with sweat.

"Thank you for bringing her," she says to the policeman. "By the by, my husband said you all have a night meeting a bit later."

"We sure do." He pops his knuckles. "Need to remind a feller about rules, if you know what I mean."

"That pastor knows better. Mixing Coloreds and whites in his service. It's just wrong."

"I'll be going."

Ooh! He tips his hat like Ruthy's beau does and leaves.

Miss Lily smiles then turns to me. Her cheeks are a little more rosy.

"Never had a mute girl here before. I'll run a bath. Get you cleaned up and into a pretty dress."

Not sure why I need to dress fancy to work in the sewing department, but getting clean does sound good.

I'll look nice and presentable when I meet up with Briar.

HAPPENINGS OF THE DAY
MAY 1921
CAUTION!
Two Years After Lake Burton
Began Filling, the Town's Church Steeple
Seen Floating Around the Lake

Timberland Lake Forest. May 1921

-23-

Briar Stewart

The day was moving along smoother than churned butter, and Taggert was in a good mood because we were back on schedule for the barrels of sap he promised. But because the sun don't shine on the same dog all the time, just like that, the day changed.

A wailing come circling out of the woods a few minutes ago, and I rush to see who done what. Tuck's on his back breathing raggedy, air and blood bubbling from his nose.

A shook-up Colored worker stands with his hands on his head, a shocked look on his face.

"Oh, Lordy," he says. His hack's lying at his feet.

I hasten to Tuck's side. "Shit! What happened here?"

Tuck's holding his nose and moaning. "Walked into his damn swing," he finally manages, with a voice choked with blood.

Taggert comes out of nowhere and is on the Colored man. He lands a slap that sounds like a pistol shot. Spit flies from the man's mouth as his head snaps sideways.

"Boss"—the Negro raises his hands to plead—"I never saw him."

Taggert hits him again, this time in the throat.

Strangling sounds come from the man.

I call out to the convict, "Hush your mouth. You only making him mad."

Tuck gets up, one knee at a time. Blood covers his mouth and runs down the front of his shirt. "It's my fault."

Taggert moves closer to study his wound. "Nose is busted. Have the cook look at it."

Tuck stumbles off.

Taggert bends and picks up the hack. Taps it against the side of his leg as he faces the convict.

Christ Almighty, is he gonna kill the man? My heart's thumping like a rabbit facing a fox, and I ain't the one in trouble.

The whites of the prisoner's eyes pop huge with terror.

I step forward. "Tuck says he wasn't looking where he was going. 'Member, we need all the convicts working. Just two days more and you prob'ly be getting a bonus."

He sends me a stink eye, but I know how much he likes making more money. He throws the axe at the convict's feet and walks away.

I let out a long breath, happy not to see another killing. I'm so tired of hate. Of violence caused by lack of understanding. Of loud men with weak morals.

Hoping the rest of the day will move along smooth, I should've been more careful with that cock strut.

It's near suppertime. Back in the tent area, the washing up begins. I don't see Taggert at first but believe he's in his tent. Always a relief to have the man outta sight.

Scuffle sounds come from behind one of the moveable cages. Taggert's raising Cain 'bout someone stealing from the cook. I shake my head. What doggone convict decided to get hisself in a fix now?

"Don't give a shit, boy." Taggert's pulling someone backwards by their shirt. The small man is backstepping to keep himself from being dragged on his ass in the dirt. "You under arrest for *thinking* 'bout stealing from the state of Georgia."

My breath leaves my chest like I been punched. It's Ilya. What is the kid doing back up here? He had a nice setup for weeks, in and round the cave.

"I talk to Ray now." Ilya looks round the camp area. I'm off to the side, and he don't see me yet.

"There's no Ray here, you Russian traitor." He shoves Ilya to the ground, but the boy pops right back up.

In my head, I yell for him to stop talking. If'n Taggert learns I helped Ilya and his brother, I'm done for. Might even get shot. Taggert don't know I told the boy my name is Ray, but I still need to act fast. I got to get him to be quiet while finding out what he needs.

"Let me take him." I rush forward and grab the boy's arm. "I'll get him in his work clothes and bring him back to you."

"R—" Ilya starts to say, but I cover his mouth and drag him backward, rougher than I want, but I need to put on a show for Taggert.

When we're in the woods near the cages, I let him go and spin him around.

"Don't tell him you know me," I say with a hiss. "He'll shoot me, and you'll be on this work gang forever."

"Okay. My brother still sick. I come for help from doctor."

"You should've gone to Euharlee."

"But no money."

Hellfire and damnation! I should've told the kid where I kept the money or left him with some.

"Look. You got to work on this gang till I can figure out how to get you outta here. Do not talk back to this boss. He's a snake waiting to strike."

I enter the storage room and bring out his convict clothes.

"Put these on."

"But…my brother?"

This is bad news all around. Ilya did nothing to warrant a workday of fourteen hours, and his brother is alone and needs help. A mistake repeated more than once is a decision, so I reckon I'm deciding to help this boy again.

"In a few days, I'll check on him when I go to Cartersville." With Tuck mending, I'm sure Taggert will send me again. He's gotten over his anger about me coming back late last time. "I'll carry him to the doctor if need be."

Tears are welling. "Zank you."

"You won't be thanking me when you learn what life is like up here." I gather his threadbare clothes and put them back in the storage cage under a poke of blue work clothes. He'll need 'em again one day. "I have to treat you like a criminal when the boss is around. Sorry."

I walk him back to where the convicts are all seated round the table, eating. I push him onto a seat at the end.

"Shut up and eat what we put in front of you," I say, harshlike.

The cook slides a tin plate and silverware in front of Ilya and ladles out vittles. Timid, the boy picks up the spoon and eats, cutting his eyes to the other convicts at the table.

They ignore him. The lesson that we borrow trouble for ourselves, but there ain't no reason to take on another feller's misfortune, is a warning they have all learned.

I shy away from Ilya, acting like I don't know him any better than Adam and Eve's housecat. But the boy is all I can think of. A heavy sack of worry drops on my back. How long can Cy stay in that cave with no help? Is he too weak to get himself out in the sunshine? Everybody knows the healing nature of the warm rays.

Later that evening, guilt storms in my guts as I lock Ilya in a mobile cage. His eyes are filled with confusion. He's scared to death. I thought about pleading with Taggert to let the young feller go and shackling Ilya with the lie that he's only thirteen. With fear marked on his face and his small size, boy looks much younger than his fifteen years. Before I lock the cage, I send him a tiny smile I hope says I'm on his side.

In my tent, I listen to the peepers and crickets as dark drops in round our camp. How am I gonna sneak back to Saltpeter Cave and not get in trouble?

I bet Taggert returns the Colored boy that hit Tuck, accident or not, to County prison. My stomach sours at the idea the feller will end up dead and buried behind the secret shed.

And another trustee will be with me to protect the new workers and the girls coming back to the mountain from Miss Lily's Threads & Things. How do I get him on my side to let me slip away and help Cy? I got to figure something by morning light. Worrying tonight won't empty tomorrow of its trouble, but it will sap me of my strength. And I'm gonna need all I can hold on to.

As I done since my arrest, I push my concerns way deep inside. They'll be back and I'll be ready for 'em.

I'm thinking of Mama. She loves watching the rising sun. On mornings like this, she thanks the good Lord for brushing the sky with pinks and yellows. The colors of promise and hope, she says.

The silence of the woods blesses the men with a moment of peace before they're forced and pushed through another day of hard labor.

The ideas I come to over the last few days don't seem so worthy in the bright on this traveling day. I juggle them now.

I'd convince Taggert that the new kid should be in the County Prison Camp.

But, I'd drop him off at the front steps of that orphanage in Cartersville.

Then, at the prison camp, me and the other trustee would ask for a more hefty worker, and none of that would make Taggert think I pulled a fast one. Trading one little kid for a strong feller.

Of course, I'd leave Ilya with how to find my money. Carrie Smith 1896 is watching over my secret stash. And eight miles ain't far from Cartersville to the cave. Ilya could leave the orphanage steps and be there in a couple hours. Next day, he can head into Euharlee with some money to ask the doctor for help. After some full workdays in these here pines, Ilya recollects why I told him to stay away from our work gang. The boy as droopy as a picked tobacco leaf.

Just gotta make sure Ilya knows to say he's only thirteen when I pitch the idea to Taggert. It's a year below legal working age in Georgia, so a fair and reasonable request.

Fingers of daylight creep through the forest floor while we finish up breakfast.

Tuck's face is still swollen and plum-colored round his eyes. He looks like a turnip two donkeys been fighting over.

"You getting any better?" I say.

"Glad I got a mouth to breathe through. Nose ain't working worth a damn."

He sounds like he got a cold. Nose all stopped up.

"Hurt much?" I ain't never had my nose busted, but one time I healed from a split lip that hurt like a hundred bee stings.

"Up through my head and back"—he slowly touches his ears—"and these have a powerful ringing going on inside."

"You think you'll be up to making the ride into town later? Mighty bumpy out there."

"No." He shakes his head. "Taggert's talking 'bout going now."

"Now?" I ain't had time to talk to Taggert 'bout Ilya leaving the work gang. I wanted to get Ilya alone to tell him how he can get back to the cave and find my money.

"He's all set on getting girls up here since he missed last month."

I set off and soon find him.

Can't hardly stand to look at him. That big ol' belly's sitting on his lap. His face is redder than a crawdad. Most likely from holding his breath whilst he leans over to tie his work boots' strings.

"You sending workers into town this morning?"

He sits up, face still red and sweat dripping off it, and shrugs.

"You wanna go? With Tuck messed up I need somebody now."

"Sure thing." This is good news. Just what I hoped for. "I want to ask something."

"What?" He stands and hooks his thumbs in his belt.

"That new kid. He's a mite young for this type of work, ain't he? Says he's just thirteen. What say I take him back and get us a big feller?"

"Thirteen?" He itches his left arm. "Seen eleven-year-olds get time for breaking the law. Why you think he's so special?"

"Don't think that. Just wanna make sure we show ourselves as able. We work the pines like the company asks, and we get to stay out here longer"—I shrug—"I think you agree. You're the only boss man in these forests with no one to answer to."

He searches the area for Ilya. The kid's been put on the job of setting the cups below the cuts.

Taggert's one of those men that their thinking shows on their face. As for him, his eyebrows come together in a mess of wrinkles above his nose, and his eyes get all catawampus.

"Not yet," he says, coming back to the moment. "Kid was slinking around. Needs a lesson." He straightens. "He can give us two weeks' worth before we trade him out."

Now I got to come up with a new plan and think out how to reach the cave with no one knowing.

"Okay. I'll get my things. Sounds like it's a trip in to get supplies and the girls. No new workers?"

"Naw. We're making out okay with these S-O-Bs, though I thought about losing the one that hit Tuck."

I nod, not wanting to rile him. Need to keep the man thinking I'm on his side.

"I can handle that. You got the list for supplies?"

His mouth jerks up into a sneer.

"You must be outside your mind, boy. You ain't going alone."

My hopes drop a mite. "Okay." I can probably convince another trustee to look the other way when I ride to the cave and back. "Who you want me to take?"

He laughs. It's a nasty sound, like rusty gears.

"Me."

I swallow hard. No way I can help Cy now, and it's two weeks till the next chance. Might mean the death of that child. And Ilya? He'll go off his rocker with worry. May even blurt out his dilemma. Our dilemma.

"Glad for the company." I force myself to meet his mean stare. "I'll hitch the wagon."

Once on the trail, Taggert smokes and relaxes in the seat next to me.

My mind is circling like a hawk round a mouse for another way to help Ilya's brother. Taggert startles me with a question.

"You from round here, ain't you? Some peckerwood town to the east?"

No way I'm telling him anything more than what's most likely in my arrest record.

"Was. Town upside of Helen. Nothing much left for me there. Brother died in the mines. Pa come home broken from the war. I left coupla years back."

"Who are your people? You mentioned a ten-year-old sister."

"Aw. Got none that care." I shake my head, adding truth to the lie. "Happens more often than not, I learned." I need to get the subject off me. "Where you from?"

"Burton. You heard of the Tallulah Gorge?"

"Yup." I'm extra careful steering the mule down the trail. The empty wagon has a mind all its own back there, jumping and bucking like a spring foal.

"Sure you have. Called the Niagara of the South. Wife writes that people are coming from all around to see it."

"That so?" With him away from the homestead, bet his wife's happy enough to be twins.

"Old town of Burton I grew up in sets at the bottom of the lake now. Since 1919. That's when the Georgia Railway and Electric Company bought Burton, built a dam 'cross the Tallulah River, and the deep valley flooded."

"Heard the whole town's underwater." When we read about it in the newspaper, I remember trying to picture a city in the wavering deep. Creepy is what came to mind.

"Yeah, but everyone had warning and moved up to the ridgeline, now lakefront." He chuckles. "The lake is haunted they say."

"They do?" Haunted ain't something to take lightly.

"The lake filled faster than the smartass dam builders said. All the graves were supposed to be raised and moved uphill, but some got missed. All them dead people left below aren't too happy."

"You don't believe in ghosts, sounds like?"

"When a man gives up the ghost, it shoots straight heavenward. Got no desire to turn back to this ugly place." He flicks his cigarette butt into the trees. "A white man's soul, that is. Just like animals, Negroes and Indians weren't given one."

I can't let that go. "Indians have powerful beliefs about their dead folk and their souls. Very protective of their burial grounds." I think of the Indian mound coming up once we cross the river.

"Bunch of horseshit to get attention and try to take land from farmers round here."

I shut up. Arguing with him is kin to spitting into a hurricane. Gonna get the bad end of it with no reward.

We reach the flats and come to a small lake where a flat-bottom boat is tied to a crooked gray dock. A slight wind sends tiny ripples 'cross the water, making shivers of silver in the late day sun. A dozen geese swim in circles in the middle. It paints a right nice picture of peacefulness. Frogs add their agreeing croaks along grassy banks.

We're heading to the Etowah River when a strange sight boils up in the road ahead. A swirling circle of black feathers and legs.

"The hell's that?" Taggert says.

We draw closer, and although some crows fly off, hundreds stay, walking round the body of a dead one.

"Crows at a funeral." I heard Pa speak of it but never seen it myself. Said magpies do the same ceremony.

They each have bits of grass or twigs and drop them next to the body, the front row moving out while the next row moves forward.

Chills skitter up my neck. Not that long ago, as in one hour past, I thought my luck had hit rock bottom. Ilya showing up. Taggert coming along with me. But with crows at a funeral, rock bottom seems to have more layers to its undersides I wasn't aware of.

Taggert pulls his gun and aims.

"Don't!" I yell. "They recollect faces, 'specially those that harm 'em."

"They're stupid birds." He squeezes the trigger.

The blast splits the air, and the crows take flight, blacking the sky for a moment.

He holsters his weapon and scowls my way.

"You getting too smart for your situation. Don't tell me what to do."

"Yessir."

We don't talk the rest of the way into Cartersville. I park at the mercantile with the list, while he walks one street over, heading to Miss Lily's Threads & Things.

How can he talk about his wife while drooling over the newest gals he plans to have his way with?

I pull the items from the shelf and pay. Many trips later, I have the back of the wagon filled. Now to wait for Taggert, and then I start wondering.

What happened in these young girls' lives so they end up here, rented out to menfolk? They sure must have kin who care 'bout 'em. I swear, people raised in the mountains know 'bout loyalty. Even though Pa told me to leave, I could've stayed up on the mountain, built my own homestead. Mama begged me to. But his words cut clean through me when he swore nobody loved me but Jesus. So's it was my choice to leave, to try to hurt him back with my absence. But, if'n I knew him or any of them was in trouble, I'd be back there, fighting whatever brought them harm.

"Hey, Stewart!" Taggert is behind two gals, both with their heads down, dressed up in frilly dresses and floppy hats. "Guess what?"

"What?" If'n he's offering me a gal, he'll soon learn I ain't interested.

"Seems you got your sentence shortened"—he laughs like he's fit to bust. "You're getting out in two months now."

What? How did he come up with that from a visit to the secret prostitution house?

"You jawing nonsense. What you mean reduced?"

"Seems you *do* have family that cares. Someone's working off two months of your time."

"Who?" My throat hitches. For sure, it ain't Pa that's come looking for me.

Then one gal lifts her head. Red hair frames a pale white face full of freckles. It's Willow! Spots float in and out of my vision. I can't believe it's her. How did she get here?

Then fear takes over when it hits me what's about to happen to her.

NURSEMAID WANTED
Room & Board + $30
White, Refined, Protestant
Prefer Widow or Spinster
Dobbs' Advertising Agency

Marietta, Georgia. May 1921

-24-

Ardith Dobbs

Baby Katherine wants to make her entrance earlier than expected. It was only yesterday Dr. Grange drove the drugged-up Josephine to the police station to have her declared crazy. Then she'd be sent to the insane asylum. The doctor said he asked that she be admitted to a locked-down unit, with neurosis due to depression. She has the option to wet-nurse the babies at the attached foundling home. I think that will do her a lot of good. Dr. Grange also let us know she didn't go inside the jailhouse willingly. I'm glad we weren't there to witness that.

The doctor called William to let him know. Not long after, William and I drove *her* dead baby to the Colored cemetery behind the Piney Grove

Missionary Baptist Church. William paid the pastor the burial fees and we drove home.

While there, I peeked behind the white two-story church. The cemetery was a sad affair. No headstones, some random cement markers, dinner plates, and household items left on mounds or sunken graves. The pastor explained leaving belongings for a loved one was customary, and no, the graveyard hadn't been abandoned. Hard to believe since it was laid out randomly, not in tidy rows. As if everyone flung their loved one from a slingshot, and where they landed was where they were buried. I walk around a grouping of five mounds with one hand-carved cross in the center with the initials GJ. No grass, and only a few trees shading the unfenced area.

It's mighty good Josephine didn't see her son's final resting place. All willy-nilly, like junk thrown onto a brown carpet.

"I'm happy we could do that for Josephine," I said to William on the way home. Wearing a solemn face all that morning, he only nodded after I spoke. Losing Josephine as our maid and nanny bothers him. The hate she threw our way puzzles him. He never can take it when people unjustly accuse him of anything.

Of course, he doesn't understand the whole picture.

He ran the advertisement in the paper for a new childcare worker. We have a week to find a new one.

Or so I thought.

My water broke this morning at breakfast, dripping on our new linoleum floor.

"Call Dr. Grange," I said to William. "Tell him we're on our way to the hospital." The doctor said he wouldn't deliver my baby, but if he knows what's good for his son, he'll be there.

William jumps up and hurries to the telephone in his office. A dull ache moves through my abdomen. But I won't be afraid of giving birth this time around. The doctor assured me they'd give me Twilight Sleep the moment I'm in my hospital bed, and it should start working right away.

I pull my packed overnight case from the closet and a small one for Oliver's stay at the Withingtons'. Nancy once confided she prays she and

York will have half-a-dozen children. She just loves a house full of noise and bother. Nancy says noise and *laughter*—bother is my word.

Another pain grips me, this one stronger. What is taking William so long? And he's still talking to someone. His voice rumbles from the other room.

"Oliver," I say, although it comes out like I'm angry. He's pulled a chair close to the kitchen window and is tracing raindrops down the glass with his fingers. "Would you get your raincoat, please? You're going to play with Clara and Paul today."

"Look, Mommy, the drops are racing, but I don't know which one will win."

"That's like life, Oliver." I inhale, trying to ward off a squeezing sensation in my back. "Grab your coat before Daddy has to get cross with you."

He slides off the chair like a boneless snake and slowly walks to the peg by the door where his yellow rubber coat hangs.

William is back with his coat on and helps me into mine.

"Can you walk?" He's flushed, but his eyes are bright with anticipation.

"Yes." I'm excited too. It'll be wonderful to bend over again, to not feel so full. And a baby girl. All her new clothes are packed away in my bureau. I can't wait to see her in ribbons, satin, and lace. "But I think we need to hurry." Another pain grips me. They seem to be quite close together since losing my water.

He grabs our cases and ushers us into the car. There's light rain today, a Scotch mist, and the street is steamy. The day is dreary and dark enough to confuse the streetlights that glow eerily behind the drizzle.

Oliver stands between us on the front seat, one hand lightly on each of our shoulders.

"We'll have to play hide-and-seek inside at Clara's today," Oliver says.

"That'll be fun." William smiles and gives Oliver's leg a squeeze.

"You'll get to sleep there too," I say. He likes going to Nancy's house. No furniture is off-limits, and it's fine and dandy to hide behind the curtains or pretend brooms are horses to be ridden inside. "And when we pick you up, we'll have our new baby to show you."

"Tell the doctor to bring the right baby this time," he says, leaning forward to study the stoplight.

My heart thuds louder. Is he going to divulge what I told him about Josephine's baby being a *mix-up*?

William chuckles. "What do you—"

"Sweet Oliver." I interrupt to keep William's questions at bay. "Whatever baby we bring home will be the right baby. Do you want a brother or a sister?"

"Both! Tell the doctor, okay?" He's hopping up and down as William pulls the car into the Withingtons' drive. "Then we can have a fun house like Clara and Paul."

William raises his eyebrows and looks my way. "I think that's a fine idea, son. We'll see what the doctor says."

The rain is heavy now, so he picks up Oliver along with his pack and runs to the front step. The boy squeals with delight.

William charges back and slips into the driver's seat. "Here we go, dear." Then gently pats my leg. "Next stop, the hospital."

The rainstorm has almost emptied the streets, and it intensifies as we take the corners faster than usual. No complaints from me. The wipers can't keep the heavy rain cleared, and the hospital is indistinct through the windshield.

William parks under the awning. His call to the doctor alerted them, and thankfully a nurse waits with a wheelchair. The cramping sharpens and shoots into my legs. I'm drawing in long breaths, and the next moments blur. William leans down and kisses my cheek.

"You'll do great. I can't wait for our little one to arrive." He accepts the paperwork from the admissions desk. "I'll be right here until the all-clear."

I try for a smile but it's more like a grimace.

"Hello, Mrs. Dobbs." The freckle-faced young nurse is cheery as she pushes me through open doors. "My name is Eve. We have your room ready."

I nod and let out a growly, "Thank you."

My ears latch on to the whir of the rubber wheels on the hallway's floor. We turn into a room with a bed, two chairs, and a small table laid out with familiar medical instruments.

"Dr. Grange here yet?" She helps me undress and pulls a maternity gown around my front. I lumber onto the bed and fall against the soft mattress and pillows. The head of the bed is upright. But the wide footholds at the bottom of the bed will be something I won't remember. "I'll be needing medication soon."

"Dr. McCorbin is delivering today. Dr. Grange is away. Took his family on a trip to Tennessee to visit relatives."

"That weasel," I mutter between clenched teeth.

"What did you say?" She stops folding and setting my clothes onto one of the chairs.

"Um…where did the weeks go? I saw him recently, and he never mentioned a vacation."

"It surprised us too. He came by yesterday late and said he'd be taking some time off."

Another pain squeezes inside. It feels like someone's twisting my parts with barbed wire.

"Is this other doctor good with the sleep medications?" Right now, I don't care who's in charge as long as it gets started.

Eve's mouth opens and closes like a dying fish.

"We have you going through the birth without sedation."

What? I don't believe this! Someone has snuck me in the side door of hell.

"That was never the plan! I cannot go through this awake." The next contraction lasts more than a few seconds, and I can't breathe as the pain rips through my back. "Go get my husband. He knows what we scheduled."

She hurries out of the room, and I clutch the sheets in my fists. Incompetence! I'm not prepared for this. It was to be peaceful. Then it suddenly occurs to me why this is happening. Everyone knows it's bad luck to walk on a grave. At the Negro cemetery yesterday, I walked on top of those haphazardly buried dead folks.

A scream escapes as a spike slices through me. Also, it must be why the baby's coming a week early. I should've brought a knife. Tucked under the mattress, it reduces labor pains. Every mountain woman attests to that.

The door opens, and Eve is back with a tall, redheaded doctor.

"Mrs. Dobbs, I'm Albert McCorbin." He nods and flashes a grin like he was given first place for his prize hog. "It sounds like this is not going to take much longer."

"Start the Twilight Sleep," I say through a gasp.

"Your husband doesn't want that for you. He said your nanny just lost her child because of it."

"Damnation!" The tears are uncontrollable, cold, streaming down the sides of my face. "That's *not* what killed her baby."

He's clearly startled but presses on.

"When a woman is heavily sedated, the baby may quit breathing." He moves to the foot of the bed. "Scoot down here and put your feet in the stirrups. I need to check on things."

"No! I can't do this!"

"Your husband said you're a strong woman. You've overcome terrible family tragedy." He shakes his head and turns to the nurse. "Her parents and close family died on the *Titanic*."

"No! I'm not strong at all. You have to give me something!"

"I want you to take in long, cooling breaths. Hum a favorite song. Or think of a place that's calming, peaceful, and picture yourself there."

Eve moves beside the bed and places a wet cloth on my forehead. No peaceful images come to mind. But I do picture Dr. Grange telling William the sleep drugs are too dangerous. This must be his revenge for what I asked the doctor to do to Josephine. The Klan will soon learn about his son *and* the Catholic woman.

Burning pain sears through me. I silently practice saying the secret Klan names for the months of the year. Appalling. Frightful. Sorrowful. Mournful. Horrible. The name for May is proving to be true. This is just horrible. I hear myself screaming for all the world like a damn banshee but can't control it. I'm so embarrassed!

Breathe. Breathe.

Okay, June. June is Terrible, then comes Alarming, Furious, Fearful, Hideous, Gloomy, and finally Bloody.

Far off, I hear a man telling me to push.

Ohhhhhh. I bear down but there's no relief.

My mind drifts backward in time. I'm climbing the ragged peaks of Hickory Nut Hollow.

Up and down. My legs burn. Now there! It's Gator Tyre, the preacher boy who got me pregnant, saying he was saving me from my rotten brother, Clem, and his dirty ways. Daddy scared the preacher away. A shotgun will do that. I thought Gator would be my ticket out of there, so I let him have his way. Now he claims he wants to live here forever, never see the outside world. This is not the plan for my future. Now I want nothing to do with his graspy cold hands.

"Push."

Who is that?

It's Clem, who has a side that's ornery as a rattlesnake on fire, especially since he learned Gator and I have been together. I let Clem know I'm 'bout to tell what he's been doing to me for years. When Gator comes toward me this time, pleading for me to stay, Clem busts his way from the trees and pokes the man to the edge of Old Baldy Ridge with a sharp stick. He's gonna push him off and that ain't the right answer.

"Push, Ardith! Push." It's a man giving me an order. I'm so tired of men in my life. Pa, my brother. All owning me. Telling me what to do. Well, I don't need them.

I rush toward my brother and Gator. Clem grabs my arm, and I'm about to teeter over the edge with him. I don't want to die. I peel his hand away myself and push with all my might. Together, Clem and the preacher boy somersault down the rocky face of the cliff, disappearing into the churning river below.

"Almost there, Mrs. Dobbs. Push again."

"No! He's dead," I yell. "I didn't mean to."

And suddenly, a huge relief flows through me. The pain subsides, and through my tears, the room clears.

"Mrs. Dobbs. There's nothing to worry about. He's not dead." The doctor stands up and points to the nurse who's busy at a sink. "You have a healthy baby boy."

Miss Lily's Threads & Things
Four Queens
Chenille Robes
ON SALE - $3.98
Add Pin-Up Girl
Glamour to Your Life!

Cartersville, Georgia. May 1921

-25-

WILLOW STEWART

Miss Lily's Threads & Things has us making bedspreads most of the day, but it's not hard work. Tufting out the material to make it into soft chenille is tiring, but we get a ten-minute break every few hours. The only rules are that we can't talk to each other—which is an easy one for me—and we can never leave the building without Miss Lily or another worker.

"You're serving out a sentence," Miss Lily reminds us. "You do what the state of Georgia says."

But I've been here a week already, and my earlier thoughts of meeting up with Briar have dwindled. Miss Lily locks us into our tiny sleeping quarters at night. The bed is comfortable, and there's a chair and one tiny table with a lamp. We have to knock to be let out to use the toilet, and we're allowed one time after lockdown or she gets out a switch and whips the backs of our legs. I learned my lesson the second night. Don't drink too much water with supper, or your legs will sting into the next day.

I ask to write a letter home, but I'm told no. As a *criminal*, as Miss Lily likes to call us, we have no outside rights. I worry what Poppy and my family is thinking. Has he come looking for me? Would the police in our county be in touch with the police in this county? Something tells me loads of people might be missing everywhere. With the way the judges deem everyone a lawbreaker, it's a wonder more people aren't lost in the shuffle of the you-go-here and you-go-there process.

Something new must be happening today because she hurries us through our baths and hands us frilly dresses to wear.

When a sweaty man arrives, Miss Lily's mood changes. She tugs down her dress, even though it hasn't gotten any shorter since she stood up to answer the door.

"I come to see that my order is filled this time." His voice is cow-manure brown.

"I apologize for last time. The girls weren't what you expected."

His face reddens. "With hundreds of girls running loose, should be easy to get what I'm wanting."

Why is this man here? He acts like he has something to do with us.

"Well"—Miss Lily tugs her dress again—"we have a special one for you this time." She turns to point to me. "You have a Briar Stewart working for you?"

"Got him with me outside."

My brain stutters for a moment, and every part of me goes on pause while my thoughts catch up. Briar is here? I was worried I would have no way to reach him. Now I'm doing my best to keep from smiling, but my eyes are betraying me. I bite my lip to not give away my mood.

"She's doing time to reduce her brother's sentence," Miss Lily says. "By two months."

"Well, I'll be," the man says. "This is one big fat surprise all around." He's shaking his head in disbelief but doesn't look happy.

Miss Lily hands him some papers. "She don't work out for you, she's to go to a home in Marietta." She clears her throat. "I mean after she's done working for you."

Oh no! That's the bad place the Colored gal was yelling about in jail. And what does Miss Lily mean by "done working for you"? I have two months of sewing work, and then Briar and I are free to go.

The man chuckles. "This is gonna be fun." He motions for the other girl named Lacy and me. "Grab your things."

Miss Lily hands us pretty hats to match our fancy dresses. I'm confused. Why are we going with this man? This doesn't set right. I hold back, and Miss Lily gives me a little push.

"Move along, gal."

Next thing I know we're on the street, and I hear our family name called and a hoot of laughter. I lift my eyes and there he is! Briar! He's thinner but looks strong.

By the color of their voices, he and the man don't like each other. Red bumping up against deep blue.

"Seems you *do* have family that cares," the man says to him. "Someone's working off two months of your time."

Briar should look surprised but happy, right? Instead, when I lift my face, his shoulders hunch together like he's trying to disappear inside himself. His face fills with massive confusion. Crumples.

He raises his hands and signs, *"Why are you here?"*

Oh, how I've missed him talking to me in our secret language. *"We need you at home."*

"Why?"

"Mama had a baby that died." I don't dare tell him about losing Mama. *"Poppy has forgiven you. He's proud of you for your travels, thankful for the money."*

"Can't be too proud of me now."

"What the hell you two doing?" The man slaps my hands down. The sting of his slap travels up my arms.

Briar lunges closer. Fierce and threatening, like a trapped mountain lion. I've never seen him like this. "Don't touch her!"

The man must be Briar's boss. My brain is trying with all its might to make sense of it all, and if I could talk, I'd be empty of words.

"My sister won't make you happy. You can't take her!"

"Says *you*?" The man's smile makes me think of how a barn cat must feel just batting around a mouse, teasing it.

"I'll serve out my four months. She only come here to bring bad news about my kin."

"The kin you say you have no connection to?"

"I did leave like I said. Ain't seen hide nor hair of 'em in over a year."

Why won't Briar let me help him? I sign again. *"Why are you sending me away?"*

He swallows hard, and I see ungodly fear in his eyes. *"This man means to take you into the woods and have his way with you and the other girl. For days and days."*

I cringe as if watching someone empty their innards. It's Mr. Coburn all over again. And the judge? Did he know what he was sending me to do for two months?

"I'll do anything," Briar says.

"Your sister was arrested outside Atlanta. Judge sentenced her to two months. This place or another."

"Where's the other?" Briar says, his voice rough, navy blue like Poppy's gets at times. Full of heart.

"A woman in Marietta," I sign. *"Dobbs."* Now that mean woman don't seem half bad.

"Knock it off! I'm sick of you two talking like that." The man lets out a long breath. "Okay, Stewart, but you gonna pay. You been pushing my patience for weeks now anyways. And this time, you went too damn far… and you know it."

The boss guides the other girl up into the wagon. He points to Briar and the girl.

"Don't move. I'll shoot you both if I have to hunt you down."

He walks me back inside, and none too kindly. I stumble into a chair at the table. Rivers of cold fear run through me. What will happen to Briar now? He's made some deal with his boss, but everything says me showing up has made things worse for my brother.

"Change of plans. I'm taking the other gal, but call Sheriff Withington and get this one reassigned." His nostrils flare like an angry horse's. "And *never* bring me a mute girl again. Shit! Half the fun is listening to 'em scream."

Within an hour, I'm in the back seat of a police car and heading to Marietta. The two policemen up front ignore me, and that's fine with me. When they picked me up at Miss Lily's Threads & Things, the woman never said goodbye. She made me change back into my dirty riding dress, which suited me just fine too. All those dolly skirts of lace and satin were wrong on me, like trying to dress up a pig. A pig for the slaughter it seems.

The policemen stopped at a small glass enclosure along the street with a telephone inside. One dropped a nickel in the telephone and talked for a few minutes before writing something down.

My insides are still all aquiver. I can't help fretting about what's next for me, but I'm more scared for Briar. The boss threatened to shoot him. Could that even happen? Oh, I have the card from Miss Burns on the train. Her beau is a lawyer and helps people in trouble. Maybe I could write to her. The girls who work for Miss Lily need help and so does Briar.

About thirty minutes later, the car pulls down a pretty street with huge houses. We stop in front of one grander than the rest. It has stately pillars and a first *and* second floor porch. Domed shade trees line both sides of the long drive.

"I'll walk her inside," the one who made the call says.

At the door with the pretty brass knocker, he finally speaks to me.

"You'll work off your two months here. Maybe you'll want to stay longer as a paid maid." He shrugs. "This is an important family in Marietta."

The door opens, and a handsome man stands there with a question-marked smile on his lips.

"Yes? May I help you?"

"Sheriff Withington says you're looking for a nanny, and this girl became available in the penal system."

"Oh." He steps back and motions for me to come inside. His voice is smooth, like polished brass. "That was fast. And just in time. My wife is barely home from the hospital with our newborn son."

"Congratulations, Mr. Dobbs." They shake hands. "You shouldn't have any trouble but call us or the sheriff if you do."

"I'm sure we will be fine here." He smiles at me and starts to close the door.

"One more thing." He hands Mr. Dobbs my arrest paper. "She can't talk, but we hear she can read some and write a few words."

Mr. Dobbs startles for a minute but recovers his manners. "Well, Mrs. Dobbs likes a quiet house. This might suit her just fine."

I think to argue, but then reckon it might benefit me to have them think less of my reading and writing skills.

He closes the door, and his eyes roam around the paper.

"Ah. You are Willow Stewart. Welcome. My name is William, my wife is Ardith, and we have Oliver, who's five…and a newborn yet to be named."

I smile. Tears are coming, but I fight not to cry. This man is the nicest person I've run into since Miss Burns on the train.

The inside of this house might as well be a princess palace. Oh-so-large rooms and high ceilings with flower patterns stamped into them. Shiny doodads decorating tables and shelves are aplenty. Mama would've loved walking through this house just to see it.

"Everyone is napping right now, but I'll show you to your room."

He leads me along a hallway with the softest carpet, like thick moss underfoot. Past the kitchen, he pulls open a small door. He closes it, and we walk out of the house.

"You will use the washroom and toilet out here."

I'm living outside?

"Here we are." He stops in front of a small one-story building fixed onto the house and pulls the door open. "I think you'll find it comfortable. Our last nanny said she was happy out here." His voice changes to rusty orange with those words.

With the way the nanny was screaming in jail about them killing her baby, I doubt she found any comfort in this little house.

I settle in. It's nicer than my room back home. The cover on the bed is so pretty and kind of matches the red roses on the tiny window's curtains. Hmm. Wonder if they got the cover from Miss Lily's sinful place. Everybody seems to know each other in these parts. There's a white wood chair, which'll be nice for reading if I'm allowed books, and a shelf with a few pegs underneath. A beautiful washstand. An indoor toilet. I set my new Red Chief notebook and pencil on the shelf and want so much to lie on the bed. But my riding dress is so dirty. Guess the rag rug will have to do till I get something clean to put on.

Mama always told us your best teacher is your last mistake. But, Mama, what does it mean when I've made so many? If I had just gone for the preacher and turned home, I wouldn't have been arrested. And I wouldn't be confined to this home, leaving my family short one soul to work the crops this summer. Worse still, Briar is now in a heap of trouble for protecting me.

I curl up on my side on the rug. The dam that held back all the pain, starting with losing Baby Luther right up till now, cracks wide open. The gush of tears comes.

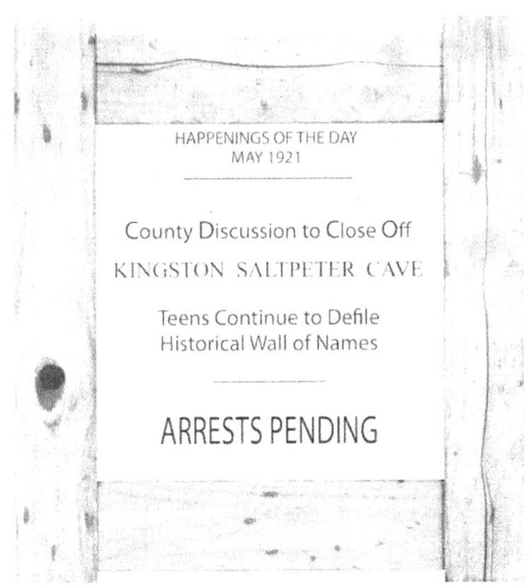

HAPPENINGS OF THE DAY
MAY 1921
County Discussion to Close Off
KINGSTON SALTPETER CAVE
Teens Continue to Defile
Historical Wall of Names
ARRESTS PENDING

Cartersville, Georgia. May 1921

-26-

Briar Stewart

"You ain't driving," Taggert growled. "*Git* in the wagon with the girl and the grub."

"These mules handle hard up that mountainside," I say. "No reason to change me out just yet." Relief and woe twist together in my mind. Willow will work in a woman's home, and I'm back to what's left of my four months. Or I think that's the deal I made. I was ready to kill Taggert if he'd taken Willow. Don't care if someone had killed me back. She don't deserve any ugliness in this world.

"You ain't going up the mountainside either." He waggles his thick fingers. "Gimme the reins and get in the back, boy."

While I hand them over, Taggert hits me with a full fist in the side of my head.

Can't see straight, so I grab the side of the wagon for balance. I shake away the blurring, climb into the back, and sit on a bag of potatoes.

The girl's neck is blotchy. She looks 'bout to cry. Her next few days will be hell, and there's no way to comfort her. No way for me to stop it. Unless. I could kill Taggert. Even if he got the law behind his actions, he's full of evilness. How he murders the workers with ease. Rapes young girls.

But they know who Willow is now. Where they can find her. Another crony of Taggert's might seek revenge after I'm dead. For sure I will be if I do something like that.

I have to finish out my time, knowing I saved Willow. Or did I? Dobbs is the name she spelled. Working for a woman has to be safe, right? And Mama had a baby boy that died? One thing for sure, she would've named him Luther II, which makes it all the sadder. And I know Willow. There was something she ain't tell me. Has Pa been beset with depression again, losing another Luther? Then they'd really need me home to plow and help out with summer chores so there's food through winter.

Taggert got the mules moving but in the wrong direction. He winds through the streets before heading up to the prison on the hill. A dark shadow descends on my soul. I'm 'bout to find myself back in black and white stripes, a slave to the state once again.

Should've known that crows at a funeral meant a helping of extra bad luck.

From the prison, things happened mighty fast. I was driven to the courthouse and ushered in front of the judge.

He smiles, but it's slippery as a boiled onion.

"You're going to be staying with us a while longer I hear, helping out south of here in Cobb County. Atlanta has been built to a spectacular showpiece by convicts the likes of you. You've seen the signs along the roads. 'Bad Boys Make Good Buildings.' Well, we need all the bricks we can get, and you're going to have a hand in that." He takes off his glasses and sets them on the raised platform he sits behind. "I sentence you to a year this round."

Good God Almighty! A year? I've done most of my time already. He's talking plumb through to *next* summer. This craziness can't be legal. A deputy steps to me to guide me to the door where the criminals exit. I dodge his reach.

"Your Honor. I got to be home just north of Helen to help my father with our homestead. My sentence was up end of August when I could help with harvest season." My mind is swirling. I'll tell any lie now to try to reduce my time.

"Son." Judge Markum's face is flushed two shades redder than when I first walked in. "You've seen my pleasant side. You don't want to rile me up."

There's no difference between a hornet and a honeybee if it's in your britches. My innards feel like I ate a bucket of lard, heavy and 'bout ready to come up.

The deputy digs his fingers into my arm and leads me to the side door. Time gets muddy.

I'm hustled into a police truck, with standing room only, chock-full of men. Another vehicle is loaded with Negroes. The whole county is as crooked as a barrel full of fishhooks. I know from my first arrest outside of this town, if you're walking the streets free as a breeze, you gonna get arrested.

The truck's metal door clanks shut, and it shivers through my boots all the way up to my back teeth.

My new sentence is bad enough, but what's to become of Ilya's brother left alone in the cave? I made a promise to Ilya I'd check on Cy. If'n Ilya don't see me come back today, he's gonna be broken. And Taggert could end up working Ilya to death out of spite just 'cause he's Russian. Damn. A year in prison working to build more fine buildings in Atlanta. Fear and shame wrestle my mind and make me dizzy. Lord, everything's gone wrong.

Two guards stand on the running boards of the paddy wagon. One slaps the roof, signaling the driver. The vehicle takes off, and I fall against two other men and quickly right myself when I see the hate in one feller's eyes.

I worry 'bout Willow. Will she get taken to Marietta, or was that just a trick to get rid of me? Sickness rises in the back of my throat when I think 'bout her innocence. She's grown into a pretty young lady since I last laid eyes on her. And she never did say how she got herself in trouble. I'm sure it points back to her setting out to find me. That don't sit well in my heart, like so many other wrongs I done.

We bounce along the roads, and I try to stay upright as the truck takes corners. Can't see enough outside to know where they're taking us. We soon head on down a bumpy back road. Dust stirs up and fills the truck bed, so I close my eyes and choke on the fine red powder.

"Chattahoochee Brick!" a guard calls from the front cab.

I try to see through the wire mesh, but all the men have their faces pressed there. A stringy feller says, "I hear it's got ghosts, so many have died here."

Men groan. This can't be good.

We unload, and the guards push us to rundown wood buildings, one story high. Once inside, they prod us past cots with thin mattresses along each side of the room. The inside is shacky, with rough boards for walls and a few iron-barred windows. We pass through the johnny where a dozen open toilets swamp the room with the stink of old shit and piss.

The men who designed the prison camps must've used a single plan. This is pert near the layout of Cartersville.

The next room is made of cinder blocks, with one door and no windows. In the center is a wooden board on uprights, akin to a hitching post. The whipping pole. A guard with a mighty mean squint stands with his hand on his gun belt. Not only does he have a pistol, but he carries a snaked bullwhip.

Sweat runs down my back. Is he gonna start right off by tearing the hide off one of us?

"Welcome to Chattahoochee Brick Company, your home for the duration of your sentence." He smiles, clasps his hands in the air in front of him, and cracks his knuckles. Confound it! That sounded like a gunshot in this shut room. "I'm Warden Rourke. Your time here will go easy if you follow the rules." He walks a few feet to the left and stops. "And they are simple. Number one. The only response you will ever utter is 'Yessir.' Is that clear?"

A handful of us mumble the response.

"That's disheartening," Rourke says. "You sons of bitches can muster a better reply than that." His face is red. His jaw tightens. "Let's try it again. *Is that clear?*"

I add my voice with the others this time round.

"Better. Number two rule. You do everything you are told to do. Since you broke the law in our fair state, you will work from sunup to sundown to make up for your disobedience. And number three. If you try to escape, you will be killed. Everyone from the governor on down agrees with these rules. You've had your say at the trial. There's no one to go bawling to. Do your time for your crime." He turned to the four guards surrounding us. "Get them into their stripes."

I swore I'd never be back in them dirty rags again. But if there ever was any reason worth going backwards, saving Willow would be just that.

Now if I can figure out how to get Ilya and Cy out of their binds.

The brickyard is sweltering hot. Full of red dust. The stripes they give me barely fit. The shirt could fit two men and the pants are too short. This wheelbarrow duty they got me on must be a devil-created hell chore. Load hot bricks from the kiln and run them across the way to the stacking yard. Yes. *Run*, or a feller hits you on the back with a stick.

That this is a place of torture became clear with my first step in the huge brickworks. Off to the side of our running trail, a man is wrapped and chained round a pickaxe, doubled in half, feet to face. He was moaning at first but in the last while fell silent.

I asked what he done, and someone said the man dropped a warm brick on accident and dented the corner. The Stamper, who puts a number 1 at the bottom of each brick, tried to help out and hide the flaw but wasn't fast enough. The inspector saw it.

The other inmates answered my questions while we loaded the bricks. The warden don't tolerate much. Men get whipped with wide leather straps like I saw at the quarry. And another torture called "getting the watering hole" I ain't heard tell of before. A man is laid back with a cloth over his nose and mouth, and a guard pours water over his face. Sometimes they don't let up in time and the feller drowns on dry land.

There's a hotbox in the full sun. And the doctor would just as soon cut off a bad hurt body part than try to doctor it. But what makes our days worse, the prison docs appointed by the state are lied to when they come by to check on the abuse of us convicts.

Nothing but Lord-awful news.

But even a barren apple tree gives up some shade. Our shade is we work with no shackles or chains.

The sun's beating down. My mouth feels dust dry. My heart pounds. 'Course, they will offer us water and vittles. We'd die out here. Even that old bastard Taggert understood that. But if I need to stop to wipe my sweat, I must ask permission by calling out, "Wipe it off, sir." I daresn't lift a hand till a guard calls back, "Wipe it off."

A truck thunders toward us, kicking up clouds of chalky dust behind it. A cough is pestering at the back of my throat, but I fight it, not knowing if I first need permission.

The prayer I send heavenward asks that God either grant me the might to keep going or send a plague of locusts to stop the work altogether.

I can accept either one.

A year of this. I could try to work my way up to trustee again, but I bet my new paperwork warns against it. No way I'm doing my full sentence. I'll figure out a way to get outta here and see that Willow is safe. Try to help Ilya and his brother.

Or die trying.

Marietta, Georgia. May 1921

27

Ardith Dobbs

Sheriff Withington worked fast. Nancy probably pushed him, knowing my dilemma with bringing a baby home and no one to help with Oliver. A runaway gal named Willow is here—got here just a day after I brought baby boy home. A mute! Who would've thought of that being a good thing, but it is. I get no sass back. To be honest, she seems sad but is remarkably good-natured for one so disadvantaged. I can't imagine not talking. They say God is the friend of silence. Look at nature. The trees, flowers, grass—they all grow in silence. The stars, the moon, and the sun. They move in silence. These aren't my thoughts, although I wish they were. I read them in a poetry book when I was in Atlanta, trying to lose my hick way of talking. Before meeting William.

Willow reminds me a bit of myself. A mountain gal who got herself into some trouble and was arrested. They assure me she isn't dangerous. Her mother is dead, she writes, although she isn't much for reading or writing. She's teaching us some hand signs. Oliver is thrilled. I admit I'm surprised a girl with her handicap is doing so well out on her own. I had a younger sister, Mable, who went missing when she was seven. Pa said he lost her while she rode along into Patch Hog to buy salt. Said she wandered off in the thick of the woods. But Clem and I always suspected he'd sold her. She had a slow mind and a crooked leg and could hardly help around the homestead. Pa came home with food aplenty that trip and never seemed too energized to go look for her, although neighbors offered for a respectful time.

This Willow must be a mite sharper than Mable.

Baby Boy cries a lot. I tried breastfeeding, but for some reason my milk isn't enough. If only Josephine's mind hadn't cracked, I'd bring her back. I'm feeding him Borden's canned milk, but it makes him gassy. And then he cries more often. William isn't thrilled with that solution. He read that it's hard to know if the cows providing the milk have tuberculosis or not.

He worries too much. I called Dr. Grange to ask if cows get TB. And yes, he's back from his "much needed" vacation. He's barely talking to me, but I'm the one who should be angry. Leaving me in incredible birthing pain. Anyway, he said if the milk isn't boiled, there's a chance of the disease passing through. Well, Borden boils their milk before it's canned.

William and I can't decide on a name. I want to name the baby after my made-up father from the *Titanic*. I found lists of the second-class passengers in the newspaper from the year it sank and adopted Alice and Charles Louch as my newly dead parents. My name then became Ardith Louch, a fine change from Sissy Belle Strunk.

And with the law looking for Sissy Belle, to find out what *she* knew about the disappearance of Preacher Gator Tyre, the name change came just in time.

Willow answers the knock on the door while I relax in bed, the baby sleeping next to me in his bassinet. Teresa and Nancy are popping by to see the baby and to catch me up on the Women of the Klan's projects. William hardly tells me anything. Secret men's stuff.

No way for me to brag, but I've kept better secrets than he's ever heard.

"Ardith!" Teresa enters the room first, followed by Nancy. They're carrying a huge vase of absolutely lovely cut flowers and a covered basket.

I raise my finger to shush them. Won't have a minute of peace if they keep hollering.

"Oh, he's darling," Nancy whispers, leaning over the baby's bed.

He is a cutie. I'm a bit disappointed he doesn't look a thing like William, but instead resembles my pa, a man that good looks sloughed off of as he aged. But Josephine's baby was the spitting image of Oliver and William. How unfair.

My friends pull my two Queen Anne chairs closer to the bed.

"We have so much to tell you," Teresa says.

"Like what?" I'm anxious to hear the news. Been out of contact for just five days, but it feels much longer.

"We finished all the baby robes and hoods," Teresa says, smiling. "They're first-rate."

"My soul-n-senses!" I shake my head. "You still had hundreds to make."

"Do you know Clara Blair?" Nancy says. "Her husband manages the bank. She's a new member and real spunky. Enlisted five of her gardening club friends. They've all joined the Klan too, and lickety-split, the robes are finished."

"It's good we have more members," I say. "I can get their dues logged in if you've brought them."

"Clara took the membership money," Teresa says. "She even was a dear to suggest she fill the Klabee position and you keep Kligrapp."

What? No. I'm treasurer *and* secretary. I often borrow from that account when necessary. I can't have this.

"Oh, she does sound like a sweetie." I wave my hand. "I enjoy doing both of those duties so much. Not only do they go hand in hand, but it's no problem now that I have my new nanny." I tap Nancy's leg. "Thanks to your husband, by the way."

"She doesn't talk, York said." Nancy wrinkles her brow. "How is she managing to talk to Oliver?"

"He doesn't need much instruction. He's such a good little boy. And she can write a few words like *Go Park*, and I tell Oliver that she's going to take him to the park. She also uses hand signs she's teaching him."

"Aren't you worried about having a girl with a criminal past in your house?" Teresa says.

I chuckle inside. If they only knew about *my* past. And besides, Willow is better than an angry Colored gal with a spiteful story to tell.

"She hardly did anything wrong. Came off the hills looking for a preacher because her mother and newborn baby brother died. Decided to look for her no-good brother. That was her mistake. Then made herself appear to be a runaway, taking money from a preacher's wife up in Helen."

"Seems safe enough," Teresa says.

"We're making final plans for the bake sale this weekend," Nancy says. "One of the Grand Dragon's Hydras will be speaking about the fight for Americanism."

William asked that I not do anything for two weeks. The bake sale is two days away.

"I'll be there. What can I do?" I've been writing a poem while lying around. Maybe they'll let me give a talk and end with it.

The Knights of the Klan,
A force with a plan,
Men and women of valor,
Fighting all that's off-color.

"We didn't know you'd be able to make it, Ardith." Teresa leans forward, her voice as if she's talking to a child. "Just come and enjoy the fundraiser in a front-row seat."

Am I being pushed out of my own Daisy Ladies' Society?

"Oh, of course I'll be there. I'll be part of the crowd but talking up membership."

"That's wonderful," Nancy says.

The doorbell rings downstairs. Soon I hear it open and a distant woman's voice rises on the stairs.

"That must be Clara," Teresa says, a smile lighting her face like she won a prize at the county fair.

"Oh, you've invited her here?" I pat my hair. "I'm such a mess right now."

"Pshaw. You look like a glowing new mother." Nancy walks to the hallway to wait. Seconds pass, then she says to someone, "Oh, we were expecting someone else. Are you here to see Mrs. Dobbs?"

"I am." The woman's voice is familiar. But who would come visiting without an invite?

My heart stops. Fiona Elsmore steps around the doorframe, looking every bit as sad as the last time I saw her.

"Fiona?" I sit up straighter in bed, unsettled. "Whatever are you doing here?" And how the dickens did she find my house?

She cuts her eyes to Teresa and Nancy while wringing her red, chapped hands.

"Roy come home night before last."

Panic grows in my chest. I can't have Teresa and Nancy hear that I took this woman's money to give her baby away. The Women of the Klan provide desperate mothers with *free* services.

I turn to Teresa and Nancy. "Thank you for coming. The flowers are beautiful, and the basket of food is much appreciated."

"Um, that's not food," Nancy says. "I knew you were expecting a girl and that you probably could use some boy clothes. They're almost new from when mine were younger."

"You told us you gave all of Oliver's baby clothes away," Teresa says. "Remember?"

I nod and start to get up. "I'll see you to the door." I tie the string on my silky pink robe. "And, I'll be there on Saturday."

"I had a baby girl," Fiona says. "I come here to ask for her back."

Lordy, why is this happening?

"We can talk about that, Fiona. Let me see my friends to the door."

"Where did your baby go?" Nancy says.

Should have known *she'd* be interested. She's the one who would like to birth a dozen children if she could.

"Mrs. Dobbs took her to be adopted out." Her face sags. "My husband was missing. I lost my mind for that time, but now we want her back."

"That shouldn't be too hard if it wasn't that long ago." Nancy turns to me, her eyebrows raised. "Where did you take her?"

Dizzy, I wobble to the bed and drop down, holding my middle. Fiona's baby has long been sold from the Beck Infantorium. Or worse. It was a sick little thing. Time to repeat the lie I told Fiona.

"The New Hope Charity Home, of course." This is the foundling home our woman's club supports. "But it's been two or so weeks now. You gave full permission to find her a new home."

"I can call over," Teresa says. "Shirley will remember you coming by."

"No!" I clear my throat. "I'm sorry"—a giggle escapes—"My goodness. I need to be the one who handles this. Besides, William has asked me to pick up the payments for some of his life insurance policies." He's done no such thing. "Fiona. I'll make the call. We can drive out tomorrow and sort this out."

"You mean pick up baby Anna?" Fiona asks.

"Yes." I need them all to leave. A dark headache is moving in, and if I don't keep my thoughts centered, I'm liable to tell what really happened. "How did you get here today?"

"Walked down Chicken Branch Road to the highway. A man gave me a ride in."

"I'll tote you back," Nancy says. "You shouldn't be walking alone. Vagrancy laws are getting tighter and tighter in these parts."

"Thank you, ma'am." She nods. "And as soon as I can save up another ten dollars, I'm going to join your ladies' group."

After they left, my heart fluttered like a rafter of turkeys were fighting in there.

I left my religion behind in Hickory Nut Holler. The preacher did that for me. Even after I was saved and all. He dunked me in the river, washing me of sins, but I should've waited another year. By then I needed a more thorough scrubbing when my brother started diddling me and I didn't fight back at first. My baptism was no different than any other after a revival came through Hickory Nut Hollow. He waded into the rushing water, a rope tied around his waist. All us sinners tied along the rope like rags along a barbed wire fence.

Haven't prayed in years but here I go.

Forgive me for what nobody knows except You. I did what I thought was best. Help me figure my way out of this mess I made. Keep me faithful to this God-given women's group I'm lucky to belong to. Let me be righteous in all things. Amen.

The Klan has a tribunal for unlawful deeds by its members. If Fiona tells them she paid to have her baby put up for adoption, I can explain I never gave the money to New Hope Charity Home. Which I hadn't, of course. I will pay her back. Give her a bit extra. Lord, she looks like twenty miles of bad road.

The most pressing problem is how to keep folks from finding out about the Beck Infantorium. I learned about the sisters' secret place years ago from a prostitute when I needed to give a baby away. I never saw that baby, and still don't know if the preacher and me had a boy or girl. He was dead, and I was busy changing my identity. You might say neither of us cared.

A thought jumps in my head. Maybe little Anna is still there. The Beck sisters would've treated her impetigo before offering her to a new family. It's only been about two weeks.

That idea feels good, like a cool breeze at a hot day's end. Yes. I'll drive out tomorrow first thing.

And there isn't a bit of use in mentioning any of this to William. He doesn't tell me about what he and the men discuss or do. Well, this is the same horse but a different color.

Women don't need men to solve their problems these days. We have each other.

HAPPENINGS OF THE DAY
MAY 1921
7 YEARS LATER
The Mystery of Missing Girl
and Hickory Nut Hollow Preacher
REMAINS UNSOLVED

Marietta, Georgia. May 1921

28

Willow Stewart

This is my second day at the Dobbses' home. I've sent a thank-you prayer skyward each day that Briar saved me from his horrible boss. I end with a wish that Briar isn't in awful bad trouble, even though my mind says he may be.

The baby boy cries a lot, and Miss Ardith says her milk isn't doing its job. She bought milk in a can, and that makes him cry more after he's done. Miss Ardith has the motherly instincts of a cowbird. That bird lays her eggs in another bird's nest and lets that fill-in mama feed and raise her babies.

She seems happy to have me here, but I know she wishes I could suckle that new baby too. She's tired from trying to soothe him, and I once heard her scolding him for not being a girl.

I'm not trying to sniff out secrets, but a body can overhear everything said through these walls and floor grates. I'm not sure if Miss Ardith is mind-fogged from having a baby, but I even heard her talking one day to a woman it seemed. She said, "Sissy Belle Strunk, you sure got yourself in some sour pickle soup."

There wasn't another person in the room that day. And her voice is strange, a mix of green and orange. I see a chameleon whenever she talks.

She and her husband belong to that secret group called the KKK. Don't know much about them but what we read in the headlines back home. They don't like lots of folks and have been accused of doing awful things to them. Don't see the hatefulness in either the Missus or Mister, but I'll be on guard.

Oliver is so cute! He snuggles in close while *reading* me his books, using his own made-up stories. His dear little voice is buttercup yellow. And he sure talks about Miss Jojo quite a lot, so I know she was good to him. She played ball with him, took him to the park, and put on puppet shows. I won't be any good at that last one. Oliver said she had a baby and it died. Jojo said as much in jail, except that her side of the tale was the Dobbses killed her son. Oliver's little face fell when he said Miss Jojo got so sad she had to go live at the hospital.

What really happened here? Mr. William is very nice, treats me like a regular hired gal, while Miss Ardith acts like she owns me. Which in a way she does through the state of Georgia. But even with her high-society attitude, I can't see either of them killing a baby.

Oliver has picked up on many of my signs. His little hands and fingers moving around warm my heart. But I had to make up some new motions for words I never needed on our mountain. The park, telephone, doorbell, traffic. That's good though.

I touch Oliver on the back. He's playing with some tiny logs and building a house that could be a tiny version of our cabin. I sigh. Gotta push away the loneliness before it takes full hold of me. He watches as I sign, "*The park,*" by putting one arm out to the side and swinging it back and forth. Looks like me holding hands with him as we walk there.

He jumps up and yells, "Hooray!"

Miss Ardith is fine for us to stay away for hours, which allows me time to learn my way round Marietta. Today, I'm stopping at the post office. I still have the stamp from the postcard I was going to send Briar before I got arrested. I've taken an envelope from Miss Ardith's desk, but I use my own paper to write home.

I let Poppy and Ruthy know I'm working for two months near Atlanta, then I'll be home. Just in time for my sister's wedding. I say I want to make money to help pay for new britches for Billy Leo and a new shirt for Poppy. That I saw Briar and he's a working man Poppy would be proud of, and he might get home when he has time off work. No way I can tell all that's really happened. Two children leave the mountain and end up arrested.

I end with *Give Jacca a good rubdown for me. I miss you all.*

I want to write to Briar but have no idea how to reach him. Sheriff Withington would know. But would he tell me how to exchange mail with my brother? The sheriff's wife was here just an hour ago, but Miss Ardith told me to take Oliver and stay out of sight. Except for answering the door, I never got a chance to slip a note to Mrs. Withington. Anyhow, it felt too, um, *brash*. Like that word! And I don't want to get on the wrong side of Miss Ardith. I've already learned there are terrible places where I could be serving my time.

One of her woman friends that stopped by late looked like she's about give up on ever finding a happy moment again. She wasn't dressed all fancy like the first two. She yelled angry words as she left with the others. The two fancy women whispered to each other, wondering what all the ruckus was about.

For now, the feeling of the wind in my hair and grass under my feet is welcome on a hot day like this. Time to chase Oliver around the park. First we're birds, then bumblebees. His sweet giggle is music to my ears. I remember doing about the same with Billy Leo when he was young. Now when I'm with Oliver, I set my worries aside. They're loyal, even though I don't like them, so they'll be waiting for me on the walk back.

The boots and new dress Miss Ardith have me gussied up in aren't the most comfortable. The boots button up the front and are prettier than a speckled pup but are too snug. This blue cotton dress is below my knees and has a tie at the waist. And these white frills outlining the bodice and hem? Whoever made this must not have minded the scratchy nature of lace, but I sure do. Miss Ardith has a huge trunk full of new clothes, shoes, and items for the house. I guess being married to an advertising man, she gets all these things sent to her.

I left my riding dress outside my little room like Miss Ardith said. Supposed it was being washed until I found burned scraps of it in the outside burn barrel. I choked back tears at that moment. Miss Ardith is too rich to understand how much work Mama put into stitching a split skirt dress for me to ride Jacca nice and proper.

Oliver and I pass the depot where a train is pulling away. Riders can travel nearabout every which way from here, according to the map on the wall. I think of pretty Miss Burns saying I can do anything I set my mind to. Over the past day, I've imagined teaching at that deaf school I just learned about from the preacher's wife. Children learning new ideas are a delight, their faces full of bliss and wonderment as they study how to get their stuck ideas out through hand signs. I know what that's like.

But my calling will be living on Stewart Mountain, taking over all of Mama's duties.

Back at the Dobbses' house, a neighbor lady has dropped off food for supper.

Miss Ardith is patting Baby Boy as Mr. William comes through a back door. I truly like his fancy car. He parks it in the driveway aside the house.

"Who brought the food this time?" he says, not looking up from the stack of mail he starts sorting through. He's dressed in a crisp white shirt, dark gray suit, and black shiny shoes. A fully grown-up copy of Oliver.

"Margaret Howard. She has that cute hat shop on Main," Miss Ardith says.

Oliver brightens at seeing his father. Quite the opposite around his mother. She need only give him a certain look of displeasure, and he becomes as silent as a gravestone. Almost like someone snatched his little soul out and hung it up until it was safe to come out again.

I help put the food on the table. They have me seated across from Oliver. Mr. William offers a prayer of grace, blessing the food and asking for the health of his family. I add on to the prayer and include my family with his thoughts.

The food is especially delicious. Parsnip and celery root soup comes first with warm bread and butter, then roasted chicken. Much higher on the hog than we Stewarts need to eat.

Anyway, the final serving is butterscotch pudding, a sweet I've never had the occasion to enjoy before. I have an English voice inside my head, speaking all hoity-toity. Yes. Butterscotch—a most delightful taste.

Mr. William asks Miss Ardith about her day. He has gray eyes and thick dark hair. When he talks, he shows more top teeth, reminding me of Jacca when he gets to talking in his horsey chit-chatter. A pang of regret for sending him home alone tightens my chest. Had he made it in fine shape?

"Teresa and Nancy came by, the dears," Ardith says. "Brought the flowers and baby clothes."

Didn't mention the other harried woman who also come knocking. I wait for her to say more, but she keeps a smile on her face intended for her husband.

"That was nice." Mr. William wipes his mouth on a napkin. "Is he eating any better now?"

"Still fussy," Miss Ardith says. "I would like to take him to Doctor Grange tomorrow."

"Are you that worried?" Mr. William sets his fork on his plate. "And tomorrow, the boys and I have a big rally in Atlanta with the Odd Fellows."

"Oh, that's right." She lets out a heavy sigh. "I guess a few more uncomfortable days for the baby won't matter."

As if on cue, the baby starts crying in his bassinet in the corner of the room.

"Willow," Miss Ardith says. "Do you mind? His bottle is in the kitchen ready to be warmed."

I push back from the table, pick up the red-faced wailing infant, and head to the kitchen.

At my back, I hear Mr. William ask if she's decided on a name yet.

"I like Karl, but with a K. What do you think, William?"

I don't hear his reply over the baby's cries.

The glass bottle sits in a pan of heated water. It's half full of Borden's Evaporated Milk, half diluted with water. I balance the baby on one arm and check the temperature of the milk by letting a little drip on my wrist. Good. Not too hot.

I settle on the bench seat by the window and feed the baby. Feed *Karl*. It's good the little rascal has a name. His eyes open up—*there you are*—and one tiny hand clutches my little finger. This is what we were all looking forward to with Mama's new baby coming.

The innocence. The sweetness. Watching new life grow.

That's why it's so sad. A pure tiny babe never had a chance. I drop my nose to his warm downy head and inhale. This has to be one of the best smells in the world, and believe me, I have a list of a hundred or so best scents. Violets. Warm bread. Moments right after it rains.

By the time Miss Ardith peeks her head into the kitchen, Karl is asleep. His mouth, every once in a while, puckers to a suck, but he's done for now.

"I'll take him while you clean up." Miss Ardith lifts him from me, and my arms suddenly feel cold and empty. It's almost a pain for a flash of a second.

"If you'll get Oliver in bed, his daddy will read to him. *Again*." Her words were light orange, but they scald like they're red hot. I overheard her complain during one of her talks with herself that nannies need to read to children, saying, "Just my luck to get a broken nanny."

Even though she's a lucky lady sitting in high cotton, she sure enough seems to spend loads of time looking for the bugs in the dirt.

Once I've cleaned up, Oliver follows me to his room.

The bedroom is stuffed with every toy ever advertised. He has a functioning metal crane and a whistle that imitates five bird sounds. There's a painting easel. Building blocks. A train track with a lifelike metal train.

I wouldn't trade my childhood with wooden carved animals or dried husk dolls for any of these toys, although that mini town by the train is the cutest thing I've ever seen. We don't have shiny store-bought niceties, but we know we're cherished. Something sorely lacking in Oliver's mind.

I fold back the fluffy quilt and top sheet, and he hops into bed and slides under the covers. I run the back of my hand along his cheek and smile. Every child needs a goodnight story. I know I most surely counted on Mama's voice lulling me to sleep. A quiver of sadness goes through me like irritable weather. Not only is Mama's voice forever gone, but I'll never read a bedtime story if I'm ever lucky enough to have children.

"Miss Jojo gives me a goodnight kiss even though she's not supposed to because she's a Negro," he whispers.

Good for Miss Jojo. Still surprised she's even considered a Colored person, her skin is so light.

I lean in and kiss him on the forehead and tuck him in tighter.

"You have to turn my table lamp on for when it gets dark." He points to a china lamp with blue and green birds decorating the base.

I search the base for a button or knob but don't find one. Seems like lamps and the lanterns we have back home should be built the same way.

"Plug it into the wall."

I follow the cord down to the prong and push it into the wall socket. The lamp imparts a bluish glow round the bedside table. I sign good night. He giggles and signs the same. Such a smart child.

The house falls quiet.

I tiptoe down the stairs and out the door to my room. Two tiny windows allow for a nice cross-breeze, while a large magnolia tree shades this side of the house.

I change into a long white nightgown folded by the bed. The mattress is so soft I'm afraid it might swallow me up. The room turns from dove gray to charcoal dark as I think about living here for another two months. Miss Ardith is "strange around the eyes," as we would say back home. There's someone inside her she hides from the sight of everyone.

I wish my time working here helped Briar shorten his sentence. The surprise on my relations' faces if he and I came walking home at the same time would brighten everyone's day.

But dreams don't come true because you dreamed them, and wishes can disappear the same way.

The door slowly opens. A tiny ghost sweeps across the room. It's Oliver, my new friend. He climbs up onto the bed, half-asleep, snuggling next to me under the thin cover. Billy Leo and I often shared a bed back home after

Briar left him to sleep alone in their room. This bed is much too empty to have all to myself.

The soft rhythmic rise and fall of his warm body next to mine almost makes me wish morning wouldn't come so fast. The sharp edges of this loneliness are dulled too. I miss my mama. My family.

Next day, I'm in an automobile again. Not so long ago, I couldn't have seen myself shuffling round so much. Oliver is in the front seat, and I'm in the tiny back seat holding the baby.

Miss Ardith has a meeting with some women at an orphanage and needs me to watch the boys. My heart stuttered at first when I heard the word orphanage. Is this a way for her to trick me into riding along and she'll leave me there? She was none too happy this morning when she come to wake me up to fix breakfast and discovered Oliver in my bed.

"We do not allow our children to sleep out here." Her mouth was tight. "He could be bitten by a mouse full of diseases."

I cut my eyes to the corners of the room. Mice? Must not care about *me* getting a disease.

She whopped the sleepy boy in the back of the head as he stumbled past her.

"You know better, Oliver."

What a start to my morning. Anyway, Oliver stands on the seat and turns around to face me as we take turns with a yoyo. Miss Ardith said she wanted only quiet toys in the car to avoid being distracted while she drives.

And I can see why. I've only been driven round by policemen, and maybe they have more training, but she's a wobbly driver, working hard to keep the car on the road. Another automobile honks at her because she's in the middle of the road. My eyes pop nearly out of my head, but I quickly cradle the children, hoping to protect them from a crash.

"Crazy driver!" she calls out after his horn stops blasting.

Thank you, Jesus! Relief sets in when we stop on the side of a large home next to an angel statue, nestled out here all by its lonesome.

The house sits in front of a small cemetery and has land and forest in all directions.

The day is muggy with giant buffaloes of clouds chasing each other, and it's going to be hot waiting in the automobile.

"I won't be but a few minutes," she says as she opens the door and reaches in next to me to grab a baby basket with frilly pink ribbons. "No reason to have you all come in, since the baby is happy for a minute."

Baby Karl is in his carrier, waving his tiny hands around, cooing. But why the other basket? She said her women friends belong to a club that donates to a foundling home, although this doesn't seem like the name she spoke. The tiny sign by the front steps reads Beck Infantorium. Her women's group supports a place with the word *hope* in it. And carrying just one basket all the way out here, when she said she was taking Karl to the doctor? To me, this is a waste of time.

"I have to wee," Oliver says, squeezing the front of his britches.

I nod. It's a right long way back to Marietta, and who knows how far to the doctor's office.

The left side of the house has a row of bushes overhung with a huge tree. It's dark and shady and offers a bit of privacy.

I scoop up Karl and take Oliver by the hand. We cross the lawn. As we draw closer, babies' wails come from inside the house. Good Lord. Is no one tending to the poor dears?

I leave Oliver peeing near a bush but keep walking alongside the house. A window is open to an office. I stay shy of it when I hear Miss Ardith's voice.

"Then give me one you have. I need a girl that's a two months old, with brown hair. Her mother won't know. Babies change so fast."

"It will cost you thirty-five dollars," a woman says, her voice a rotten apple color.

Miss Ardith is buying a baby girl? Who buys babies? And she's giving it to a mama who must've lost a different one. This seems so wrong. It *is* wrong!

"I have the money here." She pauses then tssks. "How can you stand all of this crying?"

"After a while, you only hear the ones that need your attention. I'll get you the girl."

Heavy footsteps leave the room and move farther into the house.

Curious, I duck under the window and move closer to the back-porch area. I pray Karl doesn't start a-wailing himself. I reach a wheelbarrow parked next to an icehouse with the door open. I start to peer inside but recoil like I'm snakebit.

On top of the ice are a half dozen dead babies!

I swallow hard and look again. Some are naked and some still have a tiny diaper, but they're all blue, their tiny faces frozen, some with eyes open.

This is more horrible than anything my imagination could ever create.

How could all these babies die in one home?

I fight to keep from upchucking. Oliver is walking my way, and I quickly hold my finger to my lips to signal him not to say anything. I turn him around, and we hurry back to the car and climb in.

I'm cold and sweaty all at the same time. My heart is galloping faster than Jacca ever dreamed of.

"You look sick," Oliver says. "Oh. Your eyes are running side to side."

I shake away the dizziness. Have to act like I didn't see that horrible sight by the time Miss Ardith returns. I pat Oliver's hand and nod.

"This is the place where we brought the wrong baby." He's jumping on the front seat, something he knows he can't do once his mother gets back here.

I sign, *"What baby?"*

"The day Miss Jojo's baby died. The doctor brought her a baby that looked a lot like me. Mommy said it was the wrong baby, so we came to this angel house. I got to hold him on the way here, but I don't remember going home. She gives me medicine to make me strong, but I get so sleepy."

This new story is almost as horrifying as what I just saw behind the house. Because if I'm understanding Oliver, Miss Jojo delivered a white baby boy that looked like him, and Miss Ardith brought it here.

And by the looks and sounds of things, that poor dear is probably crying his little head off.

Or dead.

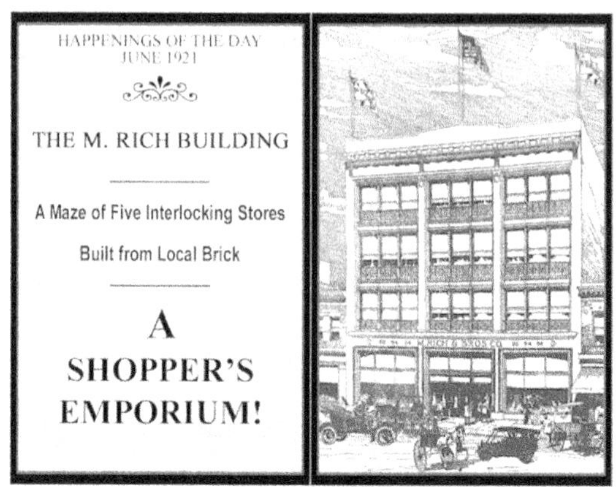

Chattahoochee Brick Company
near Atlanta, Georgia. June 1921

-29-

Briar Stewart

My mind's worn to a frazzle trying to figure out how I can get out of here. I'm plumb tuckered out, with about as much life left in me as a mashed squirrel. There's no way I'll be alive in a month let alone a year. Perhaps not even a week. Maybe that's their plan.

Today, I'm out in the clay pits. These are the messiest and hardest chores. We switch jobs every hour, from digging and dropping the earth into the mixing pans, to molding the clay by hand and forcing it into the rectangular mold. The digging blisters your hands and pains your arms and back. But filling in all the corners of the mold by pressing the clay with my fingers leaves my hands cramped and fingers nearly frozen in pain. After I drag the wooden strike ’cross the mold to remove excess clay, I leave the greeny on the ground to dry.

Been rotated through other jobs these last few days. Putting the dried greenies into the six-foot-long kilns, removing the baked bricks, or hauling them to the storage yard. None of the work’s easy. Dangit, I sure miss the scent of pines and fresh mountain air. Now my nose is clogged with dust, smoke, and the smell of sweaty men. And I got my own stink.

The warden set the quota of 140,000 bricks a day to be delivered to the kiln for drying. If’n we don’t make the daily quota, someone’s always crying out from the bite of the whip later that night.

Yesterday, I was on the kilns near sunset when the boss man yelled, “Lay ’em down.” Two trustees dropped off three dead guys. Dumped like yesterday’s washin’. I asked what was going on, and they told me to shut my yap.

When I fell in step next to a feller I got to know as Rambling Joe, he said burning the bodies is easier than digging a grave.

“How they account for no worker, no grave?”

“This whole system works best with all their bad bookkeeping. Fellers are often dropped off who didn’t pass through no court.”

Again, how can this be legal?

“Bet them folks working in the brick buildings in Atlanta don’t realize they’re surrounded by ashes and bits of people who died making blocks to build their walls.” He chuckles. “I hope they hear moans and groans at night.”

Now that he put it thataway, I hope they do too.

We’re herded back to camp housing, not so much a march as slow, shuffling feet. I meet the stare of a young feller walking next to me. Been beat up real bad, like he been sorting bobcats all night. His stare is half fear, half bewilderment.

Must be new to the chain gang business.

I recollect that feeling. When first arrested, seemed like every hour that passed came with a worse happening, one after the other. Disbelief was my only steady thought.

I nod. The feller nods back. It’s a connection. A silent vow. The saying “misery loves company” ain’t never been truer.

Back on my cot that evening, my mind turns to Ilya and Cy. I'm responsible for what's become of them two. If'n only I hadn't tried to help and just given 'em vittles or money and shooed 'em away, the young'un wouldn't be stuck in a cave while the other is slaving in the pine forest.

Taggert might kill Ilya just for having an accent. He got that much hate in him.

I roll on my side and whisper to Rambling Joe in the next cot.

"Ever heard tell of a soul escaping?"

"Some do." He squints my way. "But you better have a damn good plan. A man will die from sixty or seventy lashes from that bullwhip. And that's the price for a failed escape. Get some sleep, kid. Tomorrow's troubles roll in fast enough."

This here mixing of moaning 'n groaning men might well could be the hell I done read about in Revelations. Dying here ain't an option. Neither is working for a year or buying my way out. Heard the judge can be bought. But five hundred dollars? More money than I'll ever see.

That leaves *bugging out.*

Yep. A plan's forming in my mind, but my insides, they're wound tighter than rope around a well bucket. I'll never fall to sleep this strung out. I need to relax.

Pictures in my mind of my younger days always calm me. I page through those years, starting back to when I was ten. That'd make Willow five, and Billy Leo couldn't have been more than two. He was still stumbling and trying to get his mountain footing. We tried to playact Moses floating in a basket, using baby Billy Leo and close-by Ramson Crick. We got a sound scolding when we got back to the cabin with a broken wash basket and a sopping wet baby.

Other special memories show up. Playing Hide and Seek or Avoid the Shadow at dusk. Shade stretching from the boulders and trees became spooky shadows reaching toward us as the sun dropped behind the mountain. We chased each other, trying to make the other one be the first to step on a growing shadow. The daytime fun? Fishing a crick, watching snake doctors—townsfolk calls 'em dragonflies—walk on water, and catching pollywogs. Those were amusement enough.

I'll be satisfied knowing Willow gets home safe. She told me with her signs that Pa forgave me. I liked hearing that. And I'd sure like to see the homestead again. To hug Mama and the rest of my family. Not sure I'd stay forever, but a reunion would sit right with me after being away from my kin the past fifteen months.

Because it's Sunday, we got the afternoon off. I ain't sleeping like most the men, but lying down for a spell to rest is good enough. I still can't shake the idea that escape shouldn't be that hard. We ain't shackled and chained like in the quarry. If'n I can get to the thick of the forest, I could disappear. Know I can't outrun a coon dog but can sure outsmart one. At least that's what my mind's telling me.

Monday's the day, if'n there's any day at all, when a feller is rested and could flee. But where would I go? Leading the bounty hunters back to Stewart Mountain is a terrible idea. Another awful idea would be trying to see Willow to say goodbye. Marietta ain't that far from where I sit now, but they know she and me are related, and they'd look there. Would they add to her work sentence because of me? The thought leaves a bad taste at the back of my tongue, almost bringing on a choke.

I've lost all trust in the judges and laws.

But if I escape, I'd be on the lam forever. I read that the new Federal Bureau of Investigation don't give up, like foxes in a henhouse. They nosed out a chain-gang escapee four years after he'd got to Chicago and turned himself into a well-off working man. Back to busting rocks with the snap of a finger.

I'd be looking over my shoulder forever once I'm out.

But I need to right some wrongs. No way I can bring back Luther Junior. One day, God will sort that out. But Ilya and his poor brother. If'n I get out of here, the cave is my destination. No one knows I got a connection to it.

Okay, so I get the young'un out of there and into an orphanage. 'Course I'll have to figure out how to let Ilya know where to find his brother when his time is done working the turpentine camp. Didn't Taggert say a few weeks?

The Bible says, "And whatever you do, in word or deed, do everything in the name of the Lord Jesus."

Got a heap needs doing, and I surely will be calling out His name.

The guards skip the whippings on account of it's the Sabbath. After the same old supper, the mood is lighter in the long shack. More men talking. A few whistling mindless tunes. With no place to sit, we all take to our cots.

My innards rumble. I've made up my mind. Gonna leave tomorrow, but I need a helper. Only really talked to one guy more than any other. Rambling Joe, one got pegged for being seen holding hands with a Colored gal. 'Course he'd have been hung if'n their skin colors had been the other way round. He's done a year in prison, and his time's almost up.

I turn to my side to face Rambling Joe. "You sleep?" I say quietlike.

"Naw." His eyes stay shut. "Whatcha need?"

"Tomorrow when we're near the woods…" Am I asking the right feller? What if he don't want to help and word gets out 'bout my plan?

"What about it?" One eye cracks open, slow like a lizard sunning himself.

"I need a distraction."

"You bugging out?"

"Gonna try." I lower my voice more. "I got thirty dollars for you if you'll help."

That eye closes again. He ain't gonna help. Think I just put myself in more danger.

Seconds tick by before he slowly sits up and places his palms on his legs, leaning forward. A tiny smile grows on his lips.

"Tell me what you're thinking. I'll tell you if I think you're a dead man or not."

I push myself up to a sitting position, our heads no more than inches apart. I explain my plan and how he can find my money in the cave.

He pulls out a secret picture of his gal. I draw a quick map on the back of it. No names of places. Just lines joining dots of towns around. I tell him the names on the cave walls carved above the hidey-hole.

"It's a deal." He nods. "Could use some excitement round here. The shine done wore off this place a long time ago. And if you don't make it"—he cracks a half smile—"the money is still mine."

"It sure is."

Sleep is slipperier than an armload of eels. All night I stare at the bare wood ceiling, watching the moon move past the cracks as it travels the sky's limit. A full moon will make my night travel riskier, but I've made up my mind.

Rambling Joe and me don't say no words to each other. He just gives me a nod when we finish breakfast and head to the clay pits. The plan is to wait till after dinner when the guards are belly-full and fight to keep their eyes open.

The "All back" from dinner call comes, and we move back to our work-places. Digging clay, I stay on the outskirts of the mud fields but not so far away that it draws attention. Working hard and not resting is what the guards watch out for.

I lift my head to see Rambling Joe looking my way. He's smiling.

It's time. My heart bangs a beat. In the next few minutes, I'll be free—or dead.

Rambling Joe grabs his stomach then latches on to a guard nearby, screaming he's been poisoned. The guard tries to peel him off and yells at him to let go or he'll bust his head.

Joe throws up right on cue, slopping as many fellers as he can, hoping to catch more guards than workers. Well, that worked out better than we talked about.

The guard near me runs to the ruckus, and I dive into a near bush. I take the shovel with me so's not to leave it lying around, like a message on the open ground. I drop it in the brush and run like a duck, low and waddling toward taller, wider shrubs and the trees. No one seems to be yelling about me missing, so I stand and take off like the devil himself is at my back. I push away branches, scramble over fallen logs, aiming for the deeper woods. If'n I can get a good piece in front of them before they notice I'm gone, I got a chance.

Ain't a doubt in my mind. The coonhounds will be coming.

I cross a stream, the splashing echoing through the trees. I head northwest. If my recollecting is correct about the Southern Railroad stops, I can catch out in Sparkdale and continue northwest toward Rockmart. Ain't more than about five miles from where I am now, mostly hills and woods between.

Coonhounds start their baying behind me. I *am* missed. Some guards will hit the roads, but the two dogs will stay on my trail with their handler. Never met the feller up close, but heard he was a swamp dweller before being hired. Everybody knows you gotta be mighty tough and wily to survive in the swamp.

The wind's blowing at my back, so I'm downwind for now. I spot a field through the trees. I scan the area for buildings and see nary a one before moving into the open. Need to find some rabbit tobacco. It doesn't take long before I have two handfuls of the green leaves and flowers, and I hotfoot it back to the trees.

I strip out of my stripes and tie the shirt to one branch and the britches to another.

Left near naked 'cept for my underdrawers, I crush the plant parts, releasing the sweet, fragrant smell Pa and I always used to mask our scent while hunting deer. I rub it all over myself and stuff the rest in my boots. Sure hope it works the same for hunting dogs as it does for deer.

The hounds sound closer now. I take off running again, sighting moss on the north side of the trees to keep my direction. In front of me, a wide crick, maybe twenty feet across, bumps and splashes its way down a rocky riverbed.

I wade into the middle, where the cold water reaches my thighs. The force of the water and the slick rocky bottom conspire to knock me off my feet, but I prevail. Ahead, a tangle of tree roots and boulders strain most of the river, and I'm forced to leave the rushing waters and continue along the bank.

Somewhere behind me, the hounds must've found my clothes. They're crying like it's the end of the world.

My legs are about to give out, and I'm sucking air like broken bellows, but I push on.

I shove away the joy rising in me. Way too early to celebrate. Once on the train and heading north, I might try cracking a smile. A puny one.

The dogs' howling drops away. Hopefully, confounded by the loss of my scent. If the rabbit tobacco didn't do it, running up the middle of a wide river did.

But up ahead lie the roads, the truly dangerous part.

I weave through the trees, slapping away underbrush and jumping over rotting logs. Daresn't slow down. I can rest when I'm a free fellow.

Yonder, a train whistle blows. I come out near the back of a farm. As much as I hate to break the law, I need me some clothes. Coveralls and shirts aplenty flap from the clothesline strung between two poles in the center of the yard. The yellow house is on the other side, and I'm hidden from sight behind bedsheets.

I slip the wooden pins off some brown britches and a too big olive-green shirt, then rush back to the trees and put 'em on.

I reset my direction and run faster toward the sound. It may not completely stop, but I can catch it on the fly. Least I could nine months ago.

Blood pounds in my ears. Fellers get themselves killed all the time trying to board a moving train. Or their legs get cut off.

I break out of the bushes near the railway tracks. Not far off is a small depot and crowded platform. Steel wheels scream as the big smoking engine roars round the bend. The ground vibrates, pushing excitement through my feet up into my chest. It's a freight hauler, the best kind. Hot sparks flit from the wheels, and the smell of heated oil fills the air. The train slows and fifteen boxcars clack, knock, and groan. The engineer slows with a great *whoosh* of steam.

I dash from the trees, headed for a car. It's all a rusty blur, but I jump and seize the hot metal rung with my right hand. The movement of the train whacks me against the ladder, but I finally grip the rod with my other. I pull myself up and lay flat against the ladder, breathing hard, fear twisting through me.

Once steady, I get a foot on the rung and begin climbing.

The conductor blows the whistle again, and the train picks up speed. I hurry to the top, where I can't get ripped off by tree branches. I hold tight to the big metal beast and climb to the catwalk. I lay flat where none will notice and let out a big breath and smile at the world flying by.

The soot-belching monster shoots forward, wailing at each crossing, rattling my nerves. Eventually, I raise my head to watch the train slither along the tracks, a monstrous black snake carrying me to freedom.

I brace myself for the upcoming curves. Seen a man thrown clean off the top near Lincoln. Landed as a twisted-up mess on the other set of tracks. Tunnels is another worry, but I don't plan on sitting up. My hair's all wind-tangled and full of cinders. It's hard to stay out of the way of the long gray tail of smoke the engine stack throws over its head toward me.

Never did get myself a hobo name. What should I be called? Once thought Georgia Boy might make me a good enough name, but soon enough I'll be needing plenty of disconnect from my home state.

I try to enjoy the blur of greens, the brushstroke of farms, lakes, and hills over yonder. Young'uns along dirt roads wave at the freight train. There's only the train workers and me to wave back. I don't oblige.

The train should pass by three depots before the Brushy Mountain Tunnel. I need to slide off when the train slows for Rockmart. From there, can't be more than a fourteen-mile walk to Euharlee. Then yonder to the cave.

I drop my ear to the fearsome beast and hear the power of this metal machine, fitted together with bars and bolts and springs and wires. Obedient cars happily trailing behind. My eyes burn, and the taste of nasty thick smoke coats my tongue. But it's hard not to be pleased and a mite amazed I actually made my escape.

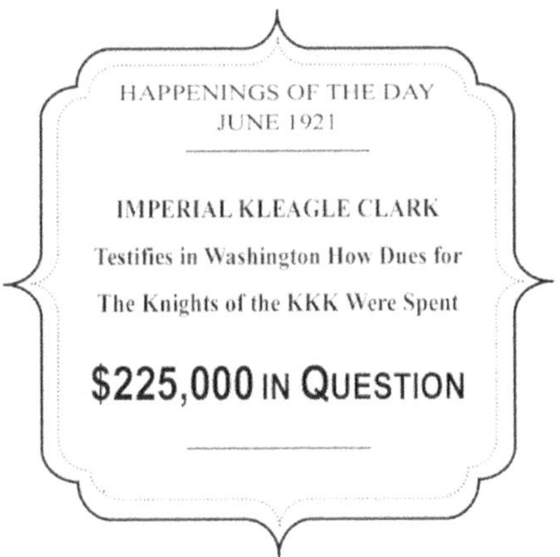
HAPPENINGS OF THE DAY
JUNE 1921

IMPERIAL KLEAGLE CLARK
Testifies in Washington How Dues for
The Knights of the KKK Were Spent

$225,000 IN QUESTION

Marietta Georgia. June 1921

-30-

ARDITH DOBBS

Supper is over, and William and I are home sitting under our magnolia tree. Oliver is playing with a new wooden airplane, and Baby Karl is asleep on my shoulder.

"I haven't talked to Teresa yet, but do you think Frank would help me fight the Legal Aid Society?" He's enjoying a pipe, a new activity he's taken up. The rich cherry tobacco aroma circles and swirls on a light breeze.

"Fight what?" He squints against the smoke as he turns his gray eyes my way.

"A woman and her husband are making trouble. The Elsmores." I shoot him my most innocent look. "Said they're going to the Legal Aid Society to get a free lawyer."

"Whatever are you talking about?" He sits up straighter and turns his wicker chair to face me. "Why do they need a lawyer?"

"Fiona Elsmore is on our charity list. Last I visited her, she said she'd been abandoned by Roy. She practically shoved the baby girl in my car and begged me to find a better home. The adoption place I took the baby to had already found a new placement by the time I went back two days ago."

"You went to the doctor that day, I thought."

He sets his lips in a line I recognize as forced patience. I've seen him use it at the office when workers ruin an ad copy.

"*Before* the doctor visit." This is a lie of course. I drove the baby to the Elsmores' place. Roy wouldn't have known the difference, and he was full of smiles and coos for the little one. The boys danced around and tried to hold their sister. Replacement sister. But Fiona, she went right out of her mind when she picked up the little girl.

All my insistence that this was their daughter couldn't calm her, and I drove away with shouts and curses trailing behind the car.

"The Legal Aid place called this morning, on a Sabbath of all days. Can you imagine?" Incredible how some people disrespect Christian values, like keeping the day holy. "I'm not worried at all, but the man said he'd be filing charges against me."

"Charges?" His mouth opens and closes twice. "If you were securing an adoption for them, what are they charging you with?"

"Using my membership in the Klan to garner favor." I circle one hand in the air to express *what a silly accusation.*

"I still don't get it." He tamps his pipe out in the glass ashtray on the table between us.

"To garner favor so I could take her money and her baby." I pat Karl's back, even though he's not awake. It soothes me too. "I feel sorry for her. She gave me the ten dollars she was saving toward our club dues to find a good home for that little girl. And she was a sick one too. All covered with impetigo blisters, sores."

William stares at his clasped hands, his arms on his knees. He's quiet. Thinking. He'll have a solution. It's what he does. He's a problem-solver.

"When was this?"

"Before Josephine had her baby. She was here cleaning while I had Oliver with me running errands."

"I remember. The day you put all those miles on the car."

This isn't good. I told him we went for a ride in the country to see the wildflowers in bloom. I nod.

He rubs his temples and closes his eyes. "And you took Oliver."

"You know I love having him around."

"No, Ardith. I don't know that, and right now I'm not even sure I know *you.*" He stands and shoves his hands in his pockets. "Going to call Frank and try to sort this out." He turns around, stops, then glares at me with a slight squint. "Is there anything else I should know about this?"

I can't tell him about the Beck Infantorium. If Frank Greer ever went there to check out my story, it might get out that the sisters knew me from years ago. *Those* are stories William can never hear. I smile and shake my head. "Thanks, hon."

I stare across the yard full of flowering gardenia and lilac bushes edged with beds of orange marigolds and red geraniums. Josephine planted them in such perfect arrangements, once I brought them home from the greenhouse. What must her life be like now at the lunatic home?

William is just short-tempered because Karl cries through most of the night. If only Josephine had accepted our story about her baby. She could be living in this wonderful house, with food aplenty and two darling children to tend to. She's a natural at mothering. Maybe the doctor went too far operating so she can never have another baby. I don't know. One day, she might have wanted to marry one of her own kind and start a family. It's all so sad she lost her mind.

Karl is awake and staring at me with these brown eyes. I can't see hide nor hair of William in him. He favors my pa, just less wrinkly, with no chin whiskers. Pa. He always smelled like the coal dust from the railroad, no matter how much he washed. That fire knocker job seeped into his skin—and eventually into his soul.

I sniff Karl's head. He smells milky sweet.

"Oliver. Time for your bath."

The boy skips over to the porch and climbs the steps. He's always so happy. He'll be a good influence on Karl.

"Willow should be done with the dishes by now. Go find her to get ready for bed."

Oliver points. "She's right there, Mommy."

I turn, and there she is, standing just inside the parlor, looking out at us.

How long has she been there? Did she hear what I told William? The windows are open to allow the fresh air inside. She knows I'm lying if she did hear. I'll have to talk to her about snooping. Of course, I'm not worried. Not really. That dumb gal can flap her hands around all day and try to tell what she saw at the Elsmores' shack. No one will understand her.

Thank goodness she was never schooled much in reading and writing.

Next morning, I'm enjoying a cup of tea and reading through the *Atlanta Constitution's* society section while Karl sleeps in his crib next to me. When I get rid of my baby bump, I'm going shopping to buy some of the styles the women pictured in the party photographs are wearing. I went from rags to riches by mimicking what I saw in newspapers and by watching women on the streets. I listened to conversations and practiced them as I rode behind genteel ladies on trolleys. Made myself worthy for any gentleman of distinction.

Pushed Sissy Belle Strunk and Hickory Nut Hollow deep down. The new me was born.

There's a knock on the front door. William is off to work, and Willow's taken Oliver for a walk. Who in the world is disrupting my free time now? The milkman knows to leave the bottles in the shady part of the porch. The coalman drives to the side of the house and unloads into the coal chute leading to the basement. Might be the bootblack always chatting with Josephine when she's out sweeping. He doesn't know she's gone. She took a new job is the easiest answer, I suppose.

I open the door with that answer on my lips, but startle to see Teresa and Nancy standing there.

"Hello, ladies." I step back to let them in. What are they doing here unannounced? "Such a nice surprise."

The women don't say anything, just take chairs across from the sofa in the parlor.

"How's the baby doing?" Teresa says.

"He's still fussy, but overall is settling down some." I tip my head to the side and smile. How nice of them to come by even if they arrive empty-handed this time.

"Good. The first few weeks are the hardest." Nancy's eyebrows look knit together as she studies me. "We need to ask you a few questions, Ardith. Frank told Teresa about the Elsmore baby."

"Oh, that dust-up." I wave the idea away and chuckle. "We try to help the less fortunate and this is what happens."

"Where did you take their baby?" Teresa just looks confused, not angry. "We called the New Hope Charity Home, and they didn't have a visit from you."

Well, great day in the dadburn morning! I didn't expect the ladies to get involved. Should Frank share legal issues with Teresa even though she's his wife? Doesn't he take a vow or something to keep folks' secrets to himself?

"That sweet baby was so sick," I say. "There's a specialty house, a little-known place that once in a while handles hard-to-adopt babies."

"What's the name?" Nancy's smile is tight.

Never seen her angry before. Heat rises in my chest, and I place a hand on my neck as if I can hide the color that must be blooming there.

"Oh, they aren't registered, I don't think. Just two good-hearted sisters trying to help a few sickly babies get a new home."

"The Elsmores say you brought a baby girl to them on Saturday that wasn't theirs." Teresa adjusts her pale blue satin skirt around her calves and crosses her ankles. "Frank said this is the part that's so confusing."

"You all know what it's like to have a baby," I say. "You're half out of your head for weeks, if not months. Fiona was so upset. The poor dear said Roy had killed himself, and she was left with no way to care for the ill baby." I slowly shake my head. "I really don't think she had time to recognize her daughter before she handed her to me."

Nancy draws in a long breath. Obviously thinking.

I'm sweating under my dress. My day is ruined, and it started out so peaceful.

"The Legal Aid Society is bringing the Women's Klan into this," Teresa says. "That's the problem, Ardith."

"With all the good we do in the community," Nancy adds, "this could become a black mark on our unblemished reputation."

"I'm sure the lawyers will find that I did nothing wrong. I do feel sorry for Fiona and Roy." I stand because I want this conversation to end. "I need to feed Karl, if you will excuse me."

"Of course," Teresa says. "But one more thing. We have replaced you as Klabee. Clara Blair will take over as treasurer. Would you mind grabbing the logbook before we leave?"

I throw my hand to my chest. "Whatever for? I do a fine job of accounting for the new members." I've borrowed about $150 from the account now. Need to get that back in there as planned.

"It's a rule from the Grand Dragon"—Nancy stands—"after a higher-up Kleagle got in trouble over two hundred twenty-five thousand dollars in dues and where he spent it. Separate duties from now on."

This day has gone all sideways all because Fiona wouldn't accept a perfectly healthy baby in return for her sick one.

I climb the stairs to my study, which is no easy task with this baby weight still clinging to me. My locked desk holds all my personal papers and the WKKK books. I slide out the leatherbound treasurer's log. Several newspaper clippings fall to the floor.

These are stories from seven years ago. From Hickory Nut Hollow. Probably should've thrown them away, but they remind me of how fortunate I've become.

I slip them back in and open the Klan log. I'm confident I've been careful not to add in all the cash deposits I've received. They won't be missed that way.

My blood's boiling. How dare they! Taking this job away from me because some dishonest man did something illegal with the funds. But I don't feel I can argue since the decree came from the top of the organization. And if it softens my lady friends' attitude toward me, that will be a relief. Even though I belong to a huge organization, I have so few close friends.

"Here you go." I hand Nancy the books. "If Clara has any questions, have her come by. I truly look forward to meeting her."

"I'll let you know if Frank needs to talk to you," Teresa says. "He's trying to make this go away as soon as possible so it never reaches the courts."

That's a relief. "Thank you." I walk them to the door and sag against it as soon as I close it behind them.

It will be my word against Fiona's. I would think and hope the wife of a prominent businessman would be believed over some dirt-poor woman.

I didn't dare ask what the Elsmores did with the new baby girl I brought to them. There would be another round of confusion if Fiona tried to return the babe to the New Hope Charity Home. The home would tell her the little girl didn't come from them.

Maybe money would keep Fiona and Roy quiet. But how much? With my inability to borrow from the dues, I have just seventy dollars stashed away. William gives me money for the groceries and to pay bills, but I can't very well ask him for a large amount.

Baby Karl lets out a squall. It's that time again. Back in the living room, I get him settled against me and reach for my tea.

It's gone cold.

Tears prick my eyes.

My friendships with Teresa and Nancy feel like they're cooling off. I've worked hard to belong in the upper levels of society. Too hard to fall from grace now over a ridiculous misunderstanding.

I vow to make this all better. What choice do I have?

I'm not sure how, but I *will* come up with a plan. I always have.

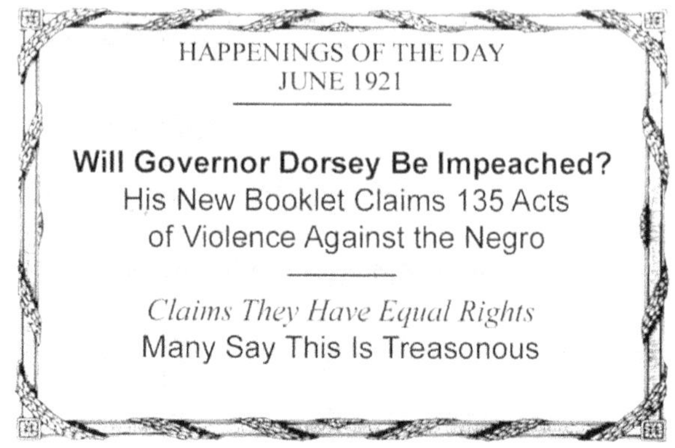
HAPPENINGS OF THE DAY
JUNE 1921

Will Governor Dorsey Be Impeached?
His New Booklet Claims 135 Acts of Violence Against the Negro

Claims They Have Equal Rights
Many Say This Is Treasonous

Marietta, Georgia. June 1921

31

Willow Stewart

Oliver and I return through the side door into the kitchen as Miss Ardith's lady friends leave through the front. I can hardly meet her gaze since we came back two days ago from the big house by the cemetery. All those dead babies. Someone needs to know about that.

And Miss Ardith didn't tell her husband about that baby girl she took from the house with the angel out front. Made him think the baby was adopted outright and proper. The woman and man in that run-down house, waiting to get their girl babe back, knew right off it wasn't their child. They were *both* yelling hateful things at the car as Miss Ardith sped away. I covered Oliver's ears to block out the ribbons of cuss words that trailed behind us.

Still, I have Miss Alice Burns's card with her address. She told me I could ask her for legal help. Not for me, but for poor Missus Elsmore. And Miss Burns's lawyer boyfriend in St. Louis might like to know what happens with those girls at Miss Lily's Threads & Things. Maybe she'll even know some way to help Briar.

When I sign that he can have molasses cookies and a cool glass of milk, Oliver climbs onto his chair at the table. I leave him there so I can hunt up Miss Ardith. She's feeding the baby in the front room, staring out the window at nothing, it seems, and doesn't notice me. Here's my chance to grab another envelope and a stamp while she's occupied.

The fact she believes I can't write is a mighty good thing.

Her office is at the top of the stairs. Her desk is a pretty piece with open areas to store things along the top. Reminds me of the inside of a beehive. I take an envelope and decide I might need two, so I grab another. I carefully tear out two stamps from the pretty little booklet they come in. She has five booklets and I take from the bottom one in the stack. I'll be long gone before she gets to that one. She can wonder her evil head off about where they went.

And do I worry about being a thief? The thought flashes through my mind like heat lightning cuts a summer sky. Noticeable, but not going to amount to anything. I accept I'm stealing from her, and although that's wrong, I reckon it's for a good purpose. Folks need to know about that bad infantorium. What does that name even mean anyway? That angel statue out in front is blasphemous, for all that's going on inside those walls.

As I'm about to leave, I notice the main desk drawer is open a smidge. I can't help my nosey thoughts since I saw Miss Ardith lock this drawer up tight just yesterday. I pull it fully open. There's a thin leather book atop a layer of old clipped-out newspaper stories.

I reach for the top clipping. It's from the Hickory Nut Hollow *Hog Mountain Herald.*

Preacher Gator Tyre still missing. Body of Clem Strunk washes up along the riverbank. Sissy Belle Strunk sought for questioning.

Why would she have a backwoods story about some missing and dead men? A woman like her wouldn't know anyone out near Hickory Nut Hollow, would she?

I pull out another clipping. Hmm. There's a seventy-dollar reward for information about the missing preacher. That's a load of money. Wonder if he was ever found since the story is seven years past.

The next newspaper snipping stops me cold. The headline reads,

Where is Sissy Belle Strunk?

But it's not the words that stun me. It's the picture below. It's a younger Miss Ardith!

Bats in my hair! Did she kill her kin *and* the preacher? The article hints at her being involved in their misfortune.

My heart's banging round as I drop the articles back in the drawer and leave it barely open. Just as I found it.

My legs shake as I head downstairs. I'm living with a woman who's somehow involved in a killing. After, she made herself from a sow's ear into a silk purse and outsmarted the law. No wonder she had no problem taking the Elsmore baby out to that unholy house to die. And she considers me a criminal?

I carry the envelopes and stamps to my tiny room and hide them under the mattress. Tonight, I'll write letters to Miss Burns. It'll be a long letter with all the sins I've witnessed.

And I need to be careful. Any woman who kills their own kin is missing a heart. I could no more kill my brother than grow wings and fly. And it's clear what she's willing to do when someone isn't kin. Very careful indeed.

Suppertime is a chilly affair. The Missus and Mister are sending looks back and forth as cold as mischief.

"Willow can take the night feedings, William." She makes quick sharp cuts on the chicken breast on her plate. "We both need sleep."

I'm used to people talking about me like I'm not there. Invisible even.

Mr. William stretches his neck, like a turtle reaching for a berry, and cracks it from side to side. "We'll try it a few nights."

Oliver's been in my bed most nights. I just make sure Miss Ardith finds him in his room by daylight. The little babe won't be a problem.

I keep eating like I don't hear. I'm anxious to get my letter-writing done after everyone's gone to bed.

"The, um…problem I talked to Frank about isn't solved yet." Mr. William gives his wife a look that could buckle iron.

"Do you know when it will be?" she says without looking up from her plate.

Now that I know some of her past, it's a marvel to watch how she keeps her face so dead still. She's been hiding secrets for years, like squirrels burying nuts for the harsher days of winter.

And maybe those harsher days are coming her way.

"Frank's trying. It's a bigger issue than you know. The Legal Aid Society is looking for a new cause to champion. And they have big donors, Coca-Cola for one. You've heard me tell how fast *that* company is growing."

"But they give the Klan money too." She dabs at her lips.

"Indirectly, yes. But not if they link the Klan to…um…to these types of doings."

As if I don't know what they're talking about.

I smile across the table at Oliver and mime he should eat more.

"I was raised to think positively, William." She bobs her head. "This will all be straightened out."

We have two sayings back home. If Miss Ardith is from Hickory Nut Hollow, she's probably heard them too. "*A crooked cornstalk can still grow a straight ear.*" That would be about someone who became a changed person for the better. But that's not what's going on here. She's the second saying. "*A stalk can grow straight and true and still be covered with rusty fungus.*"

That's a better fit.

Not long after, I'm sitting on the chair in my room, feeding Baby Karl. He's so sweet. His tiny hand wrapped round my pinky always makes me feel needed, special-like, and he's looking right at me.

Between putting Oliver to bed and Miss Ardith knocking on the door before handing me the baby, I wrote a one-page letter to Miss Burns on a sheet from the notebook she gave me. Not sure what she'll do with the information, but she'll know where to find Sissy Belle Strunk and the Beck Infantorium if she has a mind to.

Will mail it tomorrow when Oliver and I take our walk to the park.

My mind's been warring with what happens to Oliver and Karl if Miss Ardith is arrested. She's not the best of mothers, but not the worst either. Just not an upright person when dealing with everyone else. Mr. William is a good father but works long hours. I could wait and mail the letter after Baby Karl is weaned, but how many more babies will die out at the cruel sisters' house? One babe is one too many.

I startle at a faint tapping on my window. Daylight blinked off thirty minutes ago after the sky blushed deep purple. Who could be here after dark?

I stand and pull the curtain aside a tiny bit. What in tarnation? It's that Josephine looking back at me.

Not so sure if this is a good idea or not, but I motion her inside.

She quietly closes the door behind her. Goodness gracious, she looks chewed up and spit out! Her hair's a wild tangle of curls, and her dress sleeve is ripped.

"Bless your little heart for letting me in." She's breathing hard and her eyes are wide. "I done escaped from that nuthouse."

I grab my notebook and pencil. *Will they come looking for you here?* She's already in enough trouble with threatening to hurt Miss Ardith.

"I left the notion I'm heading to Virginia to be with my mama. Left a map under my bed with a line marking a trail north. I'm here to find out what happened to my baby." Her eyes drop to Karl who's fallen asleep in my arms wrapped in his blue blanket. Her face pinches together. "Miss Ardith gots a boy?"

I nod. This must be a terrible blow to Miss Jojo, as Oliver calls her. I've come to believe what Oliver said about taking the "wrong baby" to the

Beck Infantorium. Miss Ardith, for some ungodly reason, took Jojo's baby out there and brought back a dead one. But why?

"Let me hold him." She reaches out, her eyes pleading.

I hesitate. She wouldn't hurt the child, would she? Revenge is a powerful hate.

Her face softens, and her eyes fill with kindness.

She's such a natural with the babe, holding him like he's the most precious thing in the world.

"I bet Miss Ardith angry she got a boy. She only bought clothes for a little girl baby."

Wasn't here when she had him, I write. *But I heard her talking to him, scolding him for being a boy.*

"She says I has the crazy in me, but I think she crazy all along." She nuzzles her nose against Karl's tiny forehead. "Something ain't right with that white woman."

I'm sorry about your baby.

"I'm going to sneak around to see if I can figure out where she has my babe. Maybe Oliver knows."

He told me where she took him, I think.

"You know where my baby's at?" Her face lights up. Her eyes shine bright in the dimly lit room.

Maybe I shouldn't have brought this up. When I explain the Beck house of death, Jojo is liable to run inside and up the stairs and kill Miss Ardith.

Oliver said something about taking the wrong baby out to a place like a baby depositing home.

"Depositing home? Sounds like a garbage dump." Her face changes. There's hope in it. "You think my boy's still there? I know that dead brown baby they left me with weren't none of mine."

I've seen Miss Ardith take a live baby from the Beck Infantorium. No reason to believe she wouldn't have picked up a dead one from all the ones I spied in the shed and brought it back.

Why would she do this to you? I don't understand what Miss Ardith had against Miss Jojo raising her own child.

Miss Jojo sits on the side of the bed, still cradling Karl.

"I got a story that needs telling to the law, but I don't know who to trust."

I lock the door and move the chair closer to the bed so she can talk without being heard. Don't expect Miss Ardith or Mr. William to come out here this late, but don't want to be surprised.

I know a lady with legal knowledge, and her beau is a lawyer.

"I need to know that lady 'cause I sure been wronged."

Karl starts fussing.

He's not getting enough milk from Miss Ardith. Half hungry all the time.

"You poor dear. I got an answer for that." She unbuttons the top of her dress and soon the baby is latched on and making happy sounds. "I been feeding babies all week to show them I was on my best behavior."

Tell me what happened here. I can't make sense out of the little I heard.

Then Miss Jojo gets her story going, and it's worse than any haunting. Mr. William's brother raped her over and over last summer, but she was too scared to tell because she needed the job. She loved Oliver, and Mr. William treated her fine and dandy. She was so drugged when her baby was born, she didn't wake up for hours. They showed her a dead Colored baby boy, but she knows her baby should look whiter than that. Then it gets worse.

Now she's crying, holding Karl close. Tears drip onto his peach-fuzz head.

The doctor cut out her baby-making parts without her knowing he planned to do that. Said he was saving her life, but he looked like he was forced to lie by Miss Ardith.

No wonder Miss Jojo about lost her mind.

"Miss Ardith is wicked, like I said in jail." She has Karl over her shoulder and is burping him. "I don't think Mr. William know how dark her heart is, Willow."

I don't add what I know about Miss Ardith being Sissy Belle Strunk. This awful tale is enough for one sitting.

I'll help you write your story and mail it to Miss Burns. But where will Miss Jojo go now? If she stays hidden in my room, she can feed Karl, but Oliver pops in most nights. I can't trust him to keep such a big and important secret.

You stay in here. I'll sleep in Oliver's room for tonight. Miss Ardith left me in charge of Karl all night because he's been mighty fussy. I'll come back before everyone wakes.

I hope this works. I might well find myself back at Miss Lily's Threads & Things with no way out this time.

I sneak back into the house and slowly climb the stairs to the hallway. Oliver's room is two doors past his parents' bedroom. Far as I know, they never check on him once he's asleep. She doesn't want him sleeping in my room, but so far she's not stopped him.

Look at him. He's snuggled under the covers. I crawl in behind him and drop my arm over his side, pulling him close, the position he seems to prefer.

"Hi, Willow," he says, all sleepylike.

I give him a quick squeeze. My hello back.

He falls right to sleep, but I lie awake worrying about Jojo. Her coming back to the place that treated her so badly. The Dobbses had the ability to have her locked in an asylum once before. What would they do next if they found her here?

Near Rockmart, GA. June 1921

-32-

Briar Stewart

When the train begins its woeful hootin' before Rockmart, I jump off, even though it's traveling faster than I like. Learned a life-saving lesson first few times I rode. You run with the train after you jump.

My legs shake while I move away from the machine and into a field of weeds and wait for it to disappear out of sight.

I head to a line of trees, running bent over, even though no one seems to be in sight. Once in the lower bushes, I swipe my way into the saplings. A small crick gurgles a path through the center. Good chance to scrub this soot off my face and hands in the clear water, so I squat and get to it. This feels mighty good.

I follow a deer path through the woods and around a swampy area. The smell of rot and briny water fills the air. Gas bubbles rise to the surface for seemingly no good reason. A turtle parts the duckweed as it swims.

The scent of pines floods me with longing.

Walking, I think about home, about hunting coons at night. Before Luther Junior died, Poppy, Luther Junior, and me would head out at dusk. Sometimes Billy Leo would tag along, but we usually left after he fell off to sleep. The bright moon looked to me like it whirled round our heads as we moved through the trees. The air was filled with a smell of the night, of leaf mold, wet bark. Competing crickets and bullfrogs wove a thick background noise.

Sometimes we treed a coon and shot him, but nighttime was more than just shooting those troublesome varmints. Entering the forest after dark was like opening a gate. We'd leave the fuss of women behind and feel the might and main of being a man. How the good Lord made us. Our senses grew bigger in the shadowy belly of the woods.

We breathed more, saw more, and felt more.

The ancient pines whispered as their branches swayed. Their scent floated in the lowering night air.

We are one, they said. *We live inside you.*

Only been out of the pines 'bout a week, but it feels like a month. Glad to be back.

Wonder where the search party is? They might check out the house Willow is assigned to, see if I went there. And I might do that. That way, she'd learn I escaped from the gang. When I don't come home, she can tell what she knows when she gets back to the mountain. Still feel bad she got arrested on account of she was looking for me, but sure glad I got to see her one last time before I head west again.

She really is a pretty thing now. All grown up. I hope an agreeable man can see that her lack of speech ain't no handicap.

I stay to the woods, bypassing small towns and farms. Once I cross Alabama Road, I'm soon waist deep in the Etowah River. The cold water racing past revives me. But the next part of the trip is more worrisome. Getting Cy to a doc in Euharlee.

How far does a police net stretch when they're looking for a man on the run? I ain't that far from County Prison Camp right now. They told that police department for sure. Maybe I should take Cy north to Kingston. Ain't never been seen there.

Pretty soon, I reach the cave and push my way in. The damp stone smell greets me. I make my way down the steep entrance of jumbled rocks. The opening's so large, the light of day reaches in a good long piece.

I call out, "Cy?"

No sounds come back but dripping water. Wings beat the air, and a bird swoops past me and out the opening.

Ilya probably told him don't answer to nobody calling out. But seems since I left the boys here, Cy couldn't forget my voice. I take a candle and light it. Cy ain't used as many as I expected. My heart beats fast, a nuisance in my ears as I try to hear round the thumps. Then I count the days. Nine. He's been here alone *nine* days. If'n pellagra is a starvation disease, the boy should be getting better, not worse.

I sweep the light round the chamber. It's empty.

Only one way to go from here. Deeper into the cave. If the boy went exploring in the darker hollows, he might've fallen down the holes or slides that lead to the underworld, for all I can tell when I searched here.

I reach my stash of money. It's all still here. I owe Rambling Joe thirty dollars, so I take the remaining five and head through a narrow passage. The next chamber is huge and could fit my whole hilltop inside.

There! In a cranny in the wall. "Cy?" I hurry 'cross to the boy.

When I set the candle aside to see his face, my breath leaves me. It's the color of the graying stone round him.

He's given up his ghost. I pull him out of the nook. His eyes are closed, like he just fell asleep. Ain't no sign of harm on him. He just plain died in the cold and dark.

I sink to the ground and fight tears. I made a promise to Ilya to help him and his baby brother. Lord knows I did my best, but I'm still looking at one sinless boy who done nobody no harm and died anyway.

Came to this country hoping for a new start, thinking they'd left starvation and horrors behind. When the boys' kinfolk died, Ilya took over. He tried so hard to get help.

Maybe his mistake was finding me. If he'd gone to an orphanage, he might've gotten work there, even if too old to be cared for. Cy would get medical help, vittles. Most of all, they'd be together.

I throw a loose rock against the far wall. "Dammit! Dammit all to hell!"

What to do now? When Ilya gets out of his sentence in another week or so, he'll come looking for Cy. His brother's body will be a hellish sight by then.

I have to bury the boy before I can leave Georgia. Can set a marker that'll let Ilya know the sad truth when he comes back to the cave. Not much else I can do.

I pick him up. It's a rough walk back through the cave, 'specially the narrow passage where I have to lower Cy from my shoulder and drag him through, all the while carrying the candle. When I reach the chamber with their food, I search through the supplies. There's still some cheese and bread. He musta been too sick to eat. If'n he was in that inner room for a long spell, he would've shivered to death in his last hours.

I swipe the tears from my face. He died alone.

My fault. All my bad doing.

I think I should pack the bread and cheese for my journey. But I leave it. It would just remind me of another person in a cave I didn't protect.

Once outside, I carry him to an area left of the entrance. The cave opening is on a hillside, but there's a patch of flatter ground. I use a rusty old metal bucket to dig in the loose dirt, and I don't stop till I know Cy will rest deep enough not to be bothered by wild critters. His feet won't totally face east, but I figure he'll catch the Resurrection all the same. Can't believe he and all the fellers I seen thrown into open graves or left to rot in the forest won't be ready for Christ's return.

I say they'll be first to hear the trumpets.

I take one last gander at the boy. "I'm so sorry I can't give you a proper funeral, Cy."

He looks so young due to being hungry his whole life. His clothes are worn thin, but I notice something 'bout his pants pocket. One is bumpy with something inside. I reach in and find a half dozen agates, the striped and moss-colored kind.

These ain't precious as gemstones, but womenfolk do wear them in jewelry. They're surely worth something. Ilya should have 'em. These'll help him with something to start over with. A gift from Cy. Maybe that's why the little guy went deeper in the cave. Found one pretty stone and just kept on looking.

I study the area. Where can I leave 'em so Ilya can find them? Out here they'd be stolen. But what if he don't go in the cave at all? Okay, now I'm feeling as useless as tits on a boar trying to help him.

I set the agates aside and take good care as I lower Cy into the grave. Not even a fresh sawn pine box to lay him to rest. My heart feels near breaking. I can't look as I push dirt in the hole and cover him up. I find rocks to lay over the fresh dirt. Need to try to make the area look more natural. To mark his grave, I push in a cross made out of two narrows boards and rusted wire the miners left behind.

With a pointed stone, I scratch *CY* on the board. "I don't even know your last name." On the other one, I scratch *June 1921.*

Like the folks who left a piece of themselves by scratching their names in the cave, Cy now got his own record of having lived.

I gather up the agates.

Only one thing left to do.

On the back trails up to Timberland parts, it hits me that maybe the cutting gang has moved again. Been over a week and they could be anywhere by now. As I get closer, the sun's slipping down the west side of the sky. I push harder. Got to find Ilya before he's locked up for the night.

And this ain't gonna be no sorry-bout-your-brother-here's-some-stones kind of reunion. I'm getting the kid out of here.

The chopping sounds reassure me. Work hasn't stopped for the day. I circle the site like I did as a trustee, figuring out where everyone's working and trying to avoid Taggert at all costs.

If I don't spot Ilya tonight, I'll move off a piece and wait till the break of day.

I spot a couple of new fellers, but most the old gang's still here.

And then, there he is. He's smaller than I recall. Got a black eye and looks as defeated as a June bug stuck on his back with a hungry owl overhead.

My news ain't gonna lighten his load but getting him free will help. We'll hit the road together. No one's keeping him in Georgia now.

I throw a stick at him, keeping my head a peek above a bush. He startles and starts to speak, but I put my finger to my lips and motion him to me.

Closest worker is still chopping, head bent, making a good amount of noise.

I pull Ilya down to a squatting position.

"Ray. You came back." His smile 'bout breaks me in half. He ain't gonna be smiling for long.

"We're leaving," I whisper. "Gotta get you outta here. Stay quiet and trust me."

I pray this time his trust in me works out for the better.

I pull him through the woods like he's a ragged scarecrow. When he loses his footing, I get him back up and moving. We don't talk. I'm pondering the shortest way off the mountain that the hounds won't be following. The Etowah River's still a ways below, 'bout halfway down, when I hear the whistle for the end of day. It will take some time before the trustees report him missing.

But not that much time. We need to be away well before dark.

We come to an outcropping, the same one I studied Cartersville from the first time I met Ilya. Down below is where we need to get to. There's the steep way down or the winding road.

He's breathing hard, doubled over with his hands on his knees. Is the kid strong enough to get through the boulders down the rocky face? No. But I am.

I take off my too-big shirt and tell him to put it on. Then I have him press his skinny self against my back, face-first. I grab the shirttails and tie them round my waist, leaving him in a hasty-made sling. I've gotten stronger working on the gang, but it's a good thing he ain't any bigger.

I spent a lot of my younger years climbing down steeper ones, but this could be the death of us.

"Use your hands to help me grope the rocks."

His face is turned sideways against my back. I can feel him swallow.

"Okay," he chokes out.

Slowly I go over the edge, feet first, searching for my first toehold. We descend, both gripping a rock or tree root, then do it again.

I miss my footing and we slide, rocks tearing at my hands and chest. I grab ahold of a boulder and hug it close for several breaths to slow my heart. Then we get on the move again. Following cracks between the huge rocks and trees is our best route. It seems to take forever, but eventually we make it to a slight hill near the bottom.

I untie him and let him walk. My back aches, and I stretch. We just saved some time, but we still need to get farther away.

"Zanks," he says. "I vas going to die in work camp. Boss not like me."

"He the one who gave you the shiner?" I point to his eye.

"Ya. Said I vas too slow."

"Taggert's got hot liquid hate running through his veins. Don't worry 'bout it."

It was that part of the evening when the sun's gone but daylight remains. The whippoorwills call to each other, a choir of frogs sit together for critter church service in the ditch, and bats swoop overhead, swift, then gone in the gathering dusk.

"When boss man came back to camp vithout you, I vondered how you run away." He pulls leaves from his hair. "You got to cave. To Cy?"

"I was rearrested that day. For protecting my sister. I been on the work gang at a brick factory till I escaped this morning."

Has all of this happened today in the time it took the sun to cross over the sky and disappear again? Escape, the cave, a burial, to the pine area, and escape again?

"You not vith my brother all these days?"

I sigh. How do I form the next words? Once they leave my mouth, he has nothing left of his kin.

I stop and wait for him to come alongside me. "I couldn't get free. But…I went to the cave first today, to check on Cy."

A hopeful look is fixed on his face. "Vere is he now?"

"Ilya, I'm very sorry…but he died deep in the cave." I take him by the arm as he sways for a moment. "He looked at peace when I found him. Like he fell asleep."

His face is like my pa's when he came home from the war. Shell-shocked, they call it. Too long in the trenches, hearing the horror of another blast but not accepting it as real. Ilya's face crumples—he's silent, probably recollecting my promise.

"I buried him right nice." I reach in my pocket and bring out the agates. "He had these on him. They're worth something, can help when you get out on your own."

He hides his face in his hands and is whimpering like a hurt critter. A quiet sound, yet full of pain for the ages.

I let him cry, leaning up against my chest. I know what the loss of a brother feels like. 'Specially if you accept it's your fault. Hope he don't blame himself.

"You did your best to get him help." Gently, I push him away to look him in the eye. "I feel responsible for leaving him there, and there ain't enough sorrys to say how I feel, Ilya."

"I promise our mama before she die. I take care of him." He wipes a trail of snot on his sleeve. "I vill die now too. It not safe anywhere."

I can't leave him on his own. "You'll come with me." We both need to get out of here. I pause. "My real name is Briar, not Ray. What's your family name?"

"Gojack." He's gathered his emotions for now, but I suspect they'll race back like a summer storm. Sunny one minute, water busting loose the next.

"Okay. Vere you going?" he asks.

My words spill out. "Out west. Eventually. But right now, Ilya Gojack, we're going south to make sure my sister's okay."

Marietta, Georgia. June 1921

-33-

Ardith Dobbs

My idea for Baby Karl to sleep in Willow's room all night seems to be working. He's happy and doesn't need to be fed as often. And just two full nights of sleep have done wonders for me. I've even tried my hand at making supper. Tonight, I'm surprising William with breaded lamb chops, creamed potatoes, Parker House rolls, and an orange sponge cake for dessert.

He barely kissed me goodbye before leaving for work. William's been wound so tightly over the lawsuit and what it might mean for the Klan's reputation. His membership. His business dealings in town.

Frank is taking care of it from what I can tell. I've resolved not to help any more poor families with adoption. I'm sticking to giving them clothes and food and offering some a bit of advice where needed. I'll have plenty to do if I can get onto the women's planning committee for our local Klan. Bake sales, parades, visiting the elderly all alone in their homes. I never have to drive out to the sisters' Beck Infantorium again.

William parks the car and comes in through the kitchen.

"How was your day?" I say with my best smile. I'm wearing one of my prettiest dresses. Soft petal-pink with a form-fitting bodice and a lace collar. We can't be intimate for a month, but I need him to still find me attractive.

"Not the best day." He drops his briefcase by the door and hangs his hat on the rack.

"One of the printers gummed up and set us back a few hours."

His voice is tight. He's got that hard squint that says he's concentrating on something.

I point my elbow to the oven. "I found your mother's lamb chop recipe."

"It smells good." He leans against the counter with his arms folded. "I had a late lunch with Frank, but I'll eat some."

Uh-oh. That lunch must not have been served up with good news.

"Oliver and the baby are up in his room with Willow if you want to go see them."

"I need to talk to you, Ardith." He rubs his temples and then looks my way. "I want you to take the baby and go on a trip. Get away for a while."

"Whatever for?" I should go alone with Karl? I can't think of a worse *trip*. But full-time care? I'd be a washed-out rag long before I returned.

"The Legal Aid Society is not backing down. They're bringing in prominent lawyers from Washington, DC." He sighs. "To interview you and find out what happened out at that place you took the Elsmore baby to."

"My lands! This is so blown out of proportion." I wring my apron. Surely, babies are misplaced or switched around all the time. Only have to open the newspaper to read about unwanted babies abandoned in street alleys or on trash heaps. Fiona was so distraught, she might have left that baby anywhere. I was doing her a favor.

"If you're not here, you can't be interviewed." He scratches his neck, a nervous habit of his. "We hope the story will die down and go away."

I stomp my foot. "Just where do you think I should go?"

"A train tour would take you three weeks to complete. Up to Chicago, out to Yellowstone or Denver. Like in that brochure you brought home."

"Three weeks? You can't be serious. I have duties with the Daisy Ladies. And you and Oliver? How will you get by?"

"Oliver is no problem. Willow's here, and I could even take him to work some days."

"You've figured this all out without talking to me?" I fold my arms.

"We hoped the inquiry would be dropped. It's not. With the help from the Klavern—and they weren't all too eager, I tell you—I might be able to keep the story out of the local papers and maybe the regional ones. But sensational stories like this get picked up across the country. It needs to die out, and with you here speaking of it, well…"

"I don't think I can do this alone. I'll take Willow with me. She's beholden to us, even to after I get back." I picture the beautiful scenery going by my private cabin window. The spectacular dining car, meeting rich folks, because who else would be taking such an adventure. Maybe this is just what I need.

"You said Karl's less fussy. You can handle him."

The nerve! He has no idea how hard it is being a mother. He comes and goes as he pleases. Gets to go to lunch every day.

"Are you sure you don't want her here for other reasons? A girl that can't speak if *something happens to her?"*

"Ardith, of all the horrible things to think!" His face reddens. "What's happened to you?"

"Your brother Quinn had no trouble messing with the help." I wasn't going to ever tell Josephine's story, but he's got me riled. Acting like I'm a terrible person for protecting our marriage.

He starts to speak, then stops and cocks his head to the side. Like a banty rooster looking for a fight. "What are you accusing him of?"

"Josephine told Doctor Grange and me that she was raped by Quinn last August. And not just once."

He walks to the icebox and pulls out a bottle of milk, then puts it on the back of his neck and paces around the room. He returns it and reaches for my arm—none too gently. He draws a chair out from the small table where Josephine used to take her meals and pulls me to sit.

"Starting right now, you are going to tell me every secret you've been keeping from me."

No way will he hear all of them, but I *most certainly* can tell him about his immoral brother.

"Josephine's baby looked just like Oliver. Both the doctor and I thought you must have fathered him."

"The hell?" His fists are clenched now. "Doctor Grange knows me from our brotherhood. He couldn't have thought that."

"Well, he did. And he knew it would affect your membership and your businesses, so he asked what we could do." I hold my chin higher. We were saving *his* skin. "I heard of this discreet place north of here, mostly hidden away, that would take illegitimate babies and find good homes for them."

"Wait. Her baby was *alive*?"

"Yes. But what would his life be like being a white child and raised by a half-Colored gal? The doctor kept her asleep while I went to acquire and bring back a dead baby."

"Dear Lord, Ardith,"—he chuffs—"how can you sit in church after doing something like this?"

I've never seen him so angry. "That's what the Lord's forgiveness is for."

"Not always." He draws in a long breath. "The poor girl went crazy because of you. She knew it wasn't her baby."

"I, um, the doctor and I didn't think she would lose her mind. We thought she would be sad, of course, but would stay on and feed our new little one. Glad to have a baby to hold."

"Do you know you could be banished from the Klan? *We* could be banished. You'd be labeled an alien, never allowed to join again. My insurance company could come under inspection again. Already have too many babies dying that we've insured, and now you're switching live ones for dead ones."

"William, I'm too important. *We're* too important. Our Klan brothers and sisters will have our backs."

"I have to get some fresh air." He grabs his hat and stomps out the back door.

I sag in the chair. Banished? I'd go to tribunal before the Den officers, five robed and masked judges. Could even be William's friends under those hoods—York or Frank. Well, probably not Frank, since he's trying to help with the case.

I quietly recite my vows. *I will act like Jesus Christ and serve the Klan. I am in God's army against the enemies of God's chosen people. My motto is "Not for self but for others." I pay attention. I report. I preserve Marietta's protestant heritage. We are against northerners, blacks, Jews, schoolteachers, Catholics, Mormons, labor radicals, immigrants, bootleggers, theatre owners, dance hall operators, and feminists.*

I hold my head up. I can take this silly trip if that's what he wants. My marriage and my standing in the community are most important to me. I clawed my way out of the hills to be here, and I'm going to fight to stay. I am no different than the other ladies of the Klan. We all are working for a whiter world, a purer existence for our children.

William comes back and throws a question like it's a flaming spear. "Why was Josephine made sterile if all she did was have Quinn's baby? That's what made her lose her mind."

"You know uncontrolled fertility in the Negroes is bad. The diseases, poverty, and overcrowding. Many people believe the Colored mother is the least intelligent and fit to rear children properly."

"If Josephine was so *unfit* as you say, why was she caring for Oliver?" His gray eyes are chips of dark slate.

"You don't believe your vows to cleanse the country?" I lift my eyebrows.

"Yes, but through group decisions, not out there on my own giving away babies, lying to women, and bringing them a replacement child or—for goodness' sake! —a dead one. Did you take this Elsmore baby to that secret house in the country?"

"Yes. They take in the sickest and hardest to adopt."

"And Quinn's white son falls into that category?"

Okay. He's got me there. That cute boy could have gone to the New Hope

Charity Home, except they require a birth certificate and answers to questions I didn't want to provide. "The doctor and I may have made a mistake. But that healthy boy has easily found his way into a good home by now."

"I have you leaving tomorrow. Get packed! Take Willow if you need to. I'll let York know she's still serving time while helping you on this trip."

"I know the tickets are expensive. She won't need a sleeper car."

"You'll be sharing a compartment." He slides an envelope across the table. "Here's cash for extras along the way. I'll be back in the morning. I'm sure I'll simmer down before you return in three weeks, but tonight, I'm going to sleep at the Grand Dragon's apartment in town. I'll be back in the morning for Oliver."

He leaves before I get my tongue working.

William is slow to ignite, but then he explodes. He'll simmer down, of course. He's still the level-headed man I fell in love with.

As I head up the stairs to the attic space to retrieve a suitcase, I find I'm torn about leaving all this nonsense behind. What's he going to do with me away? If I stay, I believe I can talk to everyone and get this whole problem taken care of. I'm good at painting a new scenario that matches what was said and done. Not really lying—just rearranging the truth a bit.

But by the look on his face, William won't let me stay. He's determined, and I know when I can't change his mind.

I'll go and do what he says. Have to let Willow know she's going on a marvelous trip. As a hill gal, this is something she'd never get to experience. She'll have something to remember for the rest of her boring life.

I lay out the clothes the baby and I will need. I pass by my desk. The drawer is still open, but the secret newspaper articles have been rearranged! Oliver would have no interest in this drawer. That leaves the silent snoop. Of all the unmitigated gall.

But how much can she read? The picture with my birth name across the bottom is easy enough to figure out. She'd know I had another name and that I was sought after. But could she read the rest of the article?

If she has, I'll need a new plan for her.

I drop to the chair, exhausted from being the only one solving problems around here.

After a short rest, I go looking for Willow. She's not upstairs with Oliver or in the kitchen getting him a snack before bed. The house is much too quiet. Why would she be in her room with the boy? I don't like Oliver to be out there and have told her so. Karl is a different story. He's doing much better under her nightly care.

I push through the side door leading to her add-on room. She's entertaining? I hear voices, and she sure as sunrise can't talk.

With my ear to the door, I nearly drop over from shock. Josephine's in there!

I yank open the door to three startled faces. "What in Sam Hill!"

Oliver begins to cry, but he's able to blubber out words. "Don't make her leave, Mommy."

"Miss Ardith," Josephine says as she stands, holding Karl. "You've had a right handsome baby boy."

"Wha…? How are you even here?" The woman is crazy, right? But she seems put together, her face calm, her hair neat.

Willow looks defiant. She has to answer for why she let Josephine back into *my* house *without telling me*.

"I was let out." Josephine pats the head rag wrapped around her upswept hair. "They agreed bad behavior like I showed can happen after birthing a baby. Something inside a gal's mind just snaps, they say. I want to apologize for my awful conduct."

The nanny's presence answers why Karl is happy. Obviously, she's been suckling him, giving him good nutrition. He's snuggled between her heaving breasts, asleep and content. What do I do about this? William liked Josephine's ways with Oliver. And her cooking. Now she's a bonus for the baby.

"Willow. I am *so* displeased you didn't tell me Josephine was back. How *dare* you keep such a secret?"

A slow smile spreads on the mountain girl's face, and in that instant, I know she's read the newspaper articles. The truth pushes me back a step. How do I keep her from telling anyone else? Willow moves her hand in circles on her chest.

"What does that mean?" I should have taken better interest in the hand signs she uses.

"She's sorry, Mommy." Oliver mimics the same movement.

"Oliver. Run up to the baby's room and get a new burp cloth, darling." I need the boy out of earshot for my next words.

He scampers away.

"Mr. Dobbs has bought us a great getaway. Tomorrow, Willow, you and I and the baby are traveling for three weeks. Up north, out west. It'll be lovely. I need you to pack some of the nice clothes I have in the upstairs trunk."

Willow's eyes round. Is she excited or scared? She should be the latter. A girl holding the kind of secret she has about me needs to find a new place to live along the journey's route. I don't want her harmed. I quite like her. But there's no reason for her to be here, now that I have Josephine home.

I get another idea. Josephine will come too. It's a snap decision that will work out just great since William will know nothing about it until we return. A ticket in the Colored car is cheap. I'll use the cash William gave me. I can have her feed Karl at the stops, and it will be a nice adventure for her.

"And Josephine. I've decided you need to come along. But we can't let Mr. William know, or he'll send you back to the asylum." I tssk. "He doesn't much care for you." I smile. "Have you ever been out west?"

"Never been outta Georgia, ma'am."

"Then it's settled. I burned all the clothes you left behind, but you can find some in the trunk." My eyes drop to her mud-caked boots. "And shoes. Get a new pair."

This is going better than planned. Josephine is here, so Willow can finish out her sentence in another state, and Baby Karl will be taken care of.

"Oh, Oliver is staying here with Mr. William. Let's not say anything to the boy until morning." I open the door. "And Willow, why don't you let Josephine have her room, and you take the spare bedroom tonight?

Mr. William is away with the men, so it's just us ladies overseeing everything."

She nods and shoots a knowing look to Josephine.

What have they been talking about since she returned?

No worries. I have weeks to discern what they think they know.

HAPPENINGS OF THE DAY
JUNE 1921

19-Year-Old Girl Hobo, Virginia Stopher, Leaves Husband to Cross the Country Three Times

The Unwritten Code Among Hobos Kept Her Safe

Marietta, Georgia. May 1921

-34-

Willow Stewart

Miss Ardith dumps out my packed satchel on the floor of the nanny's room. The new clothes she bought me fall out along with my notebook and pencil.

"Need to see what you're packing." Her voice is tight like dried dung, never a pretty color.

She's been pinching glimpses my way since she caught me hiding Josephine. She's wary around me as if I'm a fox in her chicken coop.

And she might suspect I saw her secret articles in the desk drawer. I thought I tucked them back into place just right, but she did ask me if I'd been near her desk.

I crossed my fingers behind my back and lied by shaking my head.

And I wouldn't have thought much of her just checking out my packings, except earlier I overheard her talking to herself like she always does. "She grew troublesome, William. The St. Louis Home for Wayward Girls took her off our hands."

Thing is, Mr. William isn't there while she's talking. He's not home yet. Sounded like she's practicing up for a talk later down the road. Like when she returns without me. She doesn't know it yet, but Miss Jojo and I have other plans for the train stop in St. Louis. There, Miss Jojo can leave the train to find Miss Burns's sweetheart, the lawyer, and tell him her awful story about having her baby taken away and her baby-prevention surgery.

Miss Ardith picks up my notebook and pencil. Opens the pages and runs her finger down the jagged seam where pages are missing.

"I'll just take these. No need to write your answers anymore. Josephine does enough talking for both of us."

I keep my eyes steady on her face, smile and nod.

Thank goodness I mailed the two letters off yesterday to Miss Burns. One letter is about Sissy Belle Strunk and Miss Lily's Threads & Things, and the other detailed the babies dying at the horrible Beck Infantorium. That was a lot, now that I think about it. Everybody out here in the world is keeping secrets, staying silent when they all have perfectly good voices.

Don't know if anything'll happen, but I felt relieved in the telling. I'm a sinner, I know. I took money from Mrs. Holcombe, ran from the law, stole envelopes and stamps, and I've lied. I'll take my punishment for those things when my time comes. But I've never done the pure evil the likes of Miss Ardith's doings.

Mr. William will be gone all night, but I don't think it's for a men's meeting. A November chill flowed off him when he left earlier.

Before she took my notebook, I wrote out a few words asking to stay behind to help with Oliver. Sure don't want to be locked in no girls' home in far-off Missouri.

"Silly Willow." Her voice was the same color as a two-day-old bruise. Mottled blue with strange yellow hues. "You are indebted to me. Of course you're coming along."

That's when I knew I was in trouble. Big trouble.

How can I let Briar know what's happening? I have no way to reach him. I don't even know where he's doing his time. My only solution may be to slip away at one of the train stops. I'd be a fugitive on the run, and if the missus really wants to get rid of me, she might not report my getaway. I have to watch her closely. Make sure we don't take any side stops that don't follow the train schedule she showed me.

From Marietta, we're set to take the Southern Railway Lines to Chattanooga, Tennessee. There, we'll change trains and head west to Memphis to catch the Missouri Pacific. That's the tour train with a special car for Miss Ardith, Karl, and me. Miss Jojo will ride in the Colored car because someone named Jim Crow put that rule in writing. We're going to tour round St. Louis, and that's when Miss Jojo can go "missing." We're supposed to head out to Colorado and back, a three-week journey, but Miss Ardith won't want to care for Karl all her own.

Don't know what she plans to do after that.

And if what she's been talking to herself about comes true, *my* journey also ends in about a day's time in St. Louis.

Yes. I sure do need to watch my back.

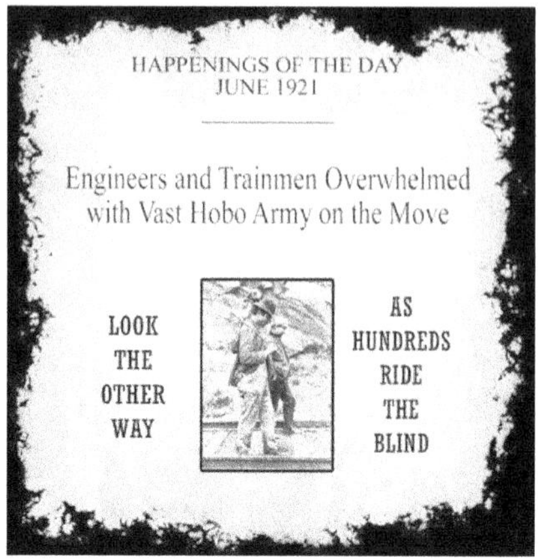
HAPPENINGS OF THE DAY
JUNE 1921

Engineers and Trainmen Overwhelmed with Vast Hobo Army on the Move

LOOK THE OTHER WAY

AS HUNDREDS RIDE THE BLIND

Near Marietta, Georgia. June 1921

-35-

Briar Stewart

Ilya and me mosey along the red clay road. The wind blows the churned-up smell of field grass and flowers and warm earth all around. This feels like one of those days where a feller needs to keep his blinders off and mind wide open.

We caught an empty coal car outside Cartersville. The floor was covered with newspapers, and heavy wires was slung halfway up like a hammock. We sat on the mesh, and I told Ilya my plan to check on my sis and then head west. He talked about Cy, about growing up under a dictator, the hardships his parents went through to get to America. I let him cry between stories, hoping he's getting his sadness poured out. 'Course it'll circle back. It's not possible to love a brother and expect to ever heal the parts he touched inside you.

A brakeman saved our bacon. He climbed down in the coal car and warned us to get off before the next stop. He was a boomer, a halftime hobo, halftime railroad worker. Said the next town was hostile and we should skirt it. Was still dark when we jumped off.

We followed a hardpacked road, ditching it every time automobile lights showed. Which wasn't too often.

The fog's still lifting from the crick, and the early morning sun sends weak blades of sunlight skyward over the distant mountains. We grabbed some clothes for Ilya off a line next to a farmhouse. The stripes he's wearing signaled work gang clothes. Didn't need nobody noticing that.

We've been sticking to back country, the wild areas, almost unpeopled. But round a bend in a crick, we come upon a sad homestead.

"Howdy." I raise my hand in greeting to a man and woman sitting on metal chairs outside a shack built on stilts. Two skinny dogs and a bushel of young'uns watch us with their heads pitched forward like we're the circus come to town. Not that I've ever seen a circus, but it's on my list of future want-to-dos. I'm 'bout to call out and ask how they're all faring, but I let the unspoken words fizzle in my head. It don't take much noticing to see the family's been living on the unlucky side of the road for more than a spell. They're scuffed up, like the dogs kept the folks living under the porch instead of the other way round.

We hotfoot it out of there.

Ilya's turning out to be good company. He's bold, like a feller counting his chickens even before he's got hisself a coop.

I can't figure where he's picked up his never-quit attitude. Seems misery has always run ahead to meet him. He's abided suffering, loss, and days of hate-filled words, but didn't shy away when I told him my plan for him. Seemed glad to have someone in charge. Told him a couple times I might need to hire someone fulltime just to answer all his questions though. Just joshing him. He's nosey in a good way, and that's not a bad quality.

We slip under barbed wire fencing, then jump over a narrow crick before heading into a field of tall grasses and wildflowers. I stop to pull a spiny burr off my britches.

A hawk circles overhead, one eye cocked toward us. At the tree line, crows caw back and forth. Their sharp barks send my mind chasing that image of the funeral, when Taggert and me went to Cartersville. Everything went bad after that, but I shake away the cockeyed notion 'bout crows and bad luck. Mama always said if superstitions died out, there wouldn't be anything for hill folk to talk about.

The sun's warm on my face, and shadows chase each other 'cross the meadows as clouds pass. I step round a slew of gopher holes. Butterflies rise from the flowers in the high grasses.

We're following a stream when I spot a tatty old shanty. The boards on the house are grayed, cracked. The owners must be too poor to paint and too proud to whitewash. A pen with two huge pigs is hooked to the backside of the house with a lean-to roof. Chickens peck the bald ground for bugs and seeds we can't see. The whole place is droopy and sunken, like it was doomed since God created the world.

"We need to hurry round this joint." I point to a scratching in a fence post. It's a triangle with raised stick arms, as if showing being held up in a robbery. I lower my voice. "It means a man with a gun lives here, and he ain't shy about using it."

We duck down and run fast along the back of his land. My heart's pounding to match my quick steps. Can't get shot before our journey's begun.

Once we've laid a safe distance between us and the property, we stop to catch our breath.

"How you know what zat sign means?" Ilya has his hands on his hips, drawing in the air.

"Learned what to look for when I rode the rails." I scratch my head. "There's over a hundred signs hobos use."

"Zanks for coming back for me." His chin's quivering. "Vat would I do on my own?"

"It is hard to know who to trust," I say with a smile. "Just 'cause a chicken has wings, don't mean it can make it over the barn. My pa always says, 'Live and learn or die and know it all.' We're still here learning, ain't we?"

"That's ze truth."

Seems we've discovered a dead-end road. Nary a car or truck have come by. I'm as jumpy as ants on a fired-up griddle because we're in a dangerous place as long as we stay in Georgia.

Yonder, a train clacks over a metal bridge.

"Bet that was ours," I say.

"Da. And I don't miss her."

The birds are gossiping from bushes nearby, as we walk along all quietlike.

Then Ilya turns and squints into the distance behind us.

"Is zat motor vehicle?"

A speck boils up red dirt and seems to be heading our way. Man, the boy has the eyes of an eagle. "Sure enough."

To hide or catch a ride? A shiver of worry runs through me. We could be poking at an ant hill with a short stick.

A feller driving an old blue farm truck pulls to a stop. He spits a stream of brown out the window and pushes a straw hat lower on his head.

"You fellers need a ride?"

"Yes, sir," I say. A man with his truck full of produce don't seem like a lawman. "We'd be right happy to get within walking distance of the Marietta Train Station, if'n you're going thataway."

The man's face is red as a crawdad, with deep lines that look a lot like a fresh plowed field.

"You all traveling men?"

"Ve are," Ilya says before I can hush him.

The driver squints at Ilya.

"Where are you from, boy?" His voice has changed from a sunny morning to a cloudy afternoon.

"Boston, sir," Ilya says, full of confidence.

"He's from South Boston." I offer up a fishy eye roll. "Got him a weird accent, I know. Can't hardly understand him myself."

"Hop in the back." He spits out the window again and switches the chaw from one cheek to the other. "Sorry, but Alice don't take too kindly to sharing the front."

I move to get a closer look. His old coon dog is sprawled 'cross the seat. She barely raises her head to look my way, the loose flesh round her eyes sagging to Sunday.

"Back of the truck works fine, sir." I nod.

"Settle in round the cabbage, and I'll try to miss the bumps in the road. Not more than twelve miles from here to Marietta. I'm bound for a warehouse close to there."

"Much obliged."

We climb into the truck bed and move the cabbage heads around to create spots for our behinds. My mouth waters when I think of Mama's cabbage and pork soup. Actually, any of her soups would do.

Red dust boils up behind the pickup truck and rolls over itself, soon dying out on the road. Ilya peeks through the glass to the feller in the cab and then leans closer to me.

"Should ve be vorried 'bout this guy?"

"Don't think so." I have the same distrustful cloud hanging over me and don't like it. "Looks like a farmer toting his produce to market to me."

We stop talking 'cause it's too hard to hear with the air blowing over the roof. I settle in to watch the scenery whip by. How will Willow take the news that this is our goodbye, that I'm heading far away? It pains me that I won't get a chance to stop by the homestead. I softened the hard protective seal I created so's I wouldn't feel hurt again, and I looked forward to a homecoming.

But I can't change the direction of water once it's headed over a cliff.

About fifteen minutes pass, and we see more motor vehicles on the road.

The truck slows going through a town.

Somewhere fresh bread is baking. The yeast scent mingles with fried meat. Once I find Willow and tell her my plan, we'll get something to eat with my five dollars.

We're on a main street, looks like. Striped awnings hang over the sidewalks, and folks are sitting round tiny tables or sweeping the cement path. Two boys race past us on bicycles, calling out to each other.

"It looks like a nice enough place."

Just past the end of the business section, a large dirt patch opens up.

Dozens of young'uns are running round, swinging like monkeys from bar to bar on ladders held up sideways high above their heads. All kinds of grab things are hanging from metal frames, like rings or other bars. A city version of what us kids spent hours doing in trees with branches or vines.

For what feels like another five minutes, the red-faced feller slowly drives down side streets before parking in front of a long red brick building with a few windows. *1902* is written above the words *Cobb County Produce Warehouse*.

The farmer reaches his hand out the window and taps on the roof. "This is my stop, boys."

We hop down. The crazy dog barks as if we just showed up.

"Train station is four blocks west of here." The man points beyond some nearby buildings.

"Thank you, sir."

We pick up our bags and turn to go.

"Hold up." He opens his door and hops down, bearing himself on one foot. He's missing his left leg below the knee, his pant-leg swinging empty. After digging in his back pocket, he pulls out a beat-looking fold of leather that may have been a new billfold at the turn of the century. "You boys came off a train, which is about the only way onto that road you was walking. I ain't judging. Was once a hobo myself. Had me twelve good years until I fell asleep one night and dropped under the wheels." He hands two dollars to Ilya.

"You look near empty," he goes on to say, rubbing his neck. "Grab you some food before you catch out again."

The farmer hops away, heading for the warehouse.

A block on, we spy a corner café called The Grill House. I go in since I imagine Ilya's accent will draw bad attention. He stays hidden behind a chimney on a brick building.

I come out carrying a small burlap poke. We head off near a stack of lumber to eat our vittles. In haste, we finish the roast beef and fried onion sandwiches and wash them down with Coca-Cola. My eyes water after the first swallow. The explosion of bubbles is a surprise, but it tastes mighty good.

If anyone knows where Willow's staying, it would be the postmaster. Barely nine o'clock by a church chiming the time, so I know one'll be open. I look around and spot a post office not far away.

"Ilya. Wait outside and don't talk to nobody."

I step inside the quaint building. The postmaster's a balding, middle-sized man with sun-cooked face and arms.

"I'm a relative just in town," I say. "Might you direct me to the Dobbses' home?" Sure hope there ain't more than one Dobbs in the city.

A map of Marietta's on the wall, and the man uses the unimportant end of a pencil to trace a short route to their house.

Not that far. A few twists and turns from here.

"You kin to William or Ardith?" He chews a toothpick, moving it like a magic show from one side of his mouth to the other.

I'm taking a gamble this man knows Mr. Dobbs more than the missus. "Mrs. Dobbs is my mama's cousin. Been a while," I shrug. "Hope she ain't forgot this scruffy face."

I tap the counter to signal I'm done jawing. Got places to be.

We follow the route in my head, through streets full of swanky homes, a new automobile in each driveway. Willow got a nice placement, and that eases my mind.

"What ve gonna do here?"

Gotta be careful with my excitement to see Willow again. After all, Ilya just lost his last kin and is raw as a just-scraped hide. And I need to see her secret-like. I'm pretty sure the sheriff let the Dobbses know her brother is on the run.

"I want to say goodbye to my sister." We turn down the street the postman said is the one. "Let's stop here for a minute."

We huddle up next to a large tree trunk, and I study the house across the street. It's got a deep front porch with fancy white posts. Trees edge both sides of the tall house. A small building is attached to the right. Looks less fancy and like someone had an afterthought putting it there. But these folks sure living high on a prize hog.

Nary a soul is outside, so we cross the street and head to the tiny add-on. If'n this ain't the nanny's quarters, I'll figure something else out.

From inside the little room, I hear a child crying. I move closer and peek in one of the windows. Willow's there giving comfort to a boy on her lap, rocking him back and forth. Another gal is breastfeeding a tiny baby.

I tap on the window. Willow lifts her eyes from the boy. Her eyes widen, then her lips stretch into a big ol' smile.

I motion her outside and tuck myself behind the tree toward the back.

Willow arrives in a flurry of hand motions, asking me what I'm doing here.

"It's a long tale, and ain't got much time," I say. "I got away from that work gang with this other feller, but we're wanted men now. Come to see if you're doing all right before I head to Colorado or Utah or somewhere out west."

She looks good, wearing a colorful dress and new shoes. But in two months, she'll leave fancy behind and travel back to Stewart Mountain. Maybe one day, I can safely come home too…at least for a visit.

Her eyes go wide, and she shakes her head no. She's up close signing and spelling words in the air. Downright flustered.

"Whoa! Slow down, sis. I'm out of practice."

She looks back over her shoulder like she's expecting a haint, then she starts over. Willow signs, *"Milk the herd without me."* Our family warning there's grave danger about.

"What's going on?" I ask. "And tell me a mite slower this time."

She signs that Miss Ardith is evil and has killed in her past. Willow found out. The woman is taking her on a train tour to St. Louis and then west, but she heard her say Willow isn't coming back.

This adds so many problems I can't stir them with a stick. If'n I can grab her now and run, she's likely to get killed jumping a train. And she can't be traveling with hobos and good-for-nothing thieves.

"When are you leaving?" My eyes are cutting from side to side, hoping no one comes out of the house. Never corner something you suspect is meaner than you. I don't know the man of this here dwelling, but I want to be ready.

She tells me they're leaving in one hour from the Marietta station.

"Who's going?" Mr. Dobbs might be a problem if he's a bigger feller than me.

I learn it's the three womenfolk and the babe.

She's truly afraid. Her chin quivers, something I ain't never seen in my sister. We once stared down a mama bear, and Willow didn't even flinch, but my legs went to wiggling worms while I waved a bush round.

A whole mess of notions shoot through my mind like stars across the sky.

She's heading the same way we're intending. Colorado, west. If'n Ilya and I catch the same trains, I can check on her all the way. And somewhere out there, maybe she can disappear along with us.

"Do you know your train stops?"

She holds up a finger and takes off round the corner to her room.

"How old your sister?"

Almost forgot Ilya's standing behind me.

"Fifteen, I reckon." I notice the look on his face. "Naw! You best not be thinking what I reckon you may be."

"Ve are same age." He smiles for the first time since I pulled him from the pines.

We have no time for this.

Willow's back and hands me a travel handout. Inside are train timetables and towns with pictures of what they'll see.

"Willow. Trust me on this." I pull her into a hug. "I'll be on these trains and won't let anything happen to you."

She wipes away a tear and tries to stretch her lips into a smile again.

I can't let her get hurt. Or worse. I carry heaps of guilt for Luther Junior's death. I remember how Willow fell to pieces when the mine owners and I came back to the mountain with Luther Junior's coffin. Her face wet with tears, her mouth open in a twisty mask of sorrow. There's no spinning the Earth backwards. No turning back time.

Losing her would surely be the end of my time on Earth.

Someone calls out, and Willow's face whitens. She signs, "*I love you*," and I cross my arms over my heart in return.

Ilya starts to do the same, and I slap his hands down.

"We gotta go," I say with a hiss.

Instead of turning back the way we come, we head through the rear yard along a fence and into the lawn of another huge house. Then we step into a street alongside the house.

"Ve going all way to Colorado?" He's a mite flushed and twitchy nervous.

"As far as Willow goes. Then we can figure out the rest."

The city is noisy and smells of oil, tar, and smoke. When did these folks get used to breathing this dirty air all day? We follow the cracked cement walk along a tree-lined street with rows of stores. Chimes jingle on an antiques' store door as a woman enters. A happy sound.

But I ain't happy, not one dang bit. How dare this Dobbs woman threaten Willow. My stomach feels twisted, and the sandwich is 'bout ready to come up.

"Right now," I say, "we need to find a safe place to jump this passenger train. Gonna be harder than grabbing a freight. Less cars to hide in." I lead us back to just shy of the railway station. The huge clock on that wall will let us know when we have to get a-running. Till then, we can stay in the trees and watch out for the railroad dicks or local police. "If we can't grab an empty," I say, "we'll ride the blind."

HAPPENINGS OF THE DAY
JUNE 1921
LEGAL AID SOCIETY
INVESTIGATES
Hundreds of Infant Deaths
Called "HOUSE OF HORROR"
by First Social Workers
on the Scene

Marietta, Georgia. June 1921

-36-

Ardith Dobbs

Everyone seems to be dragging their feet this morning. Why aren't they excited for this trip? No hillbilly gal and Negro woman have ever been offered a chance to travel, especially in this kind of luxury. I bet even the Colored car is first-rate. For *them*.

William seems to have calmed down as I knew he would. He returned home this morning and kissed Karl's head, gave me a pat on the back. Not very affectionate but it's a start. In a few moments, he'll drive us to the train station.

He's more than shocked to see Josephine. Not sure why I thought I could keep her return a secret. I explain how she's a new gal. She's put the crazies behind her, and she's sorry for her actions. I add that I'm taking her on the trip.

He can't argue. I already bought her tickets.

But he must be flustered because after he studied Josephine for a good long while, he said, "It's probably better this way." He left the room to get the car keys.

Not sure what he meant by that but glad he didn't argue about the nanny traveling along. I do hate that Josephine has her hair up in that head rag I detest so much. At least I won't have to look at her or *it* on the train.

And Oliver. Cry me a river! He won't stop bawling, even though William promised him all kinds of fun things they will do. The boy needs the soothing syrup, but William won't let me get it. Just wait. He'll be spooning that medicine into the boy after one day, I bet.

We're ready to go, and I can't find Willow. I call her and she comes scurrying around the side of her room. Can't ask her where she was since I threw her notebook away, and I certainly don't want to learn her hand flutters. How undignified! But why is she flushed and breathing fast? I need to keep her in sight.

Does she know I *know* she saw my papers? I think so. She's acting skitterish around me. Nothing but trouble since she came. What was I thinking, taking in a criminal? But now Josephine's home, and we can settle back into normal when the trip is over.

We all get into the car. Oliver clings to Josephine in the crowded back seat next to Willow. He's down to whimpering now. She's shushing him and telling him she'll be back.

The trip takes only ten minutes, and William unloads our bags onto the train platform. He pulls me into a quick hug. More for show, it seems, than loving.

"I put a bit more cash in an envelope in your suitcase." He's wearing his serious look. "Shouldn't need to open that until you've used the other money first."

"You're a dear." I peck him on the cheek. "We will be back before you know it."

"Take care of this little one." He rubs his hand gently over Karl's head and tears well in his eyes.

"I will. And you and Oliver have some fun." William peels the child off Josephine's leg, and I kiss the boy. "Bye, sweetie. Mommy will be back soon. I'll bring you lots of new toys."

"I don't want toys!" He's back to big-mouth crying.

"Sure you do." I touch William's arm. "You should go before *everyone* is staring at us."

"That's my plan." His voice is strange, almost strangled. I guess he's going to miss us more than he will admit.

He carries Oliver around the corner and out of sight.

Now it feels like an adventure.

We've switched trains in Chattanooga and then Memphis. Along the way, I enjoyed a lovely lunch in the dining car. Perfectly prepared beef stroganoff served on fine china. I love being treated like the queen I am. For the meal, a porter sat me with a couple from Savannah. He's mad about motorcar racing and she's an artist. They have two homes, one in Savannah and the other in the mountains outside Denver. I'll have to talk to William about a second house, so we can enjoy the cooler summer days out west. What the couple described about their five-month stay in Colorado sounds divine. Not hot and sticky, that's for sure.

I return to my seat, and Willow is holding the baby. We're two stops from St. Louis and Willow's exit. This next stop is Sulphur Springs, where the train takes on water. There, I'll have Willow carry Karl to Josephine. She stepped out of the Colored car to feed him at earlier stops. When I asked what her accommodations are like, Josephine said they're fine. There are only a few other riders, and they were all served cold meat sandwiches during lunch. How nice for them.

The trip has been relaxing and wonderful so far. Willow sits at the window, watching the scenery. Got to be a wonder to a child who's never been out of Georgia before.

Wish I hadn't been so angry with William when he suggested this getaway.

It's just what I need.

I remember William said there was an envelope. Might as well see how much money he left me.

"Can you give me some privacy, Willow? Maybe walk the baby for a few minutes."

She smiles, lifts Karl to her shoulder, and walks toward the front of the train. She'll have four passenger cars to move through before she reaches a dead end at the baggage car and has to return.

I pull down my suitcase and open it on the seat. I retrieve the envelope and return my suitcase to the compartment. The packet doesn't feel that thick. I tear it open and find only a folded letter around a fifty-dollar bill. The silly man has never written me a letter. How sweet.

I begin to read, and my heart drops to my stomach.

The words hardly make sense!

Ardith,

Oliver and I will not be here when you return. If you return. I suggest you start over with the baby someplace far away. The Klan wants to try me in front of the tribunal for your misdeeds. Dealing with the unscrupulous orphanage, stealing money from the women's dues. I've been exiled from the brotherhood and I can't bear the shame. Oliver could be taken away from me if I'm put in jail. I'll be run out of business according to the Grand Dragon.

I learned some other things going through your desk. Our whole marriage is built on a lie. You are built on a lie, Sissy Belle Strunk.

I don't like leaving Karl with you to raise but I have no choice.

Just like you once did, Oliver and I will recreate ourselves, and you won't find us.

William

Willow is coming through the car door. I hurriedly stuff the letter between the seat cushions and look out the window, pretending I'm falling asleep. My mind whirls. How dare he! Our marriage vows bind us together through the good times and the bad. The man only sticks around during the good? Shame on him!

And he's not going to help with my legal mess. Warns me not to return. Where am I supposed to go?

I clasp my hands tight to keep them from shaking.

An idea begins to take hold. I have sisters in the Klan in St. Louis. Or in Indiana, where Miss Barr spends most of her time. They don't know about my legal troubles.

Maybe I can start over there.

HAPPENINGS OF THE DAY
JUNE 1921
Popular Photo Spot!
The Picturesque High Trestle Bridge
Spanning Glaize Creek
Just Before It Reaches
the Mighty Mississippi River

Sulphur Springs, Missouri. June 1921

-37-

Willow Stewart

We're on the Missouri Pacific No. 32. It's beginning to slow for the next water stop in Sulphur Springs. The closer we get to St. Louis, the more my insides are slithering with a mess of baby snakes. That's where she said I was gonna be left. I get to thinking that the state of Georgia owns me, not Miss Ardith. I plan to argue that when she tries anything funny.

Sulphur Springs will be the last stop before the twenty-six miles to the big city.

Miss Ardith knows I'm suspicious of her. Early in the trip, I accidentally brushed her arm, then jerked mine back and shook it, like I was flinging off a spider.

Since then I've curled myself close to a window, watching the world blur by.

At the stop, I'll take Karl to his feeding with Miss Jojo. When we're outside together, it's the only time I'm not as nervous as a long-tailed cat in a room full of rocking chairs.

It was so painful to say goodbye to Oliver, watching him cry so hard. I signed that I'll see him soon. For both our sakes, I hope I didn't just lie to him.

Miss Ardith asked me to walk Baby Karl up and down the train aisles. I don't mind being away from her as much as possible. Once I return to our compartment, she's acting like she's fallen asleep. Her face is slack, and she suddenly looks older than I've ever seen.

She stands, covers her mouth, and hurries toward the toilet a car back. Maybe her dinner didn't sit well.

Then, I spy a letter tucked between the seats.

I glance at her departing back, shift the baby to one arm, and reach for the note. Like a chicken, I need to keep the fox in sight at all times and know what he or *she* is doing.

Oh, my lands! I can't believe what I'm reading. Mr. William found out about her evil past. I set the letter back where she left it.

What's going to happen now? He's running away, tells her not to come home. Will she change her mind about getting rid of me? Maybe she will need my help if she keeps traveling.

The train screeches to a stop, and she returns to our compartment, her eyes red.

I hold my face as even as I can and hope she doesn't see my shock.

"You go on forward again, Willow." Miss Ardith points to the baby. "Get him fed."

Should take about fifteen minutes to fill the water tender from the spigot arm on the big tank it parks under. At least that's the way it worked at the other stops.

Our passenger car is near the rear of the train, farthest away from the soot and smoke. Right now, it's parked on a high bridge over a creek. I pass through the forward cars until I see solid ground under us. Then I step out and walk outside along the tracks. Miss Jojo is standing next to the train, waiting with a big smile.

"You doing okay back there with Miss Ardith?"

I nod. I want to tell her about the surprising news in Mr. William's letter, but I have no paper and we have no time.

"Not tried to get you to stand in a doorway or anything?"

I laugh and hand her Karl. Before Miss Ardith took my notebook, I wrote a short note telling Miss Jojo about the woman's secret past, and that I feared she may know I found out. Miss Jojo doesn't trust the woman either, but she doesn't think she will kill me, just maybe pass me off someplace.

"Your brother and the other kid, they riding with the hobos on the front of the baggage car. Briar say he'll try to follow you into St. Louis if Miss Ardith tries to take you someplace."

It gives me peace to know Briar is watching over me. Literally. I spotted him and the boy on the roof for the stretch from Chattanooga to Memphis.

I look back over the tail of the train, sitting out on the high bridge. Silvery under the afternoon sun. We just came through a windy path in the hills, and not far behind the last car is a blind curve. The river below is wide, throwing up white tips where it bounces over the rocks. The earnest blast of a train horn rips apart the muggy quiet. Many passengers standing outside turn their heads in the direction of the engine, wondering why it would be laying out a warning while parked. I recognize the sound as coming from behind us. A massive black engine barrels around the curve, leading onto the trestle at the rear of the train.

I push Miss Jojo and the baby to the ground, and we roll a good distance away from the tracks onto a short slope of cinders and stones. We both look at Karl. He's fine. Even in the shock of the moment, Miss Jojo protected the baby's head and back parts as any real mother would.

"We're just fine, Willow. Thank you for the push."

The conductor jumps off as well. A prayer is on my lips as I watch for the hobos and Briar to leave the blind.

The impact is worse than what I could ever have imagined, making a gust so powerful it pushes me over. The sound of metal screaming against metal booms through the valley and echoes back from the hills, like the roar of huge animals butchered alive. Like a jumpy slow-down dream, the cars closest to us flip on their sides, folks thrown through windows. The wooden walls of the cheaper cars shatter, sending spikes of wood every which way.

In hellfire unison, the ear-busting shriek of metal splintering and grinding drowns out the people screaming and crying. And then the eeriest moment arrives. All movement stops, and for a split hair, the only sound in the remote area is the hiss of escaping steam and compressed air. Then the screams start up again, and the train lets out a death rattle like none have lived to hear. Crying rises from every direction like a slow woeful chorus. More of the same is added as time ticks on.

The air carries ribbons of hot oil and the smells of fall butchering time. The engine that plowed into us from behind forced the rear passenger cars off the trestle and into the deep canyon below, then broke them off the front portion of the train. Miss Ardith's car is gone. The big engine continued on, shrinking the dining and mail cars into one accordion-like hunk of metal.

The world is all jumpy. Survivors push and run in all directions. It's hard to focus on one sight or another.

A few bleeding men begin to lay the dead side by side on the cinder banks. A voice hollers out that help is on the way.

Above the tortured moans and agonizing cries, a man shouts orders to get to the coaches below to free trapped passengers. The rescuers stumble over bodies on the way down the riverbank.

I tug on Miss Jojo's sleeve and sign, hoping she understands but not truly caring if she doesn't. *"I want to check on the men riding the blind."* Hobos bum rides on the front of the baggage car because it has no through-passage to the other coaches, and the railroad detectives can't find them.

Two hobos stagger along the tracks toward us. Miss Jojo asks about Briar and the other boy.

He shakes his head. "Those boys had no time to jump." One held out his hand, blocking me from going forward. "Best you not see what's left."

I lose strength in my legs and fold to the ground.

All hope that anything would ever be good flees from my pained soul. Moments of our time growing up flash through my mind. The first wooden doll he carved for me. Making hammocks in the trees with Mama's old sheets. The forest, fishing, running, signing. Fleeting images of a life suddenly gone, taking a huge part of me with him.

In this instant, I wish for death. Miss Ardith can kill me if she wants. It'll be a heck of a sight easier than telling Poppy and my brother and sister that Briar isn't ever coming home.

Some men help me stand, but the world is a blur. Someone mumbles we have to get to the hobo jungle nearby. They help me down the slope through the brush and weeds to the riverbank. Miss Jojo and the baby move in and out of my wavering eyesight. I'm glad they're nearby.

At the river's edge, the scene turns eerie. The metal passenger cars are piled on top of each other like giant silver bugs mating. I hear the heart-wrenching cries as men pull the frightened and injured passengers from the partially sunken coaches.

We move on.

Baby Luther is dead, Mama's dead. Briar is dead. I'm not going back to Miss Ardith's. I'll figure out a way to get home. I need my kin. What's left of them. Got to get away from so much hate and distrust.

The men don't need to hold me up anymore. They're leading the way single file along the riverbank, heading away from the wreckage.

An almost undetectable cry sounds close by. The hobos continue on ahead, but Miss Jojo stops.

"I think it's a child, Willow." There's no way we can pass up helping a young one.

I follow her as she rushes to the water's edge, picking my way over rocks and sinking into foot-sucking muddy holes.

Among the small rocks and twisted logs lies a woman, her white hands clutching a log. She's crawled partially out of the river. Her body is clothed in a light-colored dress stretched into the shallow waters. Like a wavering ghost below the surface.

"Help me," she croaks, her head turned to the side, lying against the log. "I beg you."

It's Miss Ardith! I walk to her. She has a deep cut across her forehead, and blood runs everywhere down her face and neck. Her right leg is twisted in the wrong direction below her wavering dress. I grab her by the armpits and tug her a little farther out of the water and turn her on her back.

The woman groans, her eyes still closed. "My baby."

Miss Jojo comes closer and bends down. "I got Baby Karl. He's okay."

Miss Ardith's face is going whiter than new sheets, and one eye wobbles around as she looks our way, but she recognizes us.

"You two! This is all your fault. I wouldn't have had to leave. You're sneaky. Always making my life hard." She chokes on something. "If I go back…both of you…are going to jail."

I nudge Miss Jojo and point to the woman's head wound, cut clean to the bone.

Miss Jojo's eyes widen, and she shakes her head.

"Jesus will protect me. He heard my vow." Miss Ardith turns her head and spits out a tooth with a spray of blood. "Get some white men…to help me."

Jojo straightens, her face set in a dark mask. She hands me Karl. Looks to be recalling all the pain Miss Ardith caused her. Taking her baby away. Giving her a dead one. Having the doctor cut her so she can't have any more.

Is she gonna kill her? Miss Ardith isn't long for this life as it is.

Miss Jojo unwraps her headscarf and walks to Miss Ardith.

"*White* men will be here shortly to help you. I only got this here *rag* you once called lice-filled to help you with." She ties it round Miss Ardith's head. "That oughta help some."

"William? Where's my Baby Katherine?" Her voice is weak. Her eyes are closed. Her hands are open on her chest like she's cradling an infant.

I lay Baby Karl on her wet chest, and she closes her hands around him. He squirms against the cold wetness of her body. Moments later, her arms drop away.

"She gone," Miss Jojo says, turning her head away.

A hobo has come back to see where we are.

"We gotta get," he says. "Folks will pilfer that train and we'll get blamed for it."

He's right. If Miss Jojo and I get taken in, our arrest records will show up. My time will start over in some other place. I just want to go home.

And I want to be as far away as possible from the spot where Briar's soul left for heaven.

Miss Jojo walks away, softly talking to Karl. She turns to me.

"How we going to get this babe home?"

I haven't had a chance to explain about Mr. William's letter to Miss Ardith. Mr. William is gone, lost to wherever he took off to. I'll tell her as soon as I can get some paper.

I shrug. Then I point to Miss Jojo and mimic her rocking the infant. She needs to raise him.

"You saying I keep him?" She runs her finger down the baby's face. "I'll get arrested for stealing a baby."

I shake my head. Point to her stomach trying to say *who will know*. She has all the proof that she recently gave birth.

"We get to St. Louis and see your lawyer friend. Will we say this is my baby?"

I nod. It doesn't feel wrong. In the end, Miss Ardith owes her at least this much.

HAPPENINGS OF THE DAY
JUNE 1921

34 Killed, 150 Injured, 4 Missing in Big Wreck on the Missouri Pacific

Engineer Glen also killed
Failed to See Block Signals

Ghouls Arrested for
Stealing from the Dead

CORONER:
"Ultimate Suffering Happened Here."

Stewart Mountain, Georgia. June 1921

-38-

Willow Stewart

By the time we made it to the hobo camp that day, things were hazy for me, but my travel mate kept her head. A good Christian farmer and his wife drove us into the city, even gave us a little money for food. We read the names of the dead and injured in the newspaper. Briar and Ilya weren't listed, but they hadn't bought tickets so no one could have known their names. I cry each day when I think he was only on that train to protect me. In the end, he did our family proud.

I had Miss Jojo call Miss Burns. That's a right smart contraption that telephone. She sent Miss Jojo and me money to stay in a boarding house in St. Louis, where we spent three nights. No one is the wiser about Baby

Karl not being Miss Jojo's. She felt less guilty keeping the baby when she learned Mr. William disappeared with Oliver. The Legal Aid Society is very interested in helping Miss Jojo get her mother out of the insane asylum in Virginia so they can live together. Probably in Washington, DC. Even gave Jojo a job working in their office.

And no more trains for me.

I've been traveling by bus back home to Georgia, and early this morning got let off where the Fancy Road meets the trail, leading to my home.

I'm trying to keep my excitement tampered down, but it's running all around inside me like how Oliver used to circle the backyard. I think of him and hope he and Mr. William are doing well.

I relax a little as I soak in the combined scents of the forest around me, fresh and breezy with wild apple blossoms and honeysuckle that climbs the nearest trees. The woods feel alive. I'm back in the heartbeat of this mountain, the place that sharpens my mind, fills me with love. When I reach the first peak, I see layers of dark blue mountains stacked in the distance, darkening and then greening again under the shadows of the passing clouds.

I all but run up the long trail, along the creek, and over the bridge where Cousin Len died. A squawking comes from the trees—our pet magpie, Lucy. She hops from branch to branch, pointing me home.

Been gone six weeks. Feels like a whole year.

The family cemetery comes into view, tucked under the pines at the outer edge of the homestead. Grass grows over the newest grave. No headstone yet, but my throat hitches. Mama and Baby Luther must lie there. I send a prayer skyward, thanking the Lord for the time we had and telling Him I'm happy they're together. I turn to leave. Off to the side, another grave had been dug and filled. The wooden board stuck in the ground has the word *Outsider* carved into it.

It takes me a moment, but I realize Poppy must've come looking for me when Jacca returned home with my note under his saddle. He'd have found dead Mr. Coburn and buried him up here. That's why the police couldn't find his body.

And Poppy wouldn't know the wrong Mr. Coburn done to me. He just followed the family motto to help others in need.

The corral comes next. Jacca's back is to me, but I watch him sniff the air. Then he spins, his ears perked, and he runs to the fence, neighing and talking like I never heard before. I bury my face in his neck, breathing in his rich horse scent. I smile so wide my cheeks hurt.

By now, everyone in the cabin must know someone's here.

I give him one long rub and touch foreheads before heading up the sloping yard. Billy Leo charges my way, and I swear he's grown. Poppy is right behind him, with a huge smile stretching his lips toward his ears. He grabs me around the waist and twirls me round and round before setting me down.

"Willow. My lands!" He rubs my arms back and forth. "You made it back." His voice is husky blue. Full of emotion.

In this swimmy-headed spinning world, I see two images of my sister Ruthy on the porch.

Then my sight clears.

It's Ruthy and right beside her is…Mama? Mama! My poor eyes never stretched so big.

But how is this possible? What two buryings did Preacher Holcombe do that day?

I rush into her arms, into her wraparound hug. Her embrace never felt so warm.

"Willow." Her voice is the creamy peach sound I always hear in my head. "Thank you, Lord, for seeing her home."

When the tears and hugging are over, I sign, *"Who died the day I left?"*

"Cousin Lucille," Poppy said. "Stood up and fell right over dead not long after you left."

"I thought it was Mama."

"Bless your little heart," Mama says. "What a sad weight to be carrying all by yourself. And according to Briar, you both sure had you a passel of troubles off this mountain."

He must've written like I did. I nod. Guess it's time to tell them about him.

"And that boy, Ilya, that he helped had a mighty hard row to hoe too," Ruthy says.

Wait. How would they know about him? Once Briar escaped from the work camp with the boy, with Ilya, Briar was too busy catching trains so he could stay up with me.

The magpie swoops to the trees and sets to talking again.

Briar and Ilya come walking up the hill, carrying an axe and an armful of wood.

I burst into tears. They didn't get crushed. Not sure how Briar got off that train, but I've never been so happy in so many short moments in all my life.

And he didn't keep going to head out west. Briar's come home.

My family is back together.

"You take the slow way home, Willow?" Briar's voice is cheery orange, and his smile reaches into my chest and soothes all the pain I been carrying there. "We went looking for you after the wreck."

I laugh and cry at the same time and fall into his arms.

"The hobos said they took you to the jungle, then we heard you caught a ride into the city. Didn't take too much asking at hotels and boarding housing to learn where a silent girl with red hair might've been keeping herself. That gal you were with told us you were taking the bus home."

Ah, Miss Jojo. She stayed behind another few days to get squared away with the Legal Aid Society.

I sign, "*I couldn't bear to ride another train. How did you get off before the wreck?*"

He laughs and says, "Ilya here. The boy has eagle eyes. He spotted that other engine's smoke long before the horn. Saved our lives."

I sign, "*Thank you,*" to Ilya.

He signs, "*Good soup,*" back and we all laugh. At least he's trying.

A few nights later, we're all on the porch watching the sun lower its sleepy head to the Earth. Ruthy and I are peeling potatoes, Briar and Poppy are tinkering with a new plow head, and Billy Leo is showing Ilya his lightning bug collection.

If anybody comes looking, Briar Stewart died in Chicago, his death certificate signed by a hobo doctor in trade for six agates. Briar's new name is Cy Gojack, Ilya's brother.

Ilya's a free man as well. Not that he was ever formally charged.

Seems the turpentine camp shut down when the boss man, Taggert, got attacked by some crows one day in the woods. Pecked one of Taggert's eyes clean-out. Briar said the man had once shot at them and they didn't forget. Since there was no record of Ilya being an assigned convict at the camp, nobody's hunting him.

Before Briar returned home with Ilya, they stopped by Cy's grave. We heard some of the story about what happened at the cave, but there's more to come, I think. It'll roll out in time.

Poppy said that if the crops are good this fall, he'll pay for Cy to be moved to our family plot. Whether Ilya remains here or not, he will know where he can come visit his brother.

And part of me hopes he stays. My heart does a strange jump when he smiles my way or tries to practice the signs he sees me use.

Tonight, Mama has the newest edition of the *Atlanta Constitution* and is reading from her rocker. I told her to be on the lookout for anything on Miss Ardith or the Beck Infantorium.

"Ah, here's one."

> "The case of missing person Sissy Belle Strunk is solved. She has been masquerading in Marietta as a socialite for six years, married to a well-known businessman, William Dobbs. Information received implicates her in the death of her brother and the preacher Gator Tyre near Hickory Nut Hollow seven years earlier. Mrs. Ardith Dobbs died in the train crash outside St. Louis last month. Her infant son is thought to have been swept away in the river. Mr. Dobbs and his young son have left Marietta and have not been located. The couple has ties to the controversial Ku Klux Klan.
>
> The Klan Grand Dragon denies knowing them.
>
> In a strange twist, Mrs. Dobbs is linked to the now infamous Beck Infantorium, the horrific disposal place for unwanted babies.

> Mrs. Dobbs continued to take babies there even after learning that the two sisters who ran the house were collecting money in an adoption and insurance scam and then letting the babies die.
>
> The search for bodies around the Infantorium and in the mass graves in the cemetery behind the property continues. The Beck sisters are in jail awaiting trial."

I don't wish anyone dead, but Miss Ardith might have gotten off easy. She craved attention and praise, and none of that was going to be in her future if she had lived.

I may have a silent voice, but I'm proud I spoke up for Jojo, for the poor babies who died so horribly neglected. I told Miss Jojo she can receive the reward money for finding Sissy Belle Strunk. She'll use it to get her mother out of the asylum.

And speaking of voices, Ilya's is spring green. Fresh, like grass pushing from the ground, reaching for all that life offers. Makes me smile, hope again.

One day, I might write about all that's happened. The whole world seems to be holding on to secrets of one sort or another. Staying silent when words should be said.

Someday, I hope to understand why that is.

For now, I'm gonna watch the sun drape our mountain in golden shades each morning and bathe us in pale orange warmth every sunset. Well, except when moody weather says *not today*.

And one of these days, I might venture off our mountain again. May consider being a backwoods librarian or teacher for the deaf, those who can't talk or hear, like Miss Helen Keller.

But for now, I'm right where I've longed to be.

Home.

The End

AUTHOR'S NOTE

Women of the KKK:
In 2017, while searching for information about the beginning of the women's rights movement, I ran across an article about the women of the KKK. Several research books later, I understood why the WKKK became known as "A Poison Squad of Whispering Women." Their role in feeding their husbands the names of citizens who were "breaking the Klan's rules" or not promoting "a purer America" served the Klan well.

There were dozens of women's groups during that time. Many mentioned in the novel. One of the most frightening pictures I found was that of the Dixie Protestant Women's Political League in their regalia. (From Newspaper.org)

INDIANA EVENING GAZETTE, SATURDAY, DECEMBER 2, 1922
Women Kluxers Organize in Atlanta

Miss Daisy Barr was a highly influential Quaker woman who started out as a temperance advocate, then became an evangelist, a political organizer, the president of the Humane Society, and found her voice in 1920 with the Indiana WKKK. Over the next year, she used her revival speaker skills to organize WKKK realms in many states, personally recruiting 75,000 members in Indiana and Ohio alone in a few short months.

The WKKK ritual in the novel came from the book *Women of the Klan: Racism and Gender in the 1920s* by Kathleen M. Blee. (Berkeley Press 1991) This book was quite valuable in learning about the rise and fall of the Women's Klan and the motivation and beliefs that compelled so many women to join. Here's a quote: "By packaging its noxious ideology as traditional small-town values and wholesome fun, the Klan of the 1920s encouraged native-born white Americans to believe that bigotry, intimidation, harassment, and extralegal violence were all perfectly compatible with, if not central to, patriotic respectability."

The second Klan fizzled out by the end of the 1930s. But by then, it is estimated that 8,000,000 joined, and 500,000 were women. Ku Klux Kiddies was the youth group, and tens of thousands of babies and children were baptized in Klan ceremonies.

Another good book about the Klan in general is *Behind the Mask of Chivalry: The Making of the Second Ku Klux Klan* by Nancy Maclean. (Oxford Press 1994)

Klan members believed that Pope was coming to take over the United States and that he'd inserted his picture on the dollar bill. I spend many hours studying old 1920 bills and there is an odd object in the upper right-hand corner near the 1, but to say that it is a face, is a stretch. My only conclusion is, when you are looking for conspiracies, you can find them anywhere.

Baby Farms:

This was the hardest part of my research. The horrible stories of thousands of babies left to die or be killed or sacrificed for the life insurance money because they had no perceived value were difficult to read. Baby farming referred to a system in which infants were sent away to be nursed and boarded by private individuals for either a flat, one-time fee or a weekly or monthly charge. Baby farmers, usually middle-aged women, solicited these infants through "adoption" advertisements in newspapers, and through nurses, midwives, and the keepers of lying-in houses (private houses where poor, unwed women could pay to give birth and arrange for the transfer of their infants to baby farmers).

In 1922, in New York City, one baby a day was disposed of, some sold at bargain prices. A dramatic finding in a New York State charity study found that newspaper advertisements offered and requested children for adoption. The unmarried mother willingly paid any amount of money to dispose of her child and could be charged from as much as $15 to $65 by a maternity hospital or an individual willing to dispose of her baby. The new trade slogan of one baby seller was "it's cheaper and easier to buy a baby for $100 than to have one of your own."

The Beck Infantorium was based on a real-life horror show run by Mrs. Helene Geisen-Volk, a former German war nurse who dealt in babies. According to the evidence, some fifty-three children committed to her care died of one cause or another, usually of starvation. Conditions at her infantorium—described as a baby farm or a "baby disposal plant"—were called miserable and filthy in the extreme. A probation officer reported she had "strangled or frozen to death or otherwise disposed of babies left in her custody in order that she might reap a profit through her acts."

Like Ardith in the novel, Geisen-Volk came into the limelight after she substituted a baby for another whose fate never was discovered. After the body of another child had been exhumed, she was indicted for manslaughter. She received a three-and-a-half-year sentence for the deaths of the fifty-three children.

Babies and children gained "value" in the late 1930s when sweatshops were outlawed and adopting a child became a fad of the wealthy. A fascinating book is *Pricing the Priceless Child. The Changing Social Value of Children* by Viviana A. Zelizer. (Princeton University Press 1985) Zelizer traces the attitudes society held toward babies and children from the 1800s through modern day. Early days were not kind.

Chain Gangs:

Prior to 1900, the dilemma of operating tax-supported state prisons was solved by transforming state prisons into leased convict labor for private profit. By 1908, Georgia "prison farms" ended and the convict-leasing era wound down as a consequence of accusations that too many affluent southerners had profited from the system. Finally, there was a flicker of moral indignation over the treatment of convicts.

Then Georgia's (and other southern states') chain gang was born. Not much changed for the prisoners. The convicts on county-run chain gangs often slept in cages and were subject to brutal corporal punishment. They suffered from a host of debilitating ailments, including malnutrition, heatstroke, frostbite, contagious diseases, and shackle poisoning (infections caused by the constant rubbing of iron against the skin). These conditions caused high death rates among the prison population. Many wardens buried workers wherever they dropped, never documenting what happened to them.

A 1930s book and movie entitled *I am a Fugitive From a Georgia Chain Gang* by Robert Burns brought national attention to the Georgia penal system and eventually helped to bring reform by Governor Ellis Arnall. If you'd like to read more about the other southern states' policies and their treatment of convicts, *One Dies, Get Another* by Matthew J. Mancini (University of South Carolina Press 1996) is a detailed history of the convict-leasing program from 1866-1928.

County Prison Camp in Cartersville as described in the story is an example of all of the working chain-gang camps at the time in the South. Chain Gang Hill in Cartersville wasn't built until the early 1940's, but I used my literary license to move it twenty years earlier.

An interesting aside: Hitler stated that he learned a lot about rounding up "unwanted persons" and using them as expendable labor by studying the chain gangs in the South during the early twentieth century.

Hobos:

I've always been fascinated by hobos, the hobos' honor code, and their signs left on gates and walls. A surprise for me was that women took to the rails, escaping bad marriages or seeking their individualism. *Sisters of the Road, The Autobiography of Boxcar Bertha* (The Macauley Company 1937) follows the life of a girl named Bertha who was raised by a wandering mother, and boxcars were her playground. The book is loaded with stories of other women full of wanderlust who joined the "motley sorority," traveling the country by the thousands.

A good overall book on the human nature and character of the hobo is *The Hobo, The Sociology of the Homeless Man* by Nels Anderson (The University of Chicago 1923). It has hundreds of interviews with hobos from the 1920s.

Missouri Pacific Train Crash:

The crash in the book is based on a real crash that happened in Sulphur Springs, MO, except not in May of 1921 but on August 5th, 1922. MP No. 32 was taking water at Sulphur Springs and was standing on the main line. They had no orders against the fast train, except they were to let it pass them at the same place they let No. 1, a fast southbound train, pass. The bigger train, MP No. 4 had no orders against No. 32. It is supposed that engineer Matthew Glenn on No. 4 failed to see the block signals set against his train and did not see the halted train until too late to stop to prevent the terrible crash.

The rear end of the local train was standing on the bridge over Glaize Creek when the accident happened, and the cars were telescoped and hurled into the deep creek bed, from where many bodies were later recovered.

Death Cap mushrooms:

The deadly mushroom matures in July and August of each year, not in May. This fact was altered to conveniently fit the storyline.

Railway lines:

I did my best to study old railway maps to lay out travel for Briar and Willow. I take full credit for any mistakes made concerning train depots or which train went where.

ACKNOWLEDGEMENTS

I've had an *Appalachian story* running around in my head for twenty years and it finally broke free. It's changed over time, and I wasn't sure what this version would birth, but I knew it should involve strong family ties, injustice and wrongdoing, and survival. And the beautiful embrace of nature would paint the backdrop for the story, even as events turned ugly.

Thank you to my early readers, those brave souls, venturing into an unknown world, just as my characters often found themselves. Here's to Kristy Pappas, Kate Beckerman, Bill and Kate Chabala, Lynda Smart-Brown, Robert Dean, Jeff Lowder, Brittani Jay, and Linda Orvis for making this a better story.

Thank you to my editors, Ann Riza and Ann Suhs for their keen eye and expertise—in particular, their knowledge of Georgia's geography.

Thank you to my critique group for your enthusiasm about this story's theme.

As with my other books, thank you to Emma F. Mayo for your amazing creative skills, for your eagle eye during the very first and last versions, and for your friendship and sisterhood.

Thank you to Robert Dean for the title suggestion. For those who know me, I will fret over a title for days and days. This time the worrying ran the course of a year. Dean, you saved me.

And to my husband, John Hardy, who brainstormed with me for hours when the plot grew murky or derailed. Thank you. You've been my greatest cheerleader all these years.

AUTHOR PAGE

Karla M. Jay lives in Salt Lake City with her husband, niece, and one large gray dog. When she's not writing or reading, she's gardening or planning a trip, hoping to discover another story that needs to be told.

You can follow Karla M. Jay at:

Her website~ http://www.karlajay.com
Twitter~ http://www.twitter.com. @KarlaMJay1
Facebook~ http://www.facebook.com/AuthorKarlaJay
Instagram~ @karla.m.jay

Want more by Karla M. Jay? Check out *When We Were Brave,* an international award winner.

> "I have not read a book that has left me so broken in a long time. Ms. Jay makes you FEEL the hurt, the love, the terror of war. I have so much to say but nothing I say could do this book justice ... just read it."
>
> —Sandra Hind, *NetGalley Reviewer*

> "Jay's ... account is impressively ambitious, offering a sprawling view of the wages of war from three distinct perspectives. She ingeniously braids them into a coherent narrative tapestry, and

along the way, she realisti- cally describes the human degradation experienced by prisoners in the Nazi camps..."

—*Kirkus Reviews 2019*

"Combining excellent historical research with a compelling storyline, the hard work of author Karla M. Jay really pays off … As the plot threads and connections slowly come together, the conclusion marks the realities of war and sticks in your mind for a long time after."

—*Readers Favorite Review*

Purchase now:

https://www.amazon.com/When-Were-Brave-Karla-Jay-ebook/dp/B07QHGVPPN/ref=tmm_kin_swatch_0?_encoding=UTF8&qid=1577826883&sr=8-1

https://www.goodreads.com/book/show/44791171-when-we-were-brave

CPSIA information can be obtained
at www.ICGtesting.com
Printed in the USA
LVHW020725030121
675538LV00016BA/2660